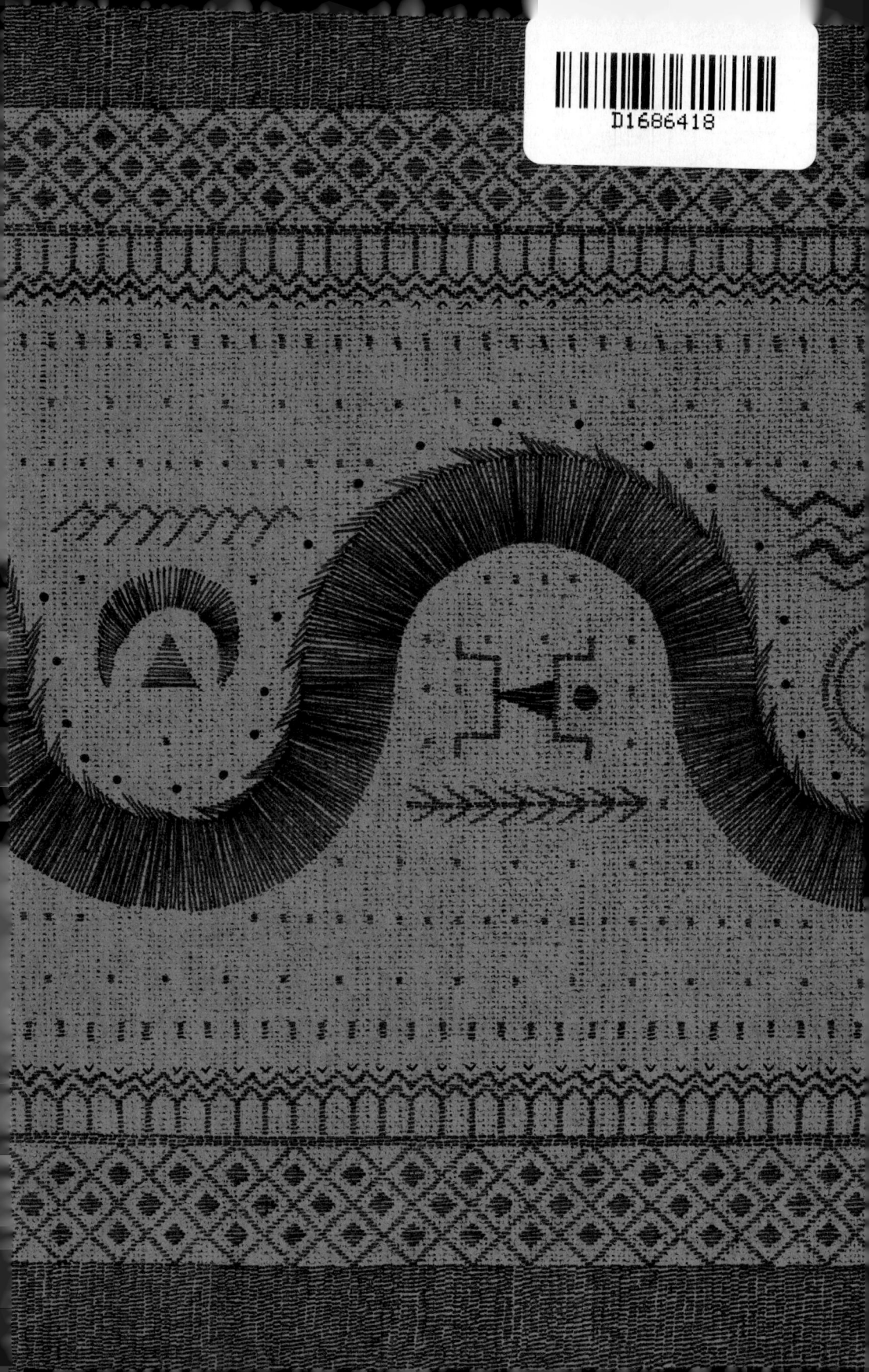

ISLES OF THE EMBERDARK

FICTION BY BRANDON SANDERSON®

THE STORMLIGHT ARCHIVE®
The Way of Kings
Words of Radiance
Oathbringer
Rhythm of War
Wind and Truth

NOVELLAS
Edgedancer
Dawnshard

THE MISTBORN® SAGA
THE ORIGINAL TRILOGY
Mistborn
The Well of Ascension
The Hero of Ages

THE WAX & WAYNE SERIES
The Alloy of Law
Shadows of Self
The Bands of Mourning
The Lost Metal

NOVELLA
Mistborn: Secret History

THE RECKONERS®
Steelheart
Mitosis: A Reckoners Story
Firefight
Calamity

SKYWARD
Skyward
Starsight
Cytonic
Defiant

NOVELLAS
Defending Elysium

SKYWARD FLIGHT, with JANCI PATTERSON
Sunreach
ReDawn
Evershore

ALCATRAZ VS. THE EVIL LIBRARIANS
Alcatraz vs. the Evil Librarians
The Scrivener's Bones
The Knights of Crystallia
The Shattered Lens
The Dark Talent
Bastille vs. the Evil Librarians WITH JANCI PATTERSON

NOVELS
Elantris
Warbreaker
The Rithmatist
Tress of the Emerald Sea
The Frugal Wizard's Handbook for Surviving Medieval England
Yumi and the Nightmare Painter
The Sunlit Man
Isles of the Emberdark

NOVELLAS
Firstborn
Perfect State
Snapshot
Children of the Nameless
The Original WITH MARY ROBINETTE KOWAL
Dark One: Forgotten WITH DAN WELLS

COLLECTIONS
Arcanum Unbounded: The Cosmere® Collection
Legion: The Many Lives of Stephen Leeds

GRAPHIC NOVELS
White Sand, A Cosmere® Graphic Novel
Dark One

PICTURE BOOKS
The Most Boring Book Ever

THE WHEEL OF TIME®, WITH ROBERT JORDAN
The Gathering Storm
Towers of Midnight
A Memory of Light

ISLES OF THE EMBERDARK

BRANDON SANDERSON

ILLUSTRATIONS BY ESTHER HI'ILANI CANDARI

DRAGONSTEEL

This is a work of fiction. All of the characters, organizations, and events portrayed in this novel are either products of the author's imagination or are used fictitiously.

ISLES OF THE EMBERDARK

Copyright © 2025 by Dragonsteel, LLC

Illustrations by Esther Hiʻilani Candari
Cover art by Rebecca Sorge Jensen
Copyright © 2025 by Dragonsteel, LLC

All rights reserved.

Edited by Kristy S. Gilbert

A Dragonsteel Book
Published by Dragonsteel, LLC
American Fork, UT

brandonsanderson.com

Brandon Sanderson®, The Stormlight Archive®, Mistborn®, Cosmere®, Reckoners®, Dragonsteel®, and the ⚜ logo are registered trademarks of Dragonsteel, LLC. The phrase "The Wheel of Time®" is a trademark of Bandersnatch Group, Inc.

ISBN 978-1-938570-50-6

First Edition: September 2025

Printed in the United States of America

0 9 8 7 6 5 4 3 2 1

For Tom Conrad,
　　Who is perhaps the oldest friend I have.
　　　And a man to whom I owe a large number of birthday
　　　　jugs of milk. (Can you believe it's been thirty years?)

ILLUSTRATIONS

BY ESTHER HIʻILANI CANDARI © DRAGONSTEEL, LLC

APPEARING ON OR IMMEDIATELY
AFTER INDICATED PAGE

Premonition   28
Roomy for a Shack   52
Cakoban Medallion   64
Industrialized Patji   82
Into the Emberdark   132
An Echo Only   182
Tug-of-War   212
Escape Plan   304
Starling Portrait   324
Warning   361
The Spirit Shores   384
Guardian   462

CONTENTS

Author's Note xi

Prologue 3

Book One: Dusk 7

Book Two: Starling 133

Book Three: The Cave of Death 233

Book Four: The Dakwara 399

Epilogue 453

Acknowledgments 463

About the Author 467

AUTHOR'S NOTE

A decade ago, I wrote a novella that just would not leave me alone. The story of a man, his birds, and the inevitable tide of progress. As I thought about the novella, I realized that there was much more here—a novel I needed to tell someday, picking up sometime after the novella ended.

I spent nine years outlining it, my enthusiasm growing with each new idea I worked out. I started writing it in 2017, though I didn't fully find time for it until 2023. As can be expected from its origin, *Isles of the Emberdark* leans upon and requires understanding of the novella *Sixth of the Dusk*. Indeed, key points of the novella are integral to the larger plot of the book.

That presented a problem. It's generally not a good idea to write a full-on novel sequel to a piece of short fiction most of your readers (probably) haven't read. I didn't want to release a novel that required homework—imagine picking this up, then realizing you had to hunt down an obscure novella to be able to appreciate it. I also didn't want to revert the character and start all over, as that wouldn't be fair to either the narrative or the people who had read the novella.

The solution, then, was to build the story of this book in such a way that I could include the novella as a set of flashbacks. This was an exciting challenge, and I found it slotted in fairly well. Therefore, the original novella *Sixth of the Dusk* is included here in the first part of the novel, set off in its own chapters, as flashbacks. Judging by the experiences of my beta readers, if you've never read that novella, you'll find it a fairly natural part of the story—and by the end of the first part, you'll be fully up to date on everything that happened in Dusk's past.

However, if you *have* read *Sixth of the Dusk*, especially recently, you may find yourself wanting to skip or skim the novella chapters. I'm here to tell you that's just fine. I *did* tweak it to better expand the mythology and worldbuilding of Dusk's world, but the changes are slight, and you can pick up on them without needing to reread. Know that there is a full-length novel here (among the longer of the secret projects I've done) even without the pages added by the novella.

Writing this book has been a delightful experience. It's quirky, not quite paced like anything I've done before. Part of that is the flashbacks, part of that is Starling and her story. Part is me dipping into the future of the Cosmere in exciting, but hopefully not too spoiler-ish, ways.

Thank you for your support of me doing strange, unexpected things with the Cosmere and these secret projects. I had a blast with this one, and within its smaller-scale story about isolation, progress, and community, I hope you find something distinctive to love.

Brandon Sanderson

ISLES OF THE EMBERDARK

Fig. 100 · **Dragon**
(head)

PROLOGUE
Fifty-Seven Years Ago

Starling hopped from one foot to the other, holding open the drapes to her balcony, staring at the dark horizon. She didn't dare blink. She didn't dare miss it.

First light. When would first light appear?

She'd barely slept, though she'd tried for *at least* a half hour. She was simply too excited, and had spent the night trying—failing—to distract herself with a book.

In the distance, across the rolling forests of Yolen, the darkness seemed to fade. Did that count? It wasn't light. It was just . . . less dark.

She went running anyway. Still wearing her nightgown, she pushed into the hallway outside her rooms in her uncle's mansion. She scrambled past smiling attendants. Starling genuinely liked most of them—and pretended to like the rest. That was what her uncle taught her: Always look for the best in both people and situations.

Today, that wasn't so difficult. Today was the day.

First light.

The day she transformed.

She burst into the grand entryway in a tizzy of white hair and fluttering nightgown, startling her uncle's priests in their formal robes and wide hats. They were up early, of course, because her uncle got up early to take the prayers of those who worshipped him.

Starling fluttered around the corner, heading for the next hallway over, which led to his reflectory. Priests, belatedly, bowed to her from the sides as she ran. She might look like an eight-year-old girl, but dragons grew slowly, and she was older than some of the priests.

She didn't feel it. She still felt like a child, which her uncle explained was the way of things. Her mental age was like that of a human child her size, but she got to experience that age far longer than they did—which would have been wonderful, except for one thing. It had forced her to wait three long decades for her transformation.

She burst into the reflectory, where her uncle sat upon his fain-wood throne. He wore his human form, which had pale skin and a sharp silver beard just on his chin, bound in cords, extending a good eight inches. He took the appearance of an older man, maybe in his sixties, though that could be deceptive for their kind.

Starling scurried up to him, but didn't touch him. With his eyes closed—wearing his brilliant white and silver robes and conical headdress—he was taking a prayer from some distant follower. She couldn't interrupt that. Not even for first light. So she waited, balancing on one foot, then the other, trying to keep from bursting from excitement.

Finally he opened his eyes. "Oh? Starling. It's early for a young dragonet like you. Why are you up?"

"It's today, Uncle! It's today!"

"Is today special?"

"Uncle!"

"Oh, your birthday," he said. "Thirty years old, unless . . . Could I have mistaken the day? A lot was happening during your birth, child. Maybe we need to wait until tomorrow."

"*UNCLE!*" she shouted.

Frost smiled, then held out his hands for her to run up and embrace him. "I just spoke with Vambrakastram—and she will take my prayers for the day. I am free, all day, for you."

"Just for me?" she whispered.

"Just for you. Are you ready?"

"I've been so, so ready," she said. "For so, so long." She pulled back. "Will my scales really be white when I am a dragon?"

"You are always a dragon," he said, raising his finger, "whether or not you have the shape of one. As for the coloring of your scales, there's no way to know until the transformation." He tapped her arm—which was powder white, like her hair. "Dragons come in all colors, and each is beautiful and unique. But I will say, every dragon I've known who was leucistic in human form—granted, there have only ever been two others—had white scales to match. A metallic, shimmering white with a sheen of mother-of-pearl. It's breathtaking."

"Only ever two," she whispered.

"Only ever two," he said, then cupped her cheek. "Plus one, Starling."

"Letsgoletsgoletsgo!" she shouted, running back out into the hallway. He followed, and—with her urging him on—they continued down the corridor, passing more smiling priests. All human, of mixed genders. Starling had been to other dragon palaces, and the priests there were stiff and stuffy. Not so here. Frost saw the best in people, and people became their best because of it. That's what he'd always said.

"Now," he said from behind, walking far too slowly for her tastes, "I'm supposed to speak to you of the ritual importance of the first transformation."

"I know the importance!" she exclaimed, spinning to walk backward. "I will be able to fly."

"We live dual lives," he said. "And there is a reason we spend thirty years in human form before reaching the age of transformation. This is Adonalsium's wisdom."

"Yes, yes," she said, spinning again as they reached the end of the hallway—and the grand balcony doors. "We live half our lives as humans so we know what it is like to be small. We live the lives of mortals before we gain the life of a dragon. That way, we'll understand."

"Do you?" he said, resting his hand on her shoulder as she stood before the closed doors, which were made of yellow stained glass. She thought . . . she could see light on the other side, from the horizon.

She was so eager, but he'd taught her to be honest, always.

"No," she admitted. "I try, but I . . . don't understand mortals. They live such hurried lives, and they are so fragile, but they don't seem to care. I try, but I don't understand."

"Yes. With our powers, even as dragonets, empathy is difficult."

"Will that ruin me?" she asked softly. She'd worried about this. "Because I don't understand? Will it stop me from flying?"

"You can never be ruined, child," he said, a smile in his voice. "Never, ever. You can learn better, and you will as you grow. Knowing that fact is how it happens! Ignorance will not hold back the transformation." He leaned back. "Sometimes, contrast is important to help us learn."

He shoved the doors open, revealing a horizon that had begun to blaze with predawn. The grand balcony was large enough to hold them in their draconic forms. It was one of the launchpads to the upper palace, which was built on a different scale—for people who were the size of buildings.

She stepped out onto the balcony, suddenly worried. What if it didn't happen to her? What if she was broken? Everyone put so much stock in her being leucistic—which was a cousin, but not exactly the same, as being albino like a human. She was more like a white tiger, she'd been told. A symbol of two worlds. But some said with every great sign came misfortune, as proven by what had happened to her parents . . .

"You are," Frost said, "so wonderful, Illistandrista. I am honored to be here, with you, on this most important of days."

He left unsaid that he wished her parents were the ones here. That was not to be. She took a deep breath, and held out her hands to her sides.

First dawn struck her, and she absorbed the light. It became part of her, and the self that had been hidden within Starling these thirty years emerged, glorious and radiant. With wings, and dragonsteel of pure silver, and scales a glittering white—faintly iridescent.

With the transformation, Starling—finally—felt that she belonged.

BOOK ONE:

DUSK

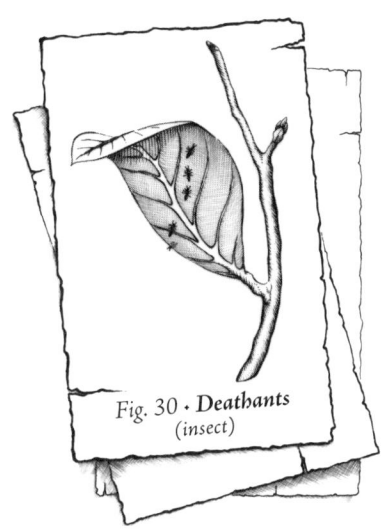

Fig. 30 • Deathants
(insect)

CHAPTER ONE

Sixth of the Dusk crept up on a deathant.

"This thing's venom," Dusk whispered, slipping forward on silent feet, "is enough to kill a horse. It would have no trouble with you or me. They call it a three-step kill. Because after its bite, you'll last only three more steps."

He kept his eyes on the tiny insect, which held to the bottom of a leaf—barely visible, imitating a natural spot on the foliage. Dusk turned a smoking brand between his fingers and slid forward. "They often cling to the bottoms of leaves," he said softly. "People rub against them, unaware, and the ants slip onto their clothing. In the jungles of Patji, you can never fully trust that you're not carrying one. Death could come with a tiny sting hours after you've passed their hive."

One more step. He raised his brand.

"Smoke," he whispered, "is your best defense. It puts them to sleep." He inched the brand up underneath the leaf, letting its smoke puff up and ooze around the insect. "Either that, or you move with extreme caution. Hoping—praying to the Father Island—that you were careful enough."

The deathant did not drop to sleep as it should have—because if you looked closely, you would see it was actually a drawing. Dots of black, painted on the leaf in the shape of the deadly insect.

He turned around to an audience of children and parents. Most were barely paying attention. He lowered his smoking brand, then rapped his other hand on the glass terrarium, which held living specimens. It was set up next to the fake display, both being used for presentations.

"You have no idea how lucky you are," he said, "to be able to look at these safely. Real, live deathants. Few people ever got that chance before the modern era."

The children stared at him blankly. One was drooling. Their juvenile Aviar—birds which clung to shoulders or heads—chattered softly at one another.

"I'm done," Dusk added.

A smattering of applause, which he always found . . . odd. He did not like being applauded. After that, the people moved on to one of the other displays, several children complaining they were bored, one crying for no reason whatsoever.

Dusk groaned and glanced back at the terrarium containing one of the deadliest creatures in all of creation. And he felt . . . sorry. These insects had once terrified even the most skilled trapper. Now they were just bugs in a jar.

It made him angry, with no good reason, for he was part of the reason they were imprisoned like this. Indeed, this entire park—with its captive displays of the dangers of the outer islands, and showy explanations for how life had once been—existed because of him. He might not have captured these animals, but he'd signed their bill of incarceration.

With a sigh, he turned from the enclosure and went to gather Sak from the Aviar roost nearby. The sleek black bird stood out among the others. Everyone here had an Aviar, all a variety of colors, but none were like Sak, with her black coloring and more pointed beak. As he put her on his shoulder, she leaned to the side, looking at his other shoulder. Empty. She never stopped looking.

"I know," Dusk said. "I miss him too."

After that, he went walking. Something that once, when he'd worked on Patji—most perilous of islands—had been rife with danger. Each step a risk of death, a new challenge around every tree and within every hollow. Five years later, and his instincts still said that walking lazily like this was dangerous. Was it strange, that he should long for those days?

He wore his old gear—cargo pants and a tight, buttoned shirt—which made him stand out in this city full of bright dresses and colorful wraps. On the street outside, he could hear new kinds of vehicles passing: the kind with motors that roared like some type of beast. Gifts of technology from the Ones Above.

He peered to the sky, and spotted the ship hanging there. More talks, more meetings, more gifts and promises. The aliens were growing impatient with this primitive planet full of stubborn people and valuable birds. How long would the Ones Above wait? He had thoughts on what could be done. He kept them to himself, as nobody asked. Couldn't Vathi send for him again? He'd only punched *one* senator. And surely the man had deserved it.

Dusk continued walking through the park. People did, occasionally, stop and point. He was a celebrity, he supposed. The last trapper of Patji, a man who had been ushered back to receive medals and awards for the secrets he'd helped discover. He'd asked them to build this park, to preserve the trapper heritage, and so they had. It was the last time they'd listened to him.

He didn't work for the park formally, but he liked to visit. To remember. Maybe that was a bad idea. Maybe that was asking for pain, seeing all these creatures in cages. Knowing that secretly, he was one of them. A relic of days that had been bulldozed. Leaving him a man with no purpose. Other than to try, and fail, to scare children.

He found Tuka, the park director, supervising one of the new exhibits. They hoped to house nightmaws here. Insanity, he'd have once said. But they'd housed Dusk, so who knew?

Tuka was a boisterous, stout woman. She had long black hair and wore orange. Always. Orange was practically a religion to Tuka.

It made her look like a fruit.

"Dusk!" she said, turning from the new construction. "I didn't know you were coming in today!"

He didn't reply. Because that had not been a question.

"What do you think?" she asked, gesturing to the enclosure—a deep pit with stone sides.

"They will get out at that point there," he said, pointing at some trees inside. "They will knock the trees down, climb up, feast upon your patrons." He paused. "It might be bad for publicity."

"Oh, you," she said, swatting him.

She thought he made jokes. He let her think that—as his gut said it would make her underestimate him.

Why would you need that kind of thinking any longer? a part of him accused. *Haven't you listened to a single thing Vathi has tried to teach you?*

"We're very lucky to have you," Tuka noted. "A real, live trapper. One who trapped Patji, no less."

The words . . . they were echoes of the ones from his presentation. The exact things he'd said about the deathants.

Father. Was this really his life? Dusk looked around at the colorful people and glass cages.

"Was it really as terrible as people say?" Tuka asked. "On the island, I mean."

"Yes," Dusk said. "And wonderful."

"Terrible . . . and wonderful?" Tuka frowned.

"Wonderful *because* it was terrible."

"I don't understand."

He wasn't surprised. All this effort to create the park, to preserve the ways of the trappers, and Dusk only now realized something. Tamed displays—no matter how vibrant and accurate—could never fully capture the truth of living on Patji.

And so, the only true displays were his memories.

Fig. 18 · Kokerlii
(Aviar)

CHAPTER TWO

Five Years Ago

Death hunted beneath the waves.

Dusk saw it approach: a vast dark shadow within the deep blue. Dusk's hands tensed on his paddle, rocking in his boat, his heartbeat racing as he immediately sought out Kokerlii.

Fortunately, the colorful bird sat in his customary place on the prow, idly biting at one clawed foot raised to his hooked beak. Kokerlii lowered his foot and puffed out his feathers, as if completely unmindful of the danger beneath.

Dusk held his breath. He always did, when unfortunate enough to run across one of these things in the open ocean. He did not know what they looked like beneath those waves. He hoped to never find out.

The shadow drew closer, almost to the boat. A school of slimfish passing nearby jumped into the air in a silvery wave, spooked by the shadow's approach. The terrified fish showered back to the water with a sound like rain, but the shadow did not deviate. The slimfish were too small a meal to interest it.

A boat's occupants, however...

It passed directly underneath. Sak chirped quietly from Dusk's shoulder; the second bird seemed to have some sense of the danger. Creatures like the shadow did not hunt by smell or sight, but by sensing the minds of prey. Dusk glanced at Kokerlii again, whose powers were their only protection. Dusk had never clipped Kokerlii's wings, but at times like this he understood why many sailors preferred protection Aviar that could not fly away.

The boat rocked softly; the jumping slimfish stilled. Waves lapped against the sides of the vessel. Had the shadow stopped? Hesitated? Did it sense them? Kokerlii's protective aura had always been enough before, but . . .

The shadow slowly vanished. It had turned to swim downward, Dusk realized. In moments, he could make out nothing through the waters. He hesitated, then forced himself to get out his new mask. It was a modern device he had acquired two supply trips back: a glass faceplate with leather at the sides. He placed it on the water's surface and leaned down, looking through it into the depths. They became as clear to him as an undisturbed lagoon.

Nothing. Just that endless deep, sunlight making streams of light like roadways into the abyss. *Fool man,* he thought, tucking away the mask and getting out his paddle. *Didn't you just think to yourself that you never wanted to see one of those?*

Still, as he started paddling again, he knew that he'd spend the rest of this trip feeling as if the shadow were down there, following him. He continued regardless, paddling his outrigger canoe until he drew a distance away—all around him was that same trembling ocean, not a speck of land in sight. He carried with him compass, map, and sextant . . . but today, he didn't reach for any of those.

Instead he dipped his hand into the water and closed his eyes, reading the lapping of the waves to judge his position. Once, those waves would have been good enough for any of the Eelakin, his people. These days, only the trappers learned the old arts, the arts of the grand navigators from long ago. It was a mark of pride to him that he almost never needed the compass, and he had yet to encounter a situation where he had to rely on the new sea charts—given as gifts by the Ones Above during their visit earlier in the year. They were said to be more accurate than even the best Eelakin surveys.

He hated that such things existed. However, you could not stop times from changing. His mother's words. You couldn't stop times from changing any more than you could stop the surf from rolling.

But he *could* remember. He pulled his hand from the ocean and got out his navigator's book, where each day he recorded observations. The rising and setting of the sun, the locations of constellations, fish he'd seen and the direction they were swimming.

Wayfinding was a puzzle. In the old days, the great navigators would not sleep for as long as a week as they traveled—for they needed to record everything in incredible detail. Distance traveled, speed of motion, the angle of each day's sailing as accounted by sun and stars.

Dusk fortunately didn't need to be quite so detailed. So long as he passed shallows now and then, a modern anchor could keep him from drifting while he slept. And he knew that if he did drift too far, the compass, map, and sextant could get him back on track.

He still loved to do it the old way. He marked the school of slimfish, and knew—without needing to look—it meant he was getting close. The birds he'd seen in the distance yesterday had been enough. At night, birds headed toward land—and that had let him turn his course slightly. The snarl of seaweed—with a hook from some previous trapper caught in it—had been an obvious sign as well. Even the clouds could help, for green reflections on the bottoms of distant clouds meant land.

He finished his notations, then used his spyglass to scan for other signs. More birds. They'd be flying away from land this time of day . . . Yes, he was close.

Again, he dipped his hand into the water. Of all the ancient techniques, this was his favorite. For while you let your fingers trail in the water, with eyes closed, you could feel the waves . . . and large islands created different wave patterns. It worked best once you were close, of course, but with his fingers in the water . . . he almost felt like the islands were talking to him. Telling him, by how they interrupted the patterns, where they were.

He smiled and took out his old string map—made with wooden sticks on a board, used to show wave patterns and indicate how to find them around certain islands. He turned his boat with confidence— his birds chirping—and paddled straight on their new path.

It was not long, after the accounting of tides, before he was rewarded with first sight of an island. He'd done it, without picking up his compass a single time this trip. That was Sori: a small island in the

Pantheon, and the most commonly visited. Her name meant "child"; Dusk vividly remembered training on her shores with his uncle.

It had been long since he'd burned an offering to Sori, despite how well she had treated him during his youth. Perhaps a small offering would not be out of line. Patji would not grow jealous. One could not be jealous of Sori, as she was the least of the islands. Just as every trapper was welcome on Sori, every other island in the Pantheon was said to be affectionate of her.

Be that as it may, Sori did not contain much valuable game. Dusk continued paddling, moving down one leg of the archipelago known as the Pantheon.

From a distance, this archipelago was not so different from the homeisles of the Eelakin, now a three-week trip behind him. Up close, they were very, very different. Over the next five hours, Dusk paddled past Sori, then her three cousins. He had never set foot on any of those three. In fact, he had not landed on many of the forty-some islands in the Pantheon. At the end of his apprenticeship, a trapper chose one island and worked there all his life.

Dusk had chosen Patji—an event some fifteen years past now. Seemed like far less.

Dusk saw no other shadows beneath the waves, but he kept watch. Not that he could do much to protect himself. Kokerlii did all of that work as he roosted happily at the prow of the ship, eyes half closed. Dusk had fed him seed; Kokerlii did like it so much more than dried fruit.

Nobody knew why beasts like the shadows lived only here, in the waters near the Pantheon. Why not travel across the seas to the homeisles, where food would be plentiful and Aviar like Kokerlii were far rarer?

Once, these questions had not been asked. The seas were what they were. Now, however, men poked and prodded into everything. They asked, "Why?" They said, "We should explain it."

Dusk shook his head, dipping his paddle into the water. That sound—wood on water—had been his companion for most of his days. He understood it, and the whisperings of the waves, far better than he did the speech of men.

Even if sometimes their questions got inside of him and refused to go free.

After the cousins, most trappers would have turned north or south, moving along branches of the archipelago until reaching their chosen island. Dusk continued forward, into the heart of the islands. He stopped briefly with harpoon and rope to spear some fish—often, in these waters, the best way to get protein.

He gutted and packed them away for later tonight at his safecamp, then continued paddling until a shape loomed before him. Patji, largest island of the Pantheon. He towered like a wedge rising from the sea, and all of the waves here bent around him. A place of inhospitable peaks, sharp cliffs, and deep jungle.

Patji. King of the Pantheon. God of the Eelakin.

Hello, old destroyer, Dusk thought. *Hello, Father.*

Fig. 3 · **Fern frond**
(plant)

CHAPTER THREE

Dusk thought perhaps he should tell Tuka about his memories. Vathi was always saying he needed to offer more in a conversation, not just wait to be prompted. However, right as he opened his mouth to speak, Tuka got called away to deal with some children who were pestering an exhibit—though as she went, she turned back for a moment.

"Oh, Dusk," she said. "Mother Frond wanted you to stop by."

Frond?

Frond was here?

"Where?" he called.

"Where else?" Tuka said, then vanished.

He started off through the park immediately, winding past natural plant displays, which were too cultivated for his taste. He kept telling them to let weeds grow, but they were resistant—a life on the homeisles seemed to make everyone want to manicure everything. Cut the wildness from it, men as well as gardens.

Frond was a heavyset older woman—a loremother who had come in from one of the outer isles last year—with a deeper brown skin than even Dusk, whose skin tone was browner than many homeislers'. She wore feathers after the traditional style, though many loremothers adopted modern costumes. He didn't mind either way. People and society changed, sometimes for the better. He would not have wanted to go trapping shirtless, as had been traditional, but there *was* something about the headdress and cloak of feathers.

Frond—ever looking for a chance to teach—crouched before some children in the small, child-sized amphitheater. Her favorite spot in the city, she'd said, though her official duties—reciting histories for chiefs and kingmakers on the outer isles—often kept her away from the capital.

She always returned, and would visit this overlooked section of the park. A shaded, tiered set of stones in what had once been a children's playground, which they had built the rest of the preserve around. People had taken to calling her Mother Frond, though her direct family lived on some distant isle.

Today, she was telling the story of Cakoban.

Dusk had heard it dozens, if not hundreds, of times. That should have made him bored, but his fingers reached absently toward his neck—for the medallion he'd once worn—as he heard the story of their ancestor.

"He sailed only at night?" one of the children asked.

"No, no," Frond whispered, leaning forward. "There was no sun back then—only night. Cakoban the Navigator sailed, then, *looking* for light."

"And he fought monsters!" a little girl said, punching the air.

"Many monsters," Frond agreed. "After Cakoban made a deal with the great winged statue, who promised to come to him when next he needed help, he escaped by sailing *between* the legs of the great giants of Epelli! First one, then the other, so they attacked each other in their confusion! He rode the waves of their falling clubs. And when their great bodies crashed to the ocean—dead—he had the grandest wave of all, which carried him *three days* across the endless sea!"

One boy eagerly raised his hand. "How," he said, "can a sea be endless!"

"If you sail it," Frond said, spinning her finger around, "can you not keep going? Past islands, always sailing toward the horizon?"

"But that's in circles!" the boy said.

"Which have no end," Frond replied, smiling. "And an ocean, young Kapu, is never the same one moment to the next—it is a road into eternity." She met Dusk's eyes and smiled. "You cannot defeat it. You can merely accompany it."

"But what *happened*?" another girl asked, her diminutive green Aviar hopping up and down on her shoulder.

"Cakoban followed a shooting star to the homeisles," the boy said, folding his arms. "He returned, then brought everyone here. The end."

"No," Frond said.

The four children regarded her with wide eyes.

"Cakoban," she whispered, "followed a brilliant shooting star, which led him past the cave of the terrible Dakwara, the monster child of a distant god. Cakoban valiantly defeated that beast, for the monster would have swallowed all the world. He blinded it with the light of a torch, as light was a thing the monster knew not, then tricked the giant serpent into tying itself in knots.

"The Dakwara was forced to acknowledge it was defeated—for with great monsters, you do not beat them by killing them, but by surviving. When Cakoban untied it, he sent it to protect his daughter and his kin for a hundred years. With a respect gained for people, when it came to our land, it served Patji—and created the islands. But that was not yet, and our story is not of those tales.

"After defeating the Dakwara, Cakoban searched long in that region, until nearly dying of starvation, for he knew that a beast such as the Dakwara must be guarding a sight truly grand! Then Patji—honoring Cakoban's courage—rose from the ocean and erupted with blazing red light, leading the way to life. A thrown ember became the sun, and Cakoban found Patji's shores. He returned to his kind, and led them to this new land, where Patji had ordered islands created. There, he found home—for all of us."

They were silent for a moment. Then the boy said, "That's what I said."

"No, child," Frond whispered. "It is not." She gave them a piece of candy each and sent them on their way, to waiting parents, before tucking her arms into her long sleeves and turning to Dusk. "How is it," she said to him, "you always arrive when I'm talking about Cakoban?"

Sak chirped softly as Frond offered a seed, and Dusk did not answer. For it seemed more an observation than a question. She offered a finger, and Sak let the woman scratch her neck, something the Aviar rarely allowed anyone but Dusk to do.

"The most wondrous of Aviar . . ." she said quietly. "What have you been showing your master these days, Sak?"

The answer was nothing. Sak's power rarely had reason to activate anymore, for Dusk was rarely in danger. Frond smiled, and touched the bird right on the forehead, scratching and whispering with a sound like ocean waves. "Guide him well." Then she glanced at Dusk.

"So quiet," Frond said. "One might think the loremothers and the trappers to be enemies, for you wield silence while we wield sound. I wish I knew what was happening in that mind of yours."

"No," he said, holding her eyes. "It would make you weep."

"That bad?"

"It is the way of things," he said. "All days must pass into shadow eventually." He looked around the park. "I think I'm finished coming here, Frond."

"What will you do instead?"

He did not answer, for he had no answer.

"Dusk . . ." she said, putting a weathered hand upon his shoulder. "What are we to do about them?" She glanced upward, toward that ship in the sky.

The Ones Above. During talks, they never showed faces or skin. Dusk imagined them as strange and terrible creatures, with faces full of fangs. Artist renditions of them from the broadsheets tended to err on the side of mystery, showing beings with dark pits where faces should be—as if representing the darkness of space itself, confined somehow in their strange outfits and helmets.

"I have nothing to do with them any longer," he said. "Vathi kicked me out. Besides, I'm just an old trapper—I belong in stories, not in the world as it has become."

"The ones I'd have dealing with those aliens," she whispered, "are people like those *from* the stories."

He considered that. He knew she liked when he thought about what she said, and he liked the silence she gave him to think.

"What could I do?" he finally asked.

"I don't know," she replied. "But I've spoken to Vathi. She might be coming around to letting you back in. You simply have to remind her."

"Of what?"

"Of who you are. Sometimes we need a person who looks in from yesterday, Dusk."

He nodded slowly. "If the chance comes, I'll . . . see what I can do. Will you do something for me? Remember us, worldspinner. When you tell stories, and train the next generation of loremothers, remember to talk of the trappers who used to be."

"I will," she said. "But I would like a promise from you in return."

"Which is?"

"Watch," she said, "for your shooting star."

"Trappers do not see the stars, Frond," he said. "We have been trained not to go out at night." He smiled in thanks, then left the park.

He was finished with this facsimile of a life he'd once lived.

Fig. 25 · Sak
(Aviar)

CHAPTER FOUR

Five Years Ago

Dusk rocked in his boat, listening to birds chirping softly, inspecting Patji—the god of all islands.

He didn't go ashore immediately. Instead, he raised his paddle and placed it in the boat. He sat, chewing on fish from last night's catch, feeding scraps to Sak. The black-plumed bird ate them with an air of solemnity, while Kokerlii continued to sit on the prow, chirping occasionally.

Kokerlii would be eager to land. Sak, though, seemed never to grow eager about anything.

Approaching Patji was not a simple task, even for one who trapped these shores. The boat continued its dance with the waves as Dusk considered which landing to make. Eventually he put the fish away, then took out his medallion, rubbing it for good luck. It was the one his uncle had carried, bearing a depiction of the hero Cakoban, ancestor to all trappers.

Dusk's uncle had carried the medallion until Patji had killed him. Dusk would now carry it until Patji killed him as well. Hopefully, that would take many years.

Finally he took up his paddle again and dipped it back into the waters—waters that remained deep and blue, despite the proximity to the island. Some members of the Pantheon had sheltered bays and gradual beaches. Patji had no patience for such foolishness. His beaches were rocky and had steep drop-offs. You were never safe on his shores. In fact, the beaches were the most dangerous part—upon them, not only could the horrors of the land get to you, but you were still within reach of the deep's monsters. Dusk's uncle had cautioned him about this time and time again. Only a fool slept on Patji's shores.

The tide was with him, and he avoided being caught in any of the swells that would crush him against those stern rock faces. Dusk approached a partially sheltered expanse of stone crags and outcroppings, Patji's version of a beach. Kokerlii fluttered off, chirping and calling as he flew toward the trees.

Dusk immediately glanced back at the waters. No shadows. Still, he felt naked as he hopped out of the canoe and pulled it up onto the rocks, warm water washing against his legs. Sak remained in her place on Dusk's shoulder.

Nearby in the surf, Dusk saw a corpse bobbing in the water.

Beginning your visions early, my friend? he thought, glancing at Sak. The Aviar usually waited until they'd fully landed before bestowing her blessing.

The black-feathered bird just watched the waves.

Dusk continued his work. The body he saw in the surf was his own. It told him to avoid that section of water. Perhaps there was a spiny anemone that would have pricked him, or perhaps a deceptive undercurrent lay in wait. Sak's visions did not show such detail; they gave only warning.

Dusk got the boat out of the water, then detached the floats and tied them more securely onto the main part of the canoe. He worked the vessel carefully up the shore—mindful not to scrape the hull on sharp rocks—to hide it in the jungle. If another trapper discovered it, Dusk would be stranded on the island for several extra weeks preparing his spare. That would—

He stopped when his heel struck something soft as he backed up the shore. He glanced down, expecting a pile of seaweed. Instead he found a damp piece of cloth. A shirt? Dusk held it up, then noticed other, more subtle signs. Broken lengths of sanded wood. Bits of paper floating in an eddy.

Those fools, he thought.

As he reached the tree line, he caught sight of his corpse hanging from a tree nearby. Those were cutaway vines lurking in the fernlike treetop. Sak squawked softly on his shoulder as Dusk hefted a large stone from the beach, then tossed it at the tree. It thumped against the wood, and sure enough, the vines dropped like a net, full of stinging barbs.

They would take a few hours to retract. Dusk pulled his canoe over and hid it in the underbrush near the tree. Hopefully, other trappers would be smart enough to stay away from the cutaway vines.

Before placing the final camouflaging fronds, Dusk pulled out his pack. Though the centuries had changed a trapper's duties very little, the modern world did offer its benefits. Instead of a simple wrap that left his legs and chest exposed, he wore thick trousers with pockets on the legs. He accompanied it with a buttoned shirt to protect his skin against sharp branches and leaves. Instead of sandals, Dusk tied on sturdy boots, and instead of a tooth-lined club, he bore a machete of the finest steel. His pack contained luxuries like a steel-hooked rope, a lantern, and a fire starter that created sparks simply by pressing the two handles together.

He looked very little like the trappers in the paintings. He didn't mind. He'd rather stay alive.

Dusk left the canoe, shouldering his pack, machete sheathed at his side. Sak moved to his other shoulder. Before leaving the beach, Dusk paused, looking up at his corpse—faintly translucent—still hanging from unseen vines by the tree.

Could he really have ever been foolish enough to be caught by cutaway vines? Near as he could tell, Sak only showed him plausible deaths. He liked to think that most were fairly unlikely—a vision of what could have happened if he'd been careless, or if his uncle's training hadn't been so extensive.

Once, Dusk had stayed away from any place where he saw his corpse. It wasn't bravery that drove him to do the opposite now. He just . . . needed to confront the possibilities. He needed to be able to walk away from this beach knowing that he could still deal with cutaway vines. If he avoided danger, he would soon lose his skills. He could not rely on Sak too much.

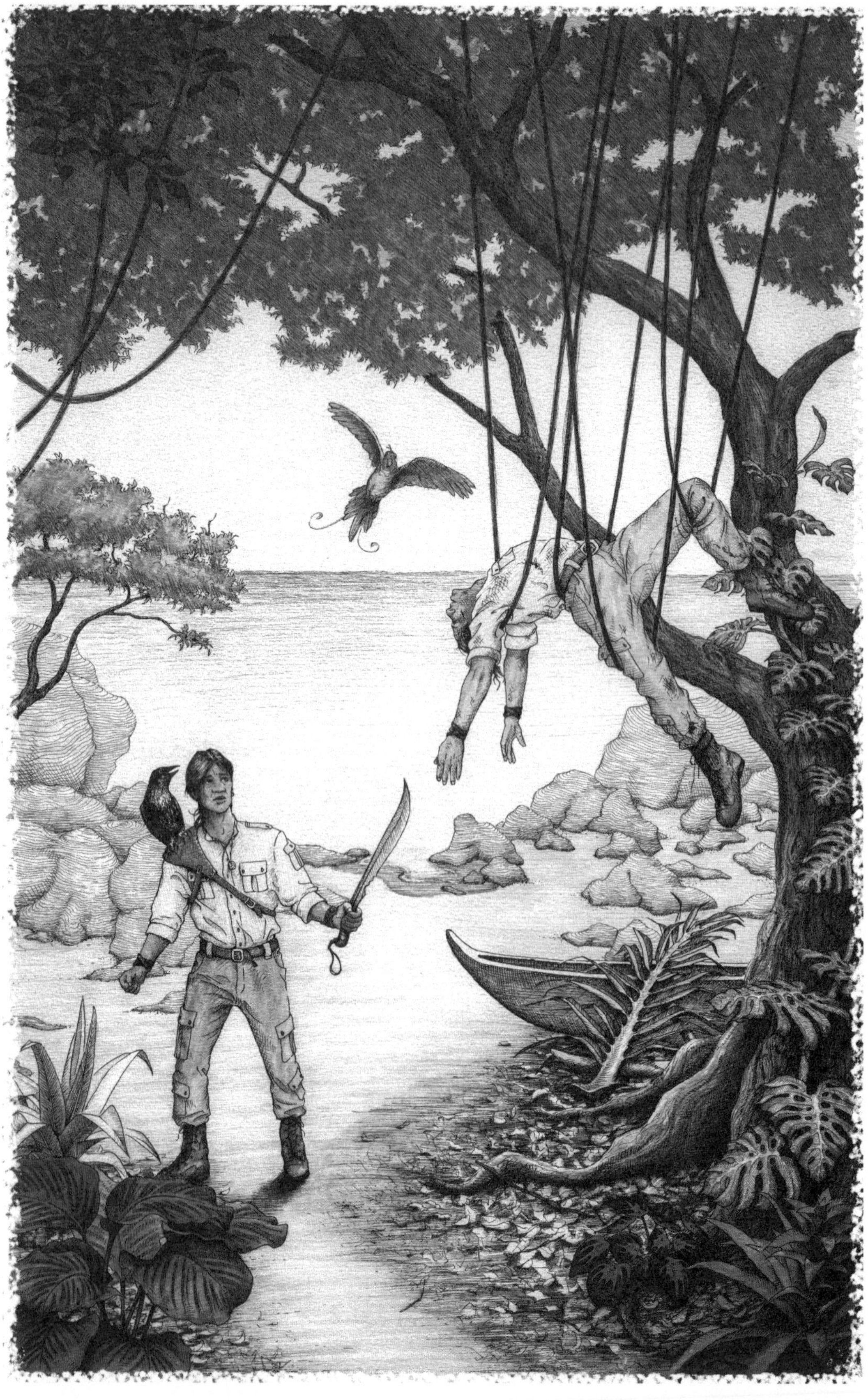

ISLES OF THE EMBERDARK

For Patji would try on every possible occasion to kill him.

Dusk turned and trudged across the rocks along the coast. Doing so went against his instincts—he normally wanted to get inland as soon as possible. Unfortunately, he could not leave without investigating the debris he had seen earlier. He had a strong suspicion of where he would find its source.

He gave a whistle, and Kokerlii trilled above, flapping out of a tree nearby and winging over the beach. With the Aviar that far away, the protections would not be as strong. But the beasts that hunted minds on the island were not as large or as strong of psyche as the shadows of the ocean. Dusk and Sak would be invisible to them, even with Kokerlii flying about.

About a half hour up the coast, Dusk found the remnants of a large camp. Broken boxes, fraying ropes lying half submerged in tidal pools, ripped canvas, shattered pieces of wood that might once have been walls. Kokerlii landed on a broken pole.

There were no signs of his corpse nearby. That could mean that the area wasn't immediately dangerous; it could also mean that whatever might kill him here would swallow the corpse whole, so Dusk trod lightly on wet stones at the edge of the broken campsite.

No. This was larger than a campsite. Dusk ran his fingers over a broken chunk of wood stenciled with the words NORTHERN INTERESTS TRADING COMPANY. A powerful mercantile force from his homeland.

He had told them. He had *told* them. Do not come to Patji. Fools. And they had camped here on the beach itself! Was nobody in that company capable of listening? He stopped beside a group of gouges in the rocks, each as wide as his upper arm, running some ten paces long. They led toward the ocean.

Shadow, he thought. *One of the deep beasts.* His uncle had spoken of seeing one once. An enormous . . . *something* that had exploded up from the depths. It had killed a dozen nell beasts that had been chewing on oceanside weeds, then had retreated into the waters with its feast.

Dusk shivered, imagining this camp on the rocks, bustling with men unpacking boxes, preparing to build the fort they had described to him. But where was their ship? The great steam-powered vessel with an iron hull they claimed could rebuff the attacks of even the deepest shadows? Did it now defend the ocean bottom, a home for slimfish and octopuses?

There were no survivors—nor even any corpses—that Dusk could see. The shadow must have consumed them. He pulled back to the slightly safer locale of the jungle's edge, then scanned the foliage, looking for signs that people had passed this way. The attack was recent, within the last day or so.

He absently gave Sak a seed from his pocket as he located a series of broken fronds leading into the jungle. So there were survivors. Maybe as many as a half dozen. They had each chosen to go in different directions in a hurry, running from the attack.

Dusk shook his head. Running through the jungle was a good way to get dead. These company types thought themselves rugged and prepared. They were wrong. He'd spoken to a number of them, trying to persuade as many of their "trappers" as possible to abandon the voyage.

It had done no good. He wanted to blame the visits of the Ones Above for causing this foolish striving for progress, but the truth was the companies had been talking of outposts on the Pantheon for years.

Dusk sighed. Well, these survivors were likely dead now. He should leave them to their fates.

Except . . . the thought of it—outsiders on Patji—made him shiver with something that mixed disgust and anxiety. They were *here*. It was *wrong*. These islands were sacred, the trappers their priests. And so, he moved beneath the dark canopy, this time trapping not birds, but humans.

Fig. 24 · **Meeker**
(rodent)

CHAPTER FIVE

Dusk went down to the subway.

A new place, with new technology—the type they'd developed on their own, not as gifts from the Ones Above. They'd begun digging their first subway just before the Ones Above had first appeared in the sky. He felt proud of that, as it proved the Eelakin weren't incapable; they were simply new to all of this.

He passed the Aviar roost along the wall, where birds could wait and chatter—and make droppings in an appropriate place. Sak didn't need to go, apparently, because she clung to his arm when he tried to offer her to the roost.

She'd been extra clingy since Kokerlii's passing. He didn't blame her. He felt the same way.

He'd hoped for a sense of comfort here beneath the ground—a place that proved that progress was doing so much for his people. Instead he felt . . . exhausted. Tired in a way that had never happened on Patji, when he'd been a trapper. There, you always needed to be alert. Here, nothing seemed to matter.

Why should that make him *more* tired? It felt backward. He shook his head, and waited on the platform with everyone else. Down here, unlike in the park, nobody recognized him. Here, he was just another person from the city, and city folk kept to themselves. He liked that about them.

His corpse appeared on the tracks.

Dusk paused, cocking his head. Yes, that *was* his corpse—something he hadn't seen in what felt like ages. He glanced at Sak. Why was she showing him this now? Was this . . . a strange way of trying to cheer him up? She chirped. Alert, feathers sticking up. No, this *was* a warning. His life was legitimately in danger, for the first time in years.

He found that invigorating.

Dusk glanced around, searching the crowd on the platform. There. That man worming toward him, with the scraggly beard and the twitching arms. Dusk stepped away from the man, back toward the wall of the platform.

The man scurried away, and Dusk's corpse vanished from the tracks. Dusk scratched Sak's neck in thanks, but then eyed the scraggly man, who was moving farther along the platform. The train was coming. He was inching toward someone else. Was he really just going to *push*?

Without further thought, Dusk dashed across the platform. The train's horn echoed and vibrated the room, and the scraggly man lunged toward a woman on the edge of the platform. Dusk arrived first, seizing the scraggly man by the arm.

The woman, leaning to look at the coming train, didn't notice what was happening behind her. Dusk tightly gripped the scraggly man, who . . . had a star tattooed on his arm?

A falling star?

Coincidence, Dusk thought. It was a popular symbol, considering how it had led Cakoban to these islands. Yet it still stunned Dusk, following the conversation with Frond. As the train pulled slowly to a stop, belching steam, the scraggly man took advantage of Dusk's momentary confusion. The man pulled free, then ran toward the steps.

Dusk smiled.

Never give a trapper something to chase.

The man barely made it to the top of the steps before Dusk—dodging around confused and nervous people—tackled him. The man screamed, claiming he was being assaulted. The police arrived, and they had experience—unfortunately—with unemployed trappers. Many of Dusk's fellows were . . . problems now that their lives had been upended—a situation for which Dusk was partially responsible.

As the police pulled him away, Dusk didn't try to explain. The police didn't like to listen to trappers. And besides, once they realized who he was, they'd call Vathi.

She was president of the First Company now, but when Dusk had met her, she'd been hanging upside down.

Fig. 74 • Mirris
(Aviar)

CHAPTER SIX
Five Years Ago

Dusk froze in the underbrush. What was that rustling? He whipped his machete about, leveling it, while reaching into his pocket for his sling. It was not a refugee who emerged from the bushes just ahead, though, or even a predator. A group of small, mouselike creatures crawled out, sniffing the air. Sak squawked. She had never liked meekers.

Let them through, Dusk commanded Kokerlii. A moment later, he could feel the minds of the meekers.

Food? the three little animals sent to Dusk. *Food?*

It was the most rudimentary of thoughts, projected directly into his mind. He sent back calmness, and fished out some dried meat for the meekers. As they huddled around it, sending him gratitude, he saw their sharp teeth and the single pointed fang at the front. One bite was enough to kill, but over the centuries, the little creatures had grown accustomed to trappers, practically tame.

They had minds beyond those of dull animals. Almost he found them as intelligent as the Aviar. *You remember?* he sent them through thoughts. *You remember your task?*

Others, they sent back gleefully. *Bite others!*

Dusk figured that maybe with some training, the meekers could provide an unexpected surprise for one of his rivals. Not wanting to pass up the opportunity, he got a few long, bright green and red feathers from his pack. They were mating plumes, which he'd taken from Kokerlii during the Aviar's most recent molting.

He moved further into the jungle, meekers following with excitement. Once he neared their den, he stuck the mating plumes into some branches, as if they had fallen there naturally. A passing trapper might see the plumes and assume that Aviar had a nest nearby, fresh with eggs for the plunder. That would draw them.

Bite others, Dusk instructed again.

Bite others! they replied.

He gave them more food. Then he hesitated, thoughtful. Had they perhaps seen something from the company wreck? *Have you seen any others?* Dusk sent them. *Recently? In the jungle?*

Bite others! came the reply.

They were intelligent . . . but not that intelligent. Dusk bade the animals farewell and struck inland, continuing to follow one of the refugee trails. He chose the one that looked as if it would pass uncomfortably close to one of his own safecamps, deep within the jungle. It was hotter here beneath the jungle's canopy, despite the shade. Comfortably sweltering. Kokerlii joined him, winging ahead to a branch where a few lesser Aviar sat chirping. Kokerlii towered over them, but sang at them with enthusiasm.

They ignored him. An Aviar raised around humans never quite fit back in among their own kind. The same could be said of a man raised around Aviar.

Dusk expected to stumble over the refugee's corpse at any moment. He did not, though his own dead body occasionally appeared along the path. He saw it lying half eaten in the mud or tucked away in a fallen log with only the foot showing. He could never grow too complacent with Sak on his shoulder, giving constant reminders of how Patji treated the unwary.

He fell into the familiar, but not comfortable, lope of a Pantheon trapper. Alert, wary, careful not to brush leaves that could carry biting insects. Cutting with the machete only when necessary, lest he leave a trail another could follow. Listening, aware of his Aviar at all times, never outstripping Kokerlii or letting him drift too far ahead.

The refugee did not fall to the common dangers of the island—he cut across game trails, rather than following them. The surest way to encounter predators was to fall in with their food. The refugee did not know how to mask his trail, but neither did he blunder into the nest of firesnap lizards, or brush the deathweed bark, or step into the patch of hungry mud.

Was this another trapper, perhaps? A youthful one, not fully trained? That seemed something the company would try. Experienced trappers were beyond recruitment; none would be foolish enough to guide a group of clerks and merchants around Patji. But a youth, who had not yet chosen his island? A youth who, perhaps, resented being required to practice only on Sori until his mentor determined his apprenticeship complete? Dusk had felt that way in *his* youth.

So the company had hired itself a real trapper at last. That would explain why they had grown so bold as to finally organize their expedition. *But Patji himself?* he thought, kneeling beside the bank of a small stream. It had no name, but it was familiar to him. *Why would they come here?*

The answer was simple. They were merchants. The biggest, to them, would be the best. Why waste time on lesser islands? Why not come for the Father himself?

Above, Kokerlii landed on a branch and began pecking at a fruit. The refugee had stopped by this river. Judging by the depth the boy's footprints had sunk in the mud, Dusk could imagine his weight and height. Sixteen? Maybe younger? Trappers apprenticed at ten, but Dusk could not imagine even this company trying to recruit one so ill trained.

Two hours gone, Dusk thought, turning a broken stem and smelling the sap. The boy's path continued toward Dusk's safecamp. How? Dusk had never spoken of it to anyone. Perhaps this youth was apprenticing under one of the other trappers who visited Patji. One of them could have found his safecamp and mentioned it.

Dusk frowned, considering. In fifteen years on Patji, he had seen another trapper in person only a handful of times. On each occasion, they had both turned and gone a different direction without saying a word. It was the way of such things. They would try to kill one another, but they didn't do it in person. Better to let Patji claim rivals than to directly stain one's hands. At least, so his uncle had taught him.

Sometimes, Dusk found himself frustrated by that. Patji would get them all eventually. Why help the Father do so? He didn't want to kill other trappers. Still, it was the way of things—and regardless, this refugee was making directly for Dusk's safecamp. Perhaps he was seeking help, afraid to go to one of his master's safecamps for fear of punishment. Or . . .

No, best to avoid pondering it. Dusk already had a mind full of conjectures. He would find what he would find. He started away from the stream, and as he did so, his corpse appeared suddenly before him.

He hopped forward, then spun backward, hearing a faint hiss. The distinctive sound was made by air escaping from a small break in the ground, followed by a flood of tiny black insects, each as small as a pinhead. A new deathant hive? If he'd stood there a little longer, disturbing their hidden nest, they would have flooded up around his boot. One bite, and he'd be dead.

He stared at that pool of scrambling insects longer than he should have. They pulled back into their nest, finding no prey, though a few remained to climb up onto nearby plants. Sometimes a small bulge in the forest floor announced their location, or perhaps you could spot their scouts on leaves, but today he had seen nothing. Only Sak's vision had saved him.

Such was life on Patji. Even the most careful trapper could make a mistake. Patji was a domineering, vengeful parent who sought the blood of all who landed on his shores.

Sak chirped on his shoulder. Dusk rubbed her neck in thanks, though her chirp sounded apologetic. The warning had come almost too late. Dusk shoved down those itching questions he should not be thinking—about why Patji was so terrible—and continued on his way, noting the hive-scorpion burrow to the side that he'd marked months ago.

He finally approached his safecamp as evening settled upon the island. Two of his tripwires had been cut, disarming them. That was not surprising; those were meant to be obvious. Dusk crept past another deathant nest in the ground—this larger one had a permanent crack as an opening, but the rift had been stoppered with a smoldering twig. Beyond it, the nightwind fungi that Dusk had spent years cultivating here had been smothered in water to keep the spores from escaping. The next two tripwires—the ones not intended to be obvious—had *also* been cut.

Nice work, kid, Dusk thought. The boy hadn't simply avoided the traps, but disarmed them, in case he needed to flee quickly back this direction. However, someone really needed to teach the boy how to move without being trackable. Though . . . perhaps those tracks were a trap unto themselves—an attempt to make Dusk himself careless. And so, he was extra careful as he edged forward . . .

Something moved in the canopy. Dusk hesitated, squinting. A woman hung from the tree branches above, trapped in a net made of jellywire vines—they left someone numb, unable to move. So one of his traps *had* worked.

"Um, hello?" she said.

A woman, Dusk thought, suddenly feeling stupid. *The smaller footprint, lighter step . . .*

"I want to make it perfectly clear," the woman said, "I have no intention of stealing your birds or infringing upon your territory."

Father. His day had just gotten so, so much worse.

Dusk stepped closer in the dimming light. He recognized this woman. She was one of the clerks who had been at his meetings with the company.

"You cut my tripwires," Dusk said. Words felt odd in his mouth, and they came out ragged, as if he'd swallowed handfuls of dust. The result of weeks without speaking.

"Er, yes, I did. I assumed you could replace them." She hesitated. "Sorry?"

Dusk settled back, squatting, considering. The woman rotated slowly in her net, and he noticed an Aviar clinging to the outside—like his own birds, it was about as tall as three fists atop one another, though this one had subdued white and green plumage. A streamer, which was a breed that did not live on Patji. He did not know much about them, other than the fact that like Kokerlii, they protected the mind from predators.

The setting sun cast long shadows, the sky darkening. Soon he would need to hunker down for the night, for darkness brought out the island's most dangerous of predators.

"I promise," the woman said from within her bindings. What was her name? He believed it had been told to him, but he could not recall. Something untraditional. "I really don't want to steal from you. You remember me, don't you? We met back in the company halls?"

He gave no reply.

"Please," she said. "I'd really rather not be hung by my ankles from a tree, slathered with blood to attract predators. If it's all the same to you."

"You are not a trapper."

"Well, no," she said. "You may have noticed my gender."

"There have been female trappers."

"One. One female trapper, Yaalani the Brave. I've heard her story a hundred times from the loremothers. She dressed as a man in order to trap, and was successful, but I'm half convinced that such stories exist so that parents can tell their daughters, 'You are not Yaalani.'"

This woman spoke. A lot. People did that back on the homeisles. The slight accent to her voice . . . he had heard it more and more when visiting. It was the accent of one who was educated.

"Can I get down?" she asked, voice bearing a faint tremor. "I cannot feel my hands. It is . . . unsettling."

"What is your name?" Dusk asked. "I have forgotten it." This was too much speaking. It hurt his ears. This place was supposed to be soft.

"Vathi."

That's right. It was an improper name. Neither a name of one of the ancients, nor a reference to her birth order. He walked over and took the rope from the nearby tree, then lowered the net. The woman's Aviar flapped down, screeching in annoyance, favoring one wing, obviously wounded. Vathi hit the ground, a bundle of dark curls and green linen skirts. She stumbled to her feet, but fell back down again. Her skin would be numb for some fifteen minutes from the vines.

She sat there and wagged her hands, as if to shake out the numbness. "So . . . uh, no ankles and blood?"

"That is a story parents tell to children," Dusk said. "It is not something we actually do."

"Oh."

"If you had been another trapper, I would have watched until you died, rather than leaving and hoping for a predator to finish you. You might have escaped to avenge yourself upon me." He walked over to her Aviar, which opened its beak in a hissing posture, raising both wings to appear bigger than it was. Sak chirped from his shoulder, but this bird didn't seem to care.

Yes, one wing was bloody. Vathi knew enough to care for the bird, however. She had pulled out the feathers near the wound, including a blood feather. She'd wrapped the wound with gauze. That wing didn't look good, though. Might be a fracture. He'd want to wrap both wings, prevent the creature from flying.

"Oh, Mirris," Vathi said, finally finding her feet. "I tried to help her. We fell, you see, when the monster—"

"Pick her up," Dusk said, checking the sky. "Follow. Step where I step."

Vathi nodded, not complaining, though her numbness would not have passed yet. She collected a small pack from the vines and straightened her skirts. She wore a tight vest above them, and the pack had some kind of metal tube sticking out of it. A map case? She fetched her Aviar, who huddled on her shoulder.

As Dusk led the way around a hive of masher wasps, she followed, and she did not attempt to attack him when his back was turned. Good. Darkness was coming upon them, but his safecamp was just ahead, and he knew by heart the steps to approach. As they walked, Kokerlii fluttered down and landed on the woman's other shoulder, then began chirping.

Dusk stopped, turning. The woman's own Aviar moved down her vest away from Kokerlii to cling near her bodice. The bird hissed softly, but Kokerlii—oblivious, as usual—continued to chirp happily. It was fortunate his breed was so mind-invisible that even deathants would consider him no more edible than a piece of bark. Because he'd likely try to befriend them.

"Is this . . ." Vathi said, looking to Dusk. "Yours . . . but of course. The one on your shoulder is not Aviar."

Sak settled back, puffing up her feathers. No, her species was not Aviar.

Dusk continued to lead the way.

Fig. 59 • Masher wasp (insect)

CHAPTER SEVEN

At the police office, Dusk found his seat. The same one he'd been in . . . what, a dozen times now? Maybe they should put his name on it.

The officers, to their credit, knew he wasn't an actual threat. They let him sit like a child sent to the corner while they called the president's office. Vathi's office.

That woman Dusk had found hanging upside down . . . well, she was kind of a big deal these days. He anticipated the call, hoping he'd be able to speak with her directly, rather than one of her many attendants. While he waited, he felt . . .

Old.

Not aged. In his early forties, he didn't yet have some of the ailments he'd heard the elderly complain about. Maybe he was a tad stiff in the mornings, but that was it.

But he felt old. Old like a horse-drawn carriage. Old like cobblestones in a city full of cement. Old like a handwritten letter when everyone was learning to type.

He had a stipend directly from the government. He could go where he wanted, do what he wanted. He needed nothing.

Except a purpose. Other than to sit in a jar and be shown to children.

Patji send that Frond was right. That Vathi might let him be part of things again. He legitimately had no idea if he could help, but perhaps . . .

An officer arrived with a phone for him, wired to the wall. Dusk breathed deeply, then answered it.

"Dusk?" It was her voice.

"Yes," he replied.

"Oh, Dusk," she said. "Not today. What is it this time? Have you been brawling again?"

"Strange man on the subway," he said. "Tried to push a woman onto the tracks. I stopped him."

"What?" Vathi said. She hesitated. "Really?"

"Sak confirmed it with a corpse."

"Father!" she said. "Why didn't you tell the police *that*?"

He could have. But then <u>he</u> wouldn't have gotten to talk to her.

"You're bored, I suppose," she said. Then she paused. "That didn't sound like a question, but it's the sort of statement that implies it wants a response."

"Oh. Thank you. Yes, I am."

She was silent on the other end of the line. He held his breath.

"You think," she finally said, "you could come give me your gut reaction to something?"

He let out a long breath. Seemed like he was forgiven. Really, he should have known better than to punch a senator. Important people had underlings you punched on their behalf, and he should have found one of those.

"I would love to help," he said. "What is it?"

"The Ones Above are coming down in person today," she said, "for more talks. You want to see what they look like, tell me what you think they *actually* want from us?"

Well look at that. He should cause problems more often.

"Where do you want me?" he asked.

"I'll send a car."

Half an hour later, Dusk climbed out of the car in front of the government offices, and was met by Second of the Soil, one of Vathi's more trusted advisors and a fairly high member in the government himself. An important man, even if he did let his Aviar ride on his head.

"You again," Soil said. "We're having important talks with the Ones Above . . . and she sends me out to fetch *you*?"

Dusk walked up beside him, glanced at his bird, then continued on.

Soil caught up on lanky legs. "Tell me really. Why does she invite you to meetings? I thought, after that last incident, it was through. Yet here you are again?"

"She hopes I will offer a different perspective."

"What kind of perspective would you possibly have?"

"The kind," Dusk said, "of one who looks in from yesterday. Where are they?"

"The talks are mostly finished," Soil said, pointing Dusk in the right direction, "but the observation room, which looks out on their ship, is over here. We should be able to catch them leaving." He paused. "They've said they'll remove their helmets and greet Vathi face-to-face for the first time before they go."

Well. That should be interesting. Dusk hastened his step, and Soil reluctantly handed him something Vathi had sent. Some transcriptions of the talks that day, as typed by the stenographer. He really was forgiven.

Her handwritten note at the bottom said, *I'm sorry.*

He read quickly as they reached the observation room. Inside, a group of generals, kingmakers, chiefs, and senators waited. They uniformly gave him nasty glares.

He didn't care. He read the notes, and realized what was happening. Vathi and the others were close to giving in. The Ones Above were finally winning.

He read that with a sinking sense of loss. However, he didn't have time to consider further as a group of people entered the courtyard beyond the observation room—including Vathi and two alien figures in strange clothing and helmets that covered their entire faces. They walked toward a small, silvery ship waiting in the center of the courtyard.

Not the main ship, which was high in the sky. This little one ferried people, like a fancy canoe. Dusk pressed against the glass. This chamber was supposed to be secret, with reflective glass on the outside, but he didn't trust that. The Ones Above had machines that could sense life.

He suspected they could see him—or at least his Aviar—regardless of the barrier.

He considered demanding to join Vathi and the diplomats on the landing platform, but he supposed he should avoid making trouble so soon after being invited back in. So he stood, waiting, watching as the aliens pushed buttons and retracted their helmets, revealing their faces.

So he was there when, for the first time, they realized the truth. The Ones Above were *human*.

The officials gathered in the room with him gasped as they saw the faces. One male, one female, with strangely pale skin. Perhaps this was what happened when people never saw the sun, living in the emptiness between planets. What were those odd pieces of metal stuck to their cheeks? Ribbed, like ripples of waves, those didn't seem like armor. More ornamental.

Sak squawked softly. Dusk glanced at the jet-black bird, then around the room, seeking signs of his corpse. She squawked again, and it took him another moment to spot the death—it had appeared out on the launchpad. One of the two aliens stood with her foot on Dusk's skull, his face smoldering as if burned by some terrible alien weapon.

What did it mean?

Sak chirped, soft, and he felt something. This . . . was a different kind of vision, wasn't it? Not an immediate danger—but something more abstract. The Ones Above were unlikely to kill him today, but that did not mean they were safe or trustworthy.

He nodded in thanks for her warning.

"Toward a new era of prosperity," one of the Ones Above said, extending a hand to Vathi, who stood at the head of the diplomats. His voice emerged from the speakers on the walls—devices developed using alien technology. "We show you ourselves now, because it is time for the masks to be down. We look forward to many fruitful exchanges between our peoples and yours, President."

Vathi took the hand, though Dusk—personally—would rather have handled a deadly asp. It seemed worse to him, somehow, that the Ones Above were human. An alien monster, with features like something from the deepest part of the ocean, would be more understandable than these smiling humans.

Familiar features should not cover such alien motives and ideas.

"To prosperity," Vathi said.

"It is good," the second alien said, speaking the language of the Eelakin as easily as if she had been born to it, "that you are finally listening to reason. Our masters do not have infinite patience."

"We are accustomed to impatient masters," Vathi said, her voice smooth and confident. "We have survived their tests for millennia."

The male laughed. "Your masters, the gods who are islands?"

"Just be ready to accept our installation when we return, yes?" the female said. "No deception." She tapped her helmet, which extended again, obscuring her features. The male did the same, and together they left, climbing aboard their sleek flying machine—a triangle pointed toward the sky.

It soon took off, streaking through the air without a sound. Its ability to fly baffled explanation; the only thing Dusk's people knew about the process was that the Ones Above had requested the courtyard launchpad be made entirely of steel.

Dusk was barely accustomed to steam-powered ships, but today he felt extra strongly the calm glow of electric lights. The hum of a fan powered by alien energy. The Ones Above had technology so advanced, so incredible, that Dusk and his people might as well have been traveling by canoe like their ancestors. They were far closer to those days than they were to sailing the stars like these aliens.

As soon as the alien ship disappeared into the sky, the generals, chiefs, senators, and First Company officials began chatting in animated ways. It was their favorite thing, talking. Like Aviar come home to roost by light of the evening sun, eager to tell the others about the worms they had eaten.

Sak pecked at the band that kept Dusk's greying hair in a tail. She wanted to hide—though she was no chick, capable of snuggling in his hair as she once had. She was as big as his head, and though he was comfortable and accustomed to her weight, he wore a shoulder pad her claws could grip without hurting him.

He lifted his hand and crooked his index finger, inviting her to stretch out her neck for a scratching. She did so, but he made a wrong move and she squawked at him, then pecked his finger in annoyance.

She got like this when she saw Vathi. Not because Sak disliked the woman, but because Kokerlii had liked her so much, so seeing her reminded them of him.

"I can't bring him back," Dusk whispered. "I'm sorry."

It had been two years since the disease, which had claimed so many Aviar. He worried that without that colorful buffoon around to chatter and stick his beak into trouble, the two of them had grown old and surly.

Sak had nearly died of the same disease. But then alien medicine from the Ones Above had arrived. The terrible Aviar plague—like those that had occasionally ravaged the population in the past—had been smothered in weeks. Gone, wiped out. Easy as tying a double half hitch.

Dusk ignored the human chattering, eventually coaxing Sak into a head scratch as they waited. He very carefully did not punch anyone, though he did watch them. Father . . . Everything about his new life—in the modern city, full of machines and people with clothing as colorful as any plumage—seemed so . . . sanitized.

Not clean. Steam machines weren't clean. Even the new gas machines felt dirty. So no, not clean, but fabricated, deliberate, confined. This room, with its smooth woods and steel beams, was an example. Here, nature was restricted to an armrest, where even the grain of the wood was oriented to be aesthetically pleasing.

She agreed. It's over. No more negotiating.

With the full arrival of the Ones Above, he doubted there would be any wilderness left on the planet. Parks, perhaps. Preserves, like the one he'd just left. Unfortunately, he'd learned that you couldn't put wilderness in a box any more than you could capture the wind. You could enclose the air, but it wasn't the same thing.

Soon, Vathi entered the observation room, Mirris on her shoulder. President of the First Company—which had once been the Northern Interests Trading Company. According to the way of the homeisles, it had made a public bid to take over government administration, and—after a yearlong campaign—had been elected to that duty by the people. Vathi, in turn, had been appointed its leader. An enormous accomplishment to achieve in the five years since she'd been a clerk. A high-ranking one, granted, but still.

ISLES OF THE EMBERDARK

She wore a colorful striped skirt of an old Eelakin pattern and a businesslike blouse and jacket. As always, she tried to embrace a meeting of old ways and new. Dusk wasn't sure you could capture tradition by putting its trappings on a skirt, no more than you could box in the wind, but he . . . appreciated the effort. She was one of the few who did try, among important officials from the various companies.

"Well?" Vathi said to the group. "We've got two months."

Two months? Dusk quickly reread the meeting transcript and found a nugget. She'd agreed *provisionally* to their demands to trade Aviar. Nothing was signed yet. The Ones Above would return in two months to collect the chicks.

Frond's words lingered with him. There was time yet to do something. But what?

"They're not," Vathi said, "going to stand any further delays. Thoughts?"

"We should prepare for the inevitable," said one general. "We've insisted they give us weapons as part of the deal. It is the best we can do."

Others nodded, though they shied away from Dusk as they did so. He had punched the senator because they'd insisted it was time to give in to the Ones Above. It seemed, in Dusk's absence, that others had begun to agree.

"Let's say we wanted to try to stall further," Vathi said. "Any ideas?"

There were a few. One suggested they feign ignorance of the deadline, or plausibly pretend that something had gone wrong with the Aviar delivery. Silly little plans. The Ones Above would not fall for that, and they would not simply trade for birds. According to the transcripts, they intended to put a production plant right on one of the outer isles to raise and ship their own Aviar.

"Maybe we fake a coup," said Tuli, Second Company strategist, who had a colorful Aviar of Kokerlii's same breed. "Overthrow your government. Force the Ones Above to deal with a new organization. Reset the talks?"

A bold idea. Far more radical than others.

"And if they decide to take us over?" said General Second of Saplings, rapping one hand on a stack of papers he held in the other. "We can't fight them. If the mathematicians are right, their orbital ships could reduce our grandest cities to *rubble* with a casual shot or two. If the Ones Above are feeling bored, they could wipe us out in a dozen more interesting ways—like shooting into the ocean so the waves wash away our infrastructure."

"They won't attack," Vathi said. "Eight years or more, and they've suffered our delays with nothing more than threats. There are rules out there, in space, that prevent them from simply conquering us."

"They've already conquered us," Dusk said softly.

Strange, how quickly the others quieted when he spoke. They complained about his presence in these meetings. They thought him a wild man, lacking social graces. They claimed to hate how he watched them, refusing to engage in conversation.

But when he spoke, they grew quiet. Words had their own economics, as sure as precious metals did. The ones in short supply were the ones that, secretly, everyone wanted.

"Dusk?" Vathi said. "What did you say?"

"We are conquered," he said, turning from the window to regard her. She didn't just grow quiet when he spoke. She listened. "The plague that took Kokerlii. How long did they sit in their ship up there, watching as our Aviar died?"

"They didn't have the medicine on hand," said Third of Waves, the First Company medical vice president—a squat man with a bright red Aviar that let him see colors invisible to everyone else. "They had to fetch it."

Dusk remained quiet.

"You imply," Vathi said, "that they *deliberately* delayed giving us the medicine until Aviar had died. What proof do you have?"

"The blackout last month," Dusk said.

The Ones Above were quick to share their more common technologies. Lights that burned cold and true, fans that circulated air in the muggy homeisle summers, ships that moved at several times the speed of steam-powered ones. But all of *these* ran on power sources supplied from above—which deactivated if opened.

"Their fish farms are a boon to our oceans," said the First Company vice president of supply. "But without the nutrients sold by those above, we can't keep the farms running."

"The medicine is invaluable," said Third of Waves. "Infant mortality has plummeted. Literally *thousands* of our people live because of what the Ones Above have traded us."

"When they were late with the power shipment last month," Dusk said, "the city slowed to a crawl. And we know *that* was intentional, from the accidentally leaked comments. They wanted to reinforce to us their control. They will do it again."

Everyone fell silent, thinking—as he wished they'd do more often. Sak squawked again, and Dusk glanced at the launchpad. His corpse was still out there, lying where the Ones Above had left. Burned and withered.

"Show in the other alien," Vathi said to the guards.

Other alien.

What?

The two men at the door, with security Aviar on their shoulders and feathers on their military caps, stepped out of the room. They returned shortly with an incredibly strange figure. The Ones Above wore uniforms and helmets—unfamiliar clothing, but still recognizable.

This creature stood seven feet tall, and was encased entirely in steel. Armor, thick and bulky, with smooth, rounded edges—and a smoky grey light glowing at the joints. The helmet likewise glowed from a slit-like visor that appeared to have glass behind it. An arcane symbol—reminding Dusk vaguely of a bird in flight—was etched into the front of the breastplate.

The ground shook beneath this being's steps as it entered the room. That armor . . . it was surreal, like interlocking plates with no visible seam. Just layered pieces of metal, covering everything from fingers to neck. Obviously airtight, the outfit had stiff iron hoses connecting helmet and armor. The other aliens might have looked human, but Dusk was certain *this* was something frightful. It was too tall, too imposing, to be human. Perhaps he was not looking at a man at all—but instead a machine that spoke as one.

"You did not tell them you have met me?" the alien said, projecting a male voice from speakers at the front of the helmet. The deep voice had a peculiar cast to it. Not an accent, like someone from a backwater isle, but still a kind of . . . unnatural air.

"No," Vathi said. "But you were right. They ignored each of my proposals, and acted as if the deal were already done. They intend to set up their facility here."

"They intend far more than you know," the stranger said. "Tell me. Is there a place on your planet where people vanish unexpectedly? A place, perhaps, where an odd pool collects something that is not quite water?"

Dusk felt a chill. He did his best not to show how much those words disturbed him.

"You have only one gem with which to bargain, people of the isles," the alien said, "and that is your loyalty. You cannot withhold it; you can merely determine to whom you offer it. If you do not accept my protection, you *will* become a vassal of the Scadrians, these 'Ones Above.' Your planet will become a farming station, like many others, used to feed their expansion efforts. Your birds will be stripped from you the moment it becomes possible to do so."

"And you offer something better?" Vathi asked.

"My people will give you back one out of a hundred birds born," the armored alien said, "and will allow you to fight alongside us, if you wish, to gain status and elevation."

"One in a *hundred*?" Second of Saplings said, the outburst unsettling his grey and brown Aviar. "Robbery!"

"Choose," the alien said. "Cooperation, slavery, or death."

"And if I choose not to be bullied?" Saplings snapped, reaching—perhaps unconsciously—for the repeating pistol he carried in a holster at his side.

The alien thrust out his armored hand, and smoke—or mist—coalesced there out of nowhere. It formed into a gun, longer than a pistol, shorter than a rifle. Wicked in shape, with flowing metal along the sides like wings, it was to Saplings's pistol what a shadowy deep beast of the ocean was to a minnow. The alien raised his other hand, snapping a small box—perhaps a power supply—to the side of the rifle, causing it to glow ominously.

"Tell me, President," the alien said to Vathi. "What are your local laws regarding challenges to my life? Do I have legal justification to shoot this man?"

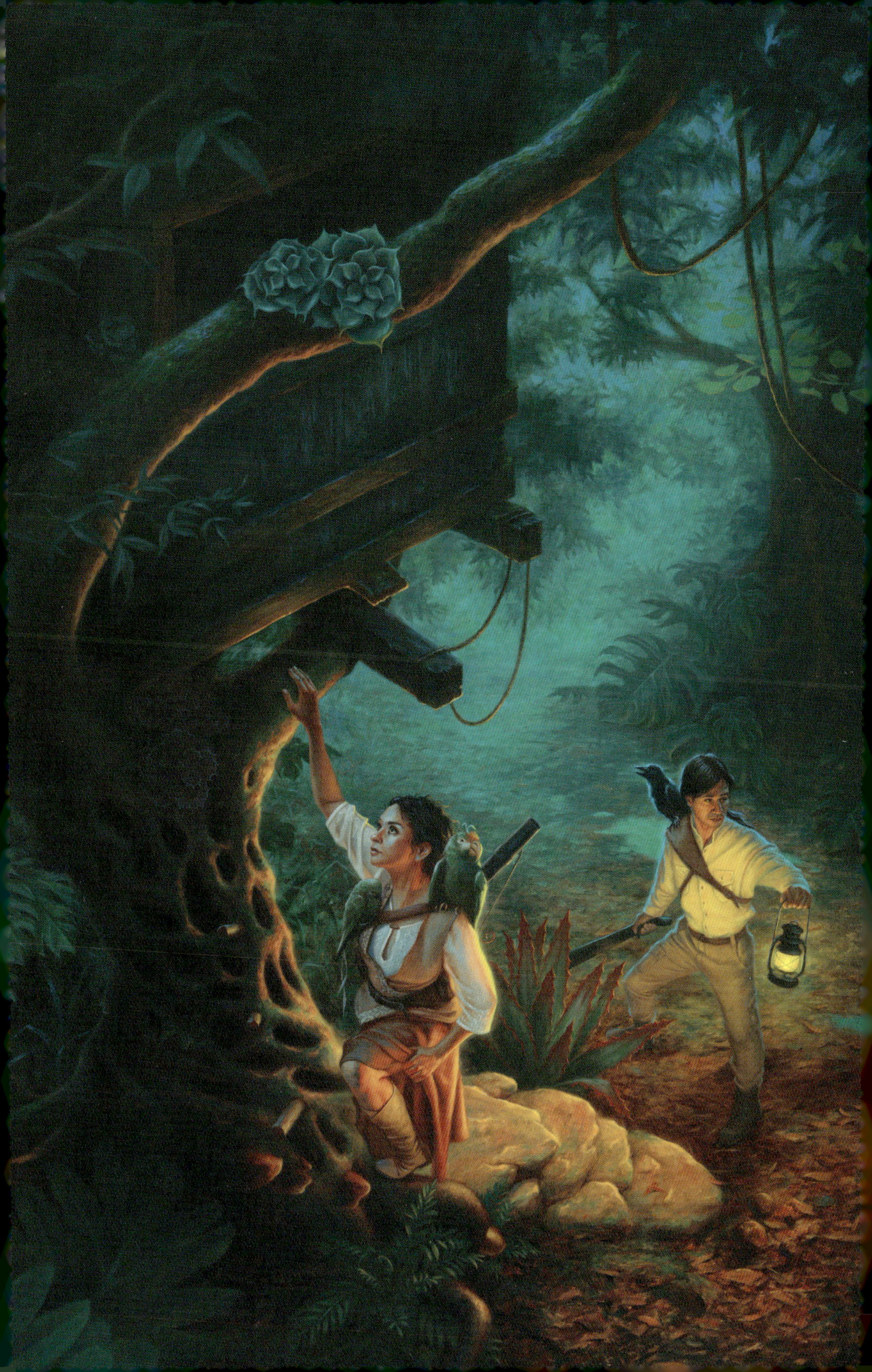

"No," Vathi said, firm—though her voice was audibly shaken. "You do not."

"I will not play games," the alien said. "I will not dance with words, like those Scadrians. You will accept my offer or you will not. If you join them, know that I will have legal right to consider you enemies."

The room remained still, Saplings carefully edging his hand away from his sidearm.

"I do not envy your decision," the armored alien said. "You have been thrust into a conflict you do not understand. But like a child who has found himself in the middle of a war zone, you *will* have to decide which direction to run."

The glowing portions of the creature's armor brightened, a glimmering silver far too inviting to come from this strange being. He lifted into the air a few inches, then finally pulled the power pack from his gun. The weapon vanished in a puff of mist.

He left without further word, gliding past the guards—who stepped away and didn't impede him.

"What was *that*?" Dusk demanded.

"He arrived early this morning," Vathi said, "with a simple offer. No negotiating." She hesitated. "He doesn't seem to need a ship to travel the stars. He . . . flew out of the sky under his own power."

"Or that of his armor," one of the kingmakers said—Dusk didn't know her name. "Perhaps that armor . . ."

The two guards took up positions at the door, sheepishly holding their rifles. But everyone in the room knew that no guard could stop a creature like that. Vathi pulled a chair over to the room's small table, then sat in a slumped posture, Mirris crawling anxiously across her back from one shoulder to the other.

"This is it," Vathi whispered. "This is our fate. Caught between the ocean wave and the unbroken stone."

This job had weathered her. Dusk missed the woman she had been—so full of life and optimism—but she was right. This was their fate, so there was no sense in offering meaningless aphorisms. Besides. She had not asked a question.

Sak chirped, and a body appeared on the table in front of Vathi. Dusk frowned. Then that frown deepened.

Because the corpse was *not his*.

Never in all his time bonded to Sak had she shown him anything other than his own corpse. Even during that dangerous time years ago, when her abilities had grown erratic, she'd shown Dusk only his own body.

He stepped across the room, and Vathi looked up, seeming relieved—as if she expected him to comfort her. She frowned when he ignored her to inspect the body on the table. It was female, very old, long hair having gone white. The corpse wore an unfamiliar uniform after the cut of the Ones Above. Commendations on the breast pocket, but in another language.

It's her, he thought, studying the aged face. *Vathi, some forty years in the future. Dead, dressed for a funeral.*

"Dusk?" the living Vathi said. "What do you see?"

"Corpse," Dusk said, causing others in the room to murmur. They were uncomfortable with Sak's power, which was unique among Aviar. He knew some disbelieved it existed, and he hadn't cared to prove anything to them.

"That's wonderfully descriptive, Dusk," Vathi said. "One might think that after *five years* you might learn to answer with more than one word."

He grunted, walking around the vision. "Corpse," he said, then met the living Vathi's eyes. "Yours."

Fig. 36 • **Memist**
(vines)

CHAPTER EIGHT
Five Years Ago

Dusk led the way through the darkness to his safecamp, where he could stay protected from the dangers of the night. But nothing could protect him from the jabbering of the homeisler he'd rescued.

"I have never seen a trapper carry a bird who was not from the islands," Vathi said from behind.

It was not a question. Dusk, therefore, felt no need to reply.

"What breed is it?" Vathi continued. "Where did you find it? Why would you keep it with your Aviar?"

Those were questions. But he didn't want to give the answers, so he kept walking. Leading her in a wide circle around a patch of memist vines. Finally, they arrived. This safecamp—he had three on the island—lay atop a short hill following a twisting trail. Here, a stout gurratree held aloft a single-room structure, marked with a few warning signs with his symbol on them. Trees—domain of the Aviar—were one of the safer places to sleep on Patji.

Dusk lit his lantern, then held it aloft, letting the orange light bathe his home. "Up," he said to the woman.

She glanced over her shoulder into the black jungle. By the lantern light, he saw that the whites of her eyes were red from lack of sleep, despite the unconcerned smile she gave him before climbing up the stakes he'd planted in the tree.

"How did you know?" he asked.

Vathi hesitated near the trapdoor leading into his home. "Know what?"

"Where my safecamp was. Who told you?"

"I followed the sound of water," she said, nodding toward the small spring that bubbled out of the mountainside here. "When I found traps, I knew I was coming the right way."

Dusk frowned. One could not hear this water from a distance, as the stream vanished a few hundred yards away, resurfacing in an unexpected location. Following it here . . . would be virtually impossible.

So was she lying, or was she just lucky?

"You wanted to find me," he said.

"I wanted to find *someone*," she said, pushing open the trapdoor, voice growing muffled as she climbed into the building. "I figured that a trapper would be my only chance for survival." Above, she stepped up to one of the netted windows, Kokerlii still on her shoulder. "This is nice. Very roomy for a shack on a mountainside in the middle of a deadly jungle on an isolated island surrounded by monsters."

Dusk climbed up, holding the lantern in his teeth. The room at the top was perhaps four paces square, tall enough to stand in, but barely. "Shake out those blankets," he said, nodding toward the stack and setting down the lantern. "Then lift every cup and bowl on the shelf and check inside of them."

Her eyes widened. "What am I looking for?"

"Deathants, scorpions, spiders, bloodscratches . . ." He shrugged, putting Sak on her perch by the window. "The room is built to be tight, but this is Patji. The Father likes surprises."

As she hesitantly set aside her pack and got to work, Dusk continued up another ladder to check the roof. There, a group of bird-sized boxes—with nests inside and holes to allow the birds to come and go freely—lay arranged in a double row. The animals would not stray far, except on special occasions, now that they had been raised with him handling them.

Kokerlii landed on top of one of the homes, trilling—but softly, now that night had fallen. More coos and chirps came from the other boxes. Dusk checked each bird for hurt wings or feet. These Aviar breeding pairs were his life's work; the chicks each one hatched became his primary stock in trade. Yes, he would trap on the island, trying to find nests and wild chicks—but that was never as efficient as raising nests.

"Your forename was Sixth, wasn't it?" Vathi said from below, voice accompanied by the sound of a blanket being shaken.

"It is."

"Large family," Vathi noted.

An ordinary family. Or so it had once been. His father had been a twelfth and his mother an eleventh.

"Sixth of what?" Vathi prompted below.

"Of the Dusk."

"So you were born in the evening," Vathi said. "I've always found the traditional names so . . . uh . . . *descriptive*."

What a meaningless comment, Dusk thought. *Why do homeislers feel the need to speak when there is nothing to say?*

He moved on to the next nest, checking the two drowsy birds inside, then inspecting their droppings. They responded to his presence with happiness. An Aviar raised around humans—particularly one that lent its talent to a person at an early age—would always see people as part of their flock. These birds were not his companions, like Sak and Kokerlii, but they were still special to him.

"No insects in the blankets," Vathi said, sticking her head up out of the trapdoor behind him, her own Aviar on her shoulder.

"The cups?"

"I'll get to those in a moment. So these are your breeding pairs, are they?"

Obviously they were, so he didn't need to reply.

She watched him check them. He felt her eyes on him. Finally he spoke. "Why did your company ignore the advice we gave you? Coming here was a disaster."

"Yes."

He turned to her.

"Yes," she continued, "this whole expedition will likely be a disaster—a disaster that takes us a step closer to our goal."

He checked Sisisru next, working by the light of the now-rising moon. "Foolish."

Vathi folded her arms before her on the roof of the building, torso still disappearing into the lit square of the trapdoor below. "Do you think that our ancestors learned to wayfind on the oceans without experiencing a few disasters along the way? Or what of the first trappers?"

"You mean Cakoban?" he asked.

"Who?"

He stopped, then turned to her, amazed. "You don't know *Cakoban*? Called Tenth the Navigator? First trapper of Patji?"

"I . . . honestly can't remember."

He stopped what he was doing and crawled across the roof, closer to her, holding out his medallion. "Here, him. You said you've studied and read about trappers; we all carry his medallion. How can you not know about him? Do you never listen to the loremothers?"

"Um . . . I've met a lot of trappers, Dusk. None of them had one of those."

"The good ones do," he said, turning away from her. "This is a reminder."

"Of . . ."

"Tradition and heritage."

"Well . . . where did tradition come from? You survive on this island using knowledge passed down for generations—knowledge earned through trial and error. If the first trappers had considered it too 'foolish' to do what is dangerous, where would you be?"

She . . . had a very small point. He returned to his birds. "The first trappers were well-trained explorers. Not a ship full of clerks and dockworkers."

"The world is changing, Sixth of the Dusk," she said softly. "And we need to change with it. We've learned so much, yet the Aviar are still an enigma. Why don't chicks raised on the homeisles bestow talents? Why—"

"Foolish arguments," Dusk said, putting Sisisru back into her nest. "I do not wish to hear them again."

"And the Ones Above?" she asked. "What of their technology, the wonders they produce?"

He hesitated, then he took out a pair of thick gloves and gestured toward her white and green Aviar. Vathi looked at Mirris, then made a comforting clicking sound and took her in two hands. The bird suffered it with a few annoyed half bites at Vathi's fingers.

Dusk carefully took the bird in his gloved hands—for him, those bites would not be as timid—and undid Vathi's bandage. Still on the rooftop, near his medical station, he cleaned the wound—much to the bird's protests—and carefully placed a new bandage. From there, he wrapped the bird's wings around its body with another bandage, not too tight, lest the creature be unable to breathe.

Mirris didn't like it, obviously, but with the fracture, flying would hurt that wing more. She'd eventually bite off the bandage, but for now, she'd get a chance to heal. He placed her with his other Aviar, who made quiet, friendly chirps, calming the flustered bird.

Vathi seemed content to let her bird remain there for the time being, though she watched the entire process with interest.

"You may sleep in my safecamp tonight," Dusk said, turning back to her.

"And then what?" she asked. "You turn me out into the jungle to die?"

"You did well on your way here," he said, grudgingly. She was not a trapper. A company woman should not have been able to do what she did. "You will probably survive."

"I got lucky. I'd never make it across the entire island."

Dusk paused. "Across the island?"

"To the main company camp."

"There are more of you?"

"I . . . Of course. You didn't think . . ."

"What happened?" *Now who is the fool?* he thought to himself. *You should have asked this first.* Talking. He had never been good with it.

She shied away from him, eyes widening. Did he look dangerous? Perhaps he had barked that last question forcefully. No matter. She spoke, so he got what he needed.

"We set up camp on the far beach," she said. "We have two ironhulls armed with cannons watching the waters. Those can take on even a deepwalker, if they have to. Two hundred soldiers, half that number in scientists and merchants. We're determined to find out, once and for all, why the Aviar must be born on one of the Pantheon Islands to be able to bestow talents.

"One team came down this direction to scout sites to place another fortress. The company is determined to hold Patji against other interests. I thought the smaller expedition a bad idea, but had my own reasons for wanting to circle the island. So I went along. And then, the deepwalker..." She looked sick.

Dusk had almost stopped listening. Two *hundred* soldiers? Crawling across Patji like ants on a fallen piece of fruit. Unbearable! He thought of the quiet jungle broken by the sounds of their racketous voices. Of humans yelling at each other, clanging on metal, stomping about. Like a city.

A flurry of dark feathers announced Sak coming up from below and landing on the lip of the trapdoor beside Vathi. The black-plumed bird limped across the roof toward Dusk, stretching her wings, showing off the long-healed scars on her left. Flying even a dozen feet was a chore for her.

Dusk reached down to scratch her neck. It was happening. An invasion of the Father. His home.

He *had* to find a way to stop it.

Fig. 53 · Tokka
(carnivorous plant)

CHAPTER NINE

"**My corpse?**" **Vathi said, rising** from her seat by the table in the observation room, which looked out at the empty courtyard and steel launchpad. She glanced at Sak, who huddled on Dusk's shoulder, feathers pulled tight. "Why? Has she ever done this before?"

Dusk shook his head, rounding the corpse. "The body wears a uniform. One of theirs. The Ones Above. There are symbols on some of the patches and awards. I cannot read the alien writing, but the body appears as if prepared for burial at sea."

One of the generals scrambled to get him paper and a pen, then backed away, regarding the table as one might a nightmaw ready to pounce.

Dusk copied the letters on the uniform's most prominent patch.

"Vathi," said the Secretary of Supply. "It really is their writing. It says . . . you are colonial governor of the occupied planet Drominad."

All eyes in the room turned toward Vathi. All but Dusk's. He knew what she looked like. So he kept writing, then nudged the Secretary of Supply again.

"A commendation for valor," the woman continued. "For putting down something called the Saoa Rebellion. The date is . . . twenty years from now? The others are similar."

If this were a glimpse of the future, it was what Vathi would be when she died. A servant of the Ones Above, apparently having turned the Eelakin militaries against dissidents. That made sense. He nodded to himself, then noticed the corpse holding something in a clutched hand. A small disk or coin, with a drawing on it?

Father. It was his medallion. The one with Cakoban on it. He had given that to her five years ago . . . on Patji.

"Dusk, you don't seem as horrified as you should be," the living Vathi said.

"Why would I be horrified?" he said. "This makes sense. It's what you would do. Probably what you *will* do."

"I'm no traitor," she said.

He didn't reply. It hadn't been a question. Even if it was an incorrect statement.

"Leave us," she said to the others. "Please. We can discuss this . . . prophecy later. I need to confer with the trapper."

They didn't like it. They never liked when Vathi listened to him. Perhaps they'd understand if they listened more themselves. Still, they filed out, leaving the two humans and two Aviar alone. Mirris hunched down and raised her wings, eyeing the table. It seemed that she could sense what Sak was doing. Curious.

"Dusk," Vathi said. "Why do you think I'd do these things?"

"Progress. It is your way."

"Progress is not worth the blood of my people."

"It will come anyway," Dusk said. "The dusk has passed. This is the night. You will presume to find a new dawn, and do what you must to guide us there." He looked to her, then tried to smile. "There is a wisdom to that, Vathi. It is what you taught me, years ago."

She wrapped her arms around herself, staring at the table. "Must it be?"

"No. I am not dead, am I, for all the times I've seen myself this way?"

She shook her head. "I want a way out, Dusk. A way to fight back, or . . . something. A way to control our own destiny. The aliens are all so confident that they own us. What I wouldn't give to surprise them . . ."

"Your corpse is holding the Cakoban medallion I gave you," Dusk said, leaning down. "Did you ever go hear his story, like I asked?"

"Cakoban," she said. "Also called Tenth the Navigator. Of course I did. But . . . it's only a story."

"Stories are important," he said. "I live because of the stories of trappers, who told me what to avoid."

"Yes, but this story? It's fanciful."

"Tell it to me."

She sighed, sitting with arms crossed on the table before her own lifeless body. "He led our people across the endless sea of night. He fought and killed the Dakwara, and—"

"He didn't kill it," Dusk said.

"He *defeated* the Dakwara, then. And was rewarded with a shooting star, which led him to Patji. Dusk, if he really was the first to visit the island, he'd have died quickly. I don't need to tell *you* how dangerous Patji is."

She was right, there. The first trappers were stupid. Not because of themselves; they just didn't have experience yet.

"We have the stories," he said. "They came from somewhere."

"You really believe there's a serpent whose tail stretches the entire ocean?" she said. "You've been out there. You've seen nothing like that."

True. But there was a great deal beneath the waves he'd never seen. And never wanted to.

"Do you deny," he said, "that our ancestors were explorers?"

"Of course not," she said. "We still are, and I appreciate the old stories—but it doesn't mean I think they are the same as accurate histories."

Perhaps she had a point. And she *had* studied, as he'd asked. She fancied herself an amateur trapper, even still, despite the fact that she had been one of those who ended the entire profession.

As Dusk studied the medallion, the vision finally vanished. Sak chirped, as if apologetic—and when Dusk looked at her, the bird's neck was drooping. She was clearly exhausted.

"I'm going to investigate stepping down," Vathi said. "A fake coup is silly, but if I simply quit, it could cause political unrest that justifies delaying negotiations. Plus, it will remove me from a position where I can do damage."

Dusk nodded. Then felt himself growing uncomfortable. For once, he found that he couldn't remain silent. "Another will do worse, Vathi. Another will cause more death. You are better than another."

"Are you sure?"

"No." How could he be? He could not see the future like Sak could. Still, he crouched beside Vathi's seat, then held his hand toward her.

She clasped it and held tight.

"You are stronger than anyone I know," he said. "But you are just one person. I learned five years ago that sometimes one person cannot stand before the tide."

"Then there's no hope."

"Of course there is. Cakoban did not give up when he was dying of starvation in endless night."

"Was he even real, though?" she asked.

"Vathi," he said softly, "have you considered that we discovered the very thing this armored stranger mentioned?"

"The pool?"

"Yes," he said. "More importantly, what's on the other side." He paused. "The endless night, Vathi. It's real. And we must tame it."

Fig. 74 • *Mirris*
(Aviar)

CHAPTER TEN
Five Years Ago

That horrid woman wouldn't stop talking.

"I'm sorry, Dusk," Vathi was saying as they sat near his birds on the roof of his safecamp. "The trappers are fascinating to me. I've read of your ways, and I respect them. But modernization of Patji was *going* to happen someday; it's inevitable. The islands *will* be tamed. The Aviar are too valuable to leave in the hands of a couple hundred eccentric woodsmen."

"The chiefs . . ."

"The hundred and twenty chiefs in council agreed to this plan," Vathi said, "by supermajority vote. I was there. They did not overrule the senate; everyone agrees. If the Eelakin do not secure these islands and the Aviar, someone else will."

Dusk stared into the night. "Go and make certain there are no insects in the cups below."

"But—"

"*Go*," he said, "and make *certain* there are no insects in the cups below!"

The woman sighed softly, but retreated down the ladder into the room below. He scratched Sak on the neck, seeking comfort in the familiar motion and in her presence. Dare he hope that the shadows would prove too deadly for the company and its iron-hulled ships? Vathi seemed confident.

She did not tell me why she joined the scouting group. She had seen a shadow, witnessed it destroying her team, but had still managed the presence of mind to find his camp. She was a strong woman. He would need to remember that.

She was also a company type, as removed from his experience as a person could get. Soldiers, craftsmen, even chiefs he could understand. But these soft-spoken scribes who had quietly conquered the world with a sword of commerce, they baffled him.

"Father," he whispered. "What do I do?"

Patji gave no reply beyond the normal sounds of night. Creatures moving, hunting, rustling. At night, the Aviar slept, and that gave opportunity to the most dangerous of the island's predators. In the distance a nightmaw called, its horrid screech echoing through the trees.

Sak spread her wings, leaning down, head darting back and forth. The sound always made her tremble. It did the same to Dusk.

He sighed and rose, placing Sak on his shoulder. He turned, and almost stumbled as he saw his corpse at his feet. He came alert immediately. What was it? Vines in the tree branches? A spider, dropping quietly from above? There wasn't supposed to be anything in his safecamp that could kill him.

Sak screeched as if in pain.

Nearby, his other Aviar cried out as well, a cacophony of squawks, screeches, chirps. No, it wasn't just them! All around . . . echoing in the distance, from both near and far, wild Aviar squawked. They rustled in their branches, a sound like a powerful wind blowing through the trees.

Dusk held his hands to his ears, eyes wide as corpses appeared around him. They piled high, one atop another, some bloated, some bloody, some skeletal. Haunting him. Dozens upon *dozens*.

He dropped to his knees, yelling. That put him eye-to-eye with one of his corpses. Only this one . . . this one was not quite dead. Blood dripped from its lips as it tried to speak, mouthing words that Dusk did not understand.

It vanished.

They all did, every last one. He spun about, wild, but saw no bodies. The sounds of the Aviar quieted, and his flock settled back into their nests. Dusk breathed in and out deeply, heart racing. He felt tense, as if at any moment a shadow would explode from the blackness around his camp and consume him.

He anticipated it, felt it coming. He wanted to run, run *somewhere*.

What had that been? In all of his years with Sak, he had never seen anything like it. What could have upset all of the Aviar at once? Was it the nightmaw he had heard?

Don't be foolish, he thought. *This was different from anything you've seen. Different from anything that has been seen on Patji.* But what? What had changed . . .

Sak had not settled down like the others. She stared northward, toward where Vathi had said the main camp of company people was setting up.

Dusk stood, then clambered down into the room below, Sak on his shoulder. "What are your people doing?"

Vathi spun at his harsh tone. She had been looking out of the window, northward. "I don't—"

He took her by the front of her vest, pulling her toward him in a two-fisted grip, meeting her eyes from only a few inches away. "*What are your people doing?*"

Her eyes widened, and he could feel her tremble in his grip, though she set her jaw and held his gaze. Scribes were not supposed to have grit like this. He had seen them scribbling away in their windowless rooms. Dusk tightened his grip on her vest, pulling the fabric so it dug into her skin, and found himself growling softly.

"Release me," she said, "and we will speak."

"Bah," he said, letting go. She dropped a few inches, hitting the floor with a thump. He hadn't realized he'd lifted her off the ground.

She backed away, putting as much space between them as the room would allow. He stalked to the window, looking through the mesh screen at the night. His corpse dropped from the roof above, hitting the ground below. He jumped back, worried that it was happening again.

It didn't, not the same way as before. However, when he turned back into the room, his corpse lay in the corner, bloody lips parted, eyes staring sightlessly. The danger, whatever it was, had not passed.

Vathi had sat down on the floor, holding her head, shaking. Had he frightened her that soundly? She did look tired, exhausted. She wrapped her arms around herself, and when she looked at him, there was a cast to her eyes that hadn't been there before—as if she were regarding a wild animal.

That seemed fitting.

"What do you know of the Ones Above?" she asked him.

"They live in the stars," Dusk said.

"We at the company have been meeting with them. As have other companies. We don't understand their ways. They look like us—two arms, two legs. They wear helmets, so we can't see their faces, but they speak our language.

"They have . . . rules, laws that they won't explain. They refuse to sell us their marvels, but in like manner, they seem forbidden from taking things from us by force. They warn it might happen, though, someday when we are more advanced. Or . . . if we keep resisting what is good for us. It's like they think we are children."

"Why should we care?" Dusk said. "If they leave us alone, we will be better for it."

"You haven't seen the things they can do," she said softly, getting a distant look in her eyes. "We have barely harnessed steamships. But the Ones Above . . . they can sail the *stars themselves*." She shook her head, reaching into the pocket of her skirt. "What interest do we hold for them? From what I've heard them say, there are many other worlds like ours, with cultures that cannot sail the stars. We are not unique, yet the Ones Above come back here time and time again. They do want something. You can see it in the questions they ask . . ."

"What is that?" Dusk asked, nodding to the thing she took from her pocket. It rested in her palm like the shell of a clam, but had a mirrorlike face on the top.

"It is a machine," she said. "Like a clock, only it never needs to be wound, and it . . . shows things."

"What things?"

"Well, it translates languages. Ours into that of the Ones Above. It also . . . shows the locations of Aviar."

"What?"

"It's like a map," she said. "It points the way to Aviar."

"*That's* how you found my camp."

"Yes." She rubbed her thumb across the machine's surface. "We aren't supposed to have this. One of their emissaries left it—and a few other things—behind by accident. They can make mistakes, stupid ones. He later returned, searching for his machines, and we will have to return them soon. But this device tells us what they are after: the Aviar. The Ones Above are always fascinated with them. They want to trade for the birds, in a way their laws allow. They hint that we might not be safe, that not everyone Above follows their laws, that we should accept their protections."

"But why did the Aviar react like they did, just now?" Dusk said, turning back to the window. "Why did . . ." *Why did I see what I saw? What I'm still seeing, to an extent?* His corpse was there, wherever he looked. Slumped by a tree outside, in the corner of the room, hanging out of the trapdoor in the roof. Sloppy. He should have closed that.

Sak had pulled into his hair like she did when a predator was near. Even Kokerlii, on his perch, seemed nervous for once—and quiet.

"There . . . is a second machine," Vathi said.

"Where?" he demanded.

"On our ship."

The direction the Aviar had looked.

"The second machine is much larger," Vathi said. "This one in my hand has limited range. The larger one can create an enormous map, one of an entire island, then *write* it out on paper. That map will include a dot marking every Aviar."

"And?"

"And we were going to engage the machine tonight," she said. "It takes hours to prepare—like an oven, growing hot—before it's ready. The schedule was to turn it on to warm up tonight just after sunset so we could use it in the morning."

"The others," Dusk demanded, "they'd use it without you?"

She grimaced. "Happily. Captain Eusto probably did a dance when I didn't return from scouting. He's been worried I would take control of this expedition. But the machine isn't harmful; it merely locates Aviar."

"Did it do *that* before?" he demanded, waving toward the night. "When you last used it, did it draw the attention of all the Aviar? Discomfort them?"

"Well, no," she said. "But the moment of discomfort has passed, hasn't it? I'm sure it's nothing."

Nothing. Sak quivered on his shoulder. Dusk saw death all around him. The moment they had engaged that machine, the corpses had piled up. If they used it again, the results would be horrible. Dusk knew it. He could *feel* it.

"We're going to stop them," he said.

"What?" Vathi asked. "Tonight?"

"Yes," Dusk said, closing the trapdoor and walking to a small hidden cabinet in the wall. He pulled it open and began to pick through the supplies inside. A second lantern. Extra oil.

"That's insane," Vathi said. "Nobody travels the islands at night."

"I've done it once before. With my uncle."

His uncle had died on that trip.

"You can't be serious, Dusk. The nightmaws are out."

"Nightmaws track minds," Dusk said, stuffing supplies into his pack. "They are almost completely deaf, and close to blind. If we move quickly and cut across the center of the island, we can be to your camp by morning. We can stop them from using the machine again."

"But why would we want to?"

He shouldered the pack. "Because if we don't, it will destroy the island."

Fig. 25 · *Sak*
(Aviar)

CHAPTER ELEVEN

The group of generals, chiefs, kingmakers, officials, and senators reluctantly convened another meeting to discuss. And even more reluctantly, they put up with Dusk being there. He had no official government position, but he *had* discovered the thing they were talking about. Plus, he got the sense that nobody wanted to fight Vathi about him right now.

They instead wanted to fight her about sending another expedition into the darkness.

"I thought we'd decided on this," said Admiral Rattu. He had a large, yellow-chested Aviar, otherwise pure green, that liked to puff out its feathers. It sat on his shoulder, looking like an owl—or maybe a soldier who had just been given his first award, standing proud, chest out.

"Let's assume," Vathi said from the head of the long table, "I want to discuss it again. The newcomer, the one in the armor, mentioned the pool. It must mean something."

Admiral Rattu sighed, and his Aviar chirped. The others in the room seemed content to let him do the talking as he stood and set up some images on a corkboard. They showed a warship full of soldiers. And a strange land with a black sky, and no sun. Endless darkness beyond.

"We *tried*," Rattu said. "Madam President, I don't think you appreciate the difficulty we had assembling a ship on the other side, in that dark dimension. It took an extreme amount of work to prepare, outfit, and launch it—not the least of which being the fact that we had to carry it across *dry land* in *pieces* to get it through the portal."

"You sent an expedition?" Dusk said, leaning forward. "You actually *tried* it? And nobody told me?"

"You were still grounded," Vathi said.

"Grounded?" he said, amused. "You called it that?"

"Internally, yes," she said. "If you punch another senator, we'll make it permanent." She waved a hand, and Rattu passed Dusk some pictures—photographs, using the newest technology—of the expedition.

"How?" Dusk asked. "How did that ship float?"

"We discovered it by accident," Vathi said. "The worms, Dusk. They float in the . . . the not-water on the other side."

The worms? The ones he and Vathi had revealed?

Interesting.

He turned to another page depicting the strange darkness. They'd found the place—the dimension—only two years ago. The clue had come from a discussion with the Ones Above, who asked—trying to make it sound offhanded and irrelevant—if anyone on the planet knew of a strange pool where people sometimes disappeared. Just as the creature in the armor had asked.

"They know," he said, looking through the images, "that this portal leads somewhere important. They're trying to reach it."

"You can't possibly know that," Admiral Rattu said. "It's conjecture."

"It's where we came from," Dusk whispered. He'd been to this dimension once, before being grounded.

"It . . . does sound like the stories," one of the senators said. "I think the trapper might have a point."

He made a mental note never to punch her.

"It's never made sense," Chief Second of the Palm said, "when people say we came from the mainland. It's a frozen wasteland. Felt like nonsense to me that we would be born somewhere so close. No, we sailed long distances—my son still practices the old arts. We came from far away."

"We crossed the night sea," another senator said. "Isn't that what the endless darkness means?"

"No," Dusk said, looking through the pages. "No, I've seen this place. It does seem endless . . . and it's where we came from. So if we crossed this long ago, we can do so again." He reached a page with a picture of their ship. "How do you float on an ocean that doesn't quite exist? You made pontoons out of the worms, perhaps?"

Vathi smiled.

"What?" he asked her.

"It took us weeks to hit on that idea."

"It's so simple, though. The worms float. So you see how much they can float."

"A trapper solution," she said. "Eminently practical."

"With some refinement of the idea," Admiral Rattu said, "we discovered that if you mash up the worms, they keep glowing. That makes a paste you can spread on the bottom of a ship, making it capable of floating upon the strange sea out in the dark place."

"Excellent," Dusk said. "What happened to the expedition?"

"Dead," Admiral Rattu said softly. "We set a radio beacon, but without something to triangulate by, it was difficult for them to navigate. They sailed for months, but could not find their way back. Radio was sporadic and warped, so they couldn't follow the beacon home. In the last message we received, the first officer—we don't know what happened to the captain—told us the ship was going down. Sinking. We think they'd run out of light—though it's hard to tell with how garbled the transmission was. They likely sailed in circles for weeks . . ."

"We must try again," Dusk said.

"Impossible," Admiral Rattu said. "It would be a waste of lives! And the resources it takes . . ."

"We have the backup ship, prepared before canceling the rescue trip," Vathi said. "We could try again."

"Yes," Admiral Rattu said, "but why would we? What makes you think this time, an expedition into that darkness will meet anything other than the same fate?"

"Because," Dusk said, throwing down the papers, "this one will have me."

Fig. 18 · Kokerlii
(Aviar)

CHAPTER TWELVE
Five Years Ago

"**Destroy the island?**" **Vathi said.** She frowned at him, cocking her head. "You can't know that if my people engage the machine, it will destroy the island. Why do you think it would?"

"Your Aviar will have to remain here, with that wound," Dusk said, ignoring the question. "She would not be able to fly away if something happened to us." The same argument could be made for Sak, but he would not be without the bird. "I will return her to you after we have stopped the machine. Come." He walked to the floor hatch and pulled it open.

Vathi rose, but pressed against the wall. "I'm staying here."

"The people of your company won't believe me," he said. "You will have to tell them to stop. You are coming."

Vathi licked her lips in what seemed to be a nervous habit. She scanned the room, looking for escape, then back at him. Right then, Dusk noticed his corpse hanging from the pegs in the tree beneath him. He jumped.

"What was that?" she demanded.

"Nothing."

"You keep glancing to the sides," Vathi said. "What do you think you see, Dusk?"

"We're going. Now."

"You've been alone on the island for a long time," she said, obviously trying to make her voice soothing. "You're upset about our arrival. You aren't thinking clearly."

Dusk drew in a deep breath. "Sak, show her."

The bird launched from his shoulder, flapped across the room, and landed on Vathi. She turned to the bird, frowning.

Then Vathi gasped, falling to her knees. She huddled back against the wall, eyes darting from side to side, mouth working but no words coming out. Dusk left her to it for a short time, then raised his arm. Sak returned to him on black wings, dropping a single dark feather to the floor. She settled in again on his shoulder. That much flying was difficult for her.

"What was *that*?" Vathi demanded.

"Come," Dusk said, taking his pack and climbing down out of the room.

Vathi scrambled to the open hatch. "No. Tell me. What *was* that?"

"You saw your corpse."

"All about me. Everywhere I looked."

"Sak grants that talent."

"There is no such talent."

Dusk looked up at her from halfway down the pegs. "You have seen your death. That is what will happen if your friends use their machine. Death. All of us. The Aviar, everyone living here. I do not know why, but I know that it *will* come."

"You've discovered a new Aviar," Vathi said. "How . . . When . . . ?"

"Hand me the lantern," Dusk said.

Looking numb, she obeyed. He held the lantern between his teeth and descended the pegs to the ground. Then he raised the light high, looking down the slope.

The inky jungle at night. Like the depths of the ocean.

He shivered, then whistled. Kokerlii fluttered down from above, landing on his other shoulder. Kokerlii would hide their minds, and with that, they had a chance. It would still not be easy. The things of the jungle relied upon mind sense, but many could still hunt by scent or other senses.

Vathi scrambled down the pegs behind him, her pack over her shoulder, the strange tube peeking out. "You have two Aviar," she said. "You use them both at once?"

"My uncle had three."

"How is that even possible?"

"They like trappers." So many questions. Could she not think about what the answers might be before asking?

"We're actually going to do this," she said, whispering, as if to herself. "The jungle at night. I should stay. I should refuse . . ."

"You've seen your death if you do."

"I've seen what you claim is my death. A new Aviar breed . . . It has been centuries." Though her voice still sounded reluctant, she walked after him as he strode down the slope and passed his traps, entering the jungle again.

His corpse sat at the base of a tree. That made him immediately look for what could kill him here, but Sak's senses seemed to be off. The island's impending death was so overpowering, it seemed to be smothering smaller dangers. He might not be able to rely upon her visions until the machine was destroyed.

The thick jungle canopy swallowed them, hot even at night; the ocean breezes didn't reach this far inland. That left the air feeling stagnant, and it dripped with the scents of the jungle. Fungus, rotting leaves, the perfumes of flowers. Accompanying those scents were the sounds of an island coming alive. A constant crinkling in the underbrush, like the sound of maggots writhing in a pile of dry leaves. The lantern's light did not extend as far as it should.

Vathi pulled up close behind him. "Why did you do this before?" she whispered. "The other time you went out at night?"

More questions. But sounds, fortunately, were not too dangerous.

"I was wounded," Dusk whispered. "We had to get from one safecamp to the other to recover my uncle's store of antivenom." Because Dusk, hands trembling, had dropped the other flask.

"You survived it? Well, obviously you did, I mean. I'm surprised, is all."

She seemed to be talking to fill the air.

"They could be watching us," she said, looking into the darkness. "Nightmaws."

"They are not."

"How can you know?" she asked, voice hushed.

"If the nightmaws had seen us, we'd be dead. That is how I know." He shook his head, sliding out his machete and cutting away a few branches before them. Any could hold deathants skittering across their leaves. In the dark, it would be difficult to spot them, so brushing against foliage seemed a poor decision.

He led the way down through a gully thick with mud, where they had to step on stones to keep from sinking in. Vathi followed with remarkable dexterity as he hopped off a stone and onto the bank of the gully. There he passed his corpse sinking into the mud. Nearby, he spotted a second corpse, so translucent it was nearly invisible. That one had been bitten by something.

He raised his lantern, hoping it wasn't happening again. Others did not appear. Just these two. And the very faint cast to the second one . . . yes, that mound meant the den of a tokka. Sak chirped softly, and he fished in his pocket for a seed to give her. She had figured out how to send him help. The fainter images were immediate dangers.

"Thank you," he whispered to her.

"What was it?" Vathi said.

"Tokka," he replied, pointing at the mound.

She seemed appropriately wary, and kept her distance from the thing's den. "That bird of yours," Vathi said, speaking softly in the gloom of night, "are there others?"

They climbed out of the gully, and he stopped them just before they wandered into a patch of deathants. Vathi looked at the trail of tiny insects, moving in a straight line.

"Dusk?" she asked as they rounded the ants. "Are there others? Why haven't you brought any chicks to market?"

"I do not have any chicks."

"So you found only the one?" she asked.

Questions, questions. Buzzing around him like flies.

Don't be foolish, he told himself, shoving down his annoyance. *You would ask the same if you saw someone with a new breed of Aviar.* He had tried to keep Sak a secret; for years, he hadn't even brought her with him when he left the island. But with her poorly healed wing these days, he hadn't wanted to abandon her.

Deep down, he'd known he couldn't keep his secret forever.

"There are many birds like her," he said. "But only she has a talent to bestow."

Vathi stopped in place as he cut them a path. He turned back, looking at her alone in a pocket of light. He had given her the lantern.

"That's a mainlander bird," she said. She held up the light. "I knew it was when I first saw it. The sharper beak, the black feathers, more sleek. I assumed it wasn't an Aviar, because mainlander birds can't bestow talents."

Dusk turned away and continued cutting.

"You brought a mainlander chick to the Pantheon," Vathi whispered. "And it *gained a talent.*"

With a hack he brought down a branch. Ahead was an entire field of tokka, so he went around them. Again, she had not asked a question, so he needed not answer.

Vathi hurried to keep up, the glow of the lantern tossing his shadow before him. "Surely someone else has tried it before. Surely . . ."

He did not know if they had.

"But why would they?" She spoke quietly, as if to herself. "The Aviar are special. Everyone knows the separate breeds and what they do. Why assume that a fish would learn to breathe air, if raised on land? Why assume a non-Aviar would become one if raised on Patji . . ."

It had to do with the pool, of course.

He would never speak of that to her. For she was not a trapper.

"Come," he said. "This way, along the slope."

Dusk led them around many dangers, though he found that he needed to rely greatly upon Sak's help. *Do not follow that stream, which has your corpse bobbing in its waters. Do not touch that tree; the bark is poisonous with rot. Turn from that path. Your corpse shows a deathant bite.*

When he stopped to let Vathi drink from her canteen, he held Sak and found her trembling. She did not peck at him as was usual when he enclosed her in his hands.

They stood in a small clearing, pure dark all around them, the sky shrouded in clouds. He heard distant rainfall on the trees. Not uncommon here.

Nightmaws screeched, one then another. They only did that when they made a kill or when they were seeking to frighten Aviar. Often, herbivore herds slept near Aviar roosts. Scatter the birds, and you could sense the prey.

Vathi had taken out her tube. The strange one from her pack that he had assumed was a scroll case. Upon reconsideration, he did not think it looked scholarly at all—not considering the way she held it as she poured something into its end. Once done, she raised it like one would a weapon.

Beneath her feet, Dusk's body lay mangled.

She fitted something that looked like a small arrow into the top end, but it didn't matter. No weapon could penetrate the thick skin of a nightmaw. You either avoided them or you died.

Kokerlii fluttered to his shoulder, chirping away, turning his head practically upside down as he inspected the surroundings. He seemed confused by the darkness. Why were they out like this at night, when birds normally made no noise?

"We must keep moving," Dusk said, placing Sak on his other shoulder and taking out his machete.

"You realize that your bird changes everything," Vathi said quietly, joining him, shouldering her pack and carrying her tube in the other hand.

"There will be a new kind of Aviar," Dusk whispered, stepping over his corpse.

"That's the *least* of it. Dusk, we assumed that chicks raised away from these islands did not develop their abilities because there was no flock to train them. We assumed that their abilities were innate, like our ability to speak—it's inborn, but we require help from others to develop it."

"That can still be true," Dusk said. "Other species, such as Sak, can merely be trained to speak."

"And your bird? Was it trained by others?"

"Perhaps." He did not say what he really thought. It was a thing of trappers. He noted a corpse on the ground before them.

It was not his. And it was not a vision.

It was a dead trapper.

*Fig. 9 • **Kalofruit***
(fruit)

CHAPTER THIRTEEN

Two days after the meeting with the Ones Above, Dusk stood on the deck of a steamship as it drew close to Patji.

Once, this solitary jungle island—steep on one side, like an axe head emerging from the water—had been the most daunting and frightening of all the Pantheon. Literally the father god, secret home of Aviar for centuries, visited by only the boldest of solitary trappers.

That god was now home to fire and steel. Dozens of steamships prowled its waters, and the mysterious shadows that lurked in the deep had been killed or driven off. Gone were the treacherous stone beaches Dusk had once used to land his canoe. Instead, long wooden docks reached their fingers into the ocean, allowing for the landing of great steamships.

Buildings covered three separate shores, and—with painstaking effort—soldiers had burned away the most dangerous insects and beasts that had inhabited the place. On the upper slope, vast Aviaries with netted sides and tops marked a distinct change in the way Aviar were gathered. No more solitary trappers worked the island, braving its dangers and passing down lore to their apprentices. Aviar were mass-produced now, like textiles or canned goods.

Patji, Dusk thought, was a god with clipped wings. He wasn't dead, but he'd been shown, in no uncertain terms, that he needed to clean

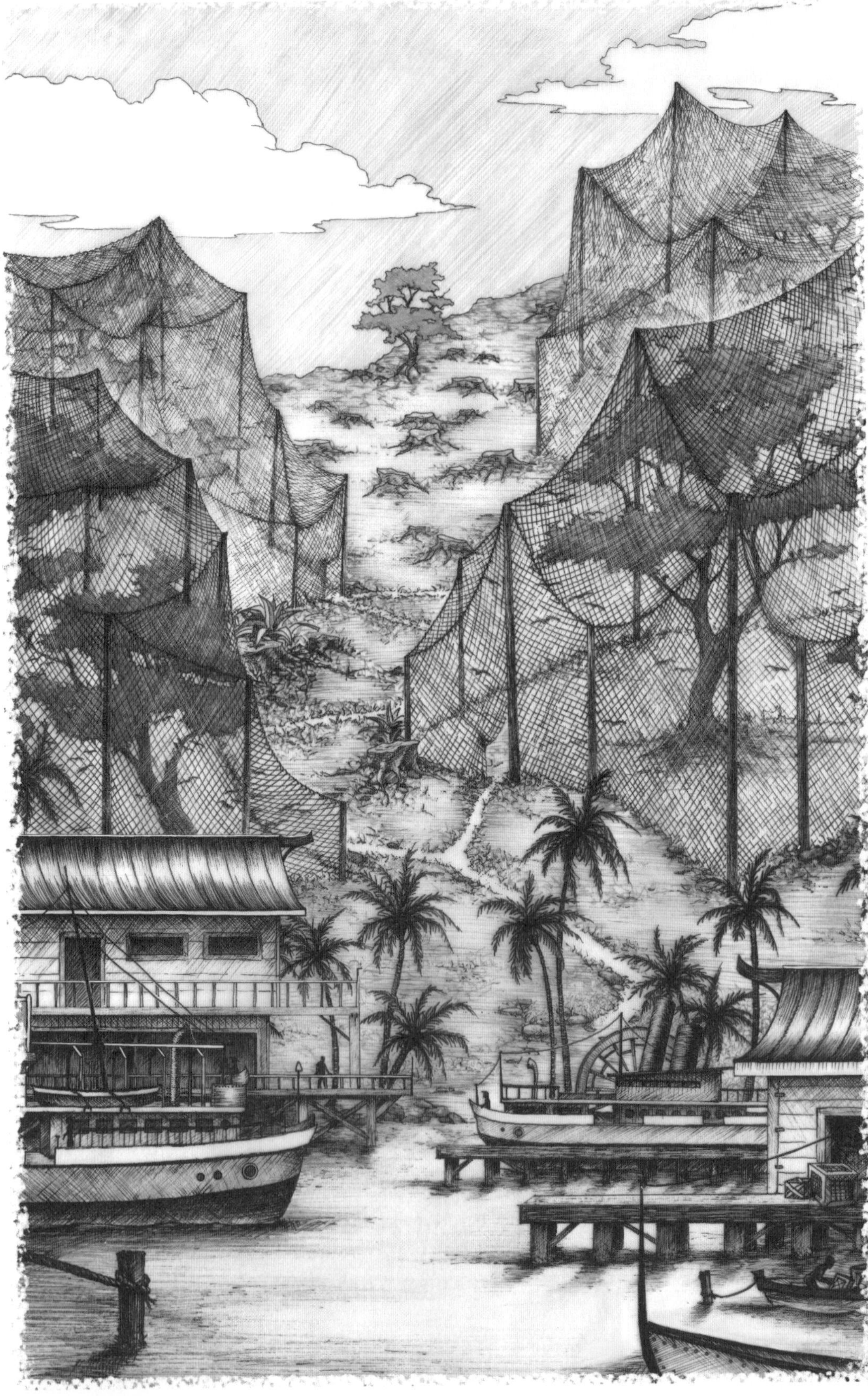

himself up. Keep his beard trimmed, his clothing neat, and show up on time for services. The people of the homeisles had no more time for wild, vengeful gods who worked against them.

As the steamship pulled into the bay, Vathi joined him at the railing. She wore a suit that, to Dusk's eyes, looked like it was trying to approximate the cut and style of the Ones Above. Large shoulder pads, slacks instead of a wrap or skirt. She wore a bandana of her village colors, a customary nod to heritage. But as they turned Patji into just another island, the dribble of technology and culture from above transformed the people.

"Does it make you sad, Dusk?" she asked, leaning against the railing and surveying the bustling dock. "To see what we did here?"

"Progress is always sad," he said. "There is no new life without death."

"Yes. I thought you might regret what we've done."

"Regret? I did not say I *regretted* anything. Only that I'm sad." He leaned down beside her. Though he'd been offered clothing of fine cuts, he still wore his trapper's outfit: cargo pants, a utilitarian vest, a sturdy and stiff buttoned shirt. Some trappers he knew had, in the face of what was happening to Patji, returned to wearing the saoa of their past—wraps, sandals, bare chests. Terrible clothing for trapping. One could revere the past without pretending everything about it had been better.

"I don't know if I want to authorize another expedition into the darkness, Dusk," she said. "It's too big, too vast."

That was wise. She was right. It was big, and vast.

She sighed. "I'm trying to engage with you, Dusk. Could you at least *try* to have a conversation for once?"

"Sorry," he said. And he was. "I am not . . . good at this, even still."

"What do you think you can accomplish out there?" she said. "Our first expedition went out three times, and had to turn back each time. The last time, the ship sank. There is nothing in the darkness. We've *determined* that."

"We've determined," Dusk said, "that the previous expedition's crew was not skilled enough to survive the darkness. That is all."

Their steamship pulled up alongside the dock, slowing itself with a great blare of its horn, startling distant Aviar in their pens and making Sak chirp in annoyance from her place on the railing nearby. Vathi wanted more of a response from him; he knew that she did. He struggled to find the right words.

During his years alone, words had never been a problem for him. Then again, during his years alone, he'd never had anyone for whom he *wanted* to find the right words.

"I don't want to send you," she said softly. "I don't want to lose you, Dusk."

He didn't reply. It was not a question.

"You won't survive," she said. "Our previous crew had an incredibly experienced team. Both scientists and soldiers."

"No trappers."

"No."

"I will go," he said.

"To find what, though?"

"Something is in that darkness. Cakoban and our people came from it, and the Ones Above are interested in it."

"Assuming I believe you—and enough of the others agree—I still don't have an answer to what you think you can accomplish."

"Perhaps I can find something to aid us against the Ones Above. And if not . . . Vathi, wouldn't you at least want to know that there is another option?"

She looked to him.

"If we can travel that darkness," he said, "and if it's truly where our ancestors came from, then there are other people out there. Perhaps we can travel, trade. Make better deals. Find out what laws and rules prevent the Ones Above from conquering us, then exploit them. So much changes if they are not our exclusive source of information."

"And if you fail?"

"Then I will die," he said. "Like Tenth the Navigator himself." Dusk touched his own forehead, then pressed his finger against hers. "I gave up Patji for the planet, Vathi, but I will not give up the planet to those people from the stars."

"Fool man."

He did not respond. Because she might be right.

He was going anyway.

"I am useless, Vathi," he said, voice rough, like a keel scraping rocks.

"That's nonsense. Your expertise was *essential* in clearing out Patji, to make it safe for workers."

"Any trapper could have done that job. *You* could have done that job, if you'd been able to spare the time. Besides, it is done now. Deathant nests smoked out, cutaway vines chopped to pieces and their roots salted. The island has been conquered." He looked to her, willing her to understand the words. The truth. "I am a canoe in a world of steamships."

"So you throw your life away?" she demanded. "Dusk, you're talking like an idiot!"

He gripped the railing hard, staring down at the waters. Vathi knew him better than any human, and she seemed to be able to read this.

She touched his arm. "That was unfair of me," she said softly.

It was. But he asked a difficult thing. It was telling, however, that she had been willing to come with him to Patji. She might be trying to talk him out of leaving, but she understood why he needed to go.

"I want," he said, "to do what you do. Help our people."

"Me?" she asked.

"You forge a new world, Vathi. You venture into the darkness, same as any explorer—only instead of deathants in the dirt, your darkness is filled with smiling aliens who want your soul. I do not regret what has been done to Patji. We *need* to change. And these five years, I've seen why. No person or Aviar will be safe in this world unless we adapt."

He reached out to Sak, who inched along the railing to eventually hop onto his offered wrist. Her jeweled eyes could see the future. How ironic that he had spent so much of his life determinedly ignoring anything but the present. "My job has always been to protect the Aviar. Here, I am nothing. But there, in the darkness, I see a chance to help. A slim, nearly impossible chance. Still a chance."

She squeezed his arm. "Dusk. I think that's the most you've ever said to me at one time. Barring lectures, I suppose."

He shrugged. Theirs had never been a romantic relationship. That just . . . never had been right. It was intense nonetheless. The politician determined to drag her people toward modernity; the trapper who taught the oldest traditions. Opposite sides of a . . . well, medallion. One that represented the soul of a people.

He embraced her, however, because it felt like the right thing to do. Sak jumped on her shoulder, and her Aviar onto his. "Goodbye, Vathi," he said into her ear.

"I'm not convinced," she said. "Don't pretend that I am. But . . . I'll gather you a crew, investigate our options. So don't say goodbye now."

"I understand," he said. "But when that is done, there won't be the time to say what I feel. Now is that time."

"You're so odd," she said, but squeezed him tightly. "I guess that's what we get for letting men like you be raised by wild animals."

"The Aviar aren't wild animals."

"I was referring to the other trappers," she said, then pulled back. "If I must say it now, then goodbye, you strange man. Thank you for putting up with me all these years. I know I've been quite the pain at times."

He didn't reply. Because yes, she had been. But she'd also been forgiving of him.

She took something from her pocket. The medallion he'd given her that first night on Patji. Now she offered it back to him.

"No," he said, pushing it toward her. "I have another, and you need the reminder. Please keep it. And think of me."

She nodded slowly. The steamship finally came to a rest in the waters, so he returned Mirris and took Sak back, then went to gather his things for the last part of the trip.

Fig. 44 · Cakoban's Finger (flower)

CHAPTER FOURTEEN
Five Years Ago

Dusk held up a hand immediately, stilling Vathi.

Another trapper? Dead? The meat had been picked off much of the bones, and the clothing lay strewn about, ripped open by animals that had feasted. Small fungus-like plants had sprouted around the ground near it, tiny red tendrils reaching up to enclose parts of the skeleton.

He looked up at the great tree, at the foot of which rested the corpse. The flowers were not in bloom. Dusk released his breath.

"What is it?" Vathi whispered. "Deathants?"

"No. Cakoban's fingers."

She frowned. "Is that . . . some kind of curse?"

"It is a type of plant," Dusk said. "Named after the man you should know. Please tell me you'll look him up, once we survive this."

"Fine. But I think you'll find that the old legends are contradictory, sometimes."

He ignored her, stepping forward carefully to inspect the corpse. Machete. Boots. Rugged gear. He *thought* he recognized the man from the clothing. An older trapper named First of the Sky.

"Cakoban's fingers," Vathi said, peeking over Dusk's shoulder. "Is that the fungus?"

"No, it's the name of the tree that killed him," Dusk said, poking the corpse's clothing, careful of insects that might lurk inside. "Raise the lamp."

"I've never heard of such a tree," she said skeptically.

"They are only on Patji."

"I have read about the flora on these islands . . ."

"Here you are a child. Light."

She sighed, raising it for him. He used a stick to prod at pockets on the ripped clothing. This man had been killed by a tuskrun pack, larger predators—almost as large as a man—that prowled mostly by day. Their movement patterns were predictable unless one happened across one of Cakoban's fingers in bloom.

There. He found a small book in the man's pocket. Dusk raised it, then backed away. Vathi peered over his shoulder. Homeislers stood so *close* to each other. Did she need to stand right by his elbow?

He checked the first pages, finding a list of dates. Yes, judging by the last date written down, this man was only a few days dead. The pages after that detailed the locations of Sky's safecamps, along with explanations of the traps guarding each one. The last page contained the farewell.

> *I am First of the Sky, taken by Patji at last. I have a brother on Suluko. Care for them, rival.*

Few words. Few words were good. Dusk carried a book like this himself, with even less on his last page.

"He wants you to care for his family?" Vathi asked.

"Don't be stupid," Dusk said, tucking the book away. "His birds."

"That's sweet," Vathi said. "I had always heard that trappers were incredibly territorial."

"We are," he said, noting how she said it. Again, her tone made it seem as if she considered trappers to be like animals. "But our birds might die without care—they are accustomed to humans. Better to give them to a rival."

"Even if that rival is the one who killed you?" Vathi asked. "The traps you set, the ways you try to interfere with one another . . ."

"It is our way."

"That is an awful excuse."

She was right.

The tree was massive, with drooping fronds. At the end of each one was a large, closed blossom, as long as two hands put together. "You don't seem worried," she noted, "though the plant seems to have killed that man."

"These are only dangerous when they bloom."

"Spores?" she asked.

"No." He picked up the fallen machete, then used it to poke around the neck until he found the man's medallion. He took this, but left the rest of Sky's things alone. Let Patji claim him. Father did so like to murder his children. Dusk continued onward, leading Vathi, ignoring his corpse draped across a log.

"Dusk?" Vathi asked, raising the lantern and hurrying to him. "If not spores, then how does the tree kill?"

"So many questions."

"My life is about questions," she replied. "And about answers. If my people are going to work on this island . . ."

He hacked at some plants with the machete.

"It is going to happen," she said, more softly. "I'm sorry, Dusk. You can't stop the world from changing. Perhaps my expedition will be defeated, but others will come."

"Because of the Ones Above," he snapped.

"They may spur it," Vathi said. "Someday we will sail the stars like they do. But change would have happened even without them. The world is progressing. One man cannot slow it, no matter how determined he is."

He stopped in the path.

You cannot stop the tides from changing, Dusk. No matter how determined you are. His mother's words. Some of the last he remembered from her.

Dusk continued on his way. Vathi followed. He would need her, though a treacherous piece of him whispered that she would be easy to end. If she died, so would her questions. More importantly, so would her answers. The ones he suspected she was very close to discovering.

You cannot change it . . .

He wanted so badly to protect this island, as his kind had done for centuries. He worked this jungle, loved its birds, was fond of its scents and sounds—despite all else. How he wished he could prove to Patji that he and the others were *worthy*.

Perhaps. Perhaps if they were . . .

Bah. Well, killing this woman would not provide any real protection. Besides, had he sunk so low that he would murder a helpless scribe? He would not even do that to another trapper, unless they approached his camp and did not retreat.

"The blossoms can think," he found himself saying as he led them away from a mound that showed the tuskrun pack had been rooting here. "The fingers of Cakoban? The trees themselves are not dangerous, even when blooming—but they attract predators, imitating the thoughts of a wounded animal that is full of pain and worry."

Vathi gasped. "A *plant*," she said, "that broadcasts a mental signature? Are you certain?"

"Yes."

"I need one of those blossoms." The light shook as she turned to go back.

Dusk spun and caught her by the arm. "We must keep moving."

"But—"

"You will have another chance." He took a deep breath. "Your people will soon infest this island like maggots on carrion. You will see other trees. Tonight we must *go*. Dawn approaches."

He let go of her and turned back to his work. He had judged her wise, for a homeisler. Perhaps she would listen.

She did. She listened, and followed. Bless her for that. And as they walked, Dusk couldn't help thinking of First of the Sky.

Cakoban's fingers. An experienced trapper should not have died in that place. The trees lived by opening many blossoms and attracting predators to come feast. The predators would then fight one another, and the tree would feed off the corpses. Sky must have stumbled across a tree as it was beginning to flower, and gotten caught in what came next.

Who would have expected a death like that? After years on the island, surviving much more terrible dangers, to be caught by those simple flowers. It almost seemed a mockery of the poor man on Patji's part.

Dusk led them past some stinging terror vines, then the slope soon grew steeper. They'd need to go uphill for a while before crossing to the downward slope that would lead to the other side of the island. Their trail, fortunately, would avoid Patji's main peak—the point of the wedge that jutted up the easternmost side of the island. Dusk's camp had been near the south, and Vathi's would be to the northeast, letting them skirt around the base of the wedge before arriving on the other beach.

They fell into a rhythm, and she was quiet for a time. Eventually, atop a particularly steep incline, he nodded for a break and squatted down to drink from his canteen. On Patji, one did not simply sit without care upon a stump or log to rest.

Consumed by worry, and not a little frustration, he didn't notice what Vathi was doing until it was too late. She'd found something tucked into a branch—a long colorful feather. A mating plume.

Dusk leapt to his feet.

Vathi reached toward the lower branches of the tree.

A set of spikes on ropes dropped from a nearby tree as Vathi pulled the branch. They swung down as Dusk reached her, one arm thrown in the way. A spike hit, the long, thin nail ripping into his skin and jutting out the other side, bloodied, stopped a hair from Vathi's cheek.

She screamed.

Many predators on Patji were hard of hearing, but still, screaming wasn't wise. He yanked the spike from his skin, unconcerned with the bleeding for now, and checked the other spikes on the drop-rope trap.

No poison. Blessedly.

"Your arm!" Vathi said.

He grunted. It didn't hurt. Yet. She began fishing in her pack for a bandage, and he accepted her ministrations without complaint or groan, even as the pain came upon him.

"I'm so sorry!" Vathi sputtered. "I found a mating plume! That meant an Aviar nest, so I thought to look in the tree. Have we stumbled across another trapper's safecamp?"

She was babbling as she worked. When *he* grew nervous, he grew even more quiet. She would do the opposite.

She was good with a bandage, and the wound had fortunately not hit any major arteries. He would be fine, though using his left hand would not be easy. This would be an annoyance. When she was done, looking sheepish and guilty, he picked up the mating plume she had dropped.

"This," he said with a harsh whisper, holding it up before her, "is a symbol of your ignorance. On the Pantheon Islands, nothing is easy, nothing is simple. That plume was placed by another trapper to catch someone who thought to find an easy prize. You cannot be that person. Never move without asking yourself, is this too easy?"

She paled. Then she took the feather in her fingers.

"We carry these," Dusk said, fishing out his medallion, "as a similar warning. Each one comes from the body of a fallen trapper. I took mine off the corpse of my uncle, after he led me through the darkness one night. Because I got bit, and then dropped the antivenom. He died by my foolishness."

She looked at the medallion. He pressed it into her hand.

"But—"

"Remember," he said, "what killed Sky. What nearly killed you."

She nodded, and seemed to understand.

"Come." He turned and walked on their way. That was the speech for an apprentice, he realized, upon their first major mistake. A ritual among trappers. What had possessed him to give it to her? And to grant her a medallion? True, he had the one he'd taken from Sky, but still.

She followed behind, head bowed, appropriately shamed. She didn't realize the honor he had just paid her, if unconsciously. They walked onward, an hour or more passing.

By the time she spoke, for some reason, he almost welcomed the words breaking upon the sounds of the jungle. "I'm sorry."

"You need not be sorry. Only careful."

"I understand." She took a deep breath, following him on the path. "And I *am* sorry. Not just about your arm. About this island. About what is coming. I think it inevitable, but I do wish that it did not mean the end of such a grand tradition."

"I . . ."

Words. He hated trying to find words.

"It . . . was not dusk when I was born," he finally said, then hacked down a swampvine and held his breath against the noxious fumes it released. They were only dangerous for a few moments.

"Excuse me?" Vathi asked, keeping her distance from the swampvine. "You were born . . ."

"My mother did not name me for the time of day. I was named because my mother saw the dusk of our people. The sun will soon set on us, she often told me." He looked back to Vathi, letting her pass him and enter a small clearing.

Oddly, she smiled at him. Why had he found *those* words to speak? He followed into the clearing, concerned at himself. He had not given those words to his uncle; only his parents knew the source of his name.

He was not certain why he'd shared them with this scribe from an evil company. But . . . it did feel good to have said them.

A nightmaw broke through between two trees behind Vathi.

Fig. 83 · **Rokke**
(Aviar)

CHAPTER FIFTEEN

Once, traveling up the slope to Patji's peak would have required passing the nests of terrible beasts like the nightmaws. Now Dusk did it in the luxury of the train's dining car. No, he did not regret change and progress. This was *so* much easier. He didn't see his corpse a single time during the trip; almost, he could forget he was on Patji.

Dusk did feel a little ashamed at how many trees had been cleared. That said, despite all the changes, something inside of him felt that Patji *approved*. Once, this island had been a deadly test where solitary trappers proved themselves worthy. Now, however, invaders had arrived from another world. The time for training was over. Either Dusk's people proved themselves, or they went extinct.

The changes to Patji were necessary. Dusk hated them, of course, but he could see that they were necessary.

At least, until the train pulled to a stop beside the fortified watchpost that marked the end of the short track. Dusk, Vathi, and several scientists were ushered out of the train and through the watchpost, into a canyon virtually untouched by industry.

It felt dark, despite the daylight, as they walked alongside the river. Into Patji's throat, toward the planet's greatest secret. Dusk held aloft his lantern, illuminating the surface of the still pool. It was small, shallow, and the edges were overgrown with trees. A few blossoms floated on the surface. These waters seemed to be responsible for so much.

Not just the Aviar. Predators that could hunt by sensing the minds of thinking beings. Rodents that were smarter than the best-trained hound—rodents that the scientists had even taught to *read* rudimentary script.

Yes, Dusk and the others had heard of a magical pool like the Ones Above described. But they'd never known it to make people vanish. Until, that was, they'd stepped into it and thought about vanishing.

It had happened, just like that.

Dusk took a deep breath, then looked to the others. Vathi nodded, as did Ruen, local head of scientific discoveries. Short. Bald. With an Aviar. Tall. Crested.

"Shall we?" Dusk said.

"Just a moment," Vathi said, waving someone over. "I've got something for you."

An attendant at the pool, who cared for the Aviar, approached. She carried something in both hands. A small bird—with a red head, and otherwise black and white markings. He knew the breed; it granted the ability to hide your mind from anything looking for thoughts. The same power Kokerlii had. There were five different breeds with that once-important ability.

Dusk immediately knew what Vathi was planning. He turned away, walking to the pool. "No."

"Dusk," Vathi said, hurrying up. "Rokke doesn't have anyone. She was kept by a trapper on one of the other islands—one of the trappers who refused to come in. He died, and she was found in his safe—"

"I don't need another bird," he said. "I won't replace Kokerlii."

"Dusk," Vathi said, taking his arm. "Please. Look at her."

He looked. The little Aviar gazed at him with wide eyes, then hid in the attendant's hands.

"I don't need another Aviar," he said, then pointed at the pool. "My corpse floats in the waters. I count it three times."

"That Aviar of yours *is* unusual," Ruen said. He was a sniffly little man with a pointed nose, like he'd slammed one too many books closed and squished his features by accident. "We still haven't been able to replicate what it can do. The other ravens we bring here gain a separate ability entirely. Do you think maybe—"

"No," Dusk said.

"But—"

"No."

"If Sak is warning you," Vathi said, "perhaps planning a second expedition is a bad idea."

It most certainly was. Dusk strode forward anyway, pack on his shoulders, wading into the pool. He'd done this before, but wasn't certain how it worked. He'd thought about disappearing, and before, that had been enough to—

The pool swallowed him. He felt a twisting sensation, and Sak's claws bit into his shoulder even through the padding. He felt as if he were sinking into an infinite depth.

And then, something new. An impression.

Something out there liked what he was planning.

Dusk splashed out of the pool, wiping his face and gasping for breath. A group of glowing golden butterflies, disturbed by his appearance, fluttered away. Sak shook herself, flinging water across his cheek as he dragged his waterproof pack to shore. However, he hadn't emerged back into the basin with the blossoms.

He was in another place. Another world. A land with a dark black sky, no sun to be seen. Streams of soft blue made lines in the air—like smoke flowing in an unseen and unfelt current. They provided some illumination, which lit a few buildings and a stone dock occupying the small strip of stable land that surrounded the pool on this side.

He stopped on the outer shore of that strip, beside a small boat, like the one he'd used as a trapper, but with a modern gas-powered motor. He was amused to find it here, a symbol from a past he thought dead. They'd probably used it to test if the larger ship could actually float.

Beyond the land was a dark abyss, though he could pick out a curious dividing line. Like the surface of the ocean, separating the sky from the waters. You could see it if you looked hard, and there was a . . .

distortion below. It seemed like water; his brain said it was water. But when he dipped his hand down, he couldn't feel it.

It was the ghost of an ocean, mostly transparent, extending into the infinite distance.

This was what he had to cross.

More dangerous, somehow, than even Patji at night.

Fig. 38 · *Nightmaw*
(predator)

CHAPTER SIXTEEN
Five Years Ago

The enormous nightmaw would have been as tall as a tree if it stood upright. Instead it crashed forward in a prowling posture, powerful rear legs bearing most of its weight, its two clawed forelegs ripping up the ground.

It extended its long neck, beak open, razor-sharp and deadly. It looked like a bird—in the same way that a wolf looked like a lapdog.

Dusk threw his machete. An instinctive reaction, for he did not have time for thought. He did not have time for fear. That snapping beak—as tall as a door—would have the two of them dead in moments.

His machete glanced off the beak and actually cut the creature on the side of the head. That drew its attention, making it hesitate for just a moment. Dusk leapt for Vathi. She stepped back from him, setting the butt of her tube against the ground. He needed to pull her away, to—

The explosion deafened him.

Smoke bloomed around Vathi, who stood—wide-eyed—having dropped the lantern, oil spilling. The sudden sound stunned Dusk, and he almost collided with her as the nightmaw lurched and fell, skidding, the ground *thumping* from the impact.

Dusk found himself on the ground. He scrambled to his feet, backing away from the twitching nightmaw mere inches from him. Lit by flickering light, it was all leathery skin, bumpy like a bird who had lost her feathers.

It was dead. Vathi had killed it.

Vathi had *killed* a nightmaw.

"Dusk!" Her voice seemed distant.

He raised a hand to his forehead, which had belatedly begun to prickle with sweat. His wounded arm throbbed, and he felt as if he should be running. He had never wanted to be so close to one of these. *Never.*

She'd actually killed it.

He turned toward her, eyes wide. Vathi was trembling, but she covered it well. "So, that worked," she said. "We weren't certain it would, even though we prepared these specifically for the nightmaws."

"It's like a cannon," Dusk said. "Like from one of the ships, only in your *hands*."

"Yes."

He turned back toward the beast. Actually, it *wasn't* dead, not completely. It twitched, and let out a plaintive screech that shocked him, even with his hearing muffled. The weapon had fired that spear right into the beast's chest.

The nightmaw quaked and thrashed a weak leg.

"We could kill them all," Dusk said. He rushed over to Vathi, taking her with his right hand, the arm that wasn't wounded. "With those weapons, we could kill them *all*. Every nightmaw. Maybe the shadows too!"

"Well, yes, it has been discussed. However, they are important parts of the ecosystem on these islands. Removing the apex predators could have undesirable results."

"Undesirable results?" Dusk ran his hand through his hair. "They'd be gone. All of them! I don't care what other problems you think it would cause. They would all be *dead*."

Vathi snorted, picking up the lantern and stamping out the small fires it had started. "I thought trappers were connected to nature."

"We are. That's how I know we would all be better off without any of these things."

"You are disabusing me of many romantic notions about your kind, Dusk," she said, circling the dying beast.

Dusk whistled, holding up his arm. Kokerlii fluttered down from high branches; in the chaos and explosion, Dusk had not seen the bird fly away. Sak still clung to his shoulder with a death grip, her claws digging into his skin through the cloth. He hadn't noticed.

Kokerlii landed on his arm and gave an apologetic chirp.

"It wasn't your fault," Dusk said soothingly. "They prowl the night. Even when they cannot sense our minds, they can smell us." This one had come up the trail behind them; it must have crossed their path and followed it.

Dangerous. His uncle always claimed the nightmaws were growing smarter, that they knew they could not hunt men only by their minds. *I should have taken us across more streams,* Dusk thought, reaching up and rubbing Sak's neck to soothe her. *There just isn't time . . .*

His corpse lay wherever he looked. Draped across a rock, hanging from the vines of trees, slumped beneath the dying nightmaw's claw . . .

The beast trembled once more, then amazingly lifted its gruesome head and let out a last screech. Not as loud as those that normally sounded in the night, but bone-chilling and horrid. Dusk stepped back despite himself, and Sak chirped nervously.

Other nightmaw screeches rose in the dark, distant. That sound . . . he had been trained to recognize it as the sound of death.

"We're going," he said, stalking across the ground and pulling Vathi away from the dying beast, which had lowered its head and fallen silent.

"Dusk?" She did not resist as he pulled her away.

One of the other nightmaws sounded again in the night. Was it closer? *Oh, Patji, please,* Dusk thought. *No. Not this.*

He pulled her faster, reaching for his machete at his side, but it was not there. He had thrown it. He took out the one he had taken from his fallen rival, then dragged her from the clearing, back into the jungle, moving quickly. He could no longer worry about brushing against deathants.

A greater danger was coming.

The calls of death came again.

"Are those getting *closer*?" Vathi asked.

Dusk did not answer. It was a question, but he did not know the answer. At least his hearing was recovering. He released her hand, moving more quickly, almost at a trot—faster than he ever wanted to go through the jungle, day or night.

"Dusk!" Vathi hissed. "Will they come? To the call of the dying one? Is that something they do?"

"How should I know? I have never known one of them to be killed before." He saw the tube, again carried over her shoulder, by the light of the lantern.

That gave him pause, though his instincts screamed at him to keep moving and he felt a fool. "Your weapon," he said. "You can use it again?"

"Yes," she said. "Once more."

"*Once* more?"

A half dozen screeches sounded in the night.

"Yes," she replied. "I only brought three spears and enough powder for three shots. I tried firing one at the deepwalker. It didn't do much."

He spoke no further, ignoring his wounded arm—the bandage was in need of changing—and towing her through the jungle. The calls came again and again. Agitated. How did one escape a *flock* of nightmaws? His Aviar clung to him, a bird on each shoulder. He had to leap over his corpse as they traversed a gulch and came up the other side.

How do you escape them? he thought, remembering his uncle's training. *You don't draw their attention in the first place!*

They were fast. Kokerlii would hide his mind, but if they picked up his scent at the dead one . . .

Water. He stopped in the night, turning right, then left. Where would he find a stream? Patji was an island. Fresh water came from rainfall, mostly. Along the eastern side, the island rose to some heights with cliffs on all sides, and rainfall did collect there, in Patji's Eye.

The river was the Father's tears. Straight from the pool itself . . . It was a dangerous place to go with Vathi in tow. Their path had skirted the slope up the heights, heading across the island toward the northern beach.

Screeches behind spurred him on. Dusk seized Vathi's hand and hauled her in a more eastern direction. She did not complain, though she did keep looking over her shoulder.

The screeches grew closer.

He ran. He ran as he had never expected to do on Patji, wild and reckless. Leaping over troughs, around fallen logs coated in moss. Through the dark underbrush, scaring away meekers and startling Aviar slumbering in the branches above. It was foolish. It was crazy. But did it matter? Somehow, he knew other deaths would not claim him.

The kings of Patji hunted him; lesser dangers would not dare steal from their betters.

Vathi followed with difficulty. Those skirts were trouble, but she caught up to Dusk each time he had to occasionally stop and cut their way through underbrush. Urgent, frantic. He expected her to keep up, and she did. A piece of him—buried deep beneath the terror—was impressed. This woman would have made a fantastic trapper.

He froze as screeches sounded behind, so close. Vathi gasped, and Dusk turned back to his work. Not far to go. He hacked through a dense patch of undergrowth and ran on, sweat streaming down the sides of his face. Jostling light came from Vathi's lantern behind; the scene before him was one of horrific shadows dancing on the jungle's boughs, leaves, ferns, and rocks.

This is your fault, Patji, he thought with an unexpected fury. The screeches seemed almost on top of him. Was that breaking brush he could hear behind? *We are your priests, and yet you hate us! You hate all.*

Dusk broke from the jungle onto the banks of the river. He led Vathi right into it, splashing into the cold waters. What else could he do? Downstream would lead closer to those sounds, the calls of death.

Of the Dusk, he thought. *Of the Dusk.*

It was time.

He turned upstream.

Fig. 82 · **Glowing butterfly**
(insect)

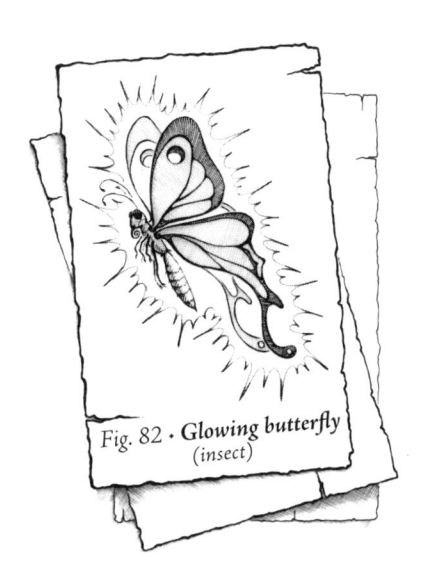

CHAPTER SEVENTEEN

Dusk lingered on the shore of the tiny island in that dimension of endless black, marked by blue smoke ribbons high in the sky. This place intimidated him. It was more than the lack of light, or the nothingness. He was accustomed to looking across an expansive ocean, but there, the horizon was only a few miles away. Here, it seemed infinitely far off. As if . . . there were no curvature to the sea on this side. As if he weren't standing on a planet, but an infinitely flat plane.

That unyielding darkness whispered, *This is where you stop. Go back to your little room in your big city. Go back to your jar.*

He'd thought, when younger, that living on Patji would make him strong enough to never fear anything else. Then he'd left, and discovered there were ideas far more frightening than any deathant. Ideas like realizing you had no future.

He finally turned away.

He forced his eyes to seek something else to study. However, the only other natural features of note in this place were little floating lights in the shape of fishhooks. Those glowed like the wick of a lantern and hovered in the air, held aloft by some unknown power. They tended to come in pairs, the hooks intertwined. He'd read in the reports what the scientists thought: These correlated exactly with the locations of people and their Aviar, as they moved around on Patji in the real world.

Indeed, several of the lights vanished, and Vathi emerged from the pool, again disturbing the strange glowing butterflies that lived on this island. Though her Aviar sputtered and complained, the president herself simply spit out a mouthful of water and stalked out of the pool.

She'd also brought the black and white Aviar with the red head. The one she wanted him to take. That woman . . . He turned his back to her as the scientists and Vathi's personal guards followed up through the pool.

"Ah!" said Ruen, the balding man with the crested Aviar. "I *always* manage to get a mouthful of the water. How is that? You'd think I could hold my breath well enough, after all these trips."

So many words. Dusk smiled at them anyway. Words didn't always have to have meaning, if their tone conveyed emotion and personality. Vathi talked about this, and he saw it now in how the sputtering man shook himself, then looked around, smiling.

The little island on this side did have a few buildings. A door in one opened, spilling welcome lantern light. Attendants rushed out, bringing towels and refreshment. The lead guard here—a man Dusk knew, named Second of the Fist—complained that he hadn't been warned that the First Company president herself would be visiting.

Dusk took the towel and wiped his face—though as soon as he did, Sak fluffed her feathers and shook herself, getting him wet again. Punishment for dragging her in here, he supposed. As he dried his face a second time, he couldn't help staring again into that vast nothingness. Here and there, glowing fishhook lights dotted the region, representing the guards in the nearby fortress or the workers and birds in the Aviaries.

Beyond that, nothing at all. Endless streams of flowing blue smoke in the sky, moving in distinct rivulets, and an infinite black "sea" below with only the slightest hint of a division between them.

It felt so stale. The ocean was always full of motion. Churning waves, even on still days. The breeze against his face, the warm waters of the currents, the sparkle of light hitting the water. The ocean was not empty just because it was empty of people.

This place, however, *defined* emptiness. Was he really thinking of traveling out into *that*? The idea frightened him, and that fright—contrastingly—made him smile. Father. Lately he had spent far too many days facing nothing more distressing than a choice of teas at breakfast. That wasn't life. Standing on an alien shore and looking into infinity . . . that was life. Somewhere out there, in that darkness, were answers. Secrets.

"The ship isn't ready yet," the head of the watchpost was saying. "It will take us a week or more to get it assembled. I thought you'd decided not to send another expedition, Madam President."

"We're reconsidering," she said, then gestured to Dusk. "Perhaps an expedition with a different kind of leader?"

"One of the old trappers, eh?" Fist said. "Dying breed, those. Pardon, President, but a life hiding in treehouses won't have prepared him for *this*."

Dusk grunted. "Show me how things float here."

Fist hesitated. But Ruen the scientist perked up. "Oh, I can show you! Come with me."

He bustled to the watchpost, and none of them—though seeming reluctant—stopped him. He came out with a small jar of glowing material.

"Worm paste?" Dusk asked.

"We're considering some appropriate names," Ruen said.

"'Worm paste' is appropriate," Dusk replied. "That's what it is."

"Not very dignified."

"Should it be?" Dusk frowned as he joined Ruen, leaving the rest standing around the watchpost, discussing pieces of a large expedition ship that had been brought through, but not assembled.

At the shoreline, Ruen carefully opened the glowing jar and took out a little fingerful of paste. "We're still experimenting," he said to Dusk as he coated a small stone from his pocket. "But, well, look."

He dropped the now-glowing stone into the not-water, and it hit—then floated. With a paddle, Ruen tapped the stone, and could push it beneath the surface. It bobbed right back up, though there was no splashing.

"There's not a lot of friction, if any," Ruen said. "But it *does* work.

Coat a propeller with this, um, worm paste and off you go. Until it wears out."

"And there's no way to navigate?" Dusk asked. "Those blue lines in the sky? Can we navigate by those?"

"Best we can tell, they are like clouds—they shift and flow. Never stable enough to use as a means of navigation. And there are no features, other than this island, that we've been able to locate."

"Compasses?"

"Do nothing," Ruen said. "As if there's nothing for them to sense. There probably isn't. To triangulate, we'd need to plant radio beacons somewhere out there. But where? There's no other land. And we get odd interference with radio anyway, making triangulation difficult even when we send multiple boats out at once. There really is no way!"

"Cakoban did it," Dusk said.

"Oh," Ruen said, eyes bright, his Aviar exclaiming excitedly. "You think that too? I think this *must* be the endless darkness from the old stories! I thought it the first time I visited."

"Some of the others think it's stupid," Dusk said. "But a scientist agrees?"

"A scientist," the man said, raising his finger, "asks questions. Plus, there's the markings. Have you seen them?"

Dusk shook his head. So Ruen led him around the small island to some stones textured like coral—and there were scratchings. Old pictures and runes. Of boats and men and a giant serpent.

"Proof!" Dusk said.

"Proof that men were here," Ruen said. "They might just have come through that pool, like we did."

That was . . . true, unfortunately. "But this *is* the story of Cakoban," Dusk said.

"Maybe. Maybe that's just what you want to see. You *do* have to take the stories with some skepticism. We've sailed for centuries, and never found any sign of a serpent with a tail as long as the ocean. But *neither* have we found signs of where we came from. We did not originate on the homeisles, best we can tell from the archaeological record."

"Some claim we're from the mainland," Dusk said, kneeling beside the ancient pictures.

"A too-simple answer to a difficult question. We have stories of empires, and vast cities, and wars with no place they could have happened, except *maybe* the frozen mainland to the south. But there is no archaeology to support those assumptions. If we lived there, we didn't leave ruins, or even arrowheads . . ."

"We came from another land," Dusk said, eager, standing and pointing. "One somewhere out there. We were summoned to this land by Patji and the gods, Cakoban being led by their signs."

"Possible, possible," Ruen said. "We—"

He cut off as Vathi started shouting.

Something was wrong. Dusk went running.

Fig. 45 · Cakoban's Finger
(fruit)

CHAPTER EIGHTEEN
Five Years Ago

Dusk led Vathi upstream, chased by the screeches of nightmaws.

This took them toward the sacred pool. Something he was *never* supposed to reveal to any but a trapper who had finished their apprenticeship.

The water came only to their calves; it was bitter cold, though he did not know why. They slipped and scrambled as they ran, best they could, upriver away from the sounds of the chasing predators. They passed through some narrows, with lichen-covered rock walls on either side twice as tall as a man, then burst out into the basin.

A cool emerald lake rested here, sequestered.

Dusk towed Vathi to the side, out of the river, toward some brush. Perhaps she would not see. He huddled with her, raising a finger to his lips, then turned down the light of the lantern she still held. Nightmaws could not see well, but perhaps dimming the light would help. In more ways than one.

They waited there, on the shore of the small lake in a basin—almost a crater—of stone. Hoping the water had washed away their scent; hoping the nightmaws would grow confused or distracted. There was no way out other than the river. If the nightmaws came up it, Dusk and Vathi would be trapped.

Screeches sounded. The creatures had reached the river. Dusk waited in near darkness, and so squeezed his eyes shut. He prayed to Patji, whom he loved, whom he hated.

Vathi gasped softly. "What . . . ?"

So she had seen. Of course she had. She was a seeker, a learner. A questioner.

Why must men ask so many questions?

"Dusk! There are Aviar here, in these branches! Hundreds of them." She spoke in a hushed, frightened tone. Even as they awaited death itself, she saw and could not help speaking. "Have you seen them? What is this place?" She hesitated. "So many juveniles. Barely able to fly . . ."

"They come here," he whispered. "Every bird from every island. In their youth, they must come here."

He opened his eyes, looking up. He had turned down the lantern, but it was still bright enough to see them roosting there. A hundred varieties, with an array of plumage. Some stirred at the light and the sound. They stirred more as the nightmaws screeched below.

Sak chirped on his shoulder, terrified. Kokerlii, for once, had nothing to say.

"Every bird from every island . . ." Vathi said. "They all come here, to this place. Are you certain?"

"Yes." It was a thing that trappers knew. You could not capture a bird before it had visited Patji.

Otherwise it would be able to bestow no talent.

"They come here," she said. "We knew they migrated between islands . . . Why do they come here?"

Was there any point in holding back now? She would figure it out. Still, he did not speak. Let her do so.

"They gain their talents here, don't they?" she asked. "How? Is it where they are trained? Is this how you made a bird who was not an Aviar into one? You brought a hatchling here, and then . . ." She frowned, raising her lantern. "I recognize those trees. They are the ones you called Cakoban's fingers."

A dozen of them grew here, the largest concentration on the island. And beneath them, their fruit littered the ground. Much of it eaten, some of it only halfway so, bites taken out by birds of all stripes.

Vathi saw him looking, and frowned. "The fruit?" she asked.

"Worms," he whispered in reply.

She grabbed a piece of half-rotten fruit nearby and pulled it apart. Tiny glowing worms squirmed in the flesh of the fruit. A similar light seemed to glow in her eyes as she realized. "It's not the birds. It never has been . . . It's a parasite. They carry a parasite that bestows talents! That's why those raised away from the islands cannot gain the abilities, and why a mainland bird you brought here could."

"Yes."

"This changes everything, Dusk. Everything."

"Yes."

Of the Dusk. Born during that dusk, or bringer of it? What had he done?

"I wish," he whispered, "everything could just stay the same."

"Nothing can."

"I can."

"No," she said. "Dusk, we're each a new person every day. The *world* changes, and is new each day, and we must change with it. That's the blessing the gods give us. The blessing to be *able* to become someone new."

Downriver, the nightmaw screeches drew closer. They had decided to search upriver. They were clever, cleverer than men off the islands thought them to be. Vathi gasped, turning toward the small river canyon.

"Isn't this dangerous?" she whispered. "The trees are blooming. The nightmaws will come! But no. So many Aviar. They can hide those blossoms, like they do a man's mind?"

"No," he said. "All minds in this place are invisible, always, regardless of Aviar."

"But . . . how? Why? The worms?"

Dusk didn't know, and for now didn't care. *I am trying to protect you, Patji!* Dusk looked toward Cakoban's fingers. *I need to stop the men and their device. I know it! Why? Why do you hunt me?*

Perhaps it was because Dusk knew so much. Too much. More than any man had known. For he had asked questions.

Men. And their questions.

"They're coming up the river, aren't they?" she asked.

The answer seemed obvious. He did not reply.

"No," she said, standing. "I won't die with this knowledge, Dusk. I *won't*. There must be a way."

"There is," he said, standing beside her. He took a deep breath. *So I finally pay for it.* He took Sak carefully in his hand, and placed her on Vathi's shoulder. He pried Kokerlii free too.

"What are you doing?" Vathi asked.

"I will go as far as I can," Dusk said, handing Kokerlii toward her. The bird bit at his hands with annoyance, although not strong enough to draw blood. "You will need to hold him. He will try to follow me."

"No, wait. We can hide in the lake. They—"

"They will find us!" Dusk said. "It isn't deep enough."

"But you can't—"

"They are nearly here, woman!" He forced Kokerlii into her hands. "The men of the company will not listen to me if I tell them to turn off the device. You are smart; you can make them stop. With Kokerlii and Sak you can reach them. Be ready to go."

She looked at him, stunned, but she seemed to realize that there was no other way. She stood, holding Kokerlii in two hands as he pulled out the journal of First of the Sky, then his own book that listed where his Aviar were, and tucked them into her pack. Then he stepped back into the river. He could hear a rushing sound downstream. He would have to go quickly to reach the end of the canyon before the nightmaws arrived. If he could draw them out into the jungle, even a short ways to the south, Vathi could slip away.

He waded farther into the stream and turned back to his birds once more. Kokerlii squirmed in Vathi's grip, but Sak met his eyes. She knew what was happening.

She gave a final chirp.

He started to run.

One of Cakoban's fingers, growing right next to the mouth of the canyon, was blooming.

"Wait!"

He should not have stopped as Vathi yelled at him. He should have continued on, for time was so precious. However, the sight of that flower—along with her yell—made him hesitate.

The flower . . .

It struck him as it must have struck Vathi. An idea. Vathi ran for her pack, letting go of Kokerlii, who immediately flew to his shoulder and started chirping at him in annoyed chastisement. Dusk didn't listen. He yanked the flower off—it was as large as a man's head, with a bulging part at the center.

It was invisible in this basin, like they all were.

"A flower that can think," Vathi said, breathing quickly, fishing in her pack. "A flower that can draw the attention of predators."

Dusk pulled out his rope as she brought out her weapon and prepared it. He lashed the flower to the end of the spear sticking out slightly from the tube.

Nightmaw screeches echoed up the canyon. He could see their shadows, hear them splashing.

He stumbled back from Vathi as she crouched, set the weapon's butt against the ground, and pulled a lever at the base.

The explosion, once again, nearly deafened him.

Aviar all around the rim of the basin screeched and called in fright, taking wing. A storm of feathers and flapping ensued, and through the middle of it, Vathi's spear shot into the air, flower on the end. It arced out over the canyon into the night.

Dusk grabbed Vathi by the shoulder and pulled her back along the river, into the lake itself. They slipped into the shallow water, Kokerlii on his shoulder, Sak on hers. They left the lantern burning, giving a quiet light to the suddenly empty basin.

The lake was not deep. Two or three feet. They had to lie down to get covered completely. While submerged in that frigid water, Dusk thought he saw something . . . glowing butterflies . . .

And an impression. Like words.

Well done.

The nightmaws stopped in the canyon. His lantern light showed a few in the shadows, large as huts, watching the sky. They were smart, but like the meekers, not as smart as men.

Patji, Dusk thought. *Patji, please . . .*

The nightmaws turned back down the canyon, following the mental signature broadcast by the flowering plant. And as Dusk watched, his corpse bobbing in the water nearby grew increasingly translucent.

Then faded away entirely.

Dusk counted to a hundred, then slipped from the waters. Vathi, sodden in her skirts, did not speak as she grabbed the lantern. They left the weapon, its shots expended.

The calls from the nightmaws grew farther and farther away as Dusk led the way out of the canyon, then directly north, slightly downslope. He kept expecting the screeches to turn and take up the chase again.

They did not.

*Fig. 3 · **Fern frond***
(plant)

CHAPTER NINETEEN

Back at the buildings on the little island in the darkness, Dusk found Vathi striding back and forth, pacing, irate. Worried. The small new Aviar, Rokke, clung to her back and hid in her hair. Sak cooed to it, while Vathi licked her lips—that old nervous habit.

So it wasn't the kind of danger that killed the body. It was the other kind of danger. The worse kind.

"What?" he asked.

"Admiral Rattu," she said to him. "You know the one?"

"Yes," Dusk said. "He has an Aviar who likes to puff out its chest."

"Well he—the man, not the Aviar—filed a motion to head off funding to my projects. He's gotten a vote of requisition to do just that, and to convene the First Company vice presidents to assess my leadership."

Dusk didn't reply. This time because he had no idea what she was saying.

"It's the first step," she explained, "in ousting me from office. It will take time for him to mount a proper offense, but he's moving to get himself installed instead. A vote of no confidence will be held in the coming weeks, and if it passes . . ." She stopped and looked at him. "Then I'm done for, politically."

"We have to launch the expedition soon," Dusk said. "Nobody else would ever authorize it."

"Dusk," she said. "*That's* what you're thinking about? At a time like this?"

"I'm thinking," he said, "about our people. You?"

She met his eyes.

"You protect them your way," he said. "I will do it mine."

She thought a moment. "I'd need proof," she said. "Not just that traveling the darkness is possible, but that doing so would help our situation."

"What would . . . that proof look like?"

"I don't know, Dusk," she said. "Proof that our ancestors did it—to quiet any doubters—would help. Proof that there are other peoples out there like us, with whom we can ally instead. Proof that trade is possible, that we can afford to anger the Ones Above. But I can't even say what that proof might look like."

"Give me a ship. A crew. If such proof exists, I'll find it."

She hesitated before nodding.

Then, uncomfortably, Ruen cleared his throat. "Um . . . if you've lost requisition abilities, Madam President . . . how are you going to fund an expedition?"

"Father!" she said. "He's right, Dusk. The admiral—really, all of the others—are against this. I won't be able to push funding for another expedition through. If I try, instead of solidifying my supporters and focusing on the attack, I'll just fall faster." She turned to him, Rokke peeking out from behind her, Mirris nuzzling the younger bird protectively. "I'm sorry. I can't get you a ship, Dusk. It's just not going to happen."

He considered that. He trusted her word. She trusted him when it came to the dangers of Patji; he would be a fool to ignore what she said about politics.

If she said there wasn't a way, there wasn't a way. So there was only one thing he could do.

He took the small jar of worm paste from Ruen, then solemnly walked to the single-person boat he'd seen on the shore nearby. Sak fluttered on his shoulder, digging in her claws, but chirped resolutely. She understood.

"I suppose," Dusk said, "I'll have to go on my own."

Fig. 13 · *Mating plume*
(feather)

CHAPTER TWENTY
Five Years Ago

The company fortress was a horridly impressive sight. A work of logs and cannons right at the edge of the water, guarded by an enormous iron-hulled ship.

Smoke rose from the fortress, the burning of morning cook fires. A short distance away, what must have been a dead shadow rotted in the sun, its mountainous carcass draped half in the water, half out. Dusk felt . . . awed at seeing it. And disbelieving, as if he expected it to rise up and attack him.

His people . . . they really *could* tame this island, couldn't they?

He didn't see his own corpse anywhere, though on the final leg of their trip to the fortress he had seen it several times. Always in a place of immediate danger. Sak's visions had returned to normal.

Dusk turned back to the fortress, which he did not enter. He preferred to remain on the rocky, familiar shore—perhaps twenty feet from the entrance—his wounded arm aching as the company people rushed out through the gate to meet Vathi. Their scouts on the upper walls kept careful watch on Dusk. A trapper was not to be trusted.

Even standing here, he could smell how wrong the place was. It was stuffed with the scents of men: sweaty bodies, the smell of oil, and other, newer scents that he recognized from his recent trips to the homeisles. Scents that made him feel like an outsider among his own people.

The company men and women wore sturdy clothing, trousers like Dusk's but far better tailored, shirts, and rugged jackets. Jackets? In Patji's heat? These people bowed to Vathi, showing her more deference than Dusk would have expected. She was better placed in the company than he'd assumed.

Vathi looked at him, then back at her people. "We must hurry to the machine," she said to them. "The one from Above. We must turn it off."

Good. She would do her part. Dusk turned to walk away. Should he give words at parting? He'd never felt the need before. But today it felt . . . wrong not to say something.

He started walking away regardless. Words. He had never been good with words.

"Turn it off?" one of the men said from behind. "What do you mean, Director Vathi?"

"You don't need to feign innocence, Winds," Vathi said. "I know you turned it on in my absence."

"But we didn't."

Dusk paused. What? The man sounded sincere. But then, Dusk was no expert on human emotions. From what he'd seen of people from the homeisles, they could fake emotion.

"What *did* you do, then?" Vathi asked them.

"We . . . opened it."

Oh no . . .

"Why would you do that?" Vathi asked.

Dusk turned to regard them, but he didn't need to hear the answer. The answer was before him, in the vision of a dead island he'd misinterpreted.

"We figured," the man said, "that we should see if we could puzzle out how the machine worked. Vathi, the insides . . . they're complex beyond what we could have imagined. But there are seeds of understanding for us there. Things we could—"

"No!" Dusk said, rushing toward them.

One of the sentries above planted an arrow at his feet. Dusk lurched to a stop, looking wildly from Vathi to the walls. Couldn't they see? The bulge in mud that announced a deathant den. The game trail. The distinctive curl of a cutaway vine. Wasn't it *obvious*?

"Don't you see . . . ?"

For a moment, they all just stared at him. He had a chance. Words. He needed *words*.

"That machine is deathants!" he said. "A den, a . . . Bah!" In his anxiety, words fled him, like Aviar fluttering away into the night.

The others finally started moving, pulling Vathi toward the safety of their treasonous fortress.

"You said the corpses are gone," Vathi said as she was ushered through the gates. "We've succeeded. I will see that the machine is not engaged on this trip! I promise you this, Dusk!"

"But," he cried back, "it was never *meant* to be engaged!"

The enormous wooden gates of the fortress creaked closed, and he lost sight of her. Dusk cursed. Why hadn't he been able to explain?

Because he didn't know how to talk. For once in his life, that seemed to matter.

Furious, frustrated, he stalked away from that place and its awful smells. Halfway to the tree line, however, he stopped, then turned back. Sak fluttered down, landing on his shoulder and cooing softly.

Questions. Those questions wanted in to his brain.

Instead of leaving, he yelled at the guards. He demanded they return Vathi to him. He even pled.

Nothing happened. They wouldn't speak to him. Finally, feeling foolish, he stormed off a second time. Once he reached the tree line, he checked a few rocks for dangers, then settled down. In the shadow of a dead sea monster, during the light of dawn, he slumped forward.

Kokerlii chirped at him, turning his head one way, then the other, then he chirped louder, imitating the way Dusk would whistle sometimes—a thing that often made Dusk happy. Today, that wasn't enough.

Dusk stared across the shore, which was empty of his corpse.

His assumptions were . . . probably wrong. Everything could go back to normal . . . To normal? Could anything *ever* be normal with that fortress looming in front of him? He forced himself to his feet and entered the canopy.

The dense humidity of Patji's jungle should have calmed him. Instead it annoyed him. As he trekked toward another of his safecamps, he was so distracted that he could have been a youth, his first time on Sori. He almost stumbled straight onto a gaping deathant den; he didn't even notice the vision Sak sent. This time, dumb luck saved him as he stubbed his toe on something, glanced down, and only then spotted both corpse and crack crawling with insects.

He growled, then sneered. "Still you try to kill me?" he shouted, looking up at the canopy. "Patji!"

Silence.

"The ones who protect you are the ones you try hardest to kill," Dusk shouted. "Why!"

The words were lost in the jungle. It consumed them.

"You deserve this, Patji," he said. "What is coming to you. You *deserve to be destroyed!*"

He breathed in gasps, sweating, satisfied at having finally said those things. Perhaps there was a purpose for words. As traitorous as Vathi and her company were, part of him was *glad* that Patji would fall to their machines.

Of course, then the company itself would fall. To the Ones Above. As would his entire people. The world itself.

He bowed his head in the shadows of the canopy, sweat dripping down the sides of his face. Then he fell to his knees, heedless of the nest just three strides away.

Sak nuzzled into his hair. Above, in the branches, Kokerlii chirped uncertainly.

"It's a trap, you see," he whispered. "The Ones Above have rules. They can't conquer us unless we're advanced enough. Just like a man can't, in good conscience, attack a child. So they have left their machines for us to discover. When we poke and prod at it, we will find explanations inside of how the device works, left as if carelessly. And at some point in the near future, we will build something like one of their machines. We will have grown more quickly than we should have. We will be childlike still, ignorant, but the laws from Above will let these visitors conquer us."

That was what he should have said. Protecting Patji was impossible. Protecting the Aviar was impossible. Protecting their entire *world* was impossible. Why hadn't he explained it?

ISLES OF THE EMBERDARK

Perhaps because it wouldn't have done any good. As Vathi had said, progress *would* come.

Dusk had arrived. At morning.

Sak left his shoulder, winging away. Dusk looked after her, then cursed. She did not land nearby. Though flying was difficult for her, she fluttered on, disappearing from his sight.

"Sak?" he asked, rising and stumbling after the Aviar. He fought back the way he had come, following Sak's squawks. A few moments later, he lurched out of the jungle.

Vathi stood on the rocks before her fortress.

Dusk hesitated at the brim of the forest. Had they cast her out? No. He could see that the gate was cracked, and people watched from inside.

Sak had landed on Vathi's shoulder down below. Dusk frowned, reaching his hand to the side and letting Kokerlii land on his arm. Then he strode forward, calmly making his way down the rocky shore, until he was standing just before Vathi.

She'd changed into a new dress, though there were still snarls in her hair. She smelled of flowers.

Her eyes were terrified.

He'd traveled the darkness with her. Had faced nightmaws. Had seen her near to death. And she had not looked this worried.

"What?" he asked, his voice hoarse.

"We found instructions in the machine," Vathi whispered. "A manual on its workings, left there as if accidentally by someone who worked on it before. The manual is in their language, but the smaller machine I have . . ."

"It translates."

"The manual details how the machine was constructed," Vathi said. "It's so complex I can barely comprehend it, but it seems to explain concepts and ideas, not just the basic workings."

"And are you not happy?" he asked. "You will have your flying machines soon, Vathi. Sooner than anyone could have imagined."

Wordless, she held something up. A single feather—a mating plume. She had kept it.

"Never move without asking yourself, is this too easy?" she whispered.

123

"You said it was a trap as I was pulled away. When we found the manual, I . . . Oh, Dusk. They are planning to do to us what . . . what we are doing to Patji, aren't they?"

Dusk nodded.

"We'll lose it all. We can't fight them. Even if we stop this time, they'll find another excuse. They'll *seize* the Aviar. It makes perfect sense. The Aviar use the worms. We use the Aviar. The Ones Above use us. It's inevitable, isn't it?"

Yes, he thought. He opened his mouth to say it, and Sak chirped. He frowned and turned back toward the island. Jutting from the ocean, arrogant. Destructive.

Patji. Father.

And finally, at long last, Dusk understood.

"No," he whispered.

"But—"

He reached into his pocket and took out Sky's medallion, with Cakoban on it. He held it up, remembering the speech he'd been given. Like every trapper.

This is the symbol of your ignorance. Nothing is easy, nothing is simple.

Vathi fished out hers. Two medallions. Two sides. Both indicating the same thing.

"They will not have us," Dusk said. "We will see through their traps, and we will not fall for their tricks. For we have been trained by the Father himself for this very day."

She stared at his medallion, then up at him.

"Do you really think that?" she asked. "They are cunning."

"They may be cunning," he said. "But they have not lived on Patji. We will not let ourselves be taken in."

She nodded hesitantly, and some of the fear seemed to leave her. She turned and waved for those behind her to open the gates. Again, the scents of mankind washed over him.

Vathi looked back, then held out her hand to him. "You will help, then?"

His corpse appeared at her feet, and Sak chirped warningly. Danger. Yes, the path ahead would include much danger.

Dusk took Vathi's hand and stepped into the fortress anyway.

Fig. 83 · Rokke
(Aviar)

CHAPTER TWENTY-ONE

Dusk wiped the bottom of the boat with the last of the small jar of worm paste. Then he settled it into the not-water.

It floated. The engine was gassed up and ready, and it even had a boiler to heat and purify salt water, not that he'd need that out in the darkness. They'd never felt it rain in here. He took a deep breath, then walked toward the building, where a sign indicated a supply dump. Here he seized a sack of rations, then took a few harpoons in his other hand before walking back to the boat.

Vathi didn't rush for anyone these days, but she did . . . walk briskly to keep up with him. "Dusk," she said under her breath, "what madness is this?"

He slung the sack into the little boat and stowed the harpoons. The boat rocked in the not-water, trembling. The substance rippled, but not quite in the correct way. More like . . . smoke than water. An infinite, mostly transparent nothing. Extending down forever. Out of curiosity, Dusk fished in his pocket, found a rock, and tossed it.

The substance did slow the rock's fall, but only slightly. You couldn't swim in this stuff unless—he supposed—you were coated in the worm paste yourself.

He watched as the rock fell, and fell, and fell . . .

Vathi's new little Aviar hid in her hair, squawking softly. Mirris cooed, comforting it.

"I need worm paste," Dusk said. "As much of it as we've gathered."

"Dusk." Vathi took him by the arm. "This is insanity. You can't travel that by yourself. Look at it!"

"Our ancestors—"

"Look. Just *look*."

He looked. Vathi had made him strange in many ways. He talked more. He cared about homeisle politics. He accepted the world was leaving—no, *had left*—trappers behind, and the Pantheon had to be tamed. Each of those changes hurt, like a sting.

She'd also taught him important things. To see the world as it was, not as he imagined it might be. For a man who prided himself on noticing every detail in a land where details could kill you, he had proven shockingly bad at actually *looking*.

So today, he looked. He saw infinity. An old friend, but coy. Normally something interrupted it. Clouds. Churning waves with sunlight streaking through. Even the horizon wasn't truly infinite, but more a . . . waypoint along an ultimate destination.

Here, he saw infinity. A horizon that seemed impossibly far away. That not-sea, it . . . just. Kept. *Going*. Look through binoculars, and it was the same. A flat expanse, completely uninterrupted. Upward, he saw only darkness and blue streaks. Downward, that smoky depth.

Infinity in three shades. Each more unnerving than the one before.

Dusk fetched a second sack of rations.

"Dusk," Vathi said, rolling her eyes as he passed her again and stowed the second sack.

"I looked," he said.

"And?"

"It's . . . big."

"It's *impossible*. Our best sailors died out there, supported by scientists and navigators. It's suicide to go on your own."

"Do you remember what you told me, when I was angry about your outpost on Patji all those years ago?" he said, striding past her.

Vathi kept her arms folded, and Sak—that traitor—flew over with difficulty and landed on her shoulder, chirping in a comforting way. That startled the new bird, Rokke, as Vathi had three on her now. It was getting crowded.

Dusk picked up a water bin. The guard standing there looked to his superior, who looked to Vathi, who said nothing as Dusk stalked right past her.

Hm. She was learning his lessons. Not talking. Father, that was annoying. Was that what it felt like when he did it?

He placed the water bin in the boat, then turned to her.

"I told you," she admitted, "that the expedition would likely be a disaster—and it kind of was, after we lost so many people to the three shadow attacks. But it would be a disaster that took us one step closer to our goals."

"You asked me," Dusk said, "if I thought the first wayfinders learned without trying, without risking themselves. You implied the first trappers needed to learn by trial and error, by doing dangerous things. Do you remember?"

"I remember," she whispered. "But Dusk . . . the first trappers all died."

"Yet we kept sending people. Because we knew someone would eventually learn the ways to explore—even live—safely on Patji and the others. Sometimes the only path forward is costly. We must travel it regardless."

"This *isn't* the only path forward," she said. "There is another. We could just . . . do as the senate wants. Accept the deals offered by the Ones Above."

It was true. He didn't reply, because contradicting a truth was . . . well, something people did in conversations far too often. But to become slaves to the Ones Above? To give away their Aviar?

Progress. At any cost. It wasn't so different from what he was proposing, was it? He nodded, understanding. Every step forward came at a cost. So this time, he took *her* by the arm and pulled her to where the strange, transparent butterflies burst into the sky. Like light shattering.

Behind, on the stones by the spring that spanned dimensions, he pointed at the ancient markings. Ships. People. A giant serpent. And was that the winged statue from the tale of Cakoban? Yes . . . and these other marks, if he remembered his schooling, indicated names. The language of the ancients, which had become their own.

"Our people were here," he said, kneeling. "This is old. Older than any we've found, maybe."

"Older ones on the inner islands may have been destroyed as people used the land."

"One interpretation. Look, Vathi. Please *look*."

To her credit, she did. She looked. She reached out as if to touch the stone, but stopped, fingers hovering an inch away. "This name," she whispered, "says Second."

"Of the what?"

". . . Of the Dawn."

A sign? A coincidence? "We did come from that darkness. Otherwise, where is our origin? Every island is explored."

She thought on that. She was a smart woman—smarter than he was, certainly. Sometimes he wondered if she spoke so much because she had so many interesting thoughts that they had to eventually spill out.

On her shoulder, Sak chirped softly and nuzzled her. And Dusk realized this wasn't Sak choosing to comfort Vathi instead of Dusk—this was Sak saying farewell to Vathi.

"You told me earlier I could go," he said. "You nodded. Because you believe, don't you?"

"I agree," she said, "that we probably came from across the darkness. It matches the stories, and exploration is our heritage."

"And so . . ."

"So you must be right. This darkness represents another way to travel between worlds. One our ancestors, using only stone tools, managed." She sighed. "But letting you go alone, then waiting on you, it's . . . a lot to ask, Dusk. We're under deadlines—and I'm suffering a challenge to my leadership."

"Stall."

"How?"

"By doing the thing you're best at, Vathi."

"Talking?" she said with a smile.

"Persuading people," he corrected. "You took a stubborn, stupid trapper and dragged him into the modern era. You can wrangle some senators and kingmakers."

"You're *not* stupid, Dusk."

"But stubborn?" he asked.

"Legendarily. Like no one else I've ever met." She paused. "But I don't know if I can continue to stall the Ones Above."

"Just a little longer, Vathi. Five years you've danced with them, and you've *won*. They never found justification for conquering us. *Five years* you've played them, and I know how frustrated they've become."

It was true. Vathi's plan had worked. Dusk's people could have had flying machines by now, but only if they'd used technology they didn't understand. Instead, they'd progressed at a rate they could understand, and built infrastructure to support it. Still incredibly quick, he suspected, but not enough for the Ones Above, whom Vathi, through numerous talks, had delicately manipulated.

Dusk and Vathi's plan, begun on a beach of Patji five years ago, had *worked*. Their people were still free. So far.

"They're trying other tactics," she said. "You spotted them—the Ones Above make us reliant on their energy sources and medicines instead of tricking us into progressing too quickly. And whatever treaties and laws they have . . . they *can* be violated. Just like any law."

"You can handle them," he said. "A little longer. Please. I will bring you proof. Not just proof that the darkness can be traveled, but proof it will help—proof our ancestors did it, and that this strange ocean will help us defy the powerful beings who pressure us."

She looked again at the petroglyphs, carved here by unknown hands years ago. But one had been named Dawn.

"Two months," she whispered. "I will give you two months."

He nodded. "Two months."

Vathi wiped her eyes with her handkerchief, then stood, speaking with the authoritative voice of a leader. "Fetch this man all of our remaining luminist."

"Luminist?" he asked.

"Because worm paste sounds so . . . gross."

"I like it," he said.

"Of course you do," she said as one of the guards brought over a tub for him.

It was smaller than he'd hoped. He'd imagined a large container, like the water jugs. What he got was a jar a handspan tall and slightly wider.

Father, he thought to Patji, *let this stuff last.*

At Vathi's orders, the guards helped Dusk load more water onto the boat. He tried his compass, but as Ruen said, it didn't work here, spinning idly as he tipped or turned it. Dusk brought it along anyway, with his basic trapping equipment, including three harpoons and rope—the new manufactured kind that was thin and extremely strong. He wasn't even certain the material *was* rope. So . . . ropeless rope. Words were stupid sometimes.

"Careful," a guard said. "We've spotted . . . something moving in the abyss down there."

"Something?" Dusk asked.

"Large something," he said. "Down deep. Like a shadow, but long."

"Good," Dusk said.

"*Good?*"

"If there are predators in here," he said, "then there is prey—something to use in wayfinding. And something for me to eat."

"Unless they're like these," the guard said, holding up his finger for one of the light butterflies to land on. The thing seemed to have no *substance*. As ephemeral as a reflection. To test his theory, Dusk snatched the thing—and felt almost nothing in holding it. Just a faint sense of pressure as the butterfly slipped out between two of his fingers. Insubstantial, as if made of liquid.

The guard glared at him. "These are holy."

"So are the Pantheon Islands," he said, "and I trap on those." If something was holy, should he *not* try to hold on to it? He shook his head; even still, homeislers sometimes made no sense to him.

He surveyed the boat, making certain the coating of worm paste was even. He put some on the propeller, but brought a good, sturdy paddle anyway. Progress made life easier, yes, but the old technologies—muscles and determination—were always the most reliable.

Sak gave Vathi a final nuzzle, then flew over to the prow of the boat. Dusk looked back, then tapped the boat with his boot. "Come on, then."

Rokke peeked a scarlet head out from behind Vathi's hair. She chirped questioningly.

Dusk tapped his foot against the boat again. So she flew down and scampered forward, hopping onto the boat with a flutter of red, white, and black feathers. She settled under one of the seats in the back, out of sight.

Last of all, he looked to Vathi. There had been many emotions shared between them. In another life, where women were allowed to be trappers, perhaps she would have been his apprentice. She'd changed those rules, but it had taken rising through corporate ranks to do things like that—and so the new world she made for younger women couldn't include her. Not in the way she'd once imagined.

Instead, he'd been her apprentice. He had worked hard, at her encouragement, to find a new place in the world. To become, awkwardly, a new man.

Turned out, they still needed the old one. Fortunately he'd never left. He'd never even really changed his clothing.

They faced one another for what might have been an uncomfortable amount of time for others. But he was used to silence, and she was used to him.

Besides, they'd already said goodbye.

"If I don't return," he finally said, "send others. Even if you take the deal, keep sending others."

She shook her head. "It's hard enough to send you."

"But—"

"I'm giving you this chance because of what you said, and what Sak showed you. Dusk, *this* is our chance."

He sighed, then nodded.

"I guess this is where—" she began.

"No," he said. "I already said goodbye. Besides, if I die, the Eelakin die." He gave her one last look, and even added a smile, because she was always encouraging him to show more of those. "So I *have* to come back. When I see you again, I'll have your proof."

He put a finger into the jar of worm paste and lightly coated one side of his oar. That might be wasteful, since the propeller was already coated, but there were things he needed to know. Did the stuff wear off faster when in use? Did more of it make a difference for how hard you could push? He would be careful, but couldn't help needing some for experiments.

He felt better starting this way. Pushing off the shore of the small island in the blackness, then leaping into the boat. Dipping his oar into the not-water, which had a satisfying, familiar resistance as he used the oldest machine—muscles—to move himself across the abyss. It might not look like water, but it felt the same to an oar.

As terrifying as this journey was, that offered him a tiny bit of reassurance.

So he didn't look back. Looking back was for people who regretted what they were about to do.

Instead, he kept paddling. One man. Two birds. Three kinds of infinity.

And an entire world that, remarkably, still needed him.

THE END OF
BOOK ONE

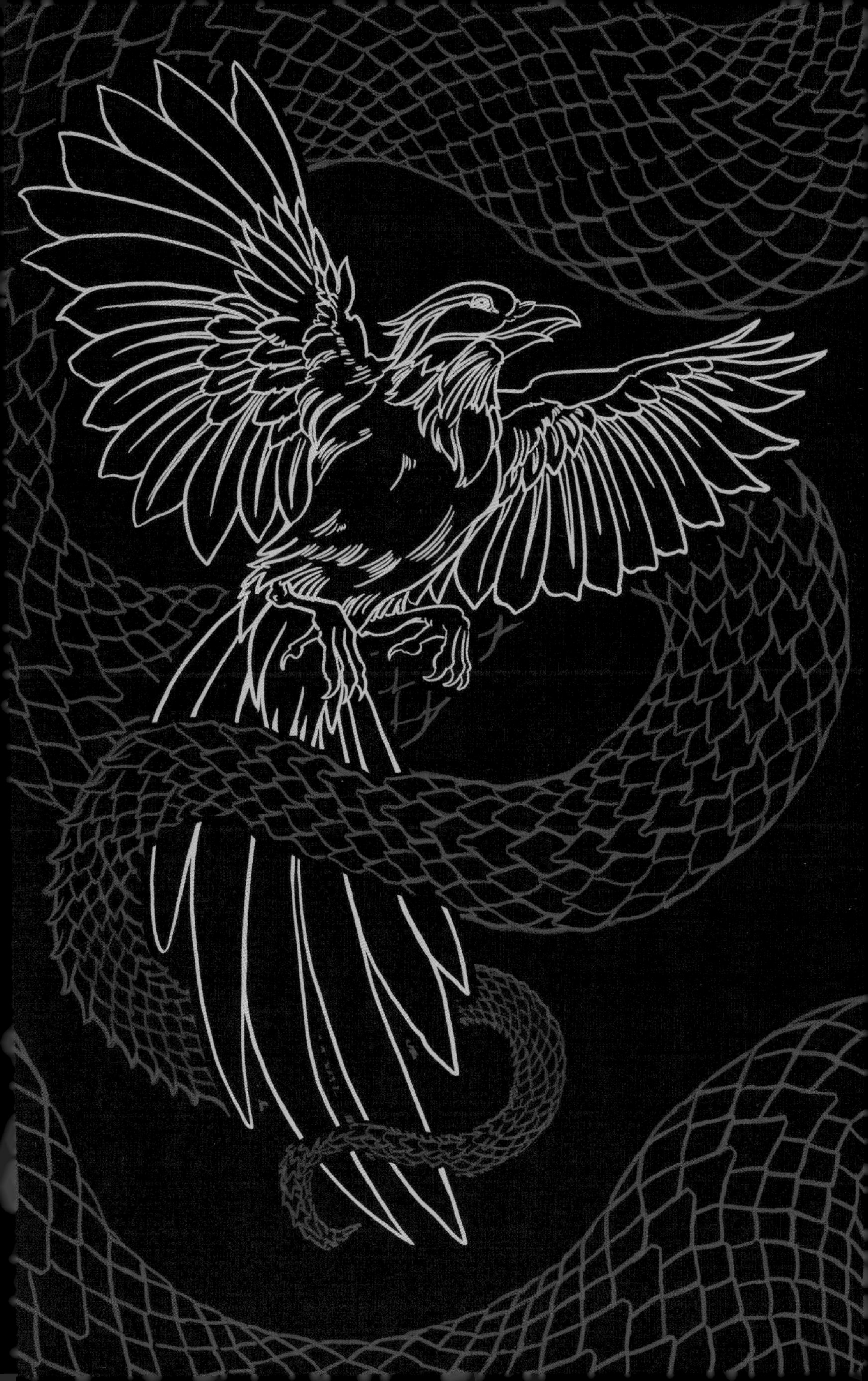

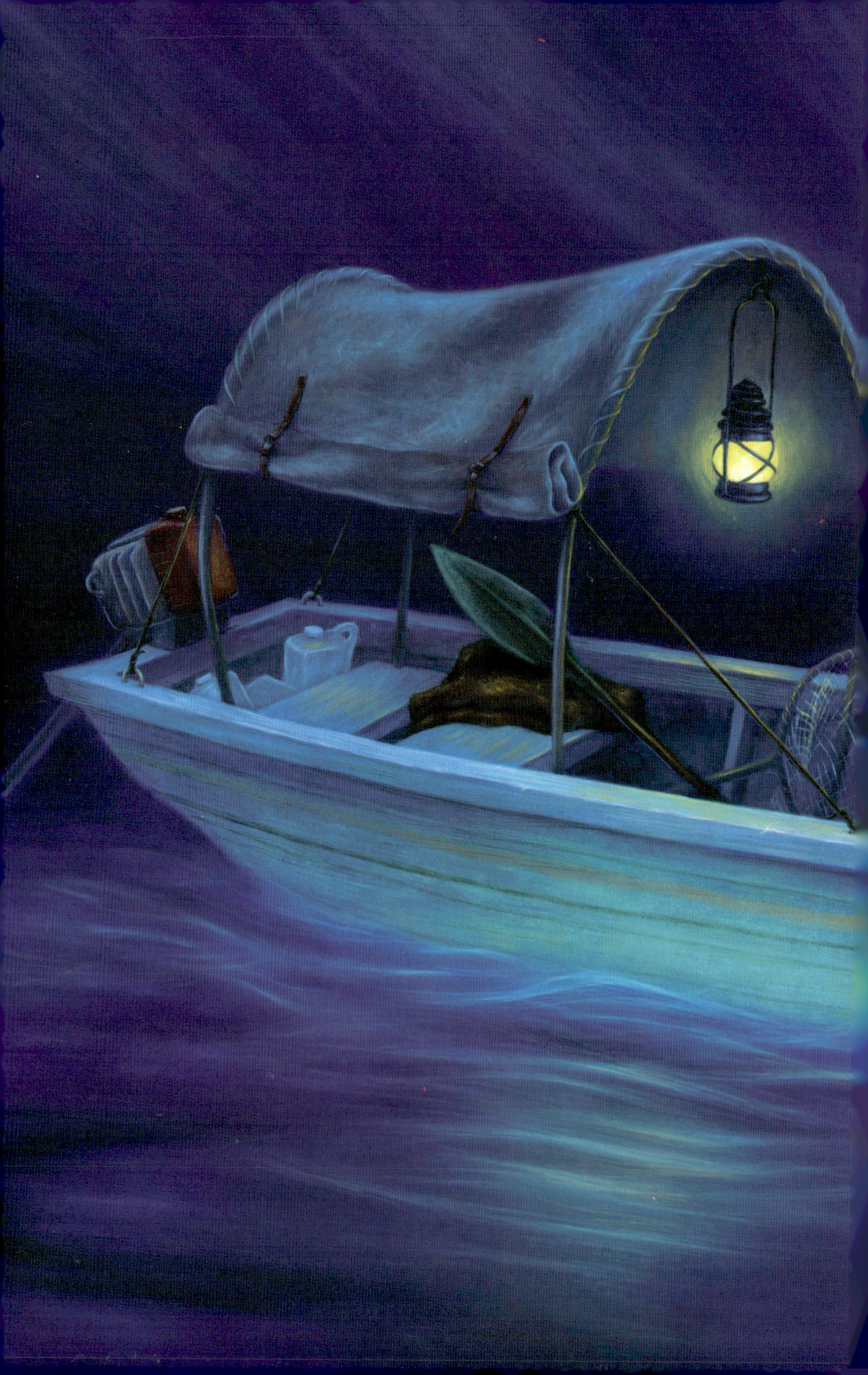

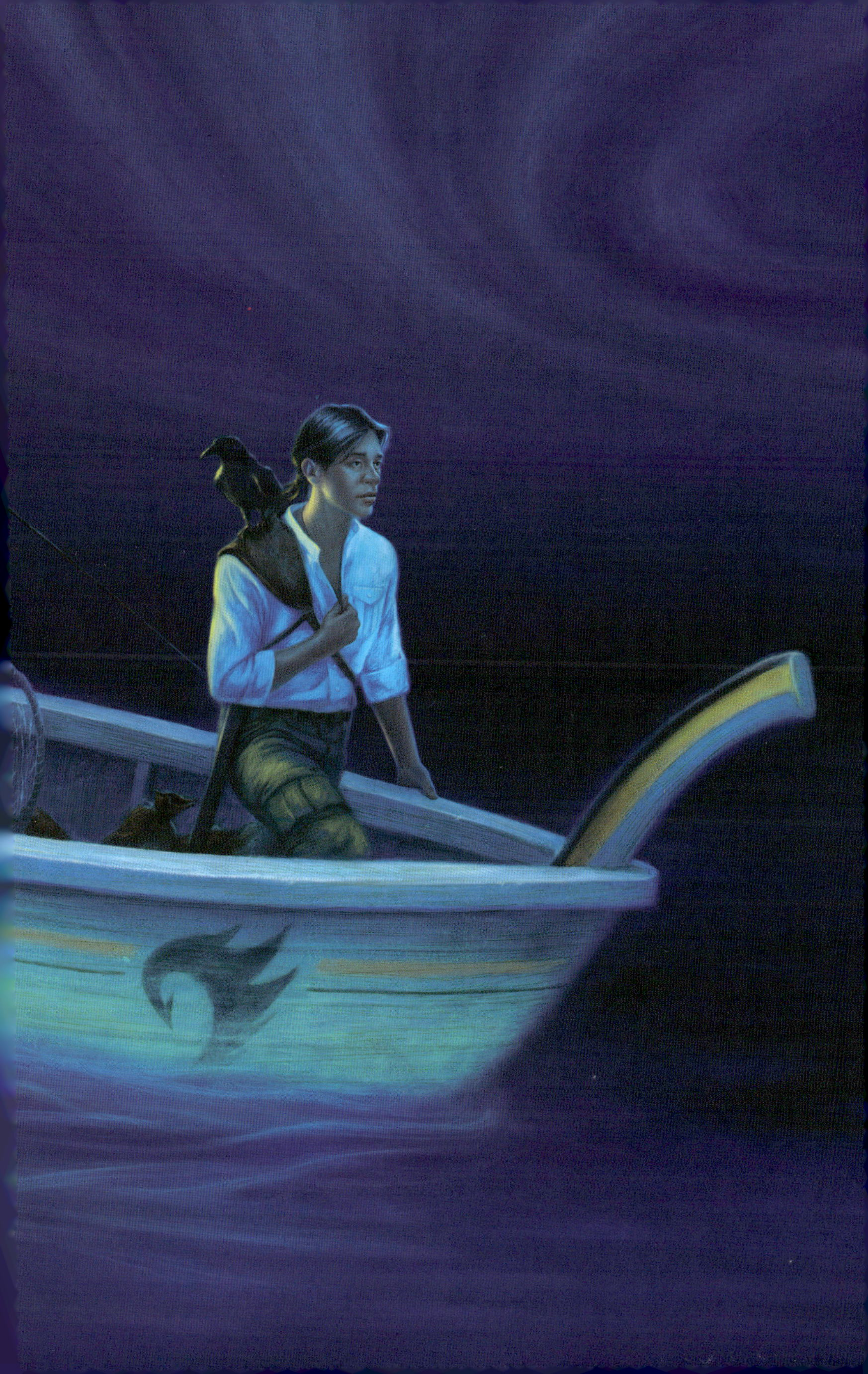

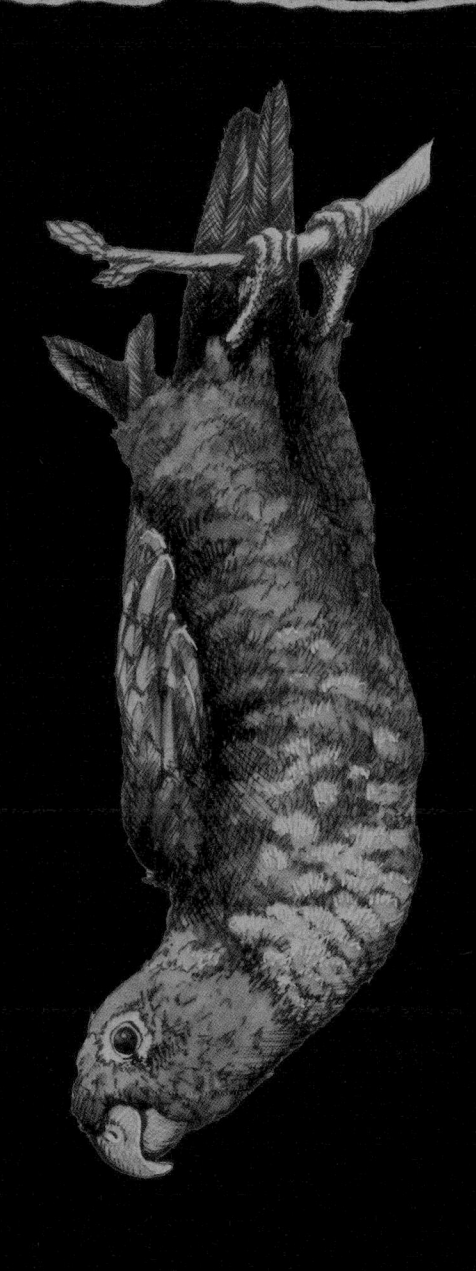

BOOK TWO:
STARLING

Fig. 99 · Dragon
(claw)

CHAPTER TWENTY-TWO

Starling crawled down the ladder in a metal tube, far from her homeworld—and even *farther*, at least emotionally, from that glorious day when she'd first transformed.

Over fifty years had passed. She was basically an adult, but she had replaced grand palaces with dimly lit corridors on a half-functional starship. She reached the last rung and turned toward engineering, wearing her human shape.

A shape she'd been magically locked into—exclusively—for *twelve years* now.

She forced a spring into her step and told herself to keep positive. There was at least one blessing about being exiled: there were a whole lot of places that *weren't* home—and many of them were vibrant, amazing. She'd never have visited them if she hadn't been forced out into the cosmere against her will.

For that, she had decided to be grateful for what had been done to her. Her master said she worked too hard to find sunlight in dark places, but what else was she to do? Darkness was commonplace, and she preferred a challenge. Besides, the cosmere really was a wondrous place.

Not that her current location was anything spectacular. A metallic corridor, with flickering fluorescent lights. Pipes for decor and barely enough space to walk upright. It took a lot of energy to keep a ship like the *Dynamic* flying, and designers learned to be economical.

She paused by one of the portholes, looking out at the bleak darkness of Shadesmar—an endless, empty black plane. Really, wasn't it the *darkness* that reminded one how wonderful the *light* was? Traveling through Shadesmar was dreary, but at least she could do it in a ship, rather than walking in a caravan like people had done in the olden days.

She tried to imagine them out there, walking the lonely obsidian expanse. Or worse, straying into regions where the ground went incorporeal and turned into the misty nothing they called the unsea. Or . . . the emberdark, people sometimes called that vast emptiness—the Rosharan term for the unexplored parts of Shadesmar.

Her ship stayed along the more frequented pathways, where the ground was solid—and had been for millennia. You often encountered other travelers on these patrolled lanes between planets. For Shadesmar, such places were conventional, understood, and safe. But her ship had strayed close to the edge of one such corridor. And out there . . . well, anything could be out there in the emberdark. Starling found that both exciting and terrifying all at once.

A figure stepped out of the wall behind her. Transparent, with a faint glow to him, Nazh had pale skin with cool undertones, and wore a dark grey formal suit: the kind with a fancy cravat that normal people wore to only the most exclusive of gatherings. He didn't have much choice, though, seeing as that was what he'd died in.

"Star?" he asked her. "Is everything all right?"

"It's strikingly beautiful," she said, running her fingers along the metal. "This corridor."

The sleeve of her jacket slipped back, exposing one of her manacles. Silver against her powder-white skin, the thick pieces of metal—more like bracers visually—were the symbols of her exile, binding her in human form, locking away her abilities. Until she "learned."

She still didn't know, years later, how much of the exile was to teach her and how much to punish her. Her people's leaders could be . . . obscure.

"Strikingly beautiful?" Nazh asked. "The . . . corridor? Star, are you having one of your moments?"

"No. Maybe. Look, I was just thinking that this ship is *almost* starting to feel like home."

"The dragon," he said with a smile, "who flies a starship."

"I don't do much flying. That's Leonore's job. I just get flown around."

Twelve years now, trapped in her human form by these manacles. Twelve years since she'd stretched her wings and taken to the sky under her own power.

Shards. She would *not* let that break her.

She would *not* let them win.

She continued on her way, Nazh joining her. He didn't walk, and he didn't really *float*. He glided, feet on the ground, as if standing still—but moving when she walked, his hands clasped behind his back.

"I shouldn't complain," she said. "I mean, there are advantages to letting someone else do the flying. Easier on the muscles this way. Plus I can sleep while we travel! Try doing that when flying with your own wings."

"Star, dear," he said, "if I still had a stomach, I believe I'd find your optimism nauseating."

"Oh, come on," she said. "You have to admit. Things could be worse. I could be dead . . ."

"One gets over such trivialities."

". . . wearing a formal suit for eternity . . ."

"I'll never be underdressed."

". . . and have a face that is . . . well, you know."

Nazh stopped in place. "I know what?"

"Never mind," she said, reaching the ladder to the bottom deck, where she'd find engineering. She descended while he floated alongside her.

"Never mind *what*?" he said.

"It wouldn't be polite to say."

"You were trained by one of the most obtuse, crass men in all of the cosmere, Star. You don't know the meaning of the word 'polite.'"

"Sure I do," she said, hopping off the ladder. "It's just that I'm a kindly young—"

"You're eighty-seven."

"I'm a kindly young—for the relative age of her species—person. Being kindly means you *don't* tell your friend about the unfortunate nature of his coiffure. You merely *imply* it is ridiculous so you can maintain plausible deniability."

He floated along, eyes forward as she reached the door to engineering. "Hairstyles of this . . . volume were quite fashionable when I died."

"Among whom? Musk oxen?"

He almost broke composure—that stern expression of near disapproval cracked, and a smile itched the corners of his mouth. It always felt like a gift when she managed to make Nazh smile. Also, his hair wasn't that bad—it had a windswept, classic look. It was just that he was a tad overly fond of it, despite it making him seem like he couldn't decide if he was a pompous prince or a rockstar.

"Hey," a commanding female voice said in Star's earpiece. "Are you wasting time again?"

"No, Captain."

"Then why isn't my engine working yet?"

"Had to stop at my rooms to fetch something, Captain," Starling said. "I'm almost to engineering."

"Did Nazrilof find you?"

"Yes, Captain."

"I explicitly told him not to."

"Tell her," Nazh said, "she can order me a hundred lashings. I'm fond of them. They tickle."

"Sorry, Captain," Starling said instead. "I'm entering engineering now."

"Warn that engineer," the captain said, "that if there is another problem, I will come down and deal with her personally. I am not known for my patience with crew who slack off." She cut the line.

"Do you suppose," Nazh said, "we could pitch her overboard and claim she jumped? I'd swear under oath she was driven mad."

"By what?"

"My ravishingly attractive hairdo, of course." He hesitated. "I mean, there *has* to be *some* musk ox in the captain's heritage. Have you *seen* the woman?"

Starling grinned, then pushed through the door. The engine room of the *Dynamic* was even more cramped than the hallway—though it had a higher ceiling, the round chamber was clogged with machinery. More than that, large bundles of tubes ran up and down the walls, tied off every few feet or so to keep them together. Like cords, only a little thicker, and sometimes pulsing with water or aether. They were a staple of the ship, and of its class. Tubes in bundles running across the ceilings, or along walls, glowing, pulsing, or thrumming. Most ships that Starling had been on, particularly the less expensive ones, had similar features.

Regardless, Starling had to squeeze between engine protrusions and the wall at several points—and step over several bundles of tubes—to make her way to the back, where a hammock hung from a rivet on the wall and a stack of large barrels, marked with symbols of various aethers.

A young woman sat up from within the hammock and hurriedly hid some items in the pocket of her blue jumpsuit. Aditil had brown skin, with light tan—almost golden—undertones. She wore her black hair in a braid, and as she moved, Starling saw the distinctive pale blue, glasslike portion of her right hand. The center of the palm was replaced—bones and all—with a transparent aether the color of the sky.

The glass was cracked, an indication that the symbiote she'd bonded was dead. Starling had never asked for the story behind that.

"L.T.!" the young woman exclaimed. "Oh hells. Captain sent you? Did I let the pressure lapse again?" She scrambled, grabbing her earpiece from the pouch in her hammock, fumbling to put it in. "Sorry. Sorry, sorry, sorry!"

Aditil slid out of the hammock, almost falling over. She hopped over a large pipe and began to monitor the engines—where she'd plugged in her lodestar to give her readouts in her native language. This was what she was *supposed* to have been doing. The old machinery needed constant attention; the *Dynamic*—as fond as Starling was of it—wasn't the most cutting-edge of ships. Indeed, it was something of a mongrel. Rosharan antigrav technology, aether spores from the Dhatrian planetary network for thrust and engine power, a Scadrian composite metal hull. Never mind that all three technological strains produced their own viable starships without the others. The *Dynamic*, like her crew, had picked up a little here and a little there. All it was missing was an Awakened metalmind, but those were expensive—and Starling had never trusted them anyway.

Aditil fiddled with machinery, often controlling the systems via her lodestar. The rectangular device—around ten inches wide and six inches tall—was a kind of controller, or input device. There were so many different kinds of mechanical architectures in the cosmere, from so many different planets, that it could be difficult to learn them all. Plus, a patchwork ship like this might have parts from a half dozen different manufacturers, each with their own languages, customs, and—most importantly—input schemes.

Having a lodestar built to your preferences helped with that. Most of them, like Aditil's—or the one that Starling wore in a holster at her belt—could be pulled apart into two pieces, each of which you plugged into a device. A little like . . . like handles for luggage that you could remove, then attach to a new piece of luggage. If those handles each had buttons, triggers, and thumbsticks made to your culture's preferences. Most had things like small foldout screens or even keypads in your local language.

Starling had spent decades customizing hers. It had a kind of stonework feel to it, though of course that was a facade for the electronics. She liked to feel that it was ancient, like her people. Aditil's was more modern, with smoother grips and . . . well, it felt more like a controller to one of the game systems she was fond of playing. It was brightly colored, almost gaudy, and the tiny readout displayed the flowing script of her people.

With the lodestar she gave inputs—but she still checked specific gauges and local readouts of things like aether levels. Someone who grew familiar with a system rarely used their lodestar for everything. In this case, Aditil actually *whispered* to the aethers themselves—but it worked, as she got the engine back up to full power. Starling leaned against the wall, noting that Nazh had chosen to remain outside. Aditil was new, and he had learned—from painful experience—to ration his time with new crewmembers. Not everyone was comfortable around shades. Indeed, there were some who'd say that bringing one on board your ship was tantamount to suicide.

"So," Starling said, "this is . . . the third time this week that Captain hasn't been able to get ahold of you?"

"Sorry, sorry, sorry!" Aditil kept her head low as she worked.

"Want to talk about it?"

"I'll do better! I need this job, L.T. Please. I . . . need to save up enough . . ."

Starling folded her arms, the edges of her manacles peeking out from beneath her jacket.

Aditil worked for a moment longer, but then slumped to the floor, leaning forward, forehead against the engine. A low humming sound came from within the machinery as zephyr aether generated gas, which created pressure—the basis for powering the ship. The fact that they could use the zephyr as propellant and for breathable air meant that the *Dynamic* was spaceworthy. They rarely needed that, as Xisis—the ship's owner—usually had them do merchant runs through Shadesmar instead.

"They're pictures of your family, aren't they?" Starling said. "The things you hide whenever I walk past?"

Aditil glanced at her, surprised.

"Can I see them?" Starling asked.

Sheepishly, the young woman fished them out of her pocket and handed them over. Only four photos, depicting a crowded family with . . . seven children? Aditil seemed the oldest. Her parents were smiling in every one, wearing the bright, colorful clothing common to her people.

"They . . . didn't want me to go," Aditil muttered. "Said I was too young, even if I'd done the apprenticing. But after . . ." She looked at her hand, pressed flat on the ground, and the cracked aether bud in the right palm. "I couldn't stay. I took the deal to work for passage offworld, but do you have any idea how much it costs to get back to Dhatri? I didn't. Stupidly, I left my family. And with them, the one place where anyone has ever wanted me . . ."

"Hey," Starling said, kneeling beside her. "You're wanted here."

"I shouldn't be," Aditil said. "I've screwed up every duty I've ever been given. You deserve a real engineer, with real experience, and a functional aether."

"Aditil, you think we can *afford* a full aetherbound? On this old piece of junk?"

"She's not a piece of junk." Aditil put a hand on the engine. "She's a good ship, L.T."

Now that was encouraging. You always wanted an engineer who cared about the ship.

"Either way," Starling said, "you're a blessing to us here. A fully trained aetherbound?"

"Without a functioning aether."

"Regardless, we get your knowledge, your skill. You always get the engine working again, when you try."

"I talk to it," she said softly. "You can only afford older spores, which tend to be drowsy. I wake them up, that's all . . ." She turned to Starling. "I'm broken, L.T. Ruined."

"You can *never* be ruined," Starling said, taking her hand. "Hey, look at me. Never ever, Aditil. It's impossible." Then she shrugged. "But here, we're all a little off, eh? Maybe that's what makes us a family." Starling had let her jacket sleeves retreat, and Aditil glanced at the manacles, thought a moment, then nodded.

"Thanks for the pep talk, L.T.," Aditil said, pulling back to work at her post. "I'll stay on it."

"Well, good," Starling said. "That's what Captain wants." She handed back the pictures, then slipped something out of her own inner jacket pocket—an envelope, fetched from her room earlier.

Aditil took it with a frown, looked to Starling, then opened it. After a moment, she registered what was inside. Her eyes went wide, and her hand went to her lips, covering a quiet gasp.

One ticket to Dhatri, Aditil's homeworld.

"But how?" Aditil asked. "Why would you . . ."

"Nobody," Starling said intently, "on *my* ship is trapped. *Everybody* on *my* ship has the right to go home. You're a great engineer, Aditil, and I love having you on this crew. But if there's another place you feel you need to be, well . . ." She nodded toward the ticket.

"What does Captain think?"

"Captain doesn't need to know," Starling said. "You're not our slave, Aditil. You're our friend and colleague."

Aditil stared at the ticket, tearing up. "How . . . how long have you known I was homesick?"

"I made a good guess. Though . . . I *did* buy a refundable ticket, in case I was wrong." She walked past and squeezed Aditil's shoulder. "When we get back to Silverlight, I'll sign your release papers. You can return home, until you're ready to leave again—if ever."

"I . . ." Aditil closed her eyes, tears leaking down her cheeks. "Thank you," she whispered.

Starling smiled. "For now, though, please just keep the ship moving. Captain keeps threatening to come down here herself, and I think she might actually do it next time."

"Thank you, L.T.," she whispered again. "Starling . . . *Thank you.*"

Starling left her working with renewed vigor, then stepped out of engineering. Nazh was waiting, one eyebrow cocked.

"What?" she asked him.

"How did you afford that?"

It *was* expensive to travel to Dhatri. The law of commerce was simple: if you could get to a location through Shadesmar, it was cheap. If not, then you had to pay. A *lot*.

Most cities were in the Physical Realm, not in Shadesmar, but you could transfer between the two dimensions with ease—if you had a special kind of portal. They were called perpendicularities, and most major planets had them. To travel, you popped into Shadesmar on one planet, traveled easily to your destination, then popped back out.

Unfortunately, Dhatri didn't have a perpendicularity anymore. Which meant you couldn't hop out of Shadesmar there to visit it. No, to get to Dhatri, you needed a faster-than-light-capable ship that traveled through space in the Physical Realm. Those were *expensive*. And mostly controlled by one military or another. Hence why Aditil could catch a ride on one leaving: a ship had needed a post filled, and recruited her. But to get back, the only reliable way was to buy an overpriced ticket.

"Well?" Nazh asked as they started walking. And gliding. "How did you afford it?"

"I had some savings," she said.

"You realize," he said, "this is only going to convince them *further* you have a hoard of gold somewhere."

Shards. She hadn't thought of that. Their crew was small—only eight people—but the myth about Starling's kind and their caverns of gold had persisted among them no matter how she tried to stamp it out. At least they'd believed her when she'd insisted that dragons *didn't* eat people.

She started up the ladder to the middle deck. Truth was, she felt good, having guessed accurately what Aditil needed. She was finally starting to feel like she understood this crew and how to be a leader, just like Master Hoid had been trying to teach her. Before he'd vanished, of course. It was . . . his way.

He'd be back. Until then, she had to do her best to guide the crew, and protect them from the interim captain. She reached the middle deck and walked through the hallway toward the stern, where she could climb up to the bridge. As she did, though, she spotted someone standing outside of the medical bay, peering in.

ZeetZi was a lawnark, a being that was basically human—except instead of hair, he had feathers. A mostly bald head, with dark brown skin that had a cool earthy tone, along with a crest of yellow and white feathers on the very top. He also had tiny feathers along his arms, almost invisible against his skin. Arcanists said lawnarks hadn't evolved from birds or anything like that—more, they were humans who had been isolated, and whose hair had evolved into something more akin to feathers. He wore a pair of trousers with suspenders over a shirt with the sleeves rolled up. His lodestar, in its case on his belt, had a shiny metallic outer shell with almost no markings on its various buttons and triggers.

ZeetZi was *supposed* to be checking on the life support systems. While Aditil handled the aethers and the engine, ZeetZi was their technician for the rest of the ship. He was a genius at mechanical devices . . . when he wasn't getting distracted by the ship's doctor.

He spotted Starling and Nazh, and his crest perked up in alarm. Then he immediately stepped forward to meet them.

"Yes," he said. "Yes, before you prod me in your relentlessly surreptitious way, L.T., I *was* checking on the doctor again. I know you encouraged me to abandon my anxiety, but I can't *help* it. We shouldn't have invited one of those on our ship, not if we value our lives or sanity."

"Zee," she said, taking his arm, "have you listened to yourself when you talk like that?"

"I know, I know," he said, crest smoothing back down. "It's unseemly, yes, but . . . you know what they did to my people. To my world."

She nodded. She'd never been to his homeworld—amazing though it sounded—but she knew what the hordes had done to other planets. It was a familiar story.

"Master Hoid," Starling said, "trusts Chrysalis. He invited her on board."

ZeetZi shivered at the name Chrysalis—and Nazh looked away. It said something that, even with a dragon and a shade on board, the crew was most frightened of the ship's doctor.

"I found one of its spies," ZeetZi hissed, "murine, sniffing around in my room again, L.T."

Well, that was a problem. Chrysalis did tend to ignore privacy.

"I'll speak to her," Starling said. She'd made a breakthrough, finally, with Aditil. Could she manage another?

"Star," Nazh said softly, "you need to stop worrying about that one. The horde will be gone from this ship as soon as Xisis finds a proper ship's doctor."

"Master Hoid told me to watch over the crew," she whispered.

"That's not a member of our crew," ZeetZi said. "L.T., show me trust in this. The creature isn't here for us, and will not lend aid if we need it. It doesn't care about us, except how it can use us to further its own arcane goals."

"We'll see," Starling said. "You two head up to the bridge. I'll meet you in a bit."

Both reluctantly withdrew. Starling approached the medical bay, looking in at a figure who wore a tight, formal uniform from a military Starling hadn't ever been able to identify. The individual worked at a cabinet, cataloging medicines, as the captain had asked.

As the figure heard Starling, it turned—revealing a face with the skin pulled back, and a network of insects beneath.

Fig. 86 · Chrysalis bug
(Sleepless)

CHAPTER TWENTY-THREE

Some called them Clemaxin's Hordes, after the first person who had discovered them. Starling used the name "Sleepless," as that was the term they seemed to prefer. There were said to be fewer than a thousand individual Sleepless in the whole cosmere—and some estimates indicated that number was closer to two or three hundred.

Though in the case of the Sleepless, "individual" was a loaded word. They were each a group intelligence, made of hundreds of hordelings: insects, like large beetles, maybe three inches from tip to tail. In Chrysalis's case, many hordelings had skin growing along them. In fact, one specific hordeling had a complete human nose growing out of its back—and was currently scurrying across the top of her head.

As Starling watched, the face resealed, insects climbing into place, skin side out. Two bugs with eyeballs on them emerged, fitting into the face, and the nose positioned itself beneath them. It all locked together, forming Chrysalis's face. At least, the face she presented to the world. Human, with tan skin and tattoos to help obscure the patchwork of lines made by the skin fitting together. Those still stood out, like scars, hiding the insects locked together beneath.

The person presented for Starling was actually hundreds of insects holding together, like the proverbial three children in a long coat. This wasn't all of Chrysalis—in fact, it might not even be the most important bits of her. The portions that held her memory and personality would be hidden safely in other places on the ship. But this *was* the portion she used to interact.

"Lieutenant," Chrysalis said with a deep yet feminine voice. Though her drones could be of either sex, and though the body didn't have secondary sex characteristics, her personality presented female. A severe, thick-bodied woman with a lean face and short blond hair. Unlike others, she didn't carry a lodestar, a subtle indication that she likely knew every possible system and could adapt to them easily. "I'm sorry you caught me with my face down. Many eyes are better for cataloging than two."

"It's all right, Chrysalis," Starling said. "I've been around Sleepless before." She didn't mention how much that experience always creeped her out. That it made her skin crawl—made her imagine she was made of insects too. She couldn't help picturing them under her flesh, crawling through the cavities in her body.

"Is there something you wanted?" Chrysalis asked.

"You heard what we talked about in the corridor," Starling said. "I know you did."

Chrysalis turned back to her cataloging.

"You have nodes, drones, all over the ship," Starling said. "I know it's the way of your people, but you *can't* keep spying on the others."

Chrysalis placed a bottle in the cabinet. If she were like others of her kind, each finger in her hand would be a separate insect, bred for that look and purpose, connected to the palm—another pair of insects—to imitate a hand.

"Chrysalis," Starling said, stepping forward. "If we're to be a crew, you—"

"Nazrilof is correct," Chrysalis said. "I will be leaving soon. You needn't worry about me."

"But—"

"What do you want, Lieutenant?" Chrysalis said, slapping a bottle down on the counter. "What do you *really* want of me?"

"I want you to try," Starling said. "Try being one of us."

"And the others?" The Sleepless turned toward her. "I watch because they will eventually try to kill me, as most crews do, and I need warning."

"I won't let that happen."

"Forgive me," Chrysalis said, "if experience has shown me otherwise. I will continue to keep watch. Tell ZeetZi he needn't worry—I, personally, have no intention of enslaving him or returning him to his homeworld."

Starling gritted her teeth. It was always like this with Chrysalis. Terse, unwavering. Stubborn.

"Chrysalis," Starling said. "Can you at least *try*?"

"Try what? To not hear when they call me 'it' instead of 'she'?"

Starling winced. "I'll talk to them."

"Don't," Chrysalis said. "Better they fear us. It is advantageous." She clicked another jar into the cabinet. "I will move on soon. Hoid has abandoned me, as he warned me he would. I don't know why I ever trusted him . . ."

Starling wanted to say more, but . . . Shards, she found herself unable to respond. Chrysalis was right—the others did treat her unfairly. But she also continued to *spy* on them, with hordelings all through the ship. Maybe it was best if she just moved on, like she said.

The idea made Starling sad. Master Hoid wouldn't have let this problem persist; he'd have fixed it somehow.

As she was trying to think of something else to say, the ship banked to starboard—hard enough that Starling, frowning, walked to the porthole.

"We've turned off the tradeway," she said. "Heading into the emberdark."

"Maybe there's a Scadrian patrol coming," Chrysalis suggested.

"Our cargo is legal this time, though."

"Captain can be paranoid," Chrysalis said, continuing her work.

"No," she said. "This close to Silverlight, even the Scadrians wouldn't dare bully a trading vessel. Something is up." She tapped her earpiece, stepping out of the room. But a moment later, before she could ask for an explanation, Nazh floated down from the floor above. He could hover through most any substance—so long as he didn't encounter any silver or aluminum.

"Distress signal," he said, voice tense. "From the emberdark."

"And the captain is willing to go help?"

"She put us on a course right for it."

That left Starling deeply unsettled.

She looked at Nazh, then immediately ran for the bridge.

Captain Crow was not the type to help out of the goodness of her heart. There was almost *certainly* another reason they were on their way to that distress beacon.

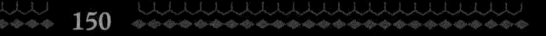

Fig. 18 · Kokerlii
(Aviar)

CHAPTER TWENTY-FOUR

Dusk stopped when the island with the pool was just out of sight.

He settled into the boat, lying back, staring at the sky with its ribbons of faint light. How unnatural to be in a boat, but not feel it rocking to any waves. Still, he liked the feel of the oar in the not-water, liked gliding through the abyss. That part felt right.

Maybe he was simply glad to be in a boat again. He watched the sky for a short while, then decided to check over the engine. As he worked, he hoped that Rokke would come out from her hiding place under the seats. She didn't, not even when Sak fluttered over and chirped at her. He smiled at that regardless. Once, Sak had been the quiet, shy one. While she certainly wasn't ever going to be boisterous, perhaps life on the homeisles had changed both of them.

He dug his binoculars out of the pack. With them, he could still see the island, but this place's too-distant horizon still unnerved him. It looked the same distance away through binoculars as it did to the naked eye, indicating that this plane just kept going.

"Sak," he said, lowering the binoculars. "Any guesses?"

She chirped, and suddenly the surface of the abyss outside the boat was filled with his corpses. Floating face down, arms spread, drifting until they—one by one—sank into that smoky not-water.

"Same in every direction," Dusk said, dissatisfied. "Equally dangerous no matter where I go."

Sak chirped apologetically. He'd hoped that maybe she could ascertain the best path for him, but her talent didn't work that way. She sent visions of what might come, but couldn't specifically read the future.

Curiously, as he'd spoken, Rokke poked her head out from underneath the seat for the first time.

"Well," he said, though normally he didn't say much to the birds, "our first goal is to discover a method of wayfinding. Grand discoveries won't accomplish anything if I can't retrace our path and bring proof back to Vathi."

It was a mouthful of words, and he felt like he was rambling, disturbing the unnerving serenity of this place. Yet Rokke liked it. She emerged fully, and even hopped up on the seat across from him.

Father. Why had Vathi given him a bird that wanted him to *speak* of all things?

He sighed and engaged the motor—which drove her back into hiding. He took them out a ways, using the binoculars to keep view on the island. Once they got far enough out that he could barely see it—which was saying something—he cut the motor and scanned for any kind of feature.

Though the butterflies had followed him out for a while, they'd long since retreated. He didn't spot even a hint of . . . well, anything at all. That's what he'd expected, unfortunately. Vathi's initial expeditions had explored in all directions, trying—as he was—to locate anything to use as a waypoint.

When her sailors had finally struck out farther, they'd almost immediately gotten lost. With nothing to use as reference, and with the strange behavior of radio out here, even getting home had proven impossible. He put his fingers into the not-water. As he brushed them back and forth, he felt almost no resistance. About as much as a soft breeze. Next, he checked his oar, and it seemed to have maintained most of its worm paste. He could maneuver with it same as when he'd first applied the coating.

With an inward sigh, he forced himself to talk. "Suppose I *could* swim in this, if I coated my arms. To that end . . ." He took the jar of paste and slipped it into a sack, which he tied to one of his ropes. Then he put it overboard.

It sank. Which confused him, but he supposed it needed to be exposed to the not-ocean to float? Rather than contained in a jar? He pulled it back up and then—curious—pressed his hand into the abyss. Before, he'd used his left hand, but he'd applied the paste to the oar with his right.

A small remnant still coated it, and with that he felt more resistance. He could feel the abyss this way, as if it really were water. Though mostly invisible.

He tied the jar to his belt with a rope. It was awkward there—but it was also the only thing that kept him from sinking into nothingness forever. He wanted that reservoir attached to him, just in case.

"Don't fancy trying to take a dip," he decided. "The boat is buoyant in this stuff, but who knows about me? Even with worm paste on my arms, I might not be able to swim back up to the boat before I run out of strength."

Rokke's head appeared again from underneath her seat.

"You can breathe under there, I read," he said. He stuck his face into the smoky substance. "Yes, I can breathe. It's not really water; it's like . . . the memory of water. Something strange like that. A poet could explain, maybe."

He looked up, and Rokke was standing on the lip of the boat, peering with one eye down into the nothing. Sak, on the boat's Aviar perch near the prow, chirped encouragingly.

Dusk closed his eyes, then rested his right hand in the not-water. Wayfinding had many different elements. In his book he'd record his best guess on how far he'd come—but without stars, compass, or sun, that wouldn't get him back. There had to be other methods, like spotting wildlife, or *some* kind of feature to use in navigation.

Or this. A hand in the water.

He reached back into the depths of ancestral memory, remembering the lessons his uncle had taught while sailing between islands. Lessons he'd applied many times in his life, until he was likely one of the greatest living experts in the skill.

Feel the currents. *Waves are the voices of the islands,* his uncle had said. *They speak as loudly as any Aviar. But you have to learn to listen with your fingers.*

If that was the case, this place wasn't just silent to the ears, but to the fingers as well. No waves. He coated his entire hand and held it in the stillness, waiting. Yearning.

Nothing.

Cakoban didn't travel this darkness blindly, he thought. *That's not the way of the explorer. Please show me. Father, please show me how they did it.*

Again, nothing. Not a hint of a sensation. So reluctantly, he made some notes in his book, took up his oar, and started paddling away from the island, into the void.

Sak squawked uncertainly.

"I know," Dusk said. "Setting off without knowing your way home is a supremely stupid thing to do."

Sak chirped a question.

"No, I don't know how we'll find our way back," Dusk admitted. "The moment we lose sight of that island, I'm unlikely to find it again."

A final chirp. And an image of Dusk's corpse, lying in the front of the boat, face up—toward the upward infinity this time. Eyes sightless.

"I know," Dusk said. "But this is what we need to do. I can take you back, if you want."

An angry chirp to the negative.

"Sometimes," Dusk said, "you can't know the way. Sometimes, you have to strike out anyway. If we turn back, that's the end of our people. Despite her admirable efforts, Vathi will fail to protect us from the Ones Above. I want to face the possible end as my ancestors did: with oar in hand."

Sak turned around on the perch, facing forward, determined. Dusk's corpse vanished, and so they continued, gliding along the surface of something that wasn't nearly real enough. He eventually engaged the motor, determinedly carrying them farther and farther from safety. He didn't check with the binoculars; he knew that the waypoint island was gone to them now. Even if he turned around and went back in what he thought was exactly the right way, he knew he wouldn't find it.

The human ability to sense direction was a liar straight from Gofi, the trickster island. People grew up in familiar environs, which led them to falsely trust instincts they didn't actually have—for memory was different from navigational sense. Without landmarks, people were helpless. His uncle had drilled that into him, teaching Dusk to watch the stars and read the waves. Teaching him how to not get lost in the jungle, where his "natural" senses would send him in circles.

For now, he sailed. Which was the proper term, even without a sail, because words were stupid sometimes. He slept at some point, woke up, ate, and fed the birds. Then continued on. There was light in this place, somehow. Too much for it to be from those ribbons in the sky, which were fading as he got farther from land. He couldn't find a source for that light, which was more than a little unnerving. No shadows. He hadn't realized how much they informed his relation to the world. Without them, this all felt like a dream.

Rokke kept hiding, so Dusk started a soft song, one his father had sung to him when he was a child. In the old version of the language, with similar sounds but words that felt off—yet in a familiar way.

> "I took a dream
> And made it mine
> I took a them
> And made they mine."

"Dream," said more like "drem," had once rhymed with the word "them." He'd always found it curious how, in the old song, "them" was a noun you could count. A group. And "they" used to mean . . . well, what "them" meant now, he supposed. He was only guessing, but there was a calming way about the sounds. A promise. He sang the verses, appreciating that words—like people—changed over time to become something new.

Perhaps he shouldn't dislike words. They were living things, and maybe they could sense his aversion. Was that why they so often turned against him?

He thought on that as he eased into the final verse.

> "I took a morrow
> And made it mine

I took a sorrow
And made it thine . . ."

Rokke came out as he sang that last part. The twist at the end of the song had always made Dusk's father laugh. So Dusk had laughed too, even before he'd understood why the twist of saying "thine" would land after four verses. Rokke, undoubtedly, didn't understand that. The Aviar were like people—they understood things—but they relied more on emotions than definitions.

That said, some breeds of Aviar chose to say words, so who knew? Either way, Rokke hopped up onto the seat beside him—not close, but not far either.

"I'm sorry," Dusk said, "to bring you on this excursion. You picked a poor time to join up, little Aviar."

She didn't say anything. But she was there, and had gotten on the boat when he indicated. She wanted to be with them. It was just . . . losing a person was hard for an Aviar. He understood. Father, he wished he didn't, but he did. Because the silence wasn't nearly as peaceful for him as it once had been.

He was crying before he realized it. Sak was asleep on her perch, but Rokke chirped to him for the first time.

"I hope I'm not doing this because of Kokerlii," Dusk whispered. "Tell me I'm not trying to die because I lost a bird. I'm doing this because it *means* something. Aren't I?"

Rokke chirped softly. Maybe Dusk couldn't know his own emotions these days, any more than he knew the way forward. He could only keep breathing, just like he kept paddling, a lonely leaf in a currentless ocean.

Rokke suddenly went alert, then in a flutter was back down under the seat. Dusk found her trembling, red feathers on her head and neck fluffed out—which *could* mean contentment, but in this case meant the opposite. What had he done wrong?

No. That's a terrified response.

His breath caught. Then, feeling an awful premonition, he turned and looked out over the side of the boat.

Something was down there.

It was long and narrow, like a snake. But it seemed larger and longer than any snake he'd seen. Dimensions were difficult to judge, but he guessed its head was a good foot wide, with a body maybe five feet long—one that was more *plated* than *scaled*. It swam with a sinuous motion, swinging in wide curves, its body lined with faint lights.

Odd, he thought. That was how he'd always imagined shadows, the beasts that prowled the seas near the Pantheon Islands. He'd seen artist drawings all his life depicting them as serpentine like this—extensions of the Dakwara, the great god of snakes, who had infinite coils extending into every ocean.

However, he'd now *seen* actual shadows, or deepwalkers, as the scientists called them. He'd seen them up close, killed by modern weapons, their carcasses pulled up on beaches. They had legs, and were more crustacean than serpentine.

That had saddened him. So this was . . . exciting? To find a monster in these depths that finally matched his mental picture?

Either way, he reached for his harpoon.

Rokke chirped an alarm, causing Sak to stir and crack an eye.

"I need to see if it can be hunted," Dusk explained to Rokke. "See how its sides glow. It's using something like the worm paste to swim. That means it might be physical, not a ghost, which means I could eat it. Maybe."

Dusk tracked the thing, and watched it suddenly turn its head to the side, slowing its swimming. It had noticed something in the distance, though not Dusk or his boat. He judged its body language, and thought it might be hunting prey. It *could* sense things in here. It *was* possible.

On the Pantheon Islands, many things—including the shadows—hunted minds. "Rokke," he thought to ask, "are you hiding us?"

She chirped. He didn't know her well, but it seemed affirmative. Good, as that was her job. But he wondered. Had . . . had the two of them started to bond already? That was fast. Faster than he was comfortable with.

Either way, her talent hid them from things that hunted for minds. You didn't need to fully bond an Aviar to be lent its talent, if it was near.

"Turn it off," Dusk said.

She squawked in a panic.

"It's all right," he said, hefting his harpoon—which was attached to a good length of modern rope from the homeisles. "I know what I'm doing."

She hid. However, she must have disengaged her ability, for the thing beneath the not-water immediately turned toward them. It sensed them.

Yes, there must *be prey here,* he thought with satisfaction. *It must have a reason for those senses.*

And it generated its own worm paste? Seemed plausible. After all, the worms generated it. He hefted his harpoon as the not-shadow swam up toward them.

And continued swimming up toward them.

And continued.

Right about then, Dusk realized his mistake. "Rokke, put the veil back up!"

Because this thing was way, *way* bigger than he'd assumed. Turned out, without landmarks or a sense of scale, it was incredibly difficult to judge the size of a monster swimming underneath you—even more so than he'd guessed. What he'd assumed was a serpent with a head a foot wide was in reality big enough to *swallow the boat.*

Rokke did as he requested, and the sudden bubble of protection caused the thing to shake and pause. Then it kept swimming up—but by then, Dusk had engaged the engine. He sent the boat skimming across the surface just before the beast broke out of the not-water behind them.

There it snapped a beak-like mouth to one side, then the other, searching. It didn't seem to have eyes—it must hunt exclusively with its ability to sense minds. The engine carried them away from danger at a good clip, and the beast didn't give chase—as it couldn't tell where they'd gone.

Sak grumbled sleepily from her perch, and didn't even seem to have noticed the danger. Rokke peeked out, glanced at Dusk in an accusatory way, and squawked.

"We *do* need to try hunting one of those," he said. "My ancestors must have hunted when they traveled this darkness."

She squawked again.

"They *did* travel here," Dusk said, stubborn. "I believe it. I . . . I have to."

All of his people knew their heritage, and celebrated it. They had come from far away; they were explorers. It wasn't just hope on his part; it was *identity*.

"If those snakes are edible," Dusk said, still guiding the boat with its motor, "then they are part of the proof we need to show Vathi that we *can* make our own way into the cosmere without the help of the Ones Above. Besides, hunting them might be a matter of survival. We can feed the two of you for months out of a few sacks—but humans take more."

Rokke squawked from the recesses of her hiding spot. Sullen.

"I'll pick a smaller snake to fight next time," he promised, looking back at the thing as it swam in a circle around the spot where they'd been. Close call or not, he was pleased. He was a trapper of Patji, where monsters hunted with their minds. He had been trained by the Father himself to survive against terrible odds.

He was increasingly certain *this* was the reason. If a beast like this could make its way in this darkness, then Dusk could too.

Fig. 30 · Deathants
(insect)

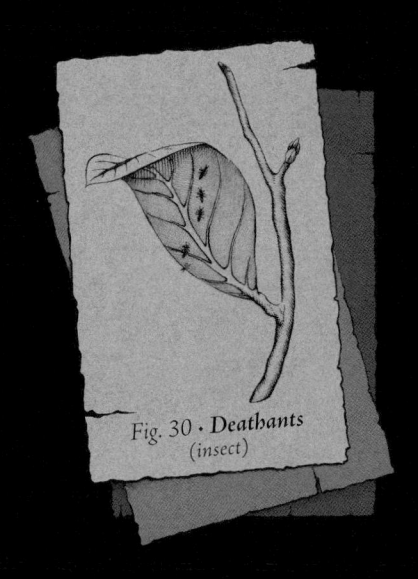

CHAPTER TWENTY-FIVE

Captain Crow had been born on a backwater planet that Starling had never visited. The captain had light tan skin with a ruddy cast to it. She was of normal height, but abnormal disposition. Starling wasn't certain when Crow had entered the service of Xisis, but when he inherited the *Dynamic*—along with its debts—following Hoid's disappearance six months before, he instantly installed Crow as captain.

She wore modern enough clothing, though her jacket had a certain old-school nautical feel to it, as did her lodestar. That, with her way of speaking, screamed that she had experience on an actual sailing ship. Crow didn't speak of her past, though, so there was no way to know when.

Starling enjoyed being first officer under Crow because it proved she could be an officer under basically anyone. Surely there was value in that realization. Surely she wasn't stretching too far to find the good in the situation.

The bridge of the *Dynamic* was, of course, cramped. The front wall was divided: The left half was a thick viewing window. The right half was a bulkhead with a Scadrian electronic control system that Starling had never learned, relying on her lodestar if she needed to access the sensors or systems there. That bulkhead had one small viewscreen that you basically had to sit directly in front of to see.

She dreamed of the grand bridges she'd seen on other ships, with huge viewscreens and a commanding seat for the captain. You found those on the larger military ships, however—not small cargo vessels. They had five seats here—a row of two at the front for using the equipment, then a cramped row of three seats behind it. Those rows took up almost all of the floor space. The ceiling was covered in a network of tubes, some of them colorful, fanning out from the controls and running to other systems in the ship. Other bundles of tubes ran up and down the walls, even more prominent here than they had been in engineering.

The occupied pilot's seat was in front of the window. Operations, with ZeetZi settled into it, was by the viewscreen and the many sensor controls. Generally, two of the seats in the back row were reserved for the captain and first officer, but Crow preferred to stand beside the doorway—as she did now—relaxing and leaning against the wall. That was the only place where one didn't have to stoop when standing, as the ceiling slanted forward above the piloting and operations stations.

Starling ducked through the small blast door entrance. She stopped beside Crow in a spot that blocked the way in, but it was the only other place to stand on the bridge.

"Captain?" she said.

Crow took a sip from her silver flagon, which she wore on her left hip, lodestar on her right. The flagon was always filled only with water, but she needed a sip every few minutes because of a specific health issue. That issue otherwise rendered her nearly indestructible, so it was an annoyance she likely didn't mind.

"Aye," the captain eventually said.

"Are we really following a distress beacon?" Starling asked.

"Aye."

"That's unexpectedly magnanimous of you!" Starling said. "Um, I'm impressed."

Crow sipped her drink. Starling nodded to Nazh, who hovered halfway out of the wall to her left, then ducked and found her way to her seat, the middle one in the row of three, centered just behind operations and the helm. To her right, Ed—their arcanist—sat in his blue robes and floppy, bulbous red hat, studying some kind of religious text. To her left was the flex seat. The engineer, the ship's doctor, or sometimes Nazh—as ship security officer—could use that one. Shades didn't need to sit, but Nazh often did if he didn't want people stumbling through the center of him and inconveniently dying. Right now, the seat was empty.

Starling strapped in to model good habits, even if she didn't personally need that protection. Then she leaned forward, between the two crewmembers in the front row. ZeetZi to her right and Leonore, the pilot, to her left. The compact woman had pale skin with a cool undertone, and wore her round, red wooden mask lifted onto the top of her head. Her lodestar—currently separated and plugged in like a set of thumbsticks to control the ship—was made of a variety of different kinds of metal that spiraled and fused together.

"Time to signal?" Starling asked.

"Several hours," Leonore said. She hesitated. "Into the emberdark. Captain never lets us fly off the paths."

They both glanced back at Crow, who sipped her canteen and gave no explanation.

It was exciting . . . though honestly, there wasn't anything to see out here. It was mostly barren wasteland, and radio interference made it frighteningly easy to get lost. Starling waited, watching, as the time passed. Eventually she caught Leonore glancing at her, cocking a smile.

"What?" Starling asked.

"You've been busy lately, L.T.," Leonore said. "And I've realized that something feels off when you're not sitting in that spot, sticking your head into our business."

"Agreed," said ZeetZi. "Your face is a great pillar, always in the corner of my vision—like my own nose, often ignored. Until it vanishes, and I am left unsettled, like a room gone too still."

"So . . ." Starling said. "Annoying? Or . . . helpful?"

"Yah," Leonore said. "Comfortably annoying."

"Like a sun: so demanding, so irritating, so essential," ZeetZi said.

"How," Leonore said, "is *sunlight* annoying, Zee?"

"Said with aplomb," he replied, "by one who has lived only in the outside, and has never known the great and comforting thrum of the Grand Apparatus as it brings your family together, room by room. Yes, said by one who knows only restless quietude."

ZeetZi studied the instruments on his dash. One hand was on half of his lodestar, which he'd plugged into the slot on the dash for it. The other, however, hovered over the built-in Scadrian control panel, and little lines of electricity—like tiny lightning bolts—connected his fingers to the panel, letting him use those native controls, which were written in the brutal, pointed, northern Scadrian script. One of his sensors would be monitoring the signal they were following. It wasn't radio, but a more expensive Invested emergency beacon.

For the moment, ZeetZi wore his vibrant crest of yellow feathers long and combed back down his neck. His eyebrows were similarly feathered. He couldn't fly, and found it amusing when people asked—he'd never seen a bird before leaving his homeworld, which sounded like one of the strangest places Starling had ever heard of. Cities made of thousands upon thousands of moving rooms, controlled by some giant mechanism? Overseen by the Sleepless and powered by unseen Investiture?

"Zee," Starling said, one arm on the side of his chair, one arm on Leonore's, "does everyone on your homeworld speak like you do? So formal?"

"Formal?" Leonore asked. "That's a strange way of saying 'convoluted.'"

ZeetZi merely smiled. Leonore and he had been flying together for over two years now, and their gibes were good-natured, best that Starling could tell. She was pretty sure the two had dated at one point, but if so, the breakup hadn't spoiled their working relationship.

"My homeworld," ZeetZi said, "is home to a multitudinous array of peoples, much as yours is, Lieutenant Starling."

"Wait," she said, and even Leonore perked up, glancing at him. "You've been to Yolen?"

"Once," he said.

"Rusting hell," Leonore said. "How did you ever manage to get passage? People wait decades and are never allowed!"

"It is a story I think I shall reserve," ZeetZi said, "until I am offered drinks in an exchange of fair compensation. It is a very good story, and deserves anticipation in the telling."

On the seat to the right of Starling, Ed had grabbed his notebook, antiquated pen at the ready. He loved the ones you had to dip, which was . . . well, inconvenient, but very Eddish. He had darker skin as well, more umber than ZeetZi's—and of course, no feathers. Ed was of Silverlight, born and raised, though of Vaxilian heritage. His lodestar wasn't on his hip; he carried it in his bag with his books and notebooks, but it was one of the arcanist ones, bigger and bulkier, with twice the number of buttons as anyone else's.

Anytime ZeetZi spoke of his homeworld, Ed took notes, likely preparing some kind of report for the other arcanists. Granted, the Grand Apparatus *did* seem unique, so she couldn't blame him. He saw that she was watching, and nudged her to keep Zee talking.

Instead, she leaned forward, looking at the instruments, reading the Scadrian outputs above ZeetZi's hand, which crackled softly with electricity as he moved fingers up and down to subtly control the systems. "Shards," she said. "That signal is weak."

"Yes," ZeetZi said. "I barely noticed its teasings, and might have lost it in the thrumming of the Current had I not been double-checking my work in anticipation of a potential scolding from the captain." He shook his head, feathers rustling. "We should have a proper navigator, Lieutenant. I am not sufficiently trained on this."

He was right, as he had plenty to monitor—and might have to leave the bridge to fix machinery if it wasn't working. They needed a copilot and navigator. Problem was, nobody wanted that job. Navigating in Shadesmar could be tough. The Knell—the name they had for the enormous natural beacon near Threnody—gave at least one data point. Anyone with a proper navigation device—or hell, even a hint of a sensory power, like Allomantic bronze—could sense the invisible waves it gave off, called the Current.

So if you wanted to go to the Knell, then great, you could just follow the Current. Unfortunately, eldritch entities born of a god's death tended to haunt the area immediately surrounding the Knell. So visiting it, and Nazh's homeworld nearby, was not advised.

Still, so long as you knew where you were, you could use the Knell as a reference point and create a heading to where you wanted to go. Things got tricky, though, if you *didn't* know where you were. If you were lucky, you'd be close to someplace inhabited, as they tended to have beacons to light the way. Most could be sensed by the same devices that could locate the Current, but many others were more mundane, like radio. Large trade routes usually had small ones all along their path.

Following one of those, you could get where you were going. But if you struck too far into the emberdark, you'd enter areas where radio grew extremely inconsistent, and even many Invested beacons weakened. You'd be left with only the Knell, and the hope that by following it you'd eventually run across civilization. Like . . . being lost in the wilderness with only a compass. Knowing the way north was vital, and you could follow that. But a compass alone couldn't tell you where you were; it only let you pick a direction and follow it.

Before his disappearance, Hoid himself had done navigation for the ship. He was gone now, leaving them to fend for themselves. While all of them knew the basics . . . well, it was a heavy duty, keeping the ship from getting lost in the emberdark. She wasn't surprised that ZeetZi would rather they hire someone else.

"We're already kinda full, Zee," Leonore said.

"The ghost requires no bunk upon which to rest his deathless eyes," ZeetZi said. "We could take on another crewmember. Consider this only a request, and a suggestion, Lieutenant. I fear my inadequacy might have cost lives today, had I not settled down to go over my work."

"But you *did* find it," Starling said.

"And were there others I missed?" he asked, studying the monitors. "We shall never know, for their voices would have died in the emberdark, like that of a distant room—cast off, lost to the city, bearing with it into the gravelands any who were unfortunate enough to occupy it."

"Gravelands?" Ed said, furiously writing. "Tell me more about gravelands, Zee. You've never mentioned that before!"

ZeetZi eyed him, then sighed. "It is a myth, Eddlin," he explained. "Of where rooms go once they are broken and worn down, discarded by the Grand Apparatus."

ISLES OF THE EMBERDARK

"You could just go see though, right?" Ed said. "Walk out of the city and find them?"

"There is no leaving the city," ZeetZi said. "The slavers made sure of that. Beyond that, you view it wrong. There are *thousands* of rooms, atop and around one another, all in motion, all part of the Grand Apparatus. If you wish to experience sunlight, my friend, you do not 'leave the city.' You request of the Grand Apparatus a room with windows, and when your time has come, a chamber will be brought to you. You will transfer, and abandon the room you've been occupying—then be taken to the perimeter, where sunlight will shine in upon you.

"It is the same when you wish to sleep—request a bedroom, and it is brought. If you need the facilities of biological necessity, you call for one, and it will be attached to your current room. No one owns any place, but merely occupies each one, as our spirits briefly occupy these hosts that form our bodies."

Ed was scribbling eagerly, though Starling still had trouble imagining the place. Apparently, ZeetZi had explained, you kept your possessions in trunks that moved with you—locking on to the new room, and going with it when you entered. But there were no houses, just thousands of communal rooms, traded between people who requested them depending on their momentary needs. All part of some insane machine built before even the Shattering, they thought. Now used by the Sleepless to run tests upon mortals.

Her master had visited the place, because of course he had. Hoid claimed to have solved a murder there, though the way he told it, she wasn't certain his help had been in any way relevant. But . . . well, that was often the case with him. She was certain he was exaggerating the annoyance of the other parties involved.

They fell silent as ZeetZi continued to track the distress beacon. Shards . . . it *was* far out here, which explained the weakness of the signal. She felt a twinge of excitement. This was something new, something she rarely got to do.

They traveled a good two hours through the emberdark, far enough that the beacons leading back to the tradeway grew faint. It unnerved her in the best way to stare into that darkness—infinite sky with a soup of blackness below, *faintly* tinged with a smoky color. The unsea, that part was called: the liquid-like nothing that formed the "ground" of the emberdark.

Its presence indicated that no inhabited planet was nearby in the Physical Realm. If there were, people's thoughts would shape Shadesmar in the region. Even places where people traveled a lot in Shadesmar itself became solid obsidian ground.

They'd spent weeks on trade routes during this trip, but were always a few hours' flight from utter nothingness. This place was dangerous, even to her. So discomforting, but also challenging. Engaging. She wished to sneak off and explore it—because this darkness was unknown, but not unknowable.

"Wait," ZeetZi said. "Slow."

Leonore did so immediately, controlling the ship via her lodestar thumbsticks, not waiting for word from the captain. When navigation said to slow, you did it.

"Captain?" ZeetZi said. "Something's out there. Not just the beacon. Something big." He pointed to a sensor that had started flashing red. Even Starling knew what that meant: an entity of negative Investiture. One of the things born from the same event that had killed a god, made the Current, erupted into the Knell.

Nazh was there a moment later, floating through the chairs, making ZeetZi lean away, whispering some quiet prayer. They all accepted Nazh, but . . . well, even the captain trod lightly around a Threnodite shade.

"The Evil," Nazh whispered. "This close to the lanes . . . Could be dangerous."

"Oh!" Ed said, flipping through one of his tomes. "They're not evil, no more than any animal is. They're more like forces of nature. As for being this close to the lanes, entities don't usually come to populated areas. Too many people thinking—it wards them away. They hate getting trapped and changed by the thoughts of mortals. At least, that's how it is unless you're close to the Knell. There . . . well, Nazh, you probably know it's different there . . ."

"Helmswoman," Crow said, not moving from her spot, "halt the ship. Operations, kindly provide a visual for us."

The ship slowed, then stopped in a hover. ZeetZi scrambled, working the ship's external cameras, which had excellent zoom. The

Dynamic didn't have weapons, but out here, you learned not to skimp on sensors.

They unbuckled and crowded around the small viewscreen. Starling and Ed jammed in next to each other to peer over ZeetZi's shoulder to get a look at the thing—a towering white mass of Investiture, translucent but not fully transparent, the size of a large building. It had a head and body, vaguely, and dozens of long, many-elbowed arms.

Eerily, it didn't move. It just . . . shifted. It was in one place, then a moment later it had changed to another posture—leaving the previous pose as a fading afterimage. Limbs jumped from one position to another, with no continuity of motion—like . . . like it existed in some other dimension, and they caught only brief blips of it. Like flashes of a strobe revealing something moving through darkness.

The camera was good, but at this distance, it was still blurry—and it took careful fine-tuning to maintain visual on the thing. Ed released a sound from the back of his throat—something Starling thought might be terror. But it was Ed, so . . .

"I can't believe I get to see one in person!" he said, practically tearing up. "A full Threnodite entity . . . a type 1-6. With my *own eyes*! Well, a monitor and my own eyes!" He held Starling's arm with one hand, clutching his tome with the other. "It could vaporize our souls with the wave of a hand! It could kill even you, or Crow, or *Nazh*! It's a being of almost pure negative Investiture!"

"Why," Leonore said, "do you sound so *excited*? I do not want to tangle with something that can take on a dragon, yah?"

"But it's so *beautiful*!" Ed said, squeezing Starling's arm out of glee. "Can you believe we found one? We get to *see* one?"

"Ah, and this is the source of the distress call," ZeetZi said, expertly dialing in with the camera. "A downed ship of diminutive stature—barely a shuttle—set adrift in the lonely dark."

Starling leaned closer and spotted the small spaceship, with flotation deployed. Out here, solid ground was rare—but things made entirely of Investiture could swim in the unsea. If your ship went down, you could deploy floats.

The poor souls had done that, then climbed out on top of their apparently powerless ship. Perhaps to wave at passing vessels, perhaps not to be trapped in the darkness of a ship with no lights. If their engines and backups had gone out completely . . . well, only the self-contained power of their Invested emergency beacon would function.

There were—ZeetZi dialed in further—yes, three people with golden Iriali hair. Seemed like two parents and a child. Huddled down, terrified at the thing approaching them.

"Ah," Ed said softly. "Their beacon likely drew the entity. The eternal conundrum of the emberdark. Radio signals die, but communication via Invested sources can draw danger. So what do you do? Each option is terrible . . ."

"Can we get there in time?" Starling asked. "It's moving slowly, but it's so close. Leonore, if we . . ."

She trailed off as she felt breath warm on her neck. She turned to find Crow looming over her, having finally approached to view ZeetZi's monitor.

"Excellent," Crow said. "Let it finish them off. When it retreats, we'll see what salvage is left."

Starling spun, standing up straight—or trying to, as the ceiling here was too low, and if she didn't crouch, she'd press against the tubes. She had to bend backward, letting Crow loom over her from behind.

"That was why we came?" Starling asked. "For *salvage*?"

Crow took a long drink from her flask, each moment letting the entity draw closer to the people. She licked her lips when done. "I figured," she said, "such a faint distress call might have been missed by everyone else. It is my duty to provide Master Xisis with returns on his investment." She nodded toward the screen. "They're as good as dead already, Lieutenant. Even if we weren't flying a broken-down garbage can of a ship, we couldn't face an entity."

Crow strolled back to her position by the doorway. Starling looked to Nazh—who was hovering halfway out of the wall, still staring at the screen, as if he hadn't even heard Crow. The entities had basically destroyed his homeworld, and the echoes of the god killed there were what made his kind persist when killed.

Ed, Leonore, and ZeetZi all turned toward her, though. Sweat trickled down the side of Starling's face, and her manacles felt heavy on her wrists. If it came to a fight between her and Crow, she'd lose. While the manacles would protect her from danger, they also stole her powers. Crow would immobilize her.

Unless Crow wasn't here.

Starling reached past Leonore and hit a switch on the dash while Crow's back was turned. The engines sputtered softly.

ZeetZi looked to her, then instantly understood. "Captain," he said. "We're losing power, just like earlier. Seems our aethers are going dull."

"Damn engineer," Crow said.

"Captain," Leonore said, catching on as well. "If that entity comes for us, I'd sure hate for our engines to be at half power!"

"They are attracted to Investiture," Ed chimed in. "That one could easily decide we are better prey than the fallen ship."

Starling glanced over her shoulder. The captain met her eyes, then turned and walked out. "That girl," Crow snapped, "will wish she'd never taken this job."

Starling gave it a count of five before running to the door, slipping it shut, and hitting the emergency lock to seal the bridge off from the rest of the ship.

But . . . she could have sworn from the look on Crow's face that she'd *known* Starling was trying to get rid of her. Why had she left, then?

Starling turned to the rest of the crew, who sat in silence. One at a time, they nodded to her. There was no need for a pep talk, or even a question. They were ready.

Shards, she loved these people.

"Nazh," she said, "make sure the captain doesn't actually accost poor Aditil—and keep Crow distracted if you can. She might be up to something. Leonore, we should already be moving!"

Nazh started off without a comment, and she could see the faintest green spark deep within his eyes. It was . . . not a sight for the faint-hearted, but at least they hadn't gone red yet.

"Right!" Leonore said, thumbing a switch on her right lodestar, then grabbing both and punching them forward—toward the downed ship.

They had full power as ZeetZi disengaged the mechanism that Starling had engaged earlier.

If the captain *hadn't* realized what Starling intended to do, she'd have sensed it as the ship started moving. Hopefully Nazh could successfully divert her.

Because they were committed now, tearing through Shadesmar toward those poor people at the best speed the *Dynamic* could manage.

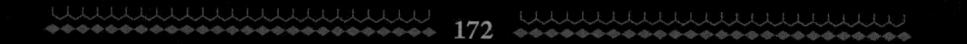

Fig. 53 · *Tokka*
(carnivorous plant)

CHAPTER TWENTY-SIX

It only took five minutes for the entity to become visible to the naked eye.

Starling had seated herself, trying to be a good example, buckles done . . . but she had them on their loosest setting so she could sit at the very edge of her seat, poking out between the helm and operations. That gave her a clear view of the thing through the front windshield as they approached—and it was even bigger than she'd expected. Less building, more skyscraper, glowing white—moving without moving, leaving afterimages in a sequence.

Leonore lowered her mask—a sign she wanted to concentrate, and not have her emotions on display to distract anyone, which meant things were getting serious—then brought them in low, skimming the surface of the unsea. Starling searched for the little shuttle and its three occupants, floating . . .

There. Her eyes were better than those of a human, and she distinctly saw the moment. That *incredible* moment when the people—huddled atop their ship—saw the *Dynamic* approaching. Their postures changed from forlorn, to shocked, to excited. If Starling had still been able to access her powers, she might have been able to feel their emotions as the woman leapt to her feet and began waving frantically, as the man clutched the child with relieved joy.

That moment, when despair became hope . . . she loved that moment. A moment like that was why she'd been exiled. And why, despite her hardships, she had never once regretted the decisions that had led her here.

"It's close to them, L.T.," Leonore said softly. "And . . . rusts, I don't know. I'm not sure I can get us near enough without getting hit. Look at those arms . . ."

"I advise against letting it touch our ship!" Ed warned, holding a different thick tome in his lap, reading up on the thing as they flew. "Its substance could rip us apart, if it wanted. Worse, though, it might just pass its arms right through our ship walls. If that negative Investiture touches our souls . . ."

"I assume it is unpleasant," ZeetZi said. "Burn our eyes out in a flash?"

"Probably an explosion, actually," Ed said. "The meeting of Investiture with so much anti-Investiture can be violent. Each of us would be vaporized in an explosion that would leave our physical forms splattered across our seats."

Leonore grunted, eyes focused, grip taut on her lodestar controls. "Don't you get off on that kind of thing, Ed?"

"What?" he said, sounding horrified.

"Being killed by some kind of bizarre monster," Leonore said. "I figured you'd . . . you know . . . like to be exploded by one someday, yah?"

"I find them fascinating!" he said. "But I don't want to be killed by one!" He paused. "Though, if I were going to go, I wonder what the most interesting way would be . . ."

Starling pushed forward against her restraints, gripping the armrests of Leonore and ZeetZi's seats. Forced to come in close, they swung only a few hundred yards from the entity. It, in turn, was maybe twice that far from the people.

The thing grew an extra hundred arms.

They appeared out of its mountainous back, each hundreds of yards long, with dozens of joints and hands made up of too many twisted, broken fingers. ZeetZi screamed, but Leonore just grunted, banking the ship out of the way as one waved toward them, then another, each using the same jarring, jumping nonmotion.

"Herr, Herr, Herr..." Leonore swore behind her mask, spinning them in a full roll away from several hands. She tried to dart back in, but another hand appeared in front of them. Starling gritted her teeth as Leonore veered the ship, barely dodging it.

Shards... that strobe effect was jarring. You *could* see the hands coming, but it was difficult.

"You can do this, Leonore," Starling whispered. "You're the best pilot the Malwish space force ever had."

"I flew *fighters*, Starling," Leonore said quietly. "Not a cargo van with wings. I can't do this. I—"

So many hands coming at once, forming a wicked, twisting snarl. Leonore was forced to dive, then roll—and their engines were *not* built for combat maneuvers. They stalled out completely, but as bad as ZeetZi was with navigation, he was a genius with ship dynamics. One hand crackling with electricity as he moved his fingers across the Scadrian panel, the other tapping buttons on his lodestar grips, he immediately engaged the emergency antigrav stabilizers—which worked without engines—and launched their Invested signal flares. Those drew the entity's attention, causing the hands to wave that way.

ZeetZi opened a line with engineering, but Aditil had already flushed the engines and refilled them with new aether, giving the ship a burst of speed. Leonore righted them and hit the thruster, taking control of the antigrav to manage elevation. She nodded to ZeetZi, eyes visible behind her wooden mask, but the hands were coming for them again.

And... Shards, the thing *hadn't* stalled at all in its advance on the people. The hands growing from its back worked independently as it blinked its way toward the stranded family.

"Leonore," Starling said, moving her hand to the pilot's shoulder. "I *know* you can do this. I know you can save them."

Leonore banked again, unable to get in.

"I've seen you running simulations when we're in dock," Starling murmured. "I've seen you take this hunk of metal and make it *soar*. I know what it is to fly, my friend. From one winged soul to another, I promise you this: you are a *maestro*."

The manacles went cold, blocking her powers. But she didn't need a dragon's abilities—traditionally used to send comfort or bravery to those who offered them prayers—to inspire. Not if every word she said was true.

Leonore's grip on her lodestar loosened, which—for her—was a good sign. Her motions grew more fluid, and while the ride was still uneven, it wasn't nearly as jerky as it had been. Unfortunately, there were hundreds of those hands. While Leonore was able to get past and approach the people, the entity continued to interfere.

"If she stops for those people," ZeetZi said, "I fear the entity will reach out and destroy us all." He made a clicking sound in the back of his throat—an indication of deep thought. "I see no obvious path forward, Lieutenant."

"Ed," Starling said. "What do you have for me?"

"Not a lot, I'm afraid," he said, still holding his tome as they banked sideways. His hat was, of course, clipped to his curly black hair. "There's a *ton* written on these things, yes, but I don't know how much of it helps. For example, I can't tell you why it is going for those three, rather than being drawn off by us. The thoughts of an entity are marvelously inscrutable.

"They're attracted to strong sources of Investiture, like a lot of predators out here, but we knew that already. I doubt we'd be able to influence its shape, size, or disposition with conscious projections of thought—it would need to be far, *far* smaller for us to influence it. Conventional weapons are useless, not that we have any . . ." He paused, cocking his head. "It would want to eat a strong source of Investiture, maybe . . ."

"We've got a cargo hold full of unkeyed Light," Starling said. "You're talking about that?"

"Absolutely."

"Dump the cargo a distance away?" ZeetZi said. "Draw it off, come back, and get the people?"

"The cargo is in aluminum housings," Ed said, "for *just* this reason.

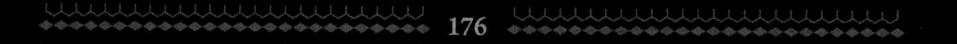

Trust me, if that thing could sense what we were carrying, it would be all over us—not just trying to swat us away."

"Then we open the containers first," ZeetZi said, hitting the button to unlock his straps. "Hopefully Nazh can keep Captain occupied . . ."

"Not to interrupt the heroism," Leonore said with a grunt, banking them, "but that thing is *close*. If we take the time to fly away and drop cargo, there won't be anybody to come back and save."

Silence. Except for some clicking from the back of ZeetZi's mouth.

Starling undid her buckles. "Ed," she said, "will that thing be frightened of me?"

"Oh!" he said, flipping a few pages. "Um . . . maybe? More likely to be curious. Yes, some of them are . . . curious about powerful and strange beings they meet. And you, um, count. No offense, but L.T. . . ." He turned his tome toward her, pointing at three names in a list in a page's sidebar.

Dragon names. She recognized one of them. Hadn't heard from him in decades, and . . . she never would. The list was titled "Notable Invested Beings Killed by Threnodite Entities."

"It might find you curious," Ed said, "but it will also want to destroy you. Nazh's people call them the Evil for a reason. They seek out and destroy Investiture. It will likely decide to eat you."

"I hear the longing in your voice, Ed . . ." Leonore said as she turned them again.

"I do *not* want to get eaten by one!" he snapped. "Yet."

"Ed, Zee," Starling said, starting toward the door, "go prep the cargo. Leonore, fly us by the ship again."

"You sure about this, L.T.?" Leonore said, not able to look at her, though the concern in her voice was evident. "I've gotta ask, since Nazh isn't here to challenge you, yah?"

"Leonore," Starling said from the door, "did you watch the posture of those people change when they saw us?"

A pause.

Then a nod.

Nothing else needed to be said. Starling unlocked the bridge door and pushed out into the corridor, and thankfully didn't find Captain

Crow waiting. She opened the flight door in the corridor as Leonore brought them in a low sweep, barely dodging another of those arms.

Starling's hearts thundered. It had been quite a long time since she'd been in a situation that could legitimately kill her.

Shards. If I die today with such a bad plan . . . Master is going to laugh himself silly at my expense.

Granted, Hoid tended to do that anyway. So as they approached, Starling gauged their speed in relation to the ship below, took a deep breath, and jumped.

Fig. 99 • Dragon
(claw)

CHAPTER TWENTY-SEVEN

Starling keenly remembered her first transformation. For that was also the first day she'd flown.

That wonderful day, at first light, with Uncle Frost. Back when, developmentally, she'd been the equivalent of a human eight-year-old. Most dragons didn't fly their first day. She had. Uncle Frost always said she had been unable to restrain her wings; they were her birthright.

Humans had trouble understanding the true nature of her kind. Many assumed that this form she wore, looking like one of them, was some false air that dragons put on. A way to hide. In reality, dragons were like amphibians. Two-stage beings. They mated and gave birth in human form, and their children grew as humans until the transformation.

After that, they lived in their draconic form for decades, mastering their abilities. From there, they lived in both forms, equally comfortable on land and in the air.

Unless they were exiled.

Unless they had their wings taken.

Unless they had to drop from the sky, like she now did.

For a moment in the air, it was like she was home again, stretching her wings. But those wings could not unfold, and her soul yearned to break free. It wasn't that her human form was onerous; she loved it.

But it was only half of Starling, and when she was falling, the other half knew it should be able to emerge.

That was when she felt most trapped. When the manacles grew cold, and her spirit roared.

But her leap had been true, gauged from decades of life with wings. She fell from the *Dynamic* at an angle, maintaining the momentum of the flyover, and hit *directly* on the top of the fallen ship, causing it to shake and bob in the unsea. Her body absorbed the shock; her manacles prevented her from using her powers overtly, but her people didn't want her dead. She could drop from any height and survive.

She glanced at the family, huddled behind her, as far from the entity as they could get. She smelled smoke and burned rubber—an electrical fire inside the small cockpit, she guessed. The reason they were outside the ship, rather than hiding inside.

Starling turned slowly, tipping her head back, looking up at the entity that approached. Despite herself, she took an involuntary step backward. It seemed as tall as the sky itself in this place where perspective was your enemy. Moving abruptly from one posture to the next, showing only frozen glimpses. With a twisted humanoid shape, but only in the most broken and unnatural way, it hunched forward, a hundred arms sprouting from its back.

Its face had no eyes, but instead cavernous holes with smooth features that evoked a skull. It advanced, relentless, towering like the sun over a withered landscape.

Its arms reached toward the occupants of the fallen ship. Yet Starling was the child of divinity and had been left with some minor methods of defending herself. At the forefront, she had the ability to show people what she was. She stood tall and tapped her manacles together to manifest her soul.

A brilliant white draconic figure burst from her, transparent and glowing. An echo only—a way of revealing herself to mortals. It was real enough for the entity, which could sense that which wasn't always seen.

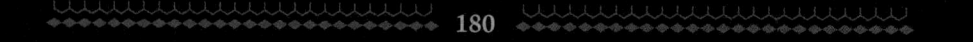

The entity froze as Starling's echo faded like one of its own afterimages. In a moment, it was bending down, crouching, until—her hearts pounding and her hands trembling—Starling found its enormous head inches from her, halfway down into the unsea. Motionless. Looking straight at her. It had a glassy white, smooth head. Within the reflection on it, she saw . . .

Eternity.

Nobody knew quite what these things were, the entities that had all but destroyed the planet Threnody—then moved out into the cosmere, hunting and exterminating life. Perhaps they searched for that which had been taken from them in the death of the god they'd once been part of.

Starling saw, in the ripped-out hollows where eyes should have been, a future. Starling, aged and withered, in her human form. Lying, bedridden, someplace dark. Watching the sky. Dying alone, with those cursed manacles still locked on her wrists.

She saw the truth that she would never be free again. That she'd been exiled not to learn a lesson, but because she'd embarrassed powerful people who wanted to make others afraid to do anything similar. A sinking despair struck her.

Then she rejected that emotion.

Her people lived to inspire others. They didn't always live up to their own ideals, but the best of them—like her uncle—spent their entire existences sending comfort, confidence, and compassion to those who prayed to them. Starling was accustomed to deliberate manipulation of emotions. So she understood.

"You could have come upon this family much faster," she whispered, looking into the thing's terrible face. "But you advanced slowly. You could have killed me, but you stopped and showed me a terrible future. You don't just want me dead. You want me *broken* and *terrified* first. Nazh is right—and for once, Ed is wrong. You're not just some force of nature . . . You're evil."

Her manacles grew cold as she rebelled against the image it projected. She *would* obtain her freedom. She *would* get her wings back. She'd find a way.

She was Illistandrista. Dragon.

And she did *not* despair.

The thing's arms froze briefly, as if rebuffed by those thoughts. It quivered, hesitated . . . just long enough. For in the distance, the *Dynamic* dropped a group of glowing barrels from its cargo hold.

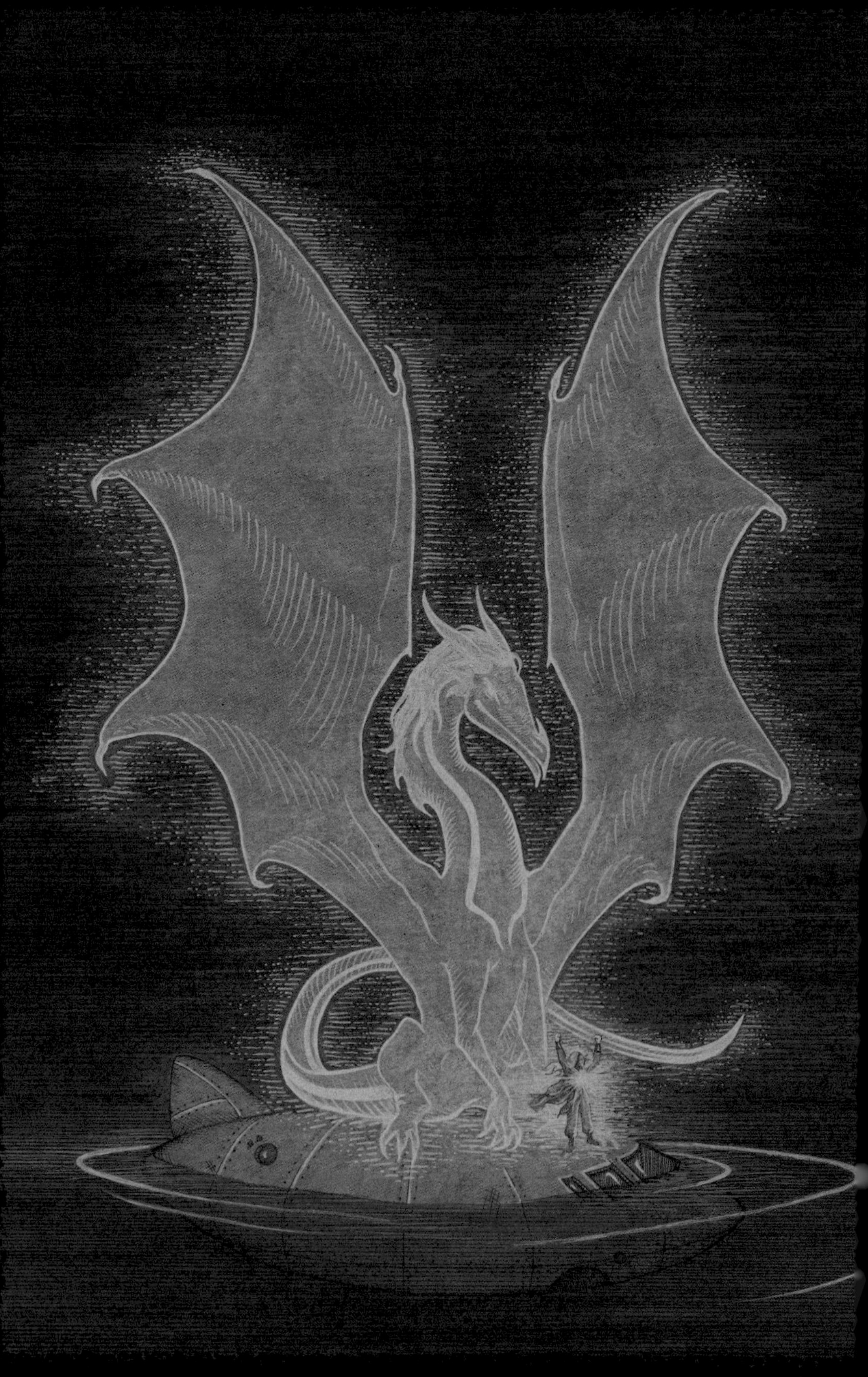

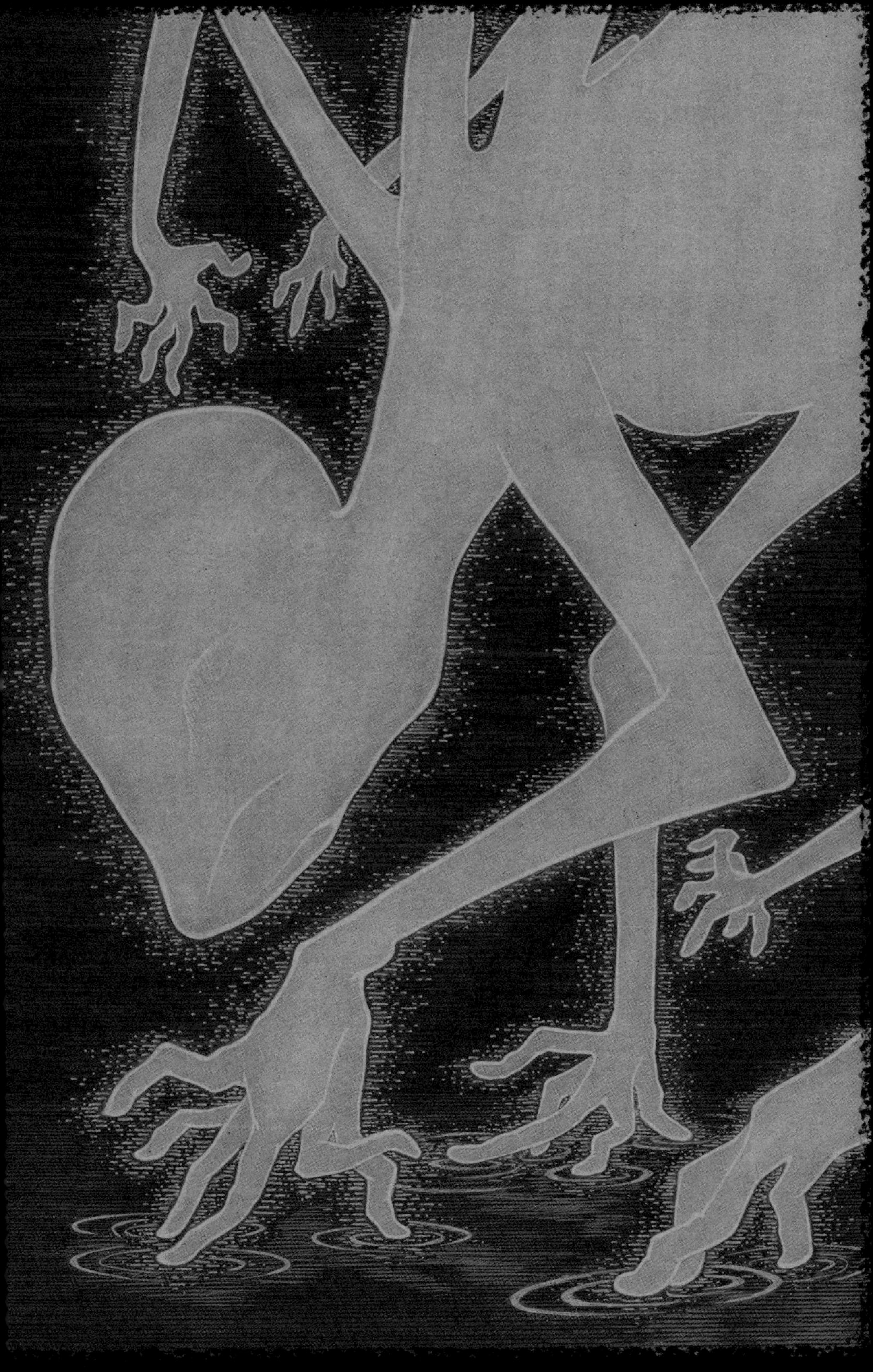

The thing's head was facing backward in an instant. It loomed large again, tall as a hundred stories. As she'd guessed, it *could* go faster—which it proved by leaving the derelict shuttle to chase after the cargo.

Starling suddenly felt as if she'd been awake far, far too long. She wobbled, legs weak. Standing before that thing, staring it head on, had somehow taken all of her strength.

She collapsed toward the rooftop, though hands caught her as she fell. The woman of the family settled her down carefully, then shot a glance at the man Starling assumed was her husband. Both looked worried.

"Your . . . Your Majesty?" the woman said in Yolish, one of the more common languages spoken in the region. "Are you all right?"

"That's . . . um . . ." Starling mumbled, hand to her head. "That's a misconception. We're not all royalty. Thank you for catching me."

The woman relaxed. "I was worried I'd done something wrong by touching your divine self."

Starling forced herself not to sigh. Surely there was a bright side to all of these fanciful stories about dragons. They . . . well, they made for icebreakers in conversation.

She managed to sit up as her unnatural enervation slowly faded. Unfortunately, the echoes of what she'd seen did not wear off so easily.

Alone. Old. Never again knowing the sky.

Dragons aged very slowly, particularly once they obtained maturity—Uncle Frost was over ten thousand years old. And though he looked like an old man in his human form, he probably had another ten thousand in him. So if she were going to die old . . . that meant twenty thousand years without ever stretching her wings again. Without feeling the sun on her scales, or the grind of claws on the stone.

No vision of the future was certain. She knew that, and even though she'd rejected despair earlier . . . now she found it lingering, hidden within a shadow of her soul. The horror of that image echoed inside her, like a fired bullet with nowhere to go, ricocheting off every vital part of her.

She felt another hand on her arm. The husband had crawled across the top of the ship to touch her.

"Thank you," he whispered, holding his child tight with one arm and clinging to her with the other. His eyes filled with tears. "Thank you so much."

She nodded, then heaved herself to her feet. Some of Ed's information had proven true—the entity was completely engaged by the feast of Light. The *Dynamic*, making a few expert moves, swung around it and came in low, the cargo hold open on the back. As the ship slowed and turned toward them, she saw ZeetZi and Ed strapped by lines to the inside, waving toward them.

"In we go," Starling said, helping the family to their feet. "I don't know how fast that entity can move when it really wants to, but let's not find out, shall we?"

Fig. 36 · Memist
(vines)

CHAPTER TWENTY-EIGHT

Starling sent Ed running for food, water, and blankets while ZeetZi closed the door to the now-empty hold of the ship. The three refugees looked exhausted as they lay on the floor, holding to one another, the child snuggled against his parents.

"Thank you again," the father said.

"We're headed to Silverlight," Starling said. "I assume that would be a fine place to drop you?"

"That would be amazing," the father said. "We have relatives at the university. Thank you."

"If you don't mind the imposition in your fatigued state," ZeetZi said, "might I inquire why you were out here, so far from regular lanes of travel?"

The mother grimaced. "We didn't realize how far out we were. We . . . we're not wealthy people. We took our inherited ship, and were trying to get home to Zidorna, but our Knell compass broke."

"Thought we'd turned back toward Silverlight . . ." the father said. "But got ourselves even more lost. Then the fire in the cabin . . ."

Starling took ZeetZi aside as Ed helped settle the people. "So," she whispered, "Crow wouldn't have found any salvage, even if we'd let her. Seems fitting."

"Indeed," ZeetZi said, though his feathers lay flat against his head, a sign of worry. "I will help Ed see that they are made comfortable, Lieutenant, but you should know that the captain is in the hallway just outside. I fear her fury could rival that of nine stars . . ."

"I'll confront her. Thank you." Starling took a deep breath, and stepped into the cramped hallway.

There wasn't a lot of space on the *Dynamic*. Just three small decks. Down here near the cargo hold was their living space and bunks; each crewmember had their own small room along this hallway.

Captain Crow stood at the very end of the hall, leaning against the bulkhead, arms folded. She was watched over by Nazh, his eyes glowing full green. Shards. Anyone who knew anything about his homeworld would understand that warning, and know not to push him into the red. But Crow . . . was difficult to read. She didn't appear frightened. She had to know that if Nazh started killing, he risked losing himself—and so would be wary to go so far. Was that why she seemed so calm?

"Nazh," Starling said. "You may go recover."

He looked to her, a question in his eyes. She nodded. Crow was dangerous, but this was not a threatening posture. Besides, the sooner Nazh went to his meditations, the better. He walked a fine line, engaging a shade's bloodlust, and she always hated asking him to.

He slipped off, passing through the wall toward his quarters—which he had, despite lacking a body.

Crow sipped quietly from her silver flask. "Was that a cargo dump I felt?" she asked between drinks. "Whole ship shaking, bobbing in the air?"

"Yes," Starling said.

"You could have gotten us all killed."

"The crew and I were agreed."

"And yet it's supposed to be my ship."

"You can discipline me," Starling said. "Confine me to quarters. Let Xisis deal with me when we return."

Crow laughed, eerily genuine and boisterous. "Lass, you ever been part of a mutiny before?"

Starling hesitated, then shook her head.

"This is my second," Crow said. "I learned some difficult lessons the first time. Once you lose a ship . . . well, there's no going back." She stepped right up to Starling, sneering. "Even if I were to haul you to that door and toss you overboard, the others would never follow me again. Fear isn't enough. Not for a crew like this."

She pushed past Starling, whose manacles went cold. Crow was Invested, the bearer of an unnatural aether. She had hidden powers Starling had seen only once, when writhing vines emerged from the captain and ripped a person clean in half. The manacles knew danger, and warned her of it. One of the few advantages to the stupid things.

Crow threw open the door to her quarters and stood there, not looking at Starling. "You can explain to Xisis yourself what you did, child. If you're wise, you'll post a guard at my door, just in case my better senses don't prevail."

She slammed the door behind her with a deafening clang.

Roughly an hour and a half later, Starling sat at a long metal table with the rest of the crew. This combined kitchen and dining area was their largest gathering space. They usually played cards here. Today, they sat solemnly, door open, giving an unobstructed view of the hallway—and therefore Crow's door.

The captain's final words itched at her. *She just wanted to intimidate you,* Starling's instincts said. *She wanted to leave you with a threat because you humiliated her. She won't actually try anything.*

Still, Starling watched that door. Normally she didn't let Crow get to her, but she was exhausted after the rescue . . . and still couldn't shake the haunting feeling from her encounter with the entity.

Nazh was last to arrive, floating in through the wall, eyes back to their normal cheery blue—with the faintest hint of a green glow to them, only visible in dim light. That made them a solemn seven, all seated save Nazh. Starling herself, ZeetZi with his feathers tight against his head, Ed with one of his notebooks—already writing about the experience with the entity. He'd be celebrated by the other arcanists after this, particularly if his essay was compelling.

Less excited was Leonore, who sipped hot chocolate, mask on top of her head. She'd set the ship in a high hover, far above the unsea. That wouldn't protect them if the entity arrived, but they'd set alarms, and the thing had not given chase once they'd flown away. Ed thought they were close enough to occupied tradeways that it would stay away.

They probably could have had this meeting an hour ago. Everyone had agreed they should just keep flying until they were absolutely certain they weren't being chased.

Aditil had accepted a cup of hot chocolate from Leonore, and sat silently. She looked so young next to the rest of them, small and worried. Chrysalis attended by way of a small insect sitting on the ledge nearby. She hadn't bothered sending her entire form, but this node could speak.

"You didn't ask me," she'd said earlier when Starling approached her, "if I agreed to the danger of the rescue. Why care about my opinion now?"

It stung. Not that Starling would have abandoned those people, but it was also true. She'd told the captain the crew had been agreed about the rescue, but she hadn't asked Aditil or the Sleepless. *You jumped into hero mode,* she thought at herself. *Like always. Save the day, without thinking about what it might cost . . .*

Her manacles felt extra heavy.

"Why the sour faces, all?" Nazh said. "We've done something grand."

"Grand and illegal, yah?" Leonore said.

Nazh cocked an eyebrow. "No court in Silverlight would convict us for mutinying to save the lives of three people on a derelict ship, Leonore."

"We'll still be disbanded as a crew," ZeetZi said. "Xisis owns the ship, and the attached debts . . . After this, he'll never let us fly for him again. And who would take us on, knowing we've mutinied?"

"I doubt the mutiny is your actual problem," Chrysalis said, voice buzzing from the ledge. "The bigger problem you'll have is this ship's historical inability to turn a profit. That, and its connection to a Silverlight outlaw in the Grand Jesk, Cephandrius Maxtori. Though of course, the fact that most of us are fugitives in one way or another won't help."

Leonore thumped her forehead against the table, mask slipping down with a click. She was wanted on her own world as a deserter from the Malwish military, and while there was no extradition treaty that would send her home . . . a pilot that couldn't fly to Scadrial—one of the biggest trading hubs in the cosmere—wasn't generally a profitable one to employ.

They all had issues like that. Aditil and her dead aether, which was terrible luck among her kind. ZeetZi had left an isolationist planet that didn't interact with others well and, beyond that, was associated with the Sleepless. People avoided his kind for both reasons. Nazh was . . . well, a ghost, and Chrysalis's people could be legally exterminated on sight on both Scadrial and Taldain, and were banned from visiting several other major planets.

Each was the type that her master collected: people cast off from their own worlds, largely forgotten or ignored, but with *stories*.

"Can I speak?" Aditil said softly, raising her hand.

"Of course," Starling said.

"I am *so proud* of you all," Aditil said.

Leonore looked up from her head-pound. ZeetZi's feathers relaxed.

"I know I don't get much of a say," Aditil continued. "I haven't been with you long. I know I hide a lot, and I haven't been the best crewmate. But when I found out what you'd done . . ." She leaned forward, voice growing softer. "You defied *her*? I have *nightmares* about that woman, and you all just spit in her face and dumped her *cargo*? Damn. Just . . . *damn*."

"It was," Nazh said, "the right decision. We'd all do it again, wouldn't we?"

"Indeed," ZeetZi said.

Leonore nodded.

Ed looked up from his scribbling. "I mean, do you need to ask me?"

Chrysalis remained silent, despite the pause giving her a chance to speak.

"Then I ask again," Nazh said. "Why the sorrowful looks?"

"The dead guy is right," Leonore said, standing. "We should be toasting. Hot choc for all!"

"Leonore," ZeetZi said, "one does not *toast* with chocolate. Haven't we a proper libation with which to celebrate?"

"Libation?" she said. "That's not a word."

"It . . ." He sputtered. "It's absolutely a word! A perfectly legitimate one!"

"Whatever," she said. "*Hot. Choc. Now!*"

He sighed, but Starling grinned, taking a cup as Leonore made and distributed them. Leonore leaned down as she put one in front of ZeetZi. "There's booze in yours," she said, which made him perk up and smile.

They toasted their victory together, all except Chrysalis, who didn't eat in the traditional way. And Nazh, being dead.

Maybe it was the hot chocolate, but the warmth Starling felt at that table almost rivaled her early days flying with her uncle. Shards. She *needed* to find a way to keep them together. If only Hoid were still with them. He'd have found a way to fix this. He always did, no matter what others said.

He left them to me, Starling thought. *He isn't here. But I am. And I got them into this.*

She wasn't going to let them be punished for saving lives. Perhaps it was her typical over-optimism, but right then, she decided. She'd find a way out.

"To our last flight," ZeetZi said, raising his cup. "It was an honor."

"No," Starling said as they began to raise their cups. "I'm going to get us out of this. I'm going to talk to Xisis and make him let us keep the ship."

They hesitated, cups half raised.

"Star, dear," Nazh said. "Xisis *hates* you."

"Xisis pretends he hates basically everyone and everything," Starling said. "He's an exceptionally old dragon, and they act grouchier than they are. I'll find an accommodation with him."

"You're not," Nazh said, "allowed to trade him something stupid, Starling. I won't have it."

"I won't have to," she said. "I promise." She placed her hand in the middle of the table, the other holding her hot chocolate. "I'm not allowed to go home and see my family. I . . . I may *never* be allowed. But as long as I'm with you all, it doesn't hurt so much. We're a crew.

We have to stay together. Anything else is unacceptable, so I'll find a way."

Leonore rested her hand on Starling's, then ZeetZi, Ed, and Aditil followed. Finally Nazh put his hand down, making the rest of theirs feel cold—and making her manacles chill with warning. But she was glad he felt comfortable joining in; when they'd first met, he hadn't been willing to touch anyone.

Starling looked at Chrysalis's hordeling, to gesture it should join. But it was flying out of the room, bobbing in the air and vanishing around the corner. So Starling sighed, and looked back at the others. Hands together.

Leonore pulled her mask down, showing determination. "Guess it's decided," she said. "We don't go down without a fight, yah?"

Together they nodded, then broke apart, heading to their stations. Aditil, oddly, lingered after the others had gone—Nazh taking up his duty to watch the captain's quarters.

Once they were all out, Aditil stood, then held out the envelope with her ticket. "I think I want to do another tour with you," the young woman said. "Before I go home."

Starling cocked her head. "You're certain? You didn't even take part in the mutiny. You can go—we wouldn't blame you."

"I know," Aditil said. "Thank you, but . . . can I please stay a little longer?"

"Glad to have you," Starling said with a smile. "But you keep that ticket safe with you for now. We'll get you another for return, so you can visit home, then come back."

Aditil nodded and bobbed off to engineering, leaving Starling carrying the weight of her own optimism. She stepped out of the kitchen, and found Nazh leaning against the wall—well, leaning *into* the wall.

"You were right about her," Nazh said. "I should know not to bet against you. It's curious how well you understand humans, never having been one yourself."

"You don't have to be the same species," Starling said, "to know what it feels like to miss your home."

Empathy. She thought, finally, she was figuring it out.

He stood up straight and met her eyes, then nodded. "They know now."

"Know?" she asked.

"They know what I know: that you are the right one to lead this crew." He leaned forward. "Hoid is immortal. Indestructible. For all of the antics he took us through, he never put himself in any real danger. Crow, basically the same—only without the antics."

"Nazh, I'm a dragon," she said. "I'm basically immortal."

"Yes," he said, pointing at her, "but today, *you* were the one who jumped out into danger. And so now they *know*. When you ask them to do something dangerous, they'll remember that you're willing to risk yourself. That's going to mean something, Star. It already does." He nodded to her in a formal way, then floated off down the corridor.

Starling watched him, feeling unreasonably proud to have had his praise. But also intimidated, as she realized that even the cynical Nazh believed that she'd make good on her word. He implied that the crew would have more chances to follow her, together, not ripped apart by Xisis's anger.

She took a deep breath. She was certain her master would have tried something like this—a way to be bold, inspire. She'd learned that lesson. Now she had to find a way to make good on it by making a deal with a dragon many thousands of years her senior—and whose very expensive cargo she'd just jettisoned.

Fortunately it was a ten-day flight to Silverlight. Because she had a lot of planning to do.

Fig. 61 · **Glowing worm**
(larvae)

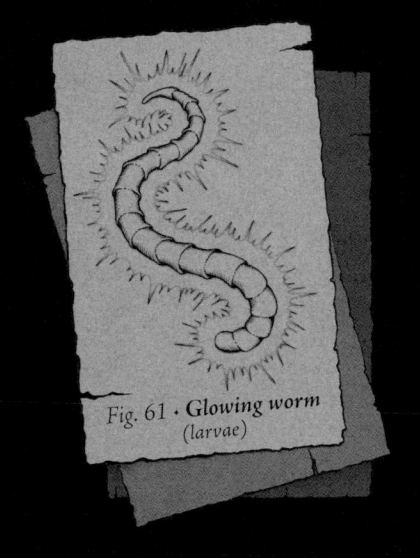

CHAPTER TWENTY-NINE

According to his watch, Dusk had been traveling six days in the abyss when he encountered a problem he'd been dreading. The worm paste on his boat was beginning to lose its effectiveness.

Starting in the morning, the boat ran lower and lower in the notwater. If he'd been in the regular world, he'd have taken this as a sign of leakage. Here, he noted that the glow on the bottom of the boat was fading.

On one hand, that was encouraging, as it meant he could run at least five days on one application. His jar would last a good long time. On the other hand, he had to figure out how to apply a new coat without a dock. The paste on the propeller had run out the day before, but he'd been able to raise it up to reapply. Now he carefully lashed all of his things in place, much of it beneath a tarp, then tied a second set of ropes around them, just to be certain.

"I'm going to have to flip the boat," he explained to the curious Rokke, who was sitting on the perch, head cocked.

Sak sat on Dusk's shoulder and kept putting her head out for scratches, something she normally only did when she was sleepy. He got the feeling she was trying to show Rokke how a proper Aviar was to act.

"I don't like the idea of upending us," Dusk continued, forcing himself to speak, as the little bird seemed comforted by words. "But this is the only option. The paste won't apply if I try to do it while under the ghostly water; the two resist each other, so if I put too much paste on my hand, it just gets pushed off as I reach under. You two, be ready to fly up."

Sak gripped the shoulder pad extra tight. He carefully tied on her harness, then tried the same for Rokke—who kept her distance, chirping at him in annoyance. Well, she had two good wings, so he was less worried about her.

That done, Dusk smeared some worm paste along the rim of the boat and prepared to perform a controlled flip. He'd done this many times in the ocean. This was a different experience, though, as he couldn't count on the water to float *him*, just the boat. He made sure he was properly hooked into place by a harness at his waist, then grabbed the side of the boat, applied leverage, and rolled it.

He was supposed to hold on to the grips at the side, letting himself hang underneath the boat.

That didn't happen.

Even prepared as he'd thought he was, there was a strong jolt to his arms as he flipped the thing and fell downward. His mind refused to accept that he wouldn't get any kind of buoyancy from the not-water. Sak screeched as his fingers slipped.

Then he dropped.

And was immediately pulled up short by his harness. He twisted, hanging from the rope—and was left swinging facedown above the abyss. His feet brushed the canvas lashing his gear tightly in place. The boat—fortunately—remained floating on top of the not-water.

His heart beating like a drum, Dusk stared down infinity. A vast nothing, only vaguely the color of white smoke. Practically invisible, like the film on glass after water dried. It seemed to want to swallow him.

Teeth clenched, ignoring the pain of Sak's talons—which had pierced the shoulder pad and dug into his flesh—he swung up and grabbed the rope. Careful, steady. He hauled himself up and seized the handles on the side of the boat. He took several deep, preparatory breaths, then moved to the prow of the boat using its handholds, with his lashed equipment and the motor providing ballast. There, muscles straining, he was able to heave up over the lip of the prow and onto the top—well, bottom—of the boat.

He flopped down, breathing heavily. A few minutes of effort had left him drained, his arms smarting. That pain and fatigue, however, was overshadowed by the memory of the expanse. Like staring into the depths of the ocean, but with nothing to hold you up. It made him painfully aware of how unnatural this place was.

Sak let out a squawk and began pecking him on the back of his head. Rokke landed beside her a moment later, and gave a few hesitant pecks herself. A clear message. *What do you think you're doing, stupid human? Don't scare us like that.*

With a groan, he righted himself and glared at the birds, who hopped over to the engine propeller and roosted there—the tether to Sak's harness reached just about that far—still grumbling at him with the occasional low chirp. Dusk stretched, then took the jar of worm paste from his belt. A small rag followed, and he dipped it, then began rubbing. He'd found, while applying the stuff to the propeller, that it wasn't like wax. Instead it was like a stain—it sank in. As he rubbed it on a section of the bottom, that section started glowing more profoundly. The wood wasn't merely coated in light; the glow *suffused* the boat.

Once it was on, it didn't scrape off, so his awkward motions lying flat on the boat's hull while applying it didn't risk sinking him. It did take a bit of effort to rub it in properly, though, so he spent two hours at work, talking softly to keep Rokke from growing too nervous. Her protection was essential; he tried not to think about what might happen if one of those skull-headed serpents found him floating like this, without access to his engine.

He found himself enjoying this part. It felt good to have something to do, something active. On a large sailing ship, there was always something important to do—but on a small vessel, most days were spent motoring along, staring at the waves, and thinking. He didn't mind that, but in reapplying the glow to his boat, he felt like he'd accomplished something for the first time this trip.

Once done, he carefully tightened the lid on the jar and tucked the glowing rag into his belt. "All right," he said to the birds, "get ready to be annoyed at me again."

This was usually the harder part. He grabbed ahold of the keel and leaned to the side, carefully rotating the boat. He found, though, this was easier in the not-water. Normally, you were fighting against the weight of the water that had gotten into the boat and soaked things. Today he met very little resistance as he rotated the boat halfway, then reached in and clipped his harness to the inside by a short tether.

From there, he balanced on the side of the boat and eased the craft upright by shifting his weight. As it flopped down, he hauled himself inside before his weight could cause it to flip back over.

The birds had plenty of time to treat the boat as a jungle gym, climbing around to the inside. They chatted energetically as he lay there, his taut nerves contrasting the ease of the work. It was only easy because he'd done it over and over—motivated, like every good trapper, by stories of those who had died. He'd determined never to be one of those who dehydrated in the middle of the ocean because he couldn't recover from a capsize. It had always sounded like such a humiliating death.

Sak chirping drew him out of his reverie. The rag he'd been using—itself now glowing with worm paste—was floating on the surface of the abyss a short distance away. It must have slipped out of his belt as he was working.

Sak hopped over to him, chirping again.

"No," he said, reaching to undo her harness. "Let's leave it. I've got a hunch."

She chirped questioningly.

"Watch and see," he said.

As it continued to float, he checked each piece of equipment and its lashing. He fed the birds a mix of dried fruit, nuts, and pellets. Then he got out his oar and paddled them a distance from the floating rag. He had a good amount of fuel left, but it wouldn't last forever. He'd been relying more and more on his own power during the last few days. It had served him most of his life, after all.

Rokke hopped onto the seat next to him, then cocked her head, looking at the rag. She chirped.

"It's just a hunch," Dusk explained, chewing on some jerky. "But you remember how those golden butterflies were attracted to the liquid in the pool?"

She chirped in the affirmative.

"Something's up with that glowing light," he said. "The worms eat it. Then you Aviar eat them as chicks. If you don't, you remain regular birds. No talents, right?"

She chirped, seeming to follow him.

"That's the big secret Vathi and I revealed," he said softly. "The secret that changed everything..."

Strange. Talking it through actually helped him formulate impressions into direct ideas. Father... was that why Vathi and everyone else talked so much? His thoughts became concrete as he wrestled them, like some nightmare beast, into a specific shape.

"The glowing butterflies are attracted to the light," he said. "And birds, they can find their way to the pool. Even birds separated a few generations from being Aviar, you bring them to the island, and they'll eventually take their fledglings to the pool to eat the worms. They know the way, Rokke. They can *sense* the way. So..."

Something moved in the depths. A short time later, one of the snake beasts breached the surface and snapped at the rag.

"It can sense the light," Dusk said. "Like it can sense minds." He took out his harpoon. "Please be ready to take down your mental shield."

Rokke immediately hid under the seat, then chirped questioningly.

"It's maybe a quarter the size of the other one," he said, hefting the harpoon in an overhand grip. "I should be able to handle it."

He wrapped the cord around the boat's side handle, eyeing the beast, which circled near the surface where the rag had been. It had swallowed the piece of refuse, though it couldn't have found that a satisfying meal.

Sak hid with Rokke this time. He smiled at them, though the expression felt stiff and fake. Vathi insisted he try that kind of thing.

"Now," he said.

In response, Rokke deactivated her talent. He could tell because the beast immediately pivoted toward the boat, then swam their direction, coils swinging wide in the not-water, eyeless head—with plates, like bone sheets—breaking the surface.

Dusk waited . . .

Waited . . .

Then *threw* precisely as the thing began to circle them. His aim was true, and he speared the thing right behind the plated head, where the skin looked less armored. The harpoon sunk in deeply. Dusk grinned, a genuine emotion this time, and laughed.

The beast screeched, a high-pitched cry with several overlapping sounds, as if it had a smaller screaming snake inside it. It bolted to the side, then started swimming. Quickly.

"Oh," Dusk said.

The line went taut.

The boat lurched.

He grunted, grabbing the line and holding it steady as the boat veered sideways after the beast. The snake stayed near the surface, fortunately—perhaps the beast didn't have the power to bring the entire boat down. Still, it had plenty of strength to pull the boat along at speed, wobbling fiercely, threatening to capsize them. And he'd undone his harness.

Maybe he should leave that on all the time. It wasn't something you did in a normal ocean, but . . .

Teeth clenched, Dusk struggled to keep the boat upright as the birds screeched in terror. He pulled out his knife, desperate, and managed to cut the line.

That lost him a harpoon as the thing immediately dove, vanishing into the depths. Dusk settled near the prow and wiped his face, then sighed and leaned back, waiting for his heart to still.

"Well," he finally said as the birds emerged, "at least we know they can be hurt."

That earned him a solid pecking as both birds laid into his foot. Which, admittedly, he probably deserved. Not that he'd stop trying to hunt the beasts. He just needed to be smarter about it.

"Let's talk through a plan for next time . . ."

Fig. 13 · Mating plume (feather)

CHAPTER THIRTY

Silverlight was a city built above a sun.

It was a full city inside Shadesmar, one of the first multicultural settlements in the cosmere, with a history going back millennia. Here, peoples from dozens of planets mixed, and many had lived here generations—coming to think of themselves as Lighters first and foremost.

The city's architectural aesthetic was to build tall instead of wide: willowy skyscrapers of a limber design, with dragonsteel supports—ultralight and extremely strong, allowing for constructions that went much higher than otherwise would have been possible. Walkways crisscrossed them, and many had hovering pods as rooms, hanging out over the expanse. ZeetZi said those reminded him of his home.

All of that was wonderful, but no construction of mortal or dragon could compete with the brilliant light of the perpendicularity. Named the Silverlight Nexus, it really was like a sun, colored a frosty white, giving the city its name. It hung in the void beneath the city, lighting everything from underneath with a calm, even glow.

This was one of the rare portals that could transfer people in and out of the Physical Realm. They referred to the regions in Shadesmar around planets as subastrals, and those regions took on unique characteristics—influenced deeply by the thoughts of the people on said planet. Around Silverlight, the subastral had hardened into a glassy, transparent window that let you see into the infinite depths underneath and let the light of the Nexus bathe you.

The Nexus was unique among perpendicularities, as it led to not one place in the Physical Realm, but *three*. One of which was hidden, shadowed: the planet of Yolen. For millennia, the dragons had kept the secret that it was the source of nearly all life in the cosmere and the origin of the Shards, though that news had been revealed quite dramatically a few decades back. Still, travel to it was strictly regulated.

As the *Dynamic* approached, the ship encountered lines of other vessels waiting their turn at the Nexus. That was always the case; traffic could be a mess near Silverlight, but flight control kept it organized. Each waited to move through holes in the glassy ground so they could fly through the unsea and approach the miniature glowing sun. Miniature, because it was *only* the size of a city, though it was the largest natural perpendicularity. Most started as small pools, barely ten feet in diameter, and had to be expanded to accommodate ships.

ZeetZi ran comms, getting them clearance. They flew down, Starling in her customary seat, leaning forward between their chairs. It felt . . . right to return to Silverlight, with its glow from below. She'd lived here—or, well, used this as her home base—ever since her exile.

Once, she'd been one of the few allowed the secret to traveling through the Nexus to emerge from the greatstar of Yolen, a glowing hole in the upper atmosphere of her homeland. The dragons had an entire infrastructure up there, with a flying city. Her manacles now prevented her from accessing that place, unless she found a way to break free from them—something even Master Hoid hadn't been able to do.

They landed on one of the many pads outside the city. There, ZeetZi and Leonore unhooked their lodestars, leaving sockets for someone to plug into after them if needed. The two halves snapped together for storage, and each slid their device into the case they carried at their hips. Now that the group had arrived, they'd normally draw lots for leave. Silverlight was relatively safe—but it was still a big city, and docking fees included only minimal security. Today though, everyone was too nervous to leave.

"Nazh and I will go," Starling said to the others as they gathered in the kitchen. "We can talk to—"

A door slammed open down the corridor. Starling jumped, and looked out to see Captain Crow striding out of her quarters. She gave the lot of them one final glance, said nothing, and made her way out via the midship gangway.

"I'll . . . reset all our codes," ZeetZi said. "Just in case."

"We need to get to our task," Starling said, turning back to the group. "Many of us have loved ones on the outside."

The powerful Nexus of Silverlight caused time dilation in the region. Each day spent in the city currently passed as ten for those on the outside, which could cause problems with relationships if one stayed in Silverlight too long.

"You sure you don't want to just . . ." Leonore made a swooping motion with her hand, a ship taking off.

The others looked to Starling.

"No," Starling said. "We would be true refugees then, forbidden from taking honest contracts, hunted by Xisis's fleet. He is not a dragon we want as our enemy. I can't put you all in that situation."

"Ah, being a fugitive ain't so bad," Leonore said, putting her mask down. "Helps with your nerves."

"Helps?" Ed asked. "How?"

"Helps," Leonore said, "in that it keeps you nervous, you know? So you never feel too comfortable anywhere. That way, nobody can ever get the jump on you—and stress doesn't bother you, because you're *already* stressed out of your *rusting gears*." She tried to laugh it off, but that died out.

ZeetZi put a hand on her shoulder. Then he turned to Starling. "We'll follow what you say, *Captain*. We trust you."

Captain. Right, that meant Starling now. "I was saying," she explained, "that I'll take Nazh and visit Xisis. Someone should go with those people we rescued and make certain they end up somewhere safe. They said they had family here, but I worry they just told me that to not be a bother."

"I'll go with them," Ed said. "I need to check in at the university anyway."

"By check in," Leonore said, "you mean brag, yah? That you saw an entity?"

"Well . . ." Ed said. "I mean, it's required by my contract. But also it *will* be satisfying to see Argent's face . . ."

Starling nodded to him, agreeing to his suggestion. Keeping an arcanist in good standing required jumping through a few hoops, but it was worth the effort. Starling and Ed made their way out through the cargo bay, gathering the Iriali family and leading them to the platform outside.

Light from underneath made shadows on their faces. It had seemed so strange, even unnerving, during her first visits here as a dragonet. Now it felt natural.

"I want to send someone to help you to your family's place," Starling said as Nazh floated through the bottom of the ship's hull to land on the ground. "I won't have you get rescued, only to end up abandoned here if your family is away or something."

"Thank you," said the wife, who was named Crux. "Once again, thank you. You don't need to go this far, but we will accept the guidance."

The husband—Nol—nodded, then met his wife's eyes. She nodded back. "Can I . . ." he started, "speak to you a moment, Captain Starling?"

Curious, she walked a few steps away with Nol, to let them speak in private. He wrung his hands, then put them through his golden hair, then wrung them again. Even still, all these years later, her first instinct was to reach out with her powers and bolster his sense of self-worth and confidence. Her manacles absorbed that intention, growing cold.

"We've lied to you," Nol finally spit out. "We weren't lost. We were . . . hunting for something."

Emboldened, he fished in his pocket, pulling out an old-looking cloth, faded with time, dirty and ragged around the edges. He thrust it toward her. "We want you to have this as our thanks. And to keep us from . . . being tempted to try something foolish again."

"What is it?" she said.

"A map," he said softly. "Supposedly. We . . . went to the location. That's where you found us. We were searching there when the fire broke out." He blushed. "We were fools, selling everything for a ship we could barely fly, trying to find this on our own..."

She held it up and found faint writing on it, in faded ink, that she couldn't read. "A map to what?"

"A hidden perpendicularity," he said, "that nobody knows about."

She looked to him, skeptical. "How much did you pay for it?"

"Nothing," he said. "I know what you're thinking, Your Majesty... This wasn't bought off a con man in a back alley. It's a family heirloom. Passed down for generations."

"So your great-great-grandmother bought it in a back alley," Starling said. "Look, I could throw a stone in Silverlight and hit someone selling ancient maps, Nol. I don't mean to be dismissive, but... if you went there and found nothing..."

"Maybe," he said, blushing again. "Either way, it's yours now. With our gratitude. It's literally all we have left, so we thought..."

"I'm grateful," Starling said. "At the very least, it's something to remember you by." She smiled at him, then walked over to the others.

"Well, shall we be off?" Ed asked. He'd broken out his formal arcanist hat—which was somehow even *floppier* than the other one. Looked like he was wearing a half-stuffed round pillow with a scoop of ice cream on the top. In her experience, though, the sillier the hat among humans, the more respectable it was.

"Um, yes," Starling said. "Nazh, will you fetch ZeetZi to see the family to their destination? As we discussed?"

Ed looked to her with a frown, but Nazh—being Nazh—picked up immediately. He did as asked, and in a few minutes, ZeetZi was leading the three off toward the shining city.

"So..." Ed said once they were out of earshot. "Um..."

"I wanted to ask you about this in private," she said, handing the folded cloth to him. "It's a fake, right?"

He took it with a curious expression, unfolding it. Then his eyes went wide. Then they went *wider*.

"It *is* a fake," Starling said again as Nazh floated up to peer over Ed's shoulder. "*Right, Ed?*"

"Grandfather of Shards," Ed said. "By gods known and unnamed..." He reached under his robes and took out his Pathian earring, holding it tight as his hand trembled. "It's the forty-seventh count . . . The numbers align . . . The text is even legible . . ."

"A *very good* fake, then?" Starling said, feeling a chill.

"This is a piece," he said, "of the Iriali Long Trail record. A *missing* piece—one we know exists, but of which no surviving tapestry fragment remains. I mean, some of the households are said to have them, but they don't share them with outsiders . . ." He looked after the retreating family again, then at Starling, eyes practically *sparkling* with joy. "If this is authentic, then it is an *incredible* find, Captain. And the fabric is . . . well, I've seen these before. It's unique, woven from their hair. Which this is. The ink . . . we could test the ink, but . . . to match it so cleanly . . ."

"It's . . . not a fake?" she said softly.

"If it is," he said, "it's an incredible one. A work of art itself, crafted by the finest of forgers."

Her hearts thumped in time with one another, fluttering. Not fake . . . Or, at least, not a fake sold on a street corner. "They said it was in their family for generations."

"It could be real," he said.

Nazh folded his arms. "Maybe we could trade it to Xisis for our freedom?"

"Put it in the hands of a private collector?" Ed said, aghast. "Besides, he wouldn't take it. By law—recognized by Silverlight—this kind of artifact belongs to the Iriali unless directly gifted. Any sale or transfer to another is forbidden! He'd have to surrender it immediately to their authorities."

"What does it say?" Starling asked.

"Oh!" he said. "All of the Long Trail tapestries have the same information! Records of visits to various planets the Iriali investigated as potential homelands on their voyage. Most of them are unsuitable, and many thought mythological, particularly ones this old. Let's see . . . Ha! They went the wrong direction, didn't they? The family?"

"Wrong direction?" Starling asked.

"Middle-old Iriali," Ed said. "It had a character shift in the 3000s—and since their numbers are letters, if you read this straight, you'll do it wrong. You need to swap a few to get the right coordinates. It's quite tricky, since—while they navigated by the Current as we do—we don't know a lot of their landmarks. Fortunately, this one uses Silverlight as a prime reference point. Funny to think of those ancient people, who kept records in tapestries instead of books and walked between worlds, visiting this place when it was just a bunch of draconic palaces."

"You like to talk a lot," Nazh said.

"Yup!" Ed said. "Oooooh . . . Look at this. They say they found a perpendicularity. Fat chance of that! Let's see . . . Birds? And bugs? A deadly island . . . Oh . . . Oh *wow*!"

"What?" Starling asked, stepping around to peer at the cloth.

"Well, Nazh does say I talk too much," Ed said.

"A lot," Nazh said in a dry monotone. "I said you like to talk 'a lot.'"

"Wouldn't want to *bore* you," Ed said, "with my proof of how this artifact is probably super, *super* important."

Starling looked to Nazh, who let out an audible breath—on purpose, being a ghost. "Fine. I appreciate it. When you talk. A lot. Ed."

"Ha! It's fun making you interact," Ed said. "You were barely human when you were human, I suspect. This is good for you, Nazh. Builds character, I think? Anyway, birds. There has *always* been talk in the arcanist community about magic birds, and there are many verified examples of them."

"I . . . met a few," Nazh admitted, "back when I was alive. Khriss has a theory on where they came from . . ."

"Oh!" Ed said. "Do you think . . . think you could introduce us?"

Ed was obsessed with Nazh's former employer. Starling, like much of the crew, had been required to listen to his frequent mentions of how she was one of his favorite arcanists, though from what Starling understood, she was from a different order from himself. Or maybe her own order?

"Khriss," Ed continued when no one replied, "recently linked historical records of these birds with a little out-of-the-way planet we're getting all sorts of reports about. It's a pre-space-travel industrial planet the Scadrians have claimed. Quite upsetting of the Scadrians, claiming someone *else's* homeworld, but you know how they are. Rusting this! Rusting that! I scowl and throw coins in your face!"

"Don't you literally worship a Scadrian?" Nazh asked.

"That's *different*," Ed said. "He is *nice*. Plus, he's the only known living Shard who has performed the—"

"Story, Ed, please?" Starling said. "Birds? Magic birds?"

"Sure," he replied. "Well, Khriss says this place has a perpendicularity—she connects it to a record of some people who encountered a well of power in Shadesmar, traveled to the other side a couple of times, and mostly all just died. Some arcanists laugh at the idea, because there *can't* be a perpendicularity on that planet, right? Because there's no known Shard Investing it. Khriss hasn't been able to prove it herself, because she can't provide coordinates."

"Shardless perpendicularities are an obsession of hers," Nazh agreed. "Anytime I was out working on another mission, she'd tinker on this problem, trying to find proof of new perpendicularities on planets that shouldn't have them. I didn't have much to do with it . . . Honestly, Star, I thought it was a waste of time. Rumors of new perpendicularities are always flying about, but they never come to anything."

"Normally I'd agree," Ed said. "But Scadrians are wild about the planet, and there's rumors of the *Rosharans* talking about it too. We thought it was because of these accounts of the locals and their cultivated Invested birds, which can supposedly initiate a Nahel bond. Everyone is *always* excited about new Investiture that can work with anyone, so it would be huge business." He looked at the map. "But it would *absolutely pale* in comparison to the existence of a perpendicularity. If Khriss is right . . . well, it would explain a lot of things. We're talking about the discovery of the *century*. Drominad—the planet—isn't near any other perpendicularities, which means it would open up an entirely new section of space for cheap travel. It could save billions in FTL expenditures, never mind the military applications . . ."

Starling sorted through that. "We should keep this," she said, "very quiet."

"I'll want to show it to a few arcanists," Ed said, "and get their opinions. I'd ask Khriss, but she's vanished."

"Not really vanished," Nazh said. "Merely drawn back to Taldain for its needs. She is a scholar first, but we all love our homeworlds."

"Regardless, I don't want to rely only on my translation of these coordinates," Ed said. "Old Iriali is tricky. And again, I could be wrong.

I don't even know how we'd go about authenticating it, honestly. Can I show it to Argent and Jess, at least? Maybe Huio, if he's not too busy?"

"You can show it to a few others," Starling said. It would have to be a calculated risk. "But be careful. And . . . the best way to authenticate it would be to go where it indicates."

"We'd need a ship for that," Nazh said.

"Fortunately," Starling said, "I'm about to go negotiate to keep this one. And I might just have the leverage we need."

Fig. 84 · Skullsnake
(creature)

CHAPTER THIRTY-ONE

Dusk crouched in his boat, watching the beast swimming nearby. He'd named them skullsnakes, and he was certain they didn't have eyes—so he felt extra foolish huddling like a child playing games. But this posture seemed to make Rokke feel better; she hid beside him, barely peeking her red-feathered head over the side of the boat.

"That's as small as they get," Dusk said.

She chirped uncertainly.

"We've lured nearly a dozen," he said, "and none of them are smaller. We have to accept it; if there are juveniles, they don't swim this abyss or they stay hidden. This is as small as we're going to find."

It wasn't much smaller than the one that had pulled the boat a week back. He glanced at Sak, who chirped in a solemn way. He didn't look, because the visions were always the same these days. His body sinking into the abyss.

"You used to be more creative with those," he noted.

She chirped, affronted.

"True," he admitted, moving to the back of the small boat. "There *were* a lot more ways to die on Patji . . ."

Father loved variety.

"Look," he said, tapping the jugs lashed behind him. "We're almost out of water. Either we kill one of these skullsnakes, or we're dead."

Rokke chirped and fluttered up on top of the motor. She turned around deliberately, head stretched out.

"Fine," he said. "One more time." He took out his binoculars and did a long, steady scan of the horizon. "Nothing. No sign of life."

Twice now, he'd glimpsed what the skullsnakes hunted: a shoal of glowing fish. One group had fluttered past yesterday, maybe some two hundred feet below, but fled as his boat neared. They hadn't been lured by his bait, and looked—to his untrained senses—like groups of ocean fish did in the real world.

He'd noted them—the direction they swam, the size of the two shoals—in his notebook. Maybe he could eventually put together their swimming patterns, and relate it to islands, forming the first hints of a wayfinding guide. Same with the skullsnakes, which he wrote about each time he saw one, along with his notes of estimated distance traveled based on his time paddling or motoring. But he didn't know enough yet to put it together into a usable wayfinding method, and he needed a way to survive.

There wasn't anything he could do now other than kill one of the skullsnakes. Sak chirped consolingly, and he felt that she agreed. Ruffled feathers and all, uncomfortable as she sat on her perch, she agreed.

Dusk unhooked one of his two remaining harpoons and checked his rope. Rokke, of course, hid under the seat.

"I've hunted deep-sea fish," he said, "that weren't much smaller than those beasts." He looked at the skullsnake, which was circling the place where he'd thrown a glowing rag. "Of course, we used bigger boats for those, and lines where you could let out a lot of slack . . ."

He hadn't brought a rifle, but he did have a small revolver in his gear. He brought this out and loaded it. He wasn't much of a shot, though he'd insisted on learning as they became commonplace these last few years. Regardless, he didn't fancy his chances of hitting one of these skullsnakes.

Fortunately he could lean on his experience with deep-sea fishing. There had only really been one way to defeat those fish, and that had been to wear them out.

He slipped the revolver into his pocket, hefted his harpoon, checked

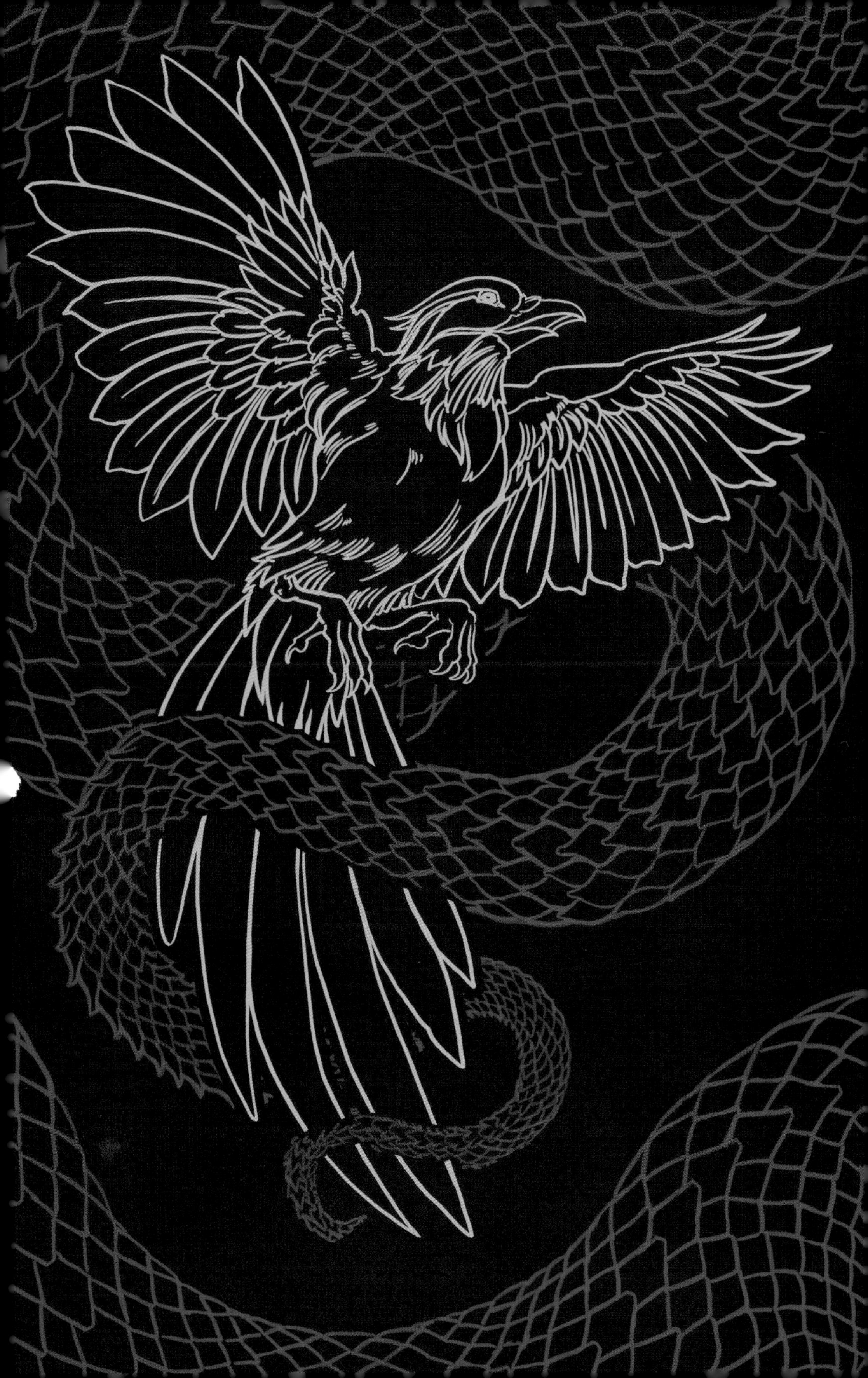

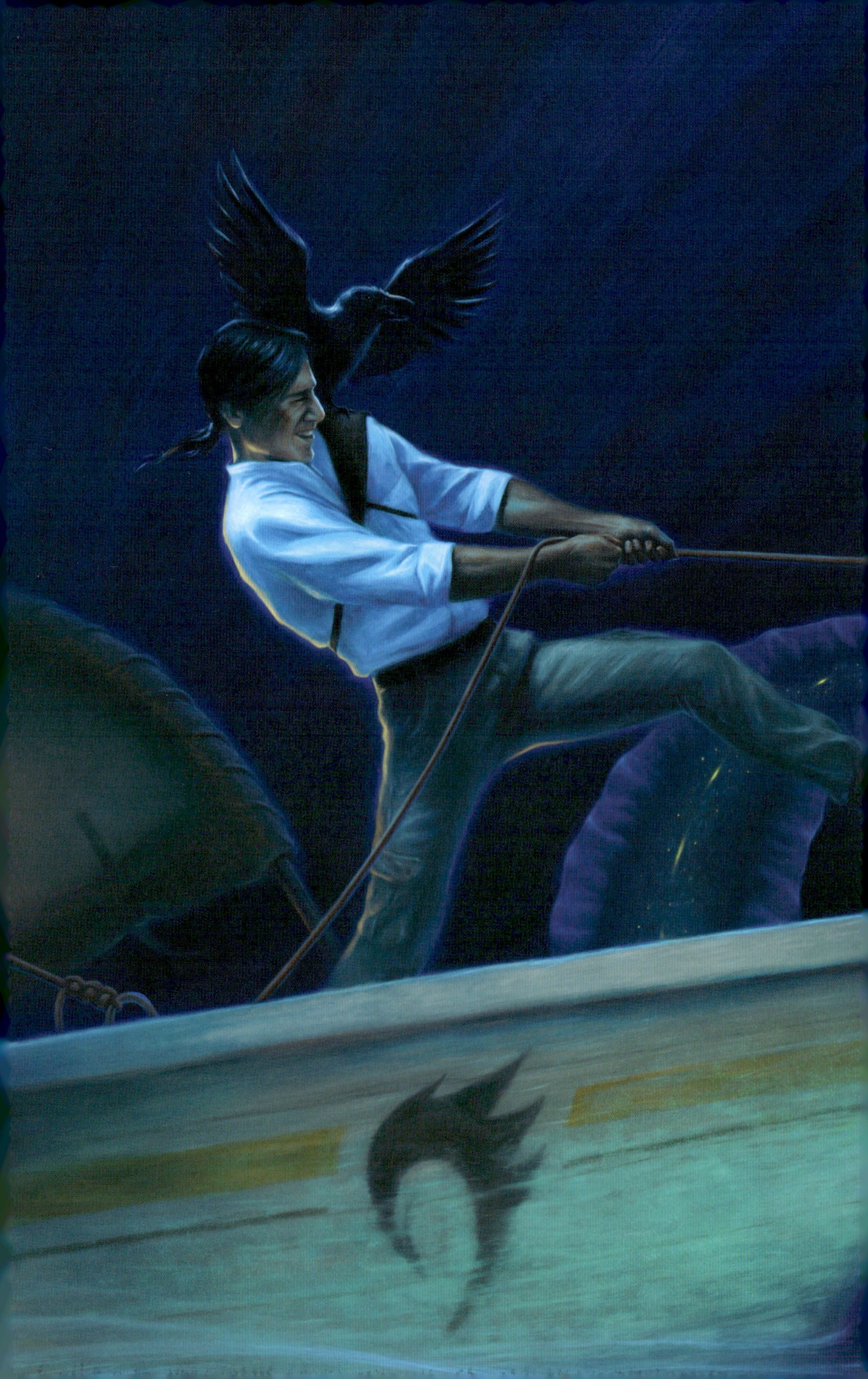

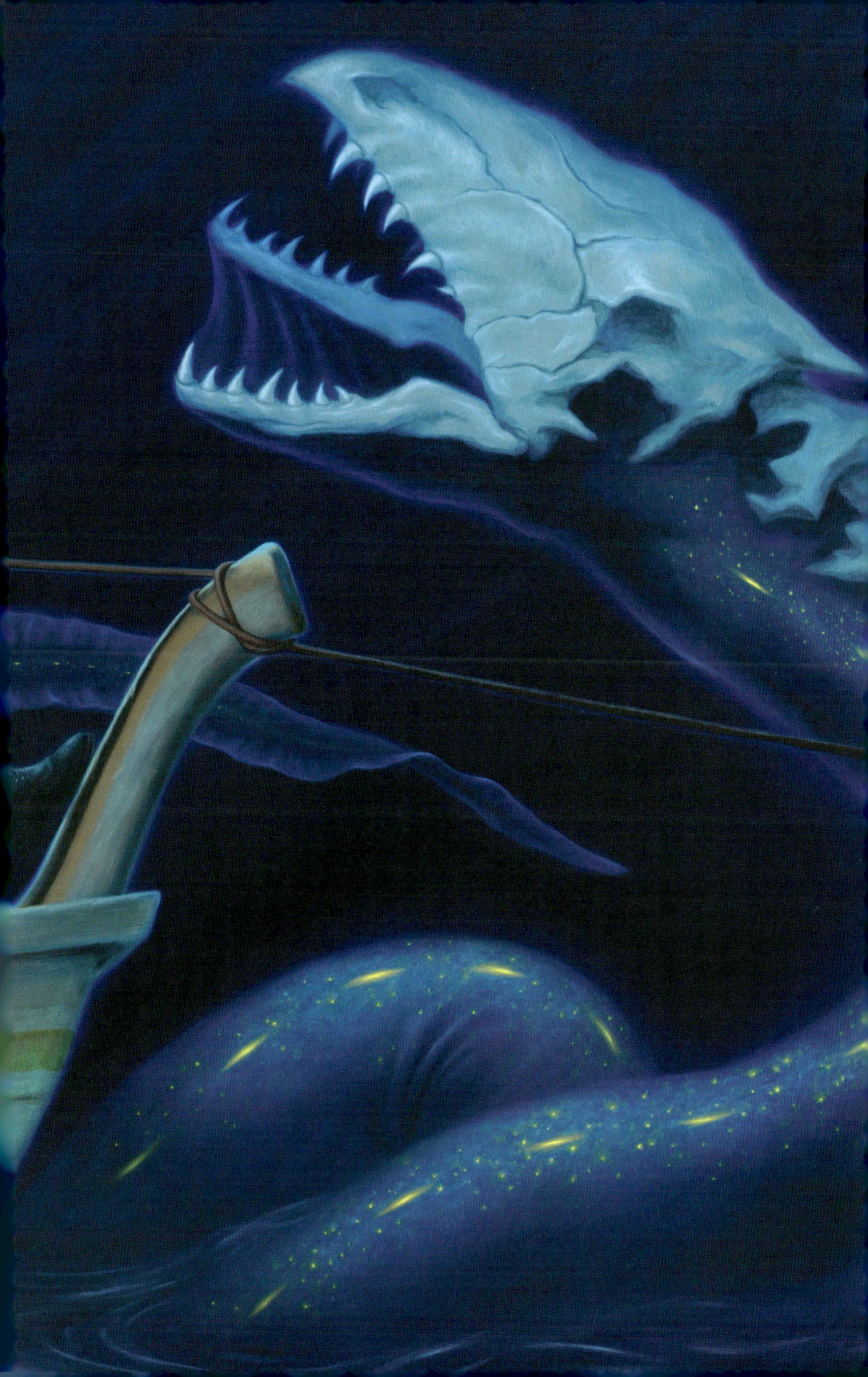

his harness, then stepped to the front of the boat. Sak flapped over beside him, wearing her harness. She had enough slack to perch on the prow and lean forward, wings out. A hunting posture. She chirped to Rokke—who chirped back from her hiding place, but did not emerge.

"It's fine, Rokke," he said. "You can hide. But I need you to drop the protection."

She did.

The skullsnake came for them immediately. These oceans were a wasteland, and finding anything to eat seemed a rare occurrence. Today, food had been located. The question was who was the predator, and who was the prey.

Dusk waited . . .

He waited . . .

He hurled the harpoon, and his aim was worse today than it had been last week. He hit, but farther back than he wanted, and to one side. Still, the harpoon sank in deeply, and the beast screamed in pain. Like before, it fled, and this time Dusk whipped the rope around the cleat at the prow—not, as he'd foolishly done before, the one at the side.

He held tight to the rope, leaning back, as the ship lurched. He was pulled after the beast, a creature—despite being the smallest he'd found—some ten feet long. How much strength did such an incredible beast have?

He was about to find out.

The thing wrenched to the side, nearly toppling them. Dusk grunted, leaning to keep the boat balanced as the birds started one of their squawking panic sessions. Agitated Aviar were a special kind of noisy, but he kept his attention on remaining upright, holding the rope with both hands. He braced one foot against the prow, straining as the skullsnake swerved the other way. Each turn threatened to capsize them—and he could only imagine the disaster that would be, upside down and dragged behind a beast like this.

He didn't dare hitch the rope all the way around the cleat for that reason—it needed to be slack enough to pull free if he let go. In addition, he needed to be able to feel the beast's tugging to help him lean the right direction in the swerves. So he could only use friction around the cleat for leverage, engaging in a tug-of-war against the beast.

More than a contest of strength, though, it was one of endurance. Grunting softly at each turn, he held tight, leaning as the beast tried to shake them free. It did try to dive, and Dusk felt an alarming panic as they actually went beneath the surface of the not-water. But the effort was too much for the beast, who soon came back up, letting them burst back onto the surface—a forceful event that nearly knocked Dusk down.

He righted himself as the thing struck out in another direction, and his frantic lean kept them from capsizing, despite the sharp turn. Almost, his boat became a board for playing in waves, like the youths did back on the homeisles. He'd never had time for that sort of thing, but he felt a thrill they'd have loved, wind in his hair as his boat moved at near-motoring speeds behind the panicked beast.

It was *hard*, but Father had trained him in tests such as this. His endurance pitted against that of the island, for decades. This was what he'd trained for, he was increasingly certain. Not this event, but this *experience*.

Father, he thought. *You knew we'd someday need to live as Cakoban did. You made sure that some of us never grew soft from a life in the homeisles. You gave us the Aviar, but made us work for them, training, testing, preparing . . .*

Vathi would have laughed. But perhaps that was why he was here and she stayed at home, fighting a different fight. Dusk was confident, for while he wouldn't have said he had *faith* in Patji, he did *respect* the god. Fear him. And after so long living in the jungle, *understand* him.

So Dusk sweated, and leaned, and gripped that rope for what felt like hours—though it was surely a shorter time. Eventually he passed beyond fatigue and pain. His arms felt like they'd been bitten by a bitterspring scorpion—which turned bones and muscles to mush. Hanging on was agony, partially because his fingers were losing their ability to grip. They kept slipping, and he started holding on with just one hand to rest the other—but each time he adjusted his grip, he lost a little of the line. And he was running out.

Letting go was the same as giving up. Giving up meant dying. He would run out of water, particularly now that he had to do the hard work of paddling himself to preserve fuel for emergencies.

Even knowing that, though, he wanted to let go. He *longed* to let go. It was too much. The skullsnake had won.

He felt a set of pinprick pains on his shoulder. With shock, he found Rokke there—perching on him for the first time. She was much smaller than Sak, and fit on the shoulder far better—even when she, trembling, opened her wings and leaned down. Imitating Sak's hunting posture.

He whipped the rope around the cleat again, leaned back, and found the strength—somewhere—to hang on. To keep leaning into the turns, which came more infrequently, and less jarringly. He couldn't hold too tightly, but he counted on the wound rope to do the rest.

This was it. He was all in. If they capsized now, there would be no untangling the rope with his worn-out fingers. So he wrapped it around again and forced himself to just hang on.

At last, the beast slowed.

Dusk took a deep breath, dug out a reserve of strength, and started hauling the line in, giving the skullsnake less and less slack. He knew what to expect—the thing would resume fleeing each time he brought it in a little more—but this felt familiar. He did it with rope and harpoon instead of line and hook, but the result was much the same. Bring the thing closer, and closer, and closer until . . .

Until its head was right in front of the boat, the core of its body writhing underneath and occasionally knocking against the hull. This part was dangerous, even if the beast was obviously exhausted. It had the mass to overturn him, maybe even smash the boat to pieces.

So Dusk took his chance quickly. He pulled out the revolver, leaned forward, and fired.

It took six shots. The first shot deflected off its skull plate, so he unloaded each subsequent round into the thing's skin just behind the head. Eventually the skullsnake sagged, then twitched, then stopped. Bleeding dark drops into the void, to fall for eternity, so far as he knew.

It didn't sink as it died, fortunately. He lashed it to the side, then lay down, resting his arms—which alternated between a throbbing pain and a sense of numb fatigue. He found the strength to reach to his neck and feel the trapper medallion he wore.

Sak hopped over, looking down at him, head cocked and black plumage ruffled. Rokke let out a cry that sent Dusk jolting upright. What was wrong? Had she seen something?

But no. That cry sounded vaguely triumphant, and she had her head tipped back, wings outstretched. She cut off after a second, noticing the two of them watching, then shrank and became a bundle of embarrassed, puffed-out feathers.

"That was wonderful," Dusk said. "Thank you."

Then he forced himself to his feet. As much as he wanted to rest, the beast was bleeding into the abyss. That seemed like a great way to draw a bigger predator—and even if it didn't, well, he'd done all of this to get some water. That blood would have to do.

Fig. 100 • *Dragon*
(head)

CHAPTER THIRTY-TWO

Xisis, or Xisisrefliel by his proper draconic name, was one of the old ones. Around since before the Shattering, an event that had happened over ten thousand years ago.

He'd owned land in Silverlight all that time. Once, this had been a den, then a palace. Now the dragon's roost was a tall skyscraper near the university—of which he was a primary patron. The things they discovered were—by his contract with the scholars—available to him first.

Starling strode through the front doors. She didn't often use her draconic name, but here it was appropriate—because while most of the bustling people in the skyscraper foyer ignored her, security had eyes on her from the moment she entered. Probably before. Starling ignored the traditional reception desk and walked straight up to their less-conspicuous station in the back right corner.

"Illistandrista," she said, placing her hands on the desk, showing her manacles. "For Xisisrefliel."

One of the guards made a quiet call, and Spring emerged from the back room to confront her. The large peakspren was—like all of his kind—made of stone, with a smoldering magma core that shone through small cracks along his "skin." He wore a guard uniform that had been tailored just for him, though he still looked like a bag of chips stuffed with far too much air, bulging at the arms, chest, and thighs.

"Foil," he said, using Xisis's common name, for when one didn't wish to invoke the religious one, "is away."

"Spring," she said dryly. "I can sense him."

"No you can't," he said, tapping one of her manacles.

"You think I need my powers to tell he's around? Professor Lake is giving his presentation about a new world in three days; Xisis wouldn't miss that, even for one of his projects. Besides, the lights on the top floor are out. He only extinguishes those when he wants people to think he's not around."

"Foil," Spring said, "is out. Until he calls me and says that he's in." He leaned down, crossing his arms on the counter. "From what I hear, you might want to not be around when that happens."

"Crow already got here?" Starling guessed.

"You think she'd go anywhere else after being subject to a mutiny?"

No surprise there. This was Silverlight. Information traded like stocks here, each nugget worth more than gold.

"I'd hoped she might stop for a drink or something on the way..." Starling said.

"Starling," Spring said. "There's optimistic, then there's stupid. Whatever you mutinied about, he isn't worth the effort. You should run."

The "he" here was just dialect—peakspren language used a gendered version of "it" that often slipped through, particularly for emphasis.

"I'll wait," she said.

"As you wish," Spring said. "I suppose he can't kill you."

"Xisis doesn't often kill people anyway," she said with a grimace. "He considers them living in misery far more entertaining."

Spring smiled, then walked back into his office.

So she waited.

And waited.

And waited until she was absolutely certain Xisis was doing it deliberately to show her just how insignificant she was. A reminder. A full dragon, of their majority and in possession of their powers, could have skipped the lobby. There was a special entrance for them at the top. All you had to do was fly there, with your own wings.

Crow sauntered past, out of the lobby. Xisis made Starling wait a half hour beyond that. Finally, Spring waved her over to the private elevator. He didn't accompany her up—she was a dragon, and deserved some measure of respect, even in her state. That meant no security guard minder.

It was a long, nerve-wracking ride to the penthouse, skipping all the levels occupied by Xisis's business enterprises, his information brokering network, his personal archives, the rooms for all his most rewarded servants. Standard dragon things. At least, for those who believed less in being old-school gods and more in being the new variety. The kind that wore suits and ran governments.

The doors opened directly into a lavish suite that took up the entire floor. Hardwoods. Dark red carpeting. Black furnishings. Xisis sat near the piano, holding a cup of ruby wine, wearing a sharp business suit. He was in his human form, of course; the draconic one didn't fit in apartments. He had ebony skin, with a cool sheen like the polish on the piano. No hair. He liked the bald look, and indeed, it did go stylishly with the suit.

The eyes were silver. Worn deliberately that way, a signal of his heritage.

He left space for her speak first. Saying nothing as he drank his wine, sitting comfortably in a chair that probably cost more than her entire life savings—and a suit that cost ten times that.

He . . . well, he'd almost certainly talk circles around her. Suddenly her small leverage in the conversation seemed ridiculous. She was going to fail utterly, wasn't she?

Again, she remembered the cold vision in the entity's eyes. Alone. Never having flown again. Her life, meaningless. She tried to force it away with the power of optimistic thinking, but she found that hard today.

What, she thought—a final shield against despair—*would Master Hoid tell me to do?*

Own the room.

She took a deep breath, then sat down next to Xisis, helping herself to a drink. "You," she said to him, "have no idea how lucky you are."

He exhaled in a suffering way. "You've grown even more ill-mannered, somehow, during your exile. I blame the jesk, and hear *him* in your voice, child. What a waste."

She finished pouring. Then she sat back, holding the cup, staring him straight in his silver eyes. Waiting. He'd ask. She grew so nervous she almost blurted out her offer, but her master's training—which had often been about *when* to speak more than *what* to say—held her back just long enough.

"All right," Xisis said. "From your posture and the crude attempt at piquing my interest, I can see you've got something you want to tell me."

"Well—" she started.

"But first," he interrupted, "tell me why."

"Why I saved those people?" she asked.

"No," he said. "That is obvious. Again, the fool's influence."

"Why . . . I came back?" she said. "Instead of dumping Crow and flying off?"

"Starling, please," he said. "Don't patronize me. We both know I'd chase you to the ends of the cosmere for such a slight, and you aren't stupid enough to try it. Shards, the young are so *aggravating*." He snapped his fingers, and a figure emerged from the edges of the large penthouse room, hurrying over.

The tall human looked maybe to be Rosharan, though the cut of his clothing was unfamiliar to her. He lifted the wine pitcher from the table just in front of Xisis, took less than one step, refilled the wine cup, then bowed and retreated.

"Really, Xisis," she said. "You couldn't do that yourself?"

"It's important to give people things to do, child," he said, then leaned forward. "That's Tumak. Once emperor of his nation. He needs a little more training in obedience before I can set him on other, more interesting tasks."

"How many monarchs do you have now?"

"Oh, just a couple. Six. Seven." He smiled, drinking, leaning back again. Xisis didn't have slaves. Such barbarism was outlawed in

Silverlight—plus, he would never keep someone for longer than a few months in such a state anyway. He didn't need to enslave people, because he could offer boons unavailable to even emperors. All the wealth in a nation could not buy an extra hundred years of life on a backwater planet—but come to serve Xisis, and he could double a mortal's lifespan with a flick of his claws.

"Your question," she finally said. "Why?"

"Why," he said, "do you care about the crew of that ship?"

"I . . ." That was not the question she'd anticipated.

"Crow is sharp," he said. "One of my best acquisitions, and bargained for by paying barely anything, except to annoy an old rival. She told me you would come to bargain to keep the crew together, because of the hardships they'd have alone—particularly if I were to publicize what they'd done. Your real fear is not what I could do to you, but to *them*. Do you know why? Can you explain it, Starling?"

"They're my friends," she said, feeling small. Hoid's training had been too brief. She . . . didn't know what to say, except the truth.

"Dragons," Xisis said softly, "do not have *friends* among mortals. It's natural to want followers; collecting them is what we do. We are meant to rule nations, found corporations, lead religions. Not fly around on *courier missions* with rejects, playing dress-up and pretending they are our *equals*."

"My uncle Frost says otherwise."

"Your uncle Frost is dead."

"No," Starling said, steeling herself. "Have you seen his soul on the Spirit Shores?"

"Souls can be destroyed before they reach that hallowed place," Xisis said.

"He's alive. He'll return from his journey. Eventually."

Xisis stood with a sigh, stepping to his piano. He settled down. "It's why you were exiled, child. Little thoughts for a little dragon who refuses to learn her lessons and grow up. I wonder how much a disservice I've done you by letting you even be part of that crew."

He began playing softly. So. He was ready to negotiate. He only sat down at the piano when he wanted to begin a *real* discussion.

His music started slow. He improvised it, crafting something that sounded as if it had been composed by a master—but to him, it was completely off the cuff. That was what happened when you played instruments for literally ten thousand years.

"What would it take," he said, punctuating the question with a building scale, "to get you to try something more in line with your heritage? I'm not your patron, and I owe you nothing, but you fell in my lap. If I were to rehabilitate you even slightly, there are those who would pay me favors."

She walked over and leaned on the side of the piano, holding her drink to keep her hand from trembling. He wanted something from her. That . . . was actually dangerous. This would have been so much easier if he were only angry at the lost cargo.

"What would that entail?" she asked quietly.

"Running a small kingdom for me," he said, "on a planet that worships me. As a demigod."

Shards. The idea nauseated Starling. It was the sort of action that would persuade the right dragons with the wrong ways of thinking that she might be worthy of coming off her exile. She hated giving in to them.

"I'm not going to do it, Xisis," she said. "Let me take the *Dynamic* and its crew. They're nothing to you."

His questioning scale became a soft, threatening minor. Shards . . . She always was amazed at how good he was. "You owe me now for both Hoid's debts *and* a hold full of unkeyed Light. I basically own that crew as well. You're a menace together, as proven by your actions. You cannot be trusted."

"You'd prefer I left those poor people to die?" she asked. "Tell me honestly, what would you have done?"

"Humans," he said, "are generally only good as meals. So I don't mind a few sinking now and then." But the subtle shift of the music—still minor—turned mocking.

"Some of them believe you when you say things like that," she said. "They keep expecting me to want to eat them."

"Good," he said. "The more misinformation, the better. You still haven't answered my question, *nor* have you offered me the secret you brought here, expecting that it would somehow be a powerful enough bargaining tool to persuade me. I am nearing the end of my song, Starling. Make your play."

"The three people we saved had a map to an unknown perpendicularity, somewhere out in the emberdark."

"I can buy sixteen of those in ten minutes," he said, music speeding up, a sign that he was preparing to compose a climax.

"Ed thinks it's authentic," she said.

The music slowed slightly. Ed could be overeager, but Xisis knew the value of his crews. He collected what was valuable, but underpriced by others—like Hoid's old ship, full of supposed misfits.

"Arcanists," Xisis said, "can be wrong."

"It's Old Iriali," she said. "It talks of them visiting a land too dangerous for settling." Now the stinger—and she hoped it was enough. "A land with birds that could form the Nahel bond."

The music stopped. Xisis looked at her.

"It's true," she said. "Drominad? The planet the Scadrians want? It's more important than people think."

"The Rosharans want it too." He continued the song, which became a complex, stately piece. "Full of those birds—Aviar, they're called. Indeed, I have a reliable report indicating there are enough birds for each inhabitant to bond one—and more to spare. That seems a great deal of Investiture for such a minor planet—and it has to come from somewhere. There are whispers it might be another of Autonomy's old dominions. Which would give the possibility . . ."

"Of a perpendicularity," she said.

"Yes," he said, continuing the song, the music of it vibrating up the piano, through her. "Though many have done their best to suppress the rumors and none have located the supposed perpendicularity in the Drominad subastral, I believe it might exist. I'm impressed. That's a play that has me *legitimately* curious. So, the deal?"

"I bring you *proof* that the perpendicularity is there," she said. "I do it within the next six months. In exchange, you cancel all of our debts—everything owed you—and give me full ownership of the *Dynamic Storyteller's Incredible Conveyance*."

"And if you fail?"

"You repossess the ship; we work off the debts." She gritted her teeth. "Split us up, if you decide that is best." It had to be something reasonable.

"And you?" he asked, song blending seamlessly once more into the rising, questioning scale of repeated measures. Four notes, as punctuation to his inquiry.

"I . . ." She took a deep breath. "Fifty years. As a demigod on your stupid planet, seeing to your interests."

It would mean more than that, of course. It would mean finally, at long last, taking a step toward what the dragons had tried to bully her into doing for so very long. She hated the mere idea, terrified that she might become like them, instead of the person Uncle Frost had wanted her to become.

But it was the only way.

"Done," Xisis said, striking a final high key. No chord. Just that last note, lingering. "Good luck."

*Fig. 101 · Sak and Rokke
(Aviar)*

CHAPTER THIRTY-THREE

Dusk watched with eagerness as the device attached to his motor processed the skullsnake blood and spat out drinking water. It was built for converting seawater, and used a remarkably simple method. It was practically just a steam engine, of the type that had been common until interactions with the Ones Above led to combustion engines instead.

Boil the water—or in this case, blood—and only pure water would rise as steam. It included a rig for capturing the steam, forcing it to condense, and that's all you needed. Indeed, with an engine generating the heat for you, it wasn't even a waste of fuel. Just process the water when you were going to use the motor anyway.

He had spent the better part of the day processing the dead skullsnake: draining the blood into one of his empty water jugs, slicing up the meat in rings, salting it for preservation, then packing it into his cooler, which could use water evaporation to help keep meat. He'd still want to jerk it using the engine's heating pad—but for now he waited to see if the little bit he'd eaten made him sick or not.

The flesh hadn't tasted off or foul, and while eating it wasn't the safest thing he'd ever done, he'd survived Patji for decades. Sometimes you just had to take risks.

He motored along—the birds snuggled together and sleeping on their roost—quietly enjoying the accomplishment. He'd captured a mythical beast in an ocean with no water, in a land with no sun. Even if he got them killed out here, surely Cakoban would be proud.

But . . . what now? He might be able to catch another skullsnake, as painful as that sounded, but what would he do when the fuel ran out and he couldn't turn blood into water? Equally concerning, the jar of worm paste wouldn't last forever.

He was lost in an endless blackness, swallowed by the three infinities. He had no destination other than to keep driving blindly forward, and no goal other than to survive. Even killing the skullsnake didn't provide much proof; he'd tasted the blood, and found it too salty for drinking. His ancestors wouldn't have had technology to make it drinkable, and so they couldn't survive on this as he could.

He leaned forward, poking at a long strip of flesh he'd laid out on a tarp. It glowed faintly in spots, like the worm paste. He'd left the carcass, but taken this. Hopefully something out there would scavenge the rest.

The strip's glow was already fading. He'd hoped for some kind of organ he could mash into more worm paste, but he'd found nothing. Why did this glow fade, and how had the beast created it? Why did the worms have it in such abundance, and why didn't theirs fade away?

To test again, he cut off a piece of the glowing flesh and tossed it over the side. It sank. Slowly, but it did sink. Earlier, it had floated. Yes, this light *was* fading very quickly. He made a note in his book, then felt foolish. What was he, a scribe? He was a trapper, not a scientist, and such questions had no place in him.

With a sigh, he checked the water. The motor had made quick work of it, boiling away the blood, leaving behind a sticky residue—and refilling enough of his water jugs to last a good week. He added the hot plate to the machine, then used it to grill some snake steak, frying it with a little oil and spice, trying not to wake the birds.

This was a useful machine, this engine. Another reminder that progress wasn't all bad. Machetes replaced obsidian or stone knives.

Motors replaced paddles. Except one day, that march of progress had turned *him* into the thing that was no longer needed. Progress was a wave. It first caught you in it and carried you, but the moment you slipped off the crest, you went crashing into the surf and maybe never came back up.

Progress had no use for men who didn't ask questions. But . . . if he was being honest with himself, such questions had always—at least in part—driven him. He, the man who had brought a non-Aviar fledgling to the pool and given her worms. He'd always pretended that he hated change, but he had been a part of it from the beginning.

Technology was a wave, yes, and it came in a flood. It wouldn't just drown him, but his entire people, unless they built higher and higher houses to survive it. Up, up, up into the stars.

The steak was good. Less fishy, more hearty, like pork. It would even sustain the birds in a pinch. They were technically omnivores, though he'd never heard of an Aviar besides Sak *liking* meat other than a worm here and there.

He cooked up a few more steaks, as they'd keep better that way, and then tried eating a piece of the glowing strip—just to see what it was like. Tasted worse, more leathery.

He cut the motor, packing away his utensils. He knew he smelled something awful, but that was nothing new for him on a long trip. But with water being so scarce, how would he clean his dining implements? Unless he got *very* good at hunting skullsnakes—and found a source of fuel—he'd never have enough water to waste on washing dishes, or even the hot plate.

He turned back to his paddle, but his arms still hadn't fully recovered. Before long, he found himself lashing it in place, then lying on the floor of the boat. He could make a spot here, folding aside one of the seats, nestling among his gear. A snug sleeping arrangement, as if the boat itself were holding him tight.

He missed the rocking sensation of being on a real sea, but there *was* something to this stillness. The serenity of floating in, literally, nothing. Of utter quiet. Alone with his thoughts in an expanse as wide as a person's imagination. Back home, there was always noise. Not just sounds, these days, but *noise*. You couldn't go anywhere to escape it, not even to what had once been the most dangerous place on the planet.

Stillness.

Beautiful nothing.

Calm serenity.

Thrum.

Dusk's eyes snapped open.

Thrum.

He leapt to his feet, scrambling for his binoculars. The birds awoke, Rokke scolding him with a chirp—but Sak could sense his anxiety. She stayed quiet, watching keenly as he searched the endless horizon.

Nothing. He looked downward, then upward. Nothing.

He glanced at Sak. "I heard something," he whispered.

Rokke chirped questioningly.

"Yes, I . . . I might have imagined it."

He closed his eyes, straining. Surely that had been his mind. There was nothing out here to—

Thrum.

Like a soft pulse. That hadn't been there before, had it? He'd slept like this every night, quiet, listening and meditating. He'd have heard it. He was certain.

Even now, he could *barely* hear it.

Thrum.

What had changed? What had . . .

His eyes fell on the slightly bloodied tarp he'd rolled up and hung from the side of the boat to dry. He'd eaten the meat.

From pool, to worms, to birds. The light transfers to each one who eats it.

Father . . . It couldn't . . .

It couldn't be that simple, could it?

He scrambled for the jar of worm paste, which he'd secured to its spot before turning in. He wrenched it out, the glow lighting his hand, making his fingers ruddily transparent. The birds squawked at his sudden motion.

He dipped a finger in, then—bracing himself—ate the paste. The flavor was foul, of course. He forced it down with some fresh water, then waited. Long enough that he felt foolish. Was he going mad? Dining on mashed-up worms, used as a stain for the hull of—

Thrum.

Thrum.

THRUM.

Eyes wide, Dusk knelt in the center of the boat, scanning around, feeling this new noise wash over him. Invisible pulses, sounding in the distance, like heartbeats.

Welcome, a far-off, masculine voice said, *my son.*

"Patji!" Dusk said, springing to his feet. "What has happened to me?"

It is the final step of your training.

"All along," he said. "If we'd eaten the worms . . . If anyone eats the worms . . ."

Anyone? The voice laughed. *Do I bless anyone?*

"No," Dusk whispered. "Only those who are tested."

And who survive, Patji said. Suddenly the medallion of Cakoban felt warmer against Dusk's chest. *What is it you want?*

"To save my people."

I have given you the tools. Go forth and discover my will, trapper. For no victory is warranted unless it is earned, and each planet must stand on its own or be consumed. Farewell, my priest.

The voice faded. Dusk stood in the wobbling boat, overawed. To have been spoken to by Patji . . .

The god had not told him what to do. Of course he hadn't. That was not his way. Dusk had the tools, so that thrumming . . . it must mean . . .

He settled down and closed his eyes, and as he concentrated, the sounds returned.

Thrum.

Thrum.

THRUM.

He could feel them, *physically*, pushing against him, like . . .

Like *waves*.

He rummaged through his things, pulling out his notepad and

charcoal. He sketched, not a picture, but the pattern of waves striking him. Just as they flowed between islands in specific ways, interacting, pushing against one another. He was reminded of the old string maps, which showed the interactions of waves around the Pantheon. An island would interrupt normal ocean swells, as would underwater ridges and chasms.

Just as he had been able to dip his hand into the water and get a sense of where he was—reading the whispers made by the ocean's very heartbeat—could he read these waves?

Both birds moved to his shoulders, Rokke flying, Sak climbing up his clothing, using her beak for purchase. One on each shoulder, they watched his frantic motions, loops, and arcs, waveforms mashing together. To many people, it would look like a mash-up of bizarre scribbles. To him, it became a map.

For he could sense something interrupting the thrums.

Just as islands interrupted waves in the ocean, something interrupted these pulses. He'd have to travel more to make a complete map, but he *could* feel what wasn't there. All because of years spent with his fingers in the water, learning to speak the language of the ocean. The abyss might not have the type of water he was used to, but it spoke the same language.

Dusk wiped tears from his eyes, wetting his fingers and charcoal. "I can see the way," he whispered, sobbing openly. "I can *see the way*."

Sak went alert, straining out her neck, and Rokke chirped in sudden confusion. What? Both of them looked around, as if . . .

As if they could *suddenly hear*.

"You can sense the pulses too? How? I didn't feed you any paste. You didn't even drink any of the blood water. Why can you . . ."

It was him.

He and the birds were bonded. All their lives, the Aviar had given their talents to their human companions. Sak, glimpses of the future, morbidly depicted. Rokke, the gift of invisibility, hiding others from the senses of predators.

Dusk had never imagined that one day, he'd have something to give back. It seemed he had a talent of his own: the ability to find the way home.

ISLES OF THE EMBERDARK

Eager for the first time since setting out, he grabbed his oar. "Come on," he said. "We need to fill in this map. There's a large interruption in that direction, warping the current of this place. It feels far away, but let's see if we can reach it."

**THE END OF
BOOK TWO**

BOOK THREE:
THE CAVE OF DEATH

Fig. 61 · *Glowing worm*
(larvae)

CHAPTER THIRTY-FOUR

Three weeks later, Dusk finally found it.

An island in the darkness. A distant spot, but unmistakable through his binoculars. He'd done it.

Dusk let out a long, relieved sigh, lowering his binoculars. In his lap sat his notebook: the start of an actual wayfinding guide for this strange place. Though he still felt like a neophyte to his uncommon senses, decades of experience on the ocean had proven surprisingly relevant.

He closed his eyes, feeling the thrumming again. That distant, invisible drumbeat, releasing waves he could describe only as energy. It intersected with *other* sources of energy, and together they amplified. That was the opposite of how waves interacted with islands, but exactly opposite—to the point that after just a few days of practice, he'd been able to account for it.

And he'd begun to sense other things. That, there, was a shoal of the strange glowing fish—he could sense it in the drumbeat, like a stone interrupting the flow of a river. They stayed away from the larger interruptions, which he now guessed were land—but not too far away. And *that* was a skullsnake, easy to miss, as he could only spot them if he was directly opposite them in a wave. They hunted the shoals, but also tended to go closer to land. He could even occasionally sense things in the air, though he hadn't identified them or how they related to his location.

He had it all carefully detailed in his notebook. If he could find other signs—the equivalent of finding seaweed floating on the waves, or reflections of land on waves—then he would be able to truly navigate in here. He opened his eyes, and for what felt like the first time in weeks, smiled.

The most important discovery was before him, visible to the naked eye only as a dot on the horizon. This island ahead, an enormous change in the pulse—though, again, it *added* to the strength of the wave, instead of *subtracting* from it. He did not know why it worked that way, but regardless, the excitement of finding land—of actually doing it—had him eager. He put paddle to not-water and continued forward.

The birds gathered on the prow of the ship, sensing his excitement, chattering to one another. As they drew closer, the dot emerged from the horizon in an unnatural way, befitting this dark place. It didn't peek up, then rise. It grew as if out of nothing. A dot, which became a blot, which became an island.

It was real. Importantly, reaching here hadn't required any modern equipment. Certainly *he* might not have survived without his motor and fuel, so he didn't know exactly how the ancients had done it. But the fact that he'd been able to traverse the darkness and locate land . . . was proof enough.

Sak climbed over and up his clothing to sit on his shoulder, feathers ruffled. Closer. He needed to get closer, tie up on it, touch the ground. As he drew near, he could make out more details. It was a flat island, without much elevation, floating on the surface of the transparent ocean. Its rocky bottom was fully visible underneath, covered in long, upside-down mountains. It reminded him of several small atolls he'd visited in the real world: the kind with only a few trees, no fresh water, and vibrant corals among the waves. This one had no trees at all, though something glowed a soft green at the center, which seemed promising. Perhaps another pool?

More, as he paddled around to survey the entire beach and check for danger, he discovered that the island had a shocking surprise for him:

people. Those were *buildings* sitting on the rocky flat portion nearest the not-water. His mysterious, lonely island in the dark was occupied.

Dusk floated quietly, considering. On one hand, he was not surprised. Most islands back home had someone living on them. A few of the small atolls had waystations, and even the Pantheon Islands—deadly though they were—had their trappers.

Humans would find a way to live anywhere, especially the places that didn't want them. But then, he had no idea if these ones would be friendly, or even if he'd be able to communicate with them. So he slipped his revolver into his pocket. Traveling so long through the darkness, and using it to hunt twice more, had left him low on bullets. And of course, he was a terrible shot—but he felt better having it than not.

The birds didn't sense his wariness. They were too excited by the sight of land. Sak flew back to the roost with difficulty, joining Rokke in calling to the island as if it were an old friend. Dusk hushed them, then took out his binoculars to inspect the people on the shore. Their buildings were all metal, maybe twenty feet square and ten high, with rounded corners. Other metallic contraptions on the beach nearby looked like vehicles.

The people he saw had metal appliances on the sides of their faces. Two others wore full masks and carried rifles. These were the *Ones Above*. They lived in this place of three infinities?

He lowered his binoculars, and the birds finally sensed his worry, hunkering down. It . . . made sense, he supposed. The Ones Above were searching for the pool where Aviar were born, and had specifically mentioned that people vanished near such pools. They were probably masters of this place.

Dusk's accomplishments didn't seem so grand now. All that work, all that struggle, and he found a whole group of his enemies casually living here.

Rokke suddenly scrambled back and hid behind him. Sak ruffled her head feathers, leaning forward, wary. What had they sensed that he had not? He turned his binoculars to the sky, searching, until he located it.

A flying vessel. Coming this direction.

Fig. 95 • Dakwara
(Entity)

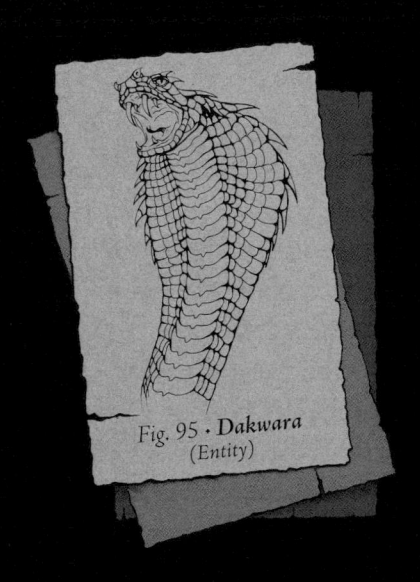

CHAPTER THIRTY-FIVE

An island.

Starling's breath caught. The bridge fell hush. An island, out here in the middle of the emberdark, near where the coordinates had led them. It was true.

Almost immediately, lights appeared in the dark black sky, zooming toward them. Starling rose from her seat on the bridge, and almost hit her head on the ceiling. She leaned to the left, looking out the bridge window.

Lights, stars, in the emberdark. Like souls . . .

They materialized into a pair of starfighters, zooming toward her ship at intercepting speed.

"Hell," Nazh said. "The Scadrians beat us here."

Starling let out her held breath. Not spirits. Not gods. Military ships, armed for dogfighting. MW-232s, it seemed. They were built for space combat, and wouldn't be quite as maneuverable in Shadesmar as they would be in a Scadrian steelfield, but they'd still be plenty dangerous. Particularly to an unarmed cargo vessel like the *Dynamic*.

"Well," Starling said, sitting back down, "at least this means the map is accurate, right?"

"Probably," Ed said. "But the Malwish Scadrians have the location too!"

"All we have to do is bring back proof of a perpendicularity's existence," Starling said. "We don't have to actually claim the thing. Xisis can worry about the Malwish."

"Uh . . ." Leonore said from the pilot's seat, "I'm worried about the Malwish, yah?"

"Let's turn back for now," Starling said.

"And you realistically posit," ZeetZi said, glancing back at her, "that upon the incredible discovery of an unknown perpendicularity, the kind souls of the Malwish Empire would just . . . let us saunter off?"

Starling didn't reply. The Malwish were a dominant force on the planet of Scadrial. A powerful force in the galaxy, and an aggressive one. Everyone tried to leave them to their war, but . . . well, Scadrians had this habit of claiming land, sending patrols, and coming up with their own rules and regulations. They patrolled half the lanes between planets in Shadesmar.

It did keep those regions safe. For a price.

She didn't have the *best* history with Scadrians, unfortunately. Her master . . . was not well liked by many of their elites. But Leonore was proof that you could get along with anyone, regardless of background. So Starling tried to remain positive about their chances.

"The island is occupied," Nazh said, squinting at the monitor, standing halfway through the wall to ZeetZi's right. "I count four more MW-232s landed there. Oh wait—five. There's another over by the supply depot. More importantly, there's a single Jagged Star gunship rising up, weapons training on us. Lovely."

Starling put her hand on Leonore's shoulder. "What if we ran?"

"You're kidding, right?" Nazh asked.

"Ha ha," Starling replied. "What if we ran? Leonore, you managed to dodge that entity. Maybe you could get us away from this lot and we could lose them in the emberdark, then see if we can sneak back to gather intel?"

Leonore didn't reply. But she did slowly lower her mask over her face.

Starling looked around the small bridge. Nazh was giving her one of his flat, ghostly stares. Ed seemed eager, but that was Ed. And—

The door behind them slammed. Chrysalis, leaving. She'd been here, watching—but had a thing about Scadrians. Her retreat seemed to indicate something, confirming some of Starling's suspicions.

"Well, Captain," Nazh said. "If we run, we will be shot down by that gunship. If it misses, one of the fighters will undoubtedly finish the job. They fly at combat speeds, and we—at our best—are still a cargo ship. They'll reach us, and you will all join me in death. It's pleasant. Except for the being-dead part."

"They're demanding we follow them to the island and land," ZeetZi said, monitoring the comm channels.

"Leonore, they're your people, right?" Starling said. "Can you talk to them? Tell them we're just lost?"

"Oh yah," Leonore said. "Members of the Malwish Planetary Guard love it when they find people like me. Capable pilots who deserted military service? Went off and joined a private ship, working for profit? We're their *favorite* people, Captain."

Starling sighed, glancing at Nazh. He moved out of the wall, standing tall in that impeccable dark grey suit with white cravat tie. He met her eyes. Tension on the bridge was thick enough to spread on toast. Shards . . . they were right.

"Follow them as they instruct, Leonore," Starling said. "Nice and easy. Warn Aditil what is happening, and get her up here on the bridge so nobody is isolated. Land when told to do so, but don't open the doors yet. Stall."

"Stall?" ZeetZi's feathers bristled on his head. "But—"

"I need to talk to Chrysalis," Starling said. "Let Nazh stall the Scadrians. He loves that sort of thing. I'll be quick."

She didn't give them further time to object, instead slipping out. She headed down the ladder to the right and into the medical and science bay, which was directly across from Ed's arcanist workshop.

Chrysalis looked over as Starling entered. Even with face tattoos and a dark tan skin, the separation lines between her various pieces were clearly visible. Perhaps if you weren't familiar, you would mistake her for someone who had a lot of scars—but Starling was familiar. Some of the hordes had managed to breed themselves to where they could pass for human. Chrysalis wasn't one of those.

"We're landing," Starling said—and felt the ship slow. "The Scadrians will almost certainly search the ship. If you have something to tell me, now would be a good time."

"I . . ." Chrysalis's skin split at the seams in a few places, which seemed a sign of stress. "I should like it very much if you did not tell them I was here."

"Can you hide?" Starling asked.

"Hoid has a hidden aluminum smuggler's box, undetectable to even modern scans," Chrysalis said, turning away from her. "I know where it is, hidden deep within the ship's machinery. It's exceptionally cramped, and there's nothing to eat or drink, let alone a way to dispose of waste. I'd die in there if I stayed too long, but I can pull inside when they scan the ship. Once they're done, I can remain hidden among the electrical systems. I've . . . hidden in there from you all before."

Starling took a deep breath. "You're going to need to start trusting me sometime, Chrysalis."

Chrysalis didn't meet her eyes.

"Two years ago," Starling said, "a Sleepless assassinated the Malwish imperial prime minister and head of party."

"I'm a doctor," Chrysalis said.

"With an excellent understanding of the anatomy of many different species, including humans."

"My kind tend toward such knowledge."

"Chrysalis," Starling said. "Are you a fugitive?"

"I . . ." Chrysalis finally met her eyes, and Shards . . . Her skin had split even further, showing tiny insectile legs sticking out, squirming.

With effort, Starling forced down her revulsion. Sleepless were people, like any other. People made up of a swarm of bugs. Skittering, twitching, buzzing insects that had learned to create flesh suits to . . .

People, she told herself. *People. Maybe not like any other, but still people. And a member of my crew.*

"I have sworn the oath of the First," Chrysalis said softly. "Hoid helped me escape a life I came to revile. I will never do harm to another again, by my sworn word. But if they find me, Starling, they will burn me. They see my kind—innocent or guilty—as abominations."

"All right," Starling said. "I'll brief the rest of the crew and we'll keep quiet about you. But Chrysalis . . . don't let this come back to bite us, all right?"

Shards, Starling thought. *Poor choice of words, perhaps.*

Chrysalis nodded, then turned away. "You will want to go. Most find my ungloving to be disconcerting."

Starling did, because she felt the ship set down. ZeetZi was still fetching Aditil, and Nazh was speaking into the comm.

". . . of course submit to an inspection team," he said. "But for your safety, I should first . . ." He saw her and—at her nod—let out a relieved sigh. "Never mind. We are at your convenience."

"Then the inspection team will arrive at your ship soon," a voice said on the other end of the line, speaking in Scadrian Malwish—a language they assumed everyone else would speak. Unfortunately, most were forced to for that reason.

"When?" Nazh asked.

"When we decide. Do not power on your engines. That will be seen as a threat, and force will be exerted to ensure your compliance." The comm went dead.

"Great," Nazh said. "So I guess we wait. And after getting yelled at for stalling . . ."

Starling settled in her seat, and softly clacked her shackles together, a nervous habit. Soon Nazh broke the tension by whistling softly in amazement. He'd moved into ZeetZi's seat, and had been looking at the viewscreen, using telescopic lenses to scan the landscape. He could just barely work simple controls by exerting the softest pressure. He had trouble interacting with physical things unless . . . well, unless things went badly.

When she didn't respond to the first whistle, he did a second one, louder.

"How do you do that?" Starling asked. "Without lips?"

"Really?" he said. "All these years, and you've never asked how I speak without lungs—and now you're curious how I whistle?"

"Sure. Why not? How?"

"Same way I put up with you, Star. Out of sheer force of will."

"Aw," she said. "Don't pretend you don't like my questions. They keep you on your toes. What are we whistling at? Hot ghost woman?"

"You're once again assuming that I'd be best matched to another ghost. As I've said, that's prejudiced."

"Why is it prejudiced? Shared experience and all that."

"And you exclusively date insufferable optimists? Shared experience and all that?"

Their eyes met. Nazh grinned. She grinned back. They'd get out of this, like they'd gotten out of everything else. It was good of him to keep her talking.

Nazh tapped an incorporeal finger on the viewfinder. "Ed, you should look at this. It's watching us." He made room for the arcanist, who pulled off his hat, exposing his curly black hair. He settled down, looking.

Starling leaned toward Leonore, putting her hand on the pilot's—which was tightly gripping the armrest, knuckles white. "You doing all right?"

"They could ship me back," Leonore whispered, mask still down. "I was court-martialed in absentia. I'm supposed to serve fifteen years in military prison, doing hard labor. Those kinds of sentences have a habit of going long, yah?"

"I won't let them take you. I promise."

But Shards . . . could she keep that promise? What had she gotten her crew into? In trying to save them, had she gotten them into something even worse?

"Captain?" Ed said, nodding to the viewfinder. "This is worth seeing. You missed it as we landed, since you were out of the room."

"What?" she asked.

"Another one is here."

"Another ship?"

"No. Another entity."

Shards. She slid into ZeetZi's seat as he made room, then leaned forward to peer at the viewscreen. The island was basically flat, but had a hole in the center—so it was actually doughnut shaped. In the center of that hole was another tiny island with some black rock formations on it. And—she squinted—maybe a cave at the center.

Perpendicularities did tend to be found in shadowed, cavernous regions. It was the case on Nalthis, for example. Unfortunately, something guarded the central island-within-an-island: a large glowing entity. It had just reared up, which was likely what had made Nazh whistle.

It was in the shape of an enormous serpent. Even with its head out, it continued to swim through the unsea there, moving in a circle. It was joined by what appeared to be hundreds—maybe thousands—of smaller creatures that were themselves like eels or snakes, only much smaller.

Unlike the one they'd faced a month back, this one moved with a smooth, undulating motion. No choppiness, no sense of a strobe. Just a monstrous glowing snake, swimming in an infinite circle.

"Relative of yours, perhaps?" Nazh asked lightly.

"Har har," she said. "Why is this one in such a normal-ish shape, Ed?"

"We don't know why they do what they do, Captain," he replied. "But I'd guess it's this shape because it's within the Drominad substral. This is why these Threnodite entities stay away from populated areas—they can get trapped into a shape if too many people are nearby. The things we love, or fear, or dream about . . . they influence beings like this."

"So it's trapped?" she asked. "Locked down?"

"In a way, but not really. It's a giant snake monster now, and wouldn't consider being anything else." He shrugged. "It's hard to say, though. Again, it could be in that shape for some other reason entirely—it could just feel like being a snake."

"That cavern," Nazh said. "You see it?"

"Yup," she said.

"That might be what we want. The perpendicularity."

"We won't be able to tell until we get closer," Ed said. "In fact, even if we find a glowing pool, we probably will need to slip through and prove that it works for accessing a planet on the other side—I doubt Lord Xisis will accept anything else as confirmation." He paused. "An entity being here is a good sign, though!"

"Yah," Leonore said. "You act like we didn't nearly get killed by one a few weeks back."

"Just being positive, like the captain!" he said in his cheerful way. "Type 1-6 Threnodite entities are attracted to sources of Investiture. If that's too technical for you, then the mere existence of land here is an even better sign."

"Because it's more proof we're near Drominad?" Starling asked, catching sight of that serpent again as it emerged from the inner unsea, then sank beneath the surface again.

"Yup! Any kind of land, particularly one with a curious shape, is a sign of a planet nearby with its people thinking and changing the shape of Shadesmar."

"Should the surface be more ground-like here if we're near a planet?" Leonore asked. "Or something different from the unsea? Scadrial's subastral is all misty, though you'll fall through if you try to walk there."

"Yes . . . subastrals are all unique, influenced by the people living in the Physical Realm nearby. Most common are variations on obsidian ground, like you see in Roshar, often inverted from the oceans. That has curious individuality when closer to the planet, but becomes a glassy, featureless plain farther out, eventually giving way to the unsea except where people travel Shadesmar with regularity. Captain, if I may." He turned and moved the view on the screen to the nearby rock beach.

Starling leaned forward, studying the black mound and the unsea just beyond. The island had the same obsidian feel, but more . . . dark stone than glassy like she'd seen elsewhere. Studying the unsea nearby, she at first missed what Ed wanted her to see. Upon looking closer, she picked it out. The unsea was thicker here, more visible. Shadowy but . . . lighter. And was that a school of *fish* swimming deep below?

"The unsea's essence *is* more ocean-like here," she said as ZeetZi and Aditil arrived.

"Each planet in the Physical Realm has a profound effect on Shadesmar," Ed said. "Near Nalthis the surface is painted colors, wet with pigment and flowers that drip ink. Roshar? Glass beads, like the gemstones they use for light, and inverted land and sea—which is common for some regions, but not all of them."

"And here it's more like water," Starling said. "Drominad is an ocean planet, I assume?"

"Exactly," Ed said. "The change here is more subtle than others, but it is a change. We sometimes see subastrals like this one near sea-faring cultures, where the unsea becomes the dominant feature, instead of fully solidifying, even for oceans. This might be why the Drominad perpendicularity, despite being less than a month's journey from important lanes of travel, hasn't been found. Because at first glance, this region seems like just any other part of the endless emberdark. These hints, though, are proof. We are absolutely within a planetary subastral."

Nazh whistled quietly.

"Again, we need more evidence of a perpendicularity," Ed said. "We're actually pretty far off from the coordinates on the map, but that's not uncommon. That map is millennia old, and Shadesmar—of course—shifts over time."

"It does?" ZeetZi settled down in Starling's customary seat. "Why does Shadesmar shift?"

"Oh!" Aditil said, raising her hand from behind him like she was in class. "I know this one! I learned it! People think about space, and the more we think about it, the more it manifests here!"

"Precisely," Ed said. "The more aware of the cosmere the people on a planet become, the larger the space between their planet and other planets grows in Shadesmar. Additional reality just . . . manifests, pushing things around, like a crumpled piece of paper unfolding!"

"That's . . . extremely unnerving," Leonore said, still huddled in her mask. "How can you sound so excited? Reality kind of . . . *poof*, appears? Planets grow farther apart?"

"It's incredibly interesting," Ed said. "Our perception creates Shadesmar! Good thing humans are really, really bad at imagining the actual distances between planets, or soon it wouldn't be any faster to travel in here than in the Physical Realm! For now, instead of light-years apart, planets just tend to be thousands upon thousands of miles apart. It's neat!"

Starling nodded, because it was—though Leonore was right, and it was also unnerving. Mortals and their minds made a mess of everything . . .

Now that everyone was there, she gave a quick explanation of how they were going to hide Chrysalis, including the smuggling box none of them, not even her, had known about. Their cover story would be that there was no current ship's doctor, but Leonore—who had some field medic training—was filling in. Starling got confirmation from everyone, including a reluctant ZeetZi, that they would hold to the story.

That done, she turned the viewfinder to watch that strange snakelike entity. A few minutes later, she noted a group of Scadrians—soldiers—finally approaching the *Dynamic*.

"Captain?" Leonore said, checking that her mask was down. "That's the inspection team."

"I'll handle them," Starling said. She glanced at the others. "Don't worry so much. This isn't as bad as it looks. Really. Even Scadrians are going to be worried about tangling with a dragon, and it's not like they have any real authority here. I'm sure I can talk us out of this."

They didn't seem convinced—and neither, really, was she. She stood up anyway.

"You sure you should go on your own?" Aditil asked.

"It's my job as captain to keep you all safe," Starling replied. "Besides, I'm virtually indestructible. What are they going to do to me?"

"Tie you up?" Ed offered. "Shoot our ship down to isolate you? Toss you in with that entity, which *can* hurt you? Oh! And—"

"Point taken," Starling said, continuing anyway.

Nazh walked with her, joining her outside the blast door. He gave her a look, the kind that said, *Really? Alone?*

"If this goes poorly," she said, "I want the rest of you to take off and run. I'll try to distract them."

"With what?"

". . . Charisma?" She met his eyes. "It will be fine. We'll find a way through this."

She braced herself, waiting for him to challenge the statement with a dose of his relentless cynicism. Instead he nodded. "We will." Then he paused. "While you're talking to them, keep an eye out for any pretty ghost ladies. I could use a date." He winked.

She grinned, took a deep breath, then raised the door and stepped out to meet the group of heavily armed fascists standing outside.

Fig. 59 · Masher wasp
(insect)

CHAPTER THIRTY-SIX

The trick in dealing with Scadrians was deciding which lies to tell. You needed to be precise and deliberate, like you were cutting diamonds for jewelry. Lots of observation, then a single strategic tap to split the stone.

The leader of the Scadrians was a red-haired man with the modern style of mask: a pair of two-inch-long metal grafts at the sides of the face, extending along the cheekbones and beneath the hair under the ears, attached directly to the skin. His had a pair of small tubes extending from them, beneath his nostrils—which wasn't standard. His uniform was immaculate, rank on display at his shoulders. He didn't carry a lodestar; none of his soldiers did. They'd have them somewhere in case they were needed, but their tech was strictly Scadrian, and they'd all be trained on it. Less need for devices to help them interface with foreign gear.

The mask meant he was Malwish, not one of the other Scadrian ethnicities. Starling knew she should have paid better attention to Scadrian politics—it was one of the cosmere's superpowers. And she'd met *some* Scadrians she got along with. Just none who wore uniforms.

The leader's lips turned down as soon as he saw her. Though the others were looking at her face, he immediately noticed the manacles. "Yolish. And a prisoner?"

"Common misconception," she said. "I'm not a prisoner. I've been assigned to live a portion of my life without my powers, as a way to . . . um . . . 'teach me humility and empathy for the mortal species of the cosmere.'" She smiled in what she hoped was a disarming way. "I'm Captain Illistandrista, Thirteenth Divinity of Shotozoko Peak. You can call me Starling—and I'm at your service, Colonel."

"You took a great long time to comply with our orders that you land and present yourself."

"We're a trading vessel, Colonel," she said. "Out of our league and completely lost. Please don't assign obstinance to what was simply chaos on our part."

He studied her, then waved to his followers. "My team will board and search your ship for contraband, as explained."

"Please," she said. "First could we—"

But they were already moving. Shards. She hoped that Chrysalis had hidden already. Starling clenched her teeth and tried not to make a scene. Dealing with people like this man was an art, and for all her faults—which she'd willingly admit—she was good with people. At least, she thought she was.

"Walk with me, Captain," the leader said, stepping away from the gangplank, across the dark ground. Rocky and black, but not like the glassy type you found elsewhere in Shadesmar. This looked more like coral, with bulbous sections full of texture.

Her boots scraped against it in a satisfying way. She liked that solid sound.

"Dragon," he said, "how ancient are you?"

"A hundred and twenty," she lied. If he'd recognized the manacles, he was well-informed and obviously knew you couldn't tell a dragon's age from their looks. He'd likely know that her true age of eighty-seven would mark her as still technically a juvenile. It wasn't a one-to-one correlation, though, comparing her aging to that of humans. She was mature, and had lived nearly a century. She was considered brash and young for her kind, but she was fully developed mentally. She just wasn't of majority by draconic terms.

"Young," he said with a nod. "You realize I can check your age?

You'll be listed on the registries as an exile, so we know not to give you passage to your homeworld."

Shards. He knew more than she'd expected, even if he'd been wrong about what specifically the manacles meant.

"You're an arcanist," she guessed.

"Close," he replied. "Two years cross-division training for a subspecialty earned me this." He tapped a badge on his chest that had the arcanist symbol. "But I chose another path for my career. You may call me Colonel Dajer, and I think you will be of use to me. Yes indeed . . ."

"Um, my crew and I," she said, "would like to be able to leave. As I said, we're a trading vessel. We've done nothing wrong, and are simply lost in the emberdark."

He barely seemed to be listening. Finally he glanced toward her. "Your kind like deals. I might be interested, though know that I am not the type to dance at your whimsical riddles and deceptive offers."

"Understood," she said, though that was a *gross* overgeneralization.

"You say you are an ordinary trading vessel," he mused. "Strange, how I always seem to meet those, and never smugglers, pirates, opportunists, or raiders."

"I guess you're just lucky," she said with a smile.

He did not smile back. Instead, he walked her past their camp. Their gunship doubled as a base camp—and had released nested pods as living or research stations, making a little town for the dozens of uniformed people who rushed about.

Dajer eventually stopped where they could look at the glowing creature in the center of the island. Coils upon coils churned as it swam in a vast circle under the surface of the unsea, accompanied by hundreds of smaller snakes.

"The little ones hunt for it," the colonel said. "The great beast sends them out for what little prey there is to be found in this forsaken land."

"Seems like a dangerous entity," she said. "If I were you, I'd head back to civilized lands, far from such creatures."

He didn't reply, though he led her to a small survey station where some people were monitoring the beast. Here, a pair of soldiers were monitoring computer equipment.

Dajer nodded toward Starling, and one of the aides began typing. "Name of your ship?" the man asked.

"Dynamic Storyteller's Incredible Conveyance."

"Scadrian registration number?"

"We don't have one," she said.

Both eyed her.

"Never needed to land there," Starling said with a shrug. "I hear it's nice." Both statements were true.

"A wise captain," Colonel Dajer said, "registers anyway. To prevent inconveniences."

"We have patrols along the Vapor–Firmament corridor," the aide said. "Malwish declarations have been very clear: this direction is off-limits, and under our exploratory jurisdiction. How is it you didn't know that?"

Now the lie. "Well . . . we maybe didn't think this through all the way. I'd heard this path could lead to a shortcut from Silverlight. I figured if I could find a shorter path, I could undercut my competitors with faster delivery times."

The aide took a call via handset, using what was obviously an expensive Invested communication device. The type that worked in the emberdark, and the aide working it—curiously—was using a lodestar for controls. He spoke softly, and Starling couldn't hear the replies, as they went into his earpiece. "Hold is full of mail," he said to the colonel.

"Is it now?" Dajer replied. "Have them check the dates."

Shards. She started sweating. Stupid human body.

"No dates," the aide said.

"Read a few," Dajer said.

"You can't do that!" Starling said. "It's not—"

Dajer raised a hand, and two guards nearby trained weapons on her. She let out a sigh, and knew what would come next.

"Same four pieces of mail," the aide said, "repeated over and over."

"You should have done a little extra work," the colonel told her. "Mail is such a convenient fake cargo. Never rots or rusts. Can be very urgent, and can explain leaving with a half-full hold, as it needs to be delivered so quickly."

ISLES OF THE EMBERDARK

"We couldn't afford anything better," she said. "But if you must know, we have—"

"A second fake cargo," he said. "Hidden, so you can pretend to be a smuggler. Something else that lasts but isn't too valuable, so the fine if you're caught is low. I don't care what it is. We both know why you're actually searching this region. How did you hear about the perpendicularity?"

Shards.

The Scadrians didn't have *actual* jurisdiction here, but they had weapons, and could get away with a lot in the name of "planetary security." Her people could be detained for months, or more.

"I don't want trouble," she said softly. "We were just chasing a dream. One of a thousand rumors, almost all of which are untrue. Betting big on the treasure we might find."

Dajer sniffed, hands behind his back, metal at the side of his face twinkling as the entity shifted in its moat beyond. "What would you have done if you'd found it? A transfer point between realms? You think you could exploit that without the protection of someone much, much more powerful than yourself?"

"Big risk," she said, "but big reward. It's . . . true then? There is one? But there's no Shard in residence here."

The colonel glanced toward the serpent. "Yes, that's the question, isn't it? How? Even most of my people don't believe it exists." He nodded toward the entity. "Beyond that Splinter of Ambition is an inner island, and on that, a cavern. I'm certain that inside it is the portal. A transfer point to a planet full of islands and birds, as detailed in the reports of my colleagues. This is the right place, close as we can determine. I will be the one to first traverse it, and then . . ." His eyes grew distant. Then the computer beeped.

"She's right," the aide said. "No ship with this description is in the logs of our patrol ships—she didn't check in with any of them before setting out this direction."

"Pity," Dajer said, "that there is no official record of your ship coming this way. As I said, it's always best to check in. It protects you from . . . inconveniences."

Starling felt a chill.

"Your ship is forfeit," Dajer said. "Your crew will be kept in one of our pods until such time as we decide to drop them off in civilized lands."

"Forfeit?" Starling exclaimed. "That's thievery! Despite your claims, you don't have authority over the emberdark. This isn't your land. Even you can't possibly—"

"You miscalculated," the colonel said, waving for the two guards to approach her. "We have a provisional treaty with the local planet, backwater though they are. That means you aren't just wandering unclaimed lands, Captain. You are trespassing on a secure Malwish military installation, and I have jurisdiction here, perfectly provable and enforceable."

Oh Shards. If he was telling the truth . . .

She had gotten her crew into serious trouble. Worse than she'd thought.

"Be glad I'm not taking more . . . extreme measures," the colonel said. "Some would not be so lax, but I am a man of great mercy, you see. Even if it is displeasing to find rats sniffing about what should be a completely hidden operation."

"Hidden for now," she said. "I mean, as soon as you find and open the perpendicularity to travelers, everyone will know. So there's really nothing to be lost by my knowledge, right?"

He watched her through dismissive eyes, narrowed slightly, lips a tight line. And finally Starling's optimism started to shake, and she admitted just how much trouble they were in. Currently, ships had to use FTL to reach Lumar for aether harvesting—either that or pay for the more powerful, but more regulated, versions available from Aditil's people. Both were enormously expensive, leading to situations like on the *Dynamic*, where only the old, stale spores were available to cargo ships. However, sublight speeds could reach the moons of the mining planet easily with this perpendicularity, perhaps within less than a year's travel time. While Dromidad wasn't super close to either Scadrial or Roshar, it was situated somewhat between them, and that was relevant to the war as well.

There was an extreme tactical advantage to this location. It was a secret worth killing for.

He wouldn't keep her crew detained for a few months. He could make them vanish for years, decades. And if he had jurisdiction here by treaty with the locals . . .

It would all be legal. Even the dragons wouldn't interfere or pay retribution, so long as Starling herself wasn't kept more than a hundred years. The dragons considered a life sentence—per a mortal definition of "life"—an acceptable slap on the wrist for dragons who let themselves get into situations like this.

She swallowed. Dajer knew he had her. In her experience, people like him loved to exercise a little authority over an immortal. They hated the idea that dragons lived, even in this modern era, as gods. Hated that there were those among her kind who *predated* the birth of his gods and the creation of his very subspecies.

That was her heritage. She was proud of it, even if these days her people weren't proud of her. Even if, long before they'd locked her into this form, she'd always felt more like an awkward girl than a divinity.

She met Dajer's gaze and held it.

"As I said before," Dajer finally said. "I think perhaps I might have a use for you. A deal."

"I'm listening," Starling said.

"Um, Colonel?" the aide interrupted.

"What?" the colonel said, not breaking eye contact with Starling.

"Do you, um, see that?" the aide asked.

She and the colonel both turned, at first, the wrong way—toward the glowing monster at the center of the atoll. When the aide cleared his throat, they turned the other direction, to the featureless abyss.

Where, impossibly, something was approaching. A solitary vessel bearing one person, gliding across the surface of the unsea, pointed right at them.

"Is that . . . a rowboat?" the colonel said.

Fig. 25 · Sak
(Aviar)

CHAPTER THIRTY-SEVEN

Dusk slowly paddled up to the beach.

More than he wanted to step onto solid stone, he needed to investigate this place. He was out of supplies.

Most of these people had uniforms on. Several with full face masks, several with helmets, a few with adornments like the Ones Above had shown on the landing pad back home. Smaller, masklike metallic bits at the edges of their faces, as if stuck there by glue. He was curious to see that while many had pale skin, some were of a more familiar, browner skin tone.

There was one woman out of uniform, and she drew his attention the most. She wore trousers and a tight shirt under a flowing knee-length overshirt—and more, she had chalk-white skin, paler than any of the other Ones Above. He didn't know enough about their worlds to know if that indicated albinism, and the shades seemed wrong for that, but it did seem similar.

Vathi had worked on him over the years, and he knew the . . . impression he tended to make. He needed to do better, for his people. So he put on a smile—kind of stapled it on, really—and raised a hand in greeting as he neared the shore. If there were entire worlds out there, then perhaps there were factions among the Ones Above. He couldn't assume that all of them were his enemies.

One of the men on the shore pointed, and two others ran for him immediately. They grabbed his boat, pulled it up—and before he could voice more than a word of complaint, they had hauled him out. They found his gun in seconds.

To avoid causing an incident, he didn't fight back. Even after they forced him to his knees on the shore, rifles held at his face.

The birds, of course, didn't take this well. They fluttered their wings, screeching. Sak clung to his shoulder as he knelt before the Ones Above. She put her wings out wide to make herself bigger, letting out her most horrific screeches. Rokke, bless her little scarlet head, even came out of her hiding place on the boat and fluttered to the roost at the prow. She screamed along with Sak.

One of the guards turned his rifle on her.

That was too far.

"Point your gun," Dusk said softly, "away from my bird."

They shouted at him in their own language, which he didn't understand. He stood up, ignoring their guns, hand at his side. They foolishly hadn't taken his knife. The motion worried them, and they stepped back, rifles both on him again. Good. But Sak was there, on his shoulder, wings out so one kept hitting his head. One rifle turned back to her.

"Point your gun *away from my bird*," Dusk said.

The other Ones Above watched with varied expressions. Dusk picked out their leader as the one with the most badges on his breast, with red hair on his head and metal pieces on his cheeks with small hoses attached to them, running under his nose. He looked like a bird, with hair like that. Under other circumstances, Dusk might have laughed. One of the leader's attendants stepped up and whispered something, pointing at Dusk. A tense moment passed.

Then the leader stapled on his own smile—he was somehow worse at it than Dusk was. When he spoke, the words were in Dusk's language. Even his lips moved correctly.

"Why, you're one of the people from the ocean planet!" the man said. "With your birds! You're no trespasser here! Ha, perish the thought. You're a welcome guest!"

He waved for the guards to lower their weapons, which they did immediately. The leader stepped forward, hands out, welcoming. "Now, now. How embarrassed you must be, to be caught in your lie. You people knew all along about the portal, did you? Ha! You certainly know how to bargain. On your way home, are you? Past the snake, through to the other side?"

Dusk didn't reply. The man seemed to think he knew everything, so why disabuse him?

"Come now," the man said, moving as if to put his arm around Dusk's shoulders. Sak glared at him, beak open and ready to snap, wings up. The man backed away. "Um, yes. Come now, friend. What was your name, again?"

"I am Sixth of the Dusk."

"Sixth, yes, Sixth. Let's get some refreshment, shall we? You've had a long journey, I must assume, since . . . well, I'll admit it. We've been here for three *weeks* studying this conundrum, and you couldn't possibly have slipped out while we were here. So you went out earlier than that?"

"I did," Dusk said. He *had* left more than three weeks ago. Why did the man assume he'd done so from this location?

Dusk collected Rokke, who hopped onto his shoulder with a little coaxing. Then he let the man lead him forward. He made it only a short distance before he saw it.

The god of all skullsnakes. Writhing ahead of him, filling a moat at the center of this atoll. He'd assumed the ones he'd seen earlier had been big, but this one . . .

Father. If they were dinghies, this was a steamship. It reared up, and he saw that she was a true snake—no bone protrusions marring her features. She unfurled a massive hood and opened a mouth that could have swallowed a battleship, with fangs as long as a person.

This was her. The Dakwara. The serpent whose length was said to stretch the ocean itself. Dusk grabbed his knife. A sign of respect and reverence for the demigod before him.

"That is a surprise," the leader of the Ones Above said, narrowing his eyes. "You didn't come from here? Then where?"

In that moment Dusk knew he *had* to protect the actual location of the portal. Otherwise this man would find it, claim it, and cut them off from this strange land. So he lied.

"We dream," Dusk said, "and in so dreaming, emerge into this place. Always, we must find our way home by defeating the Dakwara. The great serpent, demigod."

"The portal pulls you through, does it?" the man said. "Now *that* is interesting. Almost as interesting as your Invested birds. The Nahel bond, found in such a strange place as this. But what spirits do your birds bond to?"

"Spirits?" Dusk said.

"Yes, that's the way of it," the man said. "Spirits, or sprites, or whatever your local tongue might call them. That's how the birds get their uncanny abilities, is it not?"

Again, the man seemed to think he had the answers. Dusk gave him nothing further.

"Well," the man said, "how do you pass the serpent?"

"It is different for everyone," Dusk said, happy he could rely upon legends and speak the truth this time. "I do not know the way, but it is dangerous. She is . . . hungry."

"Oh, I know!" the man said.

Dusk cocked his head.

"We've lost three people to it," he explained. "Your snake god does not like it when people step past the line over there. Hard times, hard times. Lots of spousal pensions to pay." He paused, looking back at his friends—specifically, the woman who wasn't wearing a uniform. She watched with folded arms, and a guard had a gun subtly trained on her.

Interesting. What was the situation here?

"My name is Colonel Dajer," the man said to Dusk. "I have something I need to take care of, yah?" He slapped Dusk on the shoulder, and nearly got bitten. He glared at Sak before stapling on another imitation smile. "You go on ahead. I will leave orders that your things aren't to be touched! You're my guest here. I'd very much like to hear more of your legends, Sixth. If you're willing."

Dusk doubted that "willingness" had any relevance. But Patji had urged him to this quest, trained him, and given him a final blessing.

After that, this was where Dusk had come: following the shape of invisible waves to the Dakwara herself. At the very least, maybe there was something here to eat other than snake steaks and month-old rations—that would be a welcome change. And a bath . . . well, a bath would be *marvelous*.

He would play this man's game. Dusk might not be the best with words, but he felt he understood them better these days. Like the battered driftwood understood the waves. Unfortunately, before he could be led to a place where he could find drink, meat, or bath, shouting came from a building along the way.

He'd barely remarked on the strange structures here; he'd been too distracted by the presence of the Dakwara. Colonel Dajer and his guards went toward the disturbance, following the woman without the uniform. They didn't seem to be bothered by Dusk, or to even consider him a threat. They just left him there.

So, curious, he followed.

Fig. 9 • Kalofruit
(fruit)

CHAPTER THIRTY-EIGHT

Starling started running toward the *Dynamic.* That was *ZeetZi* shouting.

The Scadrian soldiers gave chase, guns on her. Dajer followed at a more casual stroll as she dashed over to the ship to find her crew—save Nazh and Chrysalis—in a line, under guard. That part wasn't unexpected, but one of the guards had a gun to Leonore's head while another held her arms from behind. ZeetZi was screaming at the guard, while others held weapons on him. Aditil stood back, looking terrified. Ed was backing up ZeetZi, though all he held was a large tome.

"Stop!" Starling said as she arrived. "What's going on?"

They all reoriented to her, and ZeetZi spoke first. "They're forcibly taking her, Captain! They ordered us down here in a line, and we complied. Now they're trying to sequester Leonore!"

Leonore sagged in the soldier's grip, resigned. She had her mask up and met Starling's eyes.

"Well, well," Dajer said, strolling up. "What is this? I asked only for them to be questioned."

"Sir!" one of the soldiers called. "I know this woman. She's a deserter. Former pilot!"

"Oh, is that so? Well, carry on with the execution then."

"*What?*" Starling demanded. "No! What if you're wrong? Even the Malwish aren't so callous!"

The order started a scuffle as Ed and ZeetZi tried to rescue Leonore. They got pushed away, and Leonore was shoved to the ground. Starling screamed, engaging the image of her soul—a brilliant white draconic figure—in hopes it might distract them. This time it didn't work. Barely anyone even looked.

At that moment something rose from the ground—a faintly transparent figure in antiquated clothing.

Nazh's eyes burned a sudden red.

"He's emerged!" Dajer snapped. "Go!"

Two soldiers that had been standing at the sides of the fight burst into motion as the one holding a gun toward Leonore ducked and rolled away. In a flash, the two newcomers had positioned themselves on either side of Nazh, who—naturally—was fighting his bloodlust. He always tried to back down when people fled.

The two soldiers raised weapons, unleashing columns of light some three feet wide—and catching Nazh in the center. Starling gasped. That was a light trap, shining Investiture that would act as a *solid* to a being like Nazh. Effectively, a way of binding him.

Another approached with a shade prison in the form of a large metal box with equipment inside. It took a lot of juice to engage it—the lights on several buildings flickered as the device drew Nazh in, transforming him to glowing white smoke. He screamed as he went, but the box held secure.

These devices weren't as effective as Rosharan fabrials, but the Scadrians tended to prefer their electronics.

Starling let her image vanish, trying to process all this. They'd been ready. They'd . . .

They'd lured Nazh out by threatening Leonore.

"That's it!" Dajer said. "Well *done*, everyone. Threat neutralized."

"You . . ." Starling looked to him. "You knew."

"We ran your ship profile the moment we spotted you," Dajer said. "Knew there was a shade on board before you landed. We had to capture *that*, of course." He waved to his soldiers, who rounded up the rest of the crew but made no further threats.

"Leonore?" Starling asked. "What are you going to do with her?"

"I'm far too preoccupied with changing the cosmere to bother with one defector," Dajer said. "So she'll share the same fate as the rest of them." He turned to Starling. "And that depends entirely on *you*." He smiled in his predatory way.

An aide trotted up, handing him a datapad and whispering something. Dajer turned it around, showing Starling a list of crewmembers. Her crewmembers.

Chrysalis wasn't on the list, blessedly. If they'd known about her . . . well, the reaction would have been even more extreme than the reaction to Nazh.

"What of this one?" Dajer asked, tapping the top.

"Crow?" Starling said. "Relieved of duty. I'm in command. She didn't come with us." She paused. "You can check easily; she'll still be in Silverlight."

"Run it through the spanreader," Dajer said to the aide. "Pay an information broker in Silverlight. Check to see if our draconic friend is telling the truth."

Starling watched them move and felt . . . trapped, her stomach in knots. Dajer had been playing her since they landed, pulling her away so the crew could be used to lure out Nazh. Shards.

"What are you going to do with him?" she asked as several soldiers carried away the prison, which was connected by a thick cord to the main power supply provided by the gunship. They weren't taking any chances.

"Again, I turn the question to you," Dajer said. "How eager are you to see him free?"

She fell quiet.

"Put my crew someplace," she finally said, "where they can relax and don't have guns on them. Then we'll talk."

Dusk didn't understand much of the display that had unfolded before him. But he took from it at least one valuable lesson: the Ones Above didn't all get along.

What had they just done, and how? Taken a person, turned them to light, and trapped them in a box? Almost, Dusk thought it a display to intimidate him, but the emotional reactions of the others seemed genuine, even if Dusk couldn't understand what anyone was saying.

Dajer, their leader, didn't seem to have emotions. Rather, he took them off and put new ones on, like a man might wear clothing. He gave some orders to his soldiers, and they led away the captives. All but the woman with the white skin, who the soldiers seemed more timid around.

The shape that had emerged from her. What had it been? She was protected by some . . . glowing bird? He knew so little. She turned and stalked past Dajer, then noticed Dusk again. Her eyes narrowed and she brushed past him, pressing something into his fingers.

"Whoever you are," she whispered, somehow, in his language. "Be careful with these people. This will let you speak their tongue. Think that you need to speak it, and it will happen. Put it somewhere it can touch your skin."

She walked off then, joined by guards, who didn't seem to notice what she'd done. Dusk turned over the item in his fingers, feeling it without displaying it. A medallion, like the one he wore? No. A coin, perhaps?

Dajer approached, and Dusk tucked the coin into his waistband, against his skin. Dajer put on a fake smile and again tried to put his arm around Dusk. Again, the birds would have none of that.

"Come with me, Sixth," the man said. "Let's chat some more. Are you hungry?"

"Yes," Dusk admitted.

"And surely you have questions."

"I have many."

"Well, out with them! Speak up."

Dajer. What an odd name, pronounced with a strange cadence and inflection. He expected something from Dusk, who hadn't moved despite the man trying to lead him toward one of the buildings close by.

Beyond them a number of flying ships—like the one the emissaries had left in—were pointed toward the sky. They seemed far too small to have carried the large central structure into place.

"These buildings," Dusk said, pointing. "You told me you've been here for only three weeks, yet these look well-built. How did you move them here and erect them so quickly?"

"Buildings . . ." Dajer said, then he laughed. "Oh, you primitives are wonderful." He touched one of the metal bits that covered the side of his face. "Kallib? You're scheduled for a scouting flight, correct? When? Excellent. Yes, if you don't mind . . ."

Dusk watched the exchange, then realized something. He had understood that part, even though Dajer had most certainly been speaking in another language. He put his hand down to touch the little coin. Whatever it was, it worked.

Nearby, one of their ships lifted into the sky. Dajer looked to him expectantly. As if he should be awed by . . .

Ah. He didn't realize Dusk recognized that as a ship. He was making a display. Which meant . . . "That large structure is a ship too," Dusk said, nodding. "They don't all look the same."

His assumptions had misled him; that happened sometimes when you were figuring things out. But why would their ships look the same? They didn't need to cut through water, so why would they need a prow or a keel?

His question had served a purpose, then. He should ask more, perhaps, as Vathi always said. It was just that observation and figuring it out yourself was . . . well, it involved less noise.

Dajer seemed disappointed at Dusk's lack of awe. Even the birds weren't impressed, preening quietly, as if to project indifference. Sak didn't like the idea of things that could fly without feathers. She found them offensive.

"These," Dajer said, waving, "are the very best fighters in all of the cosmere. They can maneuver on conventional aether engines, of course, but get them on a battlefield up in space and . . ." He kissed his fingers. Did he love himself that much? "With starship anchors placed in a proper steelfield, these fighters can Push and Pull with extreme accuracy and nimbleness, outmaneuvering any *ordinary* ship. No one can withstand them in battle."

That was a whole pile of words. The kind that heaped atop one another, smothering the ones before. Really, all Dusk took from it was that Dajer felt the need to brag about his fighters. Which meant there was someone out there who stood against him. Dusk wondered how they'd tell him that *their* fighters were the best.

"But come along," Dajer said. "If you please." He opened the door to one of the pods, and inside—on a smooth metal table—Dusk spotted plates of fruit. He could not help salivating.

"You eat fruit, I take it?" Dajer said. "Scout reports say that whatever Shard created your planet placed some familiar foods for you."

"Our world was created by Patji," Dusk said, walking into the building—wary for a trap, as always. "He gave power to the Dakwara—whom you've met—and she birthed the islands we live upon. Then once it was good, the other gods came down and became islands to join Patji."

"Charming." Dajer entered and shut the door.

No traps. Dusk still inspected the room before going to the food. Bookshelves. A desk. A board with writing on it, though he didn't think it was a chalkboard, and he saw no charcoal or pens. Carpet. Who put carpet in a ship? The Ones Above, apparently.

Two exits, plus windows that he doubted he could break. They were, after all, for traveling quickly through the sky—they'd be of thick glass. He took a kalofruit, which was long, thin, and orange. Picked it up by the tip of the rind and turned it all the way around to look for deathants.

Dajer watched him with an amused expression. Though when the man thought Dusk *wasn't* looking, he eyed the Aviar hungrily.

Dusk picked out three fruits that were free of insects, then settled down at the desk.

"That's . . . my chair," Dajer said.

"I know. It will be the safest spot in the room."

"Safest spot . . ." Dajer laughed. "You are an interesting man, Sixth."

Dusk gave no reply, as that wasn't a question. Though he did note to himself that he didn't *want* to be interesting. He'd tried his entire life to *avoid* being interesting. Interesting people drew attention, and attention killed you on Patji.

Sak chirped softly.

"Rubbish bin?" Dusk asked.

"Right there," Dajer said, arms folded as he leaned against the nearby wall. "To your left, underneath."

Dusk held Sak over it so that she could do her business. He then offered the same to Rokke, who didn't seem to want to go—she was watching Dajer like she would a scorpion, expecting its stinger at any moment.

Still, she puffed out her feathers and let a dropping out once he encouraged her. From there, he set both birds on Dajer's desk. He gave a chunk of fruit to each one before letting himself have any.

Father. It tasted wonderful—the sweetness nearly set his mouth aflame. Had he grown so soft on the homeisles that a month on rations left him panting for a little sugar? He peeled a second fruit, and watched Dajer. Perhaps being so forward as Dusk had been was rude, but he was a trapper, and the man had offered his safecamp as respite. A rare privilege among those who tried to kill one another.

Rudeness, in this case, was a sign of accepting the hospitality. That was true regardless of what homeislers and their stupid rules of etiquette said. Vathi *still* hadn't gotten over that time she'd invited Dusk to a senator's home, and he'd gone off to sleep in the man's bed during the party.

"They are so *fascinating*," Dajer said, watching the birds. "And highly valuable, if you didn't know. But of course you *do* know. We've tried trading for them. Not one has been released to us, despite the fact that the scouts report there are plenty to go around. *You* even have *two*. Curious."

Dusk kept eating.

"I thought they were a story when I first heard of them," Dajer continued. "Birds who grant powers, like they're some kind of medallion? Like they're *metal*. Nonsense, I thought. Arcanists *do* like their tales of strange manifestations of Investiture. Yet I read reports. I saw footage. Then I believed. Now, here they are."

Dusk again fingered the coin the woman had given him. Medallions and metal were some kind of technology to these people, were they? Interesting, the things you could learn without questions if you let someone fill the air with their thoughts.

"I know about the coin, by the way," Dajer said. "One of my soldiers saw her give it to you. I let you keep it so you can understand some of the wonders we offer."

Dusk nodded in thanks, because that was generous.

"I need to know why your people are being so stubborn," Dajer said. "Why they continue to stall, and stall, and stall."

Bless Vathi with each of Patji's blessings. She was *still stalling*.

"We knew you were hiding a portal," Dajer said, wandering past the fruit bowl. "Impossibly, you have a perpendicularity on your planet. Reports exist of those birds on Roshar, in the past. This means some of them *had* to have gotten offworld before the modern era."

"How?"

Dajer paused, as if surprised to hear Dusk finally speak. Then he smiled. "How what?"

"How would anyone have found our world?" Dusk asked. "Through this darkness?"

"By luck," Dajer said. "Navigation here, as I'm sure you know, is virtually impossible. You're lucky your god dropped you within sight of the island here. If you'd needed to cross the true darkness of the unsea . . . well, you'd wander forever, and die. Regardless, we have reports of people finding this island—then losing it. In the deep past, perhaps some of your people traveled through and got very, very lucky in finding civilization beyond the darkness."

Ah. So the Ones Above could not sense the way in here, at least not easily. They could not read the waves of that current that, even still, Dusk felt pulsing softly. He knew that he was unique in Patji's blessing, but perhaps there were other gods, with other blessings from other places. If so, however, these people did not have them.

"Who is that woman with the white skin?" Dusk asked. "And why did you lock away the people who were with her?"

"Ah, but it's my turn," Dajer said. "I answered truthfully. You'll do me the same service, won't you?"

That was a trouble with questions. But it *was* a fair request, and Dajer *had* invited Dusk into his safecamp. This man was a snake, but snakes had their uses. Some were food along the path. Others created the oceans.

"You arrived on a boat coated across the bottom in Investiture," Dajer said. "Where did you get it?"

"Investiture?"

"The glowing energy."

Dusk thought of the jar he'd left among his gear. Like a fool. The man smiled, and though he didn't say it, Dusk knew that his people had thoroughly searched Dusk's things—and found the jar. Despite saying they'd leave his belongings alone.

"It comes from the pool you seek," Dusk admitted. He knew too little to lie, but just enough to tell the truth.

"Why is it applied to a mash?" Dajer said.

"That's how we get it," Dusk said with a shrug.

"So the portal is beyond the serpent," Dajer said, "but you've already visited it?"

"On the other side, I did," Dusk said—another truth. "We have only recently discovered it. I am one of the caretakers of the place where it is found." He held out his hand. "I would like my glowing mash back. I will tell you more."

Dajer studied him, then tapped the metal on his face and whispered a command. A moment later, a soldier entered and handed the jar to Dusk. They would have taken a sample, of course. Dusk would have done the same.

"My god," he said, "is Patji, the island."

"I thought your god was a snake."

"The snake serves my god," Dusk explained patiently. "After she created the waters, my god then made his home in the ocean." He held up the jar. "I serve on the island as a trapper. I care for Aviar, the birds. I used to bring them home, to my people, but . . ."

"But . . ."

"I feel this is more than one question," Dusk said, "that you have asked me."

Dajer laughed. It did not reach his eyes. "The 'woman' is very dangerous—she might look human, but she belongs to a race of thieves who are very difficult to hurt or kill. She's a treasure hunter, and tried to sneak up on us to claim your portal for herself. To plunder your people. You will note that *we* have not *forced* you to do anything. *We* are trustworthy."

It was mostly true. Except for the fact that they'd sent devices that were deliberately designed to hide their purpose and spy on his people. And the fact that they were starving the Eelakin for supplies, once offered freely. And the fact that they had *let Kokerlii die* by withholding medicine until it was obvious how bad the plague would be. Until *they* could be the ones who saved everyone.

Dusk seethed at this man's tone, and more at what his people had done, but kept it to himself. Either way, Dusk was certain that something *compelled* them not to steal from his people. Other powers, opposed to them, kept them in check. Perhaps powers like those of the glowing knight who had flown into the sky.

"A treasure hunter?" Dusk said.

"Intending to rob your people."

He liked treasure hunters. Some of the greatest trappers in history had been treasure hunters. He and the woman were kindred, then. He would have to be careful not to trust her. She'd be the type who knew when to perform a calculated betrayal.

"I am no longer needed as a trapper," Dusk explained. "My way of life is over. We industrialize, and raise Aviar in large Aviaries with fleets of caretakers. I am a relic." He touched the jar. "Perhaps that is why Patji decided I should go on this quest. I'm expendable."

"It's a difficult thing, isn't it?" Dajer said. "To lack purpose?"

"It hurts," Dusk admitted, "like no sting or venom I've ever experienced. To be unneeded is a wound . . ." He tapped his chest. "A wound deep in here."

"I know that wound," Dajer said, tossing up a fruit and catching it. "I was a soldier. Ground combat. Fought in the Battle of Aheleha. They burned the very sky around us . . . So much smoke . . . Like it was suddenly midnight, and the darkness was strangling us . . ."

Dusk remained quiet. This seemed the sort of old pain that a platitude couldn't fix, while silence could reverence.

"Well, that was it for my frontline days," Dajer said, then stroked his side mask. The hoses that extended from the metal portions released a small hiss of gas in front of his nose. "I need these to function now. Without them, I'd be wheezing on the ground, my lungs enflamed."

"So . . . you're no longer a soldier?"

"Oh, I'm very much still a soldier. I've evolved into a different kind." He pointed to one of the insignia patches on his chest. "Military engineer corps."

Dusk knew of engineers. But military engineers? "You . . . design weapons?"

"Ha! So innocent. No, no. Not *that* kind of engineering. I build structures. Or I remove them." He tossed the fruit, then caught it again. "In my old brigade, they didn't fully use the talents of men like myself. I was simply another grunt with a gun. Now I'm a full colonel, and I *order around* the grunts. Purpose. You see how important it is?"

"Your purpose is . . . ordering people around?"

"That's but a means to an end! My purpose, dear friend, is to deal with *obstructions*." He caught the fruit, then smashed it in his hand—but instead of squishing, the pressure expertly forced the flesh inside out the two ends, where he could pluck each piece and eat it. He tossed the rind into the bin nearby. Sak tried to catch it as it passed.

As he chewed, Dajer walked to the shelf and took a very large metal nut—for keeping a bolt in place—from where it held up some books. It was as big as his fist, and heavy, from the way he hefted it. He dropped it with a thump on the desk in front of Dusk.

"That's a nut," he said, "for holding together two max-weight structural girders. In this case, it was applied to a bolt on the Hannerdam Bridge, just outside the great city on my homeworld. The bridge was a bold, brilliant engineering project that was supposed to greatly speed up traffic in and out of the city—which it did. Until the bridge collapsed with much of that traffic still on it."

Dusk hefted the nut. "Forgot to put this on?"

"No, but the team didn't bind them tightly enough," Dajer explained. "Forgot the washers, didn't double-check their work. The engineer was fired halfway through the project for spending too much—and they went with a lesser." He nodded. "I keep it. That nut is both a reminder to double-check our work, and a reminder of the value of a good engineer.

"My people's empire is like that bridge. It has the same purpose: getting people from where they are to where they need to be. Every little bolt and nut in the contraption is *vitally* important, but only if it does its job *right*. My job, my little piece of it all, is bridging the gaps. That's why I need you."

"For our portal," Dusk said. "And our birds."

"Oh, that's not why *I'm* here. Negotiators can handle the contracts; we all know the birds will be for sale soon. The question is cost, price, and how long you can pretend you don't need what we're offering."

For sale soon? His birds would *never* be for sale to outsiders.

Dajer tapped the nut. "We need a waystop in this region, Sixth. A friendly anchorage, you might say."

"A safecamp," Dusk said, checking his anger again. He could deal with someone he detested. He'd met trappers before in the homeisles, and been forced to interact with people he would have otherwise killed. "Every trapper needs a safecamp."

"Exactly! You get it. The presence of the birds caused quite a stir among my people, then we realized the implications. Someone had gotten birds off your world *before* the days of space travel. *That* meant a portal. *That* meant an opportunity.

"I have spent incredible resources searching Shadesmar near your planet for the portal," Dajer said. "I've stuck out my neck, bet my entire career on it existing. But the unsea out here is unpredictable, and navigation so difficult. Even with all I spent—each day having more trouble convincing my superiors to let me continue—I found nothing. Only a tip from an arcanist friend a few weeks back led me to this specific island, after someone discovered an ancient map."

Dusk quietly fed more fruit to the Aviar.

"I am here," Dajer said, "because I have a specialty. I am the remover of obstructions, the builder of bridges. You can help me, Sixth."

"Help you," he said, "enslave my people."

Dajer hesitated, perhaps realizing he'd gone too far. He stapled on another smile. "If your people have access to an unattended perpendicularity—undiscovered, unknown, uncontrolled—then congratulations. You've entered galactic politics in a dramatic way, and there's no going back. You feel obsolete, Sixth? Well, that just happened to your *entire planet*. So. Time to find a new purpose. Quickly. That is how we help each other."

He stepped closer, offering a bit of fruit to the Aviar. Neither would take it. Rokke was scared near to death of this man—as evidenced by her pooping on the desk, despite having recently gone. A flight mechanism in birds, making herself lighter so she could escape more easily. Dusk clicked his tongue softly, a soothing sound to most Aviar.

Not that they weren't in danger. It merely wasn't the type you could escape by running.

"I know what happened to you, Sixth," Dajer said, leaning down near him, hand on the table, eating the bit of fruit the birds wouldn't take. "I know the parts you *aren't* telling me. You stepped into the pool deliberately, didn't you? To go on this spirit quest? That's why you have the jar of Investiture. Why you have a boat.

"I'm curious how when you pass through, you drop into the general region, not the exact location of the portal. That's not unheard of, as the overlap between Shadesmar and the Physical Realm is askew. Still, most full-blown perpendicularities work as a stabilizing point on the map, a place where the two realms overlap identically."

Dusk didn't understand much of that, but he did know that Dajer was still making a single, terrible miscalculation. Like Dusk had done when mistaking the ship for a building. In this case, Dajer assumed that the portal must be near, because he'd found a location that contained a spectacular monster. And surely the Dakwara would be guarding *something*.

It wasn't the portal. Dajer had come to a simple, but wrong, conclusion. He'd combined that with another, which was also very reasonable: that no man like Dusk could find his way in the darkness. Seeing Dusk here, then, reinforced the previous belief. If a primitive man was floating about in the region, the portal *must* be nearby.

A faulty belief built of reasonable logical leaps. Dusk had to be very, *very* careful not to disabuse the Ones Above of their incorrect ideas. Doing so immediately became almost as important as bringing proof back to Vathi.

He didn't have that proof yet. Yes, he could travel the darkness, but she needed more: evidence that this strange place could offer valid opportunities worth denying the Ones Above. So far, he'd found those same people here, which didn't seem encouraging. However, Patji had sent him on this task; he had to assume he could find what his people needed.

Dusk *was* expendable. Trappers *were* dying. But he was going to do something important as he heaved his last gasps.

"It hurts," Dajer said, "thinking about all of this? Knowing what your people must go through?"

"Yes," Dusk admitted.

"You want things to be as they were before?"

"Is there . . . a way?" Dusk asked, feeling foolish as he asked it. He'd learned this lesson from Vathi, years before on Patji. Expressing a wish for something he knew he couldn't have—perhaps *shouldn't* have—was childish.

It made Dajer's smile genuine. He walked to the writing board on the wall and tapped it. The words vanished as if by magic, then the entire wall became a window into another world.

Dusk found that interesting.

He stood, absently picking up a bird in each hand, crossing the room to the window. It showed a place with tall buildings, and many small vehicles flying on what seemed to be roadways in the sky. Electric lights in a variety of colors illuminated bustling people with a variety of ethnic features and distinctive clothing.

"My homeworld," Dajer noted.

"Is this a portal?" Dusk asked softly. "Can we go there?"

Dajer laughed. "What a delight you are. No, this is a viewing device only." He tapped the window, and it changed to another sight. Then another, then another, then another.

Each seemed to be a different world. Different suns, different dress, different architecture. Some had vehicles that flew; others had dirt roads, with vehicles pulled by beasts. One world had oceans and pale people who had four arms. Were these the albinos from the stories? Another had flowers like from his homeworld, though the people's skin was a coppery color. They wore colors of beautiful variety.

"Does it make you feel small?" Dajer asked. "Seeing all of this? For centuries, your people assumed they were alone. Center of the cosmere, with important gods who paid attention to you only. But see, there are dozens like you. Hundreds. Worlds like the stars of the sky. You are so, so small."

Why . . . would that make Dusk feel small?

He frowned at this idea. He'd already *known* he was small. He'd sailed the oceans, knowing that one turn of the weather could sink him, with no word of it reaching any person who knew him. He'd huddled with his birds as shadows the size of buildings moved beneath the waves. He'd trapped *Patji*, the island that killed even its fondest children.

Who cared if the cosmere was big? The ocean was big, and Dusk couldn't even comprehend *that*.

"I know what this does to a person," Dajer said, tapping again, lingering on a planet where enormous, ghostly apparitions dominated the skyline. "I have a special interest in visiting primitives. *Some* of those to whom I show these wonders overcome their fear. They are daunted, yes, but decide they *have* to explore it. Visit each land in turn. Discover new ones, and new peoples living on them."

If there were people in those lands, it seemed to Dusk they'd have already discovered themselves.

"You could be that person," Dajer whispered. "I see in you the soul of an explorer, Sixth. I know you. I know you thirst for new experiences. Wouldn't you like to be the *first* to go to some world?"

There was . . . a little truth to this final assumption. Crossing the darkness, as his ancestors had, invigorated Dusk. He put his fingers to the Cakoban medallion. Once, all he'd wanted was for everything to stay the same, but now he needed a challenge. A new danger to tame.

He didn't necessarily want to visit these places, though. Seemed like strangers from another world coming to visit wouldn't be good for them, any more than the Ones Above visiting had been good for his people.

Except it was good, in some ways, he thought. *We have new medicines, new technology.* If only there had been a way to acquire such advances *without* reaching into a nest of asps to snare them.

"I asked if you wanted life to go back to how it was before," Dajer said, finally shifting the screen—uncomfortably—to a picture of the senate building of Dusk's own world. Seen from some distance above, but still very recognizable. "What do you think?"

"We can't go back," Dusk whispered. Sak cooed, sensing the pain in his voice, but he'd already confronted this. He lived with it now. "Dusk has come. We must look for new dawns, not old sunsets."

"That's right, Sixth," Dajer said, nodding in approval. "Change is inevitable—and you won't be the only one who suffers upheaval by the future. See those lights on your world? Gas, I assume?"

"Yes."

"Self-lighting electric lights are coming. What will happen to the man who lights the gas lamp each night?"

"He will be like me," Dusk said. "It's already begun."

"I offer you a place with my people. Join me, traveling to new worlds."

There *was* something tempting in this. Someone needed to visit these lands, learn of them, and decide if they were a threat. But was that for him? If he could not find a purpose among his own kind, what made him think there would be one for him out among the stars?

"I like you, Sixth," Dajer said. "I like your bluntness. Your uncivilized, simple sense of pure morality."

Did Dajer . . . think people were *honest* because they were less *advanced* in technology? Did he think that people on Dusk's planet were somehow *nicer* than ones from the stars?

It was an incredibly stupid perspective. It stood out in this man, who was otherwise so calculating and expert at maneuvering conversations. This flaw in Dajer was like a long scratch, leaking water, in an otherwise well-crafted hull.

But Dusk supposed everyone had their flaws; that was part of what made them people. And not . . . beings from some story, with an "uncivilized, simple sense of pure morality." Dajer had exposed a weakness to be exploited; Dusk could only hope that he had not unwittingly done the same thing.

Dajer seemed to make a decision, clapping his hands once. "I'm going to show you something, Sixth. Something extremely interesting. You've never been on this island before, yes? You knew about the serpent, but you'd never seen it?"

"That is correct," Dusk said.

"Do you know about the cave?"

"What cave?"

"The cave," Dajer said, "of death."

Fig. 30 · Deathants
(insect)

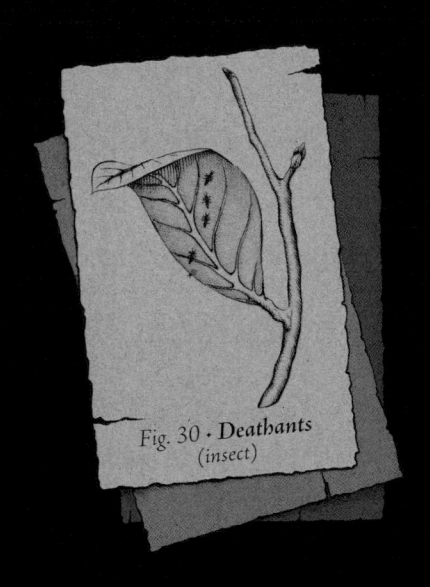

CHAPTER THIRTY-NINE

Cave of Death.

Dusk liked the name. Vathi had an entire *team* who decided how to name things, and they always shied away from names that were too descriptive. They said things like, "A name like that is too on the nose." Or, "That's the first thing you'd think of. We need something more inventive." Or simply, "That's boring."

Names of places *should* be boring. They *should* be descriptive. Hearing the name should tell you what the place is for, what it's like, or what to expect from it. And, as he found out, this *was* a cave of death. Three soldiers had died in it so far.

Though perhaps "cave" was inaccurate. It was a tunnel, burrowed into the black-coral rock of the island. There was a rise here, a hillside, and the tunnel broke out one end of it—leading downward at a shallow angle. Lights illuminated it for a while, but the rest was lost to shadows.

"We think it must run underneath the moat in the atoll here," Dajer said, pointing. "It then comes out, I'll bet, on that island at the center, providing a secret passageway past the serpent."

Dusk knelt at the mouth of the tunnel. It looked natural, rather than carved by human hands, and . . . were those *plants* growing inside? Yes, thick fronds, lush, near the lights. The air that came out of the cavern was humid, and smelled earthy. Familiar.

"Certainly," Dajer said, "it lets out *somewhere*. Otherwise, there wouldn't be that breeze."

"You think there is an island beyond the Dakwara?" Dusk asked.

"We know there is," Dajer said. "We've surveyed it by ship, but that *thing* attacked. It chews through ship hulls—and shields of all sorts, whether they be Allomantic bullet shields, Awakened deflection shields, or even Aonic force fields. I did *not* like being forced to write a loss report on one of our starfighters. Expensive, particularly these days."

"The Dakwara pulled the islands up from the ocean," Dusk said. "You are surprised she is strong?"

"Ah, Sixth," Dajer said. "You have no idea what an Invested entity even is, do you? To you, it's some god of myth."

"It ate your ship," Dusk said. "I will worship it over you. Is there anything on the island in the center?"

"A cavern like this one," Dajer said. "We flew below this larger island, and found portions of stone under the surface that connect to the center. One might contain a tunnel. This tunnel."

Dusk nodded, then started walking into the cave.

"Sixth, my friend!" Dajer said. "I *just* told you that this place killed three people!"

"Your soldiers placed those lights," Dusk said. "And there is soil there, with many footprints. The danger starts beyond."

"Well, I suppose it does! Clever man!" Dajer laughed.

Dusk hated that sound. It was the laugh of a man who had never had to care what his noises did to other people.

It felt good when Dusk's boot hit soil, maybe ten feet inside the opening. He continued another ten until he reached the lights. The tunnel became taller here, and short trees grew from the rock, accompanied by a variety of ferns, vines—overgrown foliage of all varieties.

Where did the plants get light to grow? Or water? It was *mystifying*. Worse, it smelled of home. Of rain, and the ponds stagnating beneath a canopy that blocked light. Of things dead, becoming loam, and of things living that feasted upon it. Of bark, and moss.

Sak squawked softly, and she was the *real* reason Dusk felt little fear coming this far. His corpse was only *beyond* this portion. He thought he'd seen it earlier, and now he could make it out easily, his foot sticking out from some fronds ahead, his hand flopped to the loam, his dead eyes barely visible in the shadows.

He stooped down, wishing he had his pack and a walking stick to turn over soil, stones, or fronds. Still, he could get the angle to look underneath the frond and find—crawling there—a handful of tiny black insects.

Deathants. Here, surviving somehow. Those lived *only* on Patji, or so he'd thought.

Footsteps thumped on soil behind him, and he turned to note Dajer himself approaching—though the man's soldiers remained outside, hovering by the mouth of the tunnel.

"They're afraid," Dajer said softly. He took a deep breath, and Dusk could just hear a faint hiss from the tubes by his nose. "I cannot afford to lose any more soldiers. Six dead already. Three to the snake—one of those in a ship—and three in here. If I lose a seventh, I'll be subject to a mandatory external review."

"What killed those who came inside?" Dusk asked.

"The first one died to some kind of insect," Dajer said. "The rest . . . well, whatever it was, it made them scream." He held up some mechanical device. "It's remarkable. We were able to remain in audio contact, but *every* kind of drone or camera we send into this place *stops transmitting*." He squatted near Dusk and muttered, "Cursed nephilim."

"Nephilim?"

"Eidoliths. Splinters of Ambition. Pieces of the Evil. Snake gods. Entities. Whatever you prefer to call them." He shook his device. "None of the rules ever seem to work around them . . . Even our most advanced healing devices just . . . give out . . ."

Dusk nodded in understanding. Dajer seemed the type of man who appreciated it when things worked as he wanted them to. In a way, Dusk could empathize. His own life had been upended by the world refusing to work by expected rules.

Not that he *liked* the man, of course. Dajer was a bigoted opportunist, looking to take Dusk's people and enslave them. However, he was also a man who would walk into this tunnel when all of his soldiers—presumably brave men and women—stayed outside. That was worthy of respect.

"You see the specks moving on the underside of that frond?" Dusk asked.

"Barely."

"Deathants," Dusk said. "Deadly."

"They're barely motes of dust!"

"Yes," Dusk said. "That, over there, is a hive-scorpion burrow. Their stings can go through an inch of rubber, so don't step on them. And that tree beyond there? That is nightwind fungus on the bark—it releases deadly spores if you lean against it. Defense mechanism."

Dajer looked to him, and for once seemed to show genuine emotion in the horror on his face. "How do you know this?"

"They are all common," Dusk said, "where I'm from."

"*Common?* How do you survive?"

"Many do not."

Dajer gaped at him. Rokke peeked out from underneath Dusk's ponytail—where she'd been hiding and hanging on the collar of his shirt—and opened her mouth at the foreigner. Warding him back. She was too big to hide properly, but that didn't stop her.

Dusk, however, was *worried*.

This should not be. None of this should be. The deadly protections of Patji should not be here. He needed to think.

"Sixth," the man said, "can you travel this tunnel?"

"Yes." He might die, of course. But he could travel it, at least some distance.

"Could you . . . lead some of my soldiers through it?"

"They would almost certainly die," Dusk said. "Taking care of those who have no knowledge of the jungle would be . . . eventful for a few minutes. Then silent. I am not so good a trapper that I can lead a group of neophytes."

That, of course, reminded him of Vathi, whom he missed. Dusk had never had friends before her. He had never wanted friends. He had one now. And he missed her.

I should not have been so difficult during our last days together, he thought.

Then amended the thought. *I should not have been so difficult to her during all of our days together.*

She had survived Patji, but only after careful study. To get a group of offworlders through this? He assumed they'd be able to learn—people were people—but it would take *months*.

"If I were to train your soldiers to traverse this tunnel," Dusk said, thoughtful, "could you promise me, in writing with authority, that your people would leave mine alone and stop trying to dominate us?"

"Of course," Dajer said immediately. "How long would it take?"

So. He would lie to Dusk if it suited him. That had seemed obvious, but it was still good to check.

"Months," Dusk said. "Perhaps years." He narrowed his eyes at the tunnel. "But perhaps a simpler accommodation at first. I travel through this, and see if it leads where you want. If it does, we can speak of your greater promises."

"Excellent! I'll need you to take some recording equipment."

Dusk thought that sort of machinery didn't work, but perhaps recording was different than transmitting.

Naturally, Dajer didn't trust Dusk. Men who were untrustworthy had that problem. Well, Dusk considered. Then considered some more. Long enough that he knew most people, Dajer included, would find his considering uncomfortable.

"I will need time to think," Dusk said. "Then we can discuss my payment."

"Freedom for your people?"

"No, not yet," Dusk said. "Something smaller. Payment to me, which *you* can deliver."

"Sixth, my friend," Dajer said. "I'm allowing you access to my tunnel. Free of charge. Now you want me to pay you?"

His tunnel. Like the people of the homeisles, presuming to own a piece of land. Dajer couldn't *own* this land, as it was occupied. By a glowing serpent, for one.

Still, Dusk stood. "I will require payment. It will be small. Something you personally can pay."

Dajer sighed. "We'll see."

"For now, a place to rest, please. Some more fruit and the things from my boat. All of them."

Dajer rose and met his eyes. The little tubes under his nose made a hissing sound.

"Gladly," Dajer said. "You are, of course, my honored guest." He paused. "Is there something we can . . . put at the mouth of this cavern to keep those ants in?"

"If they haven't come out to kill you already," Dusk said, "they won't do so. I suspect they have enough to feed on for some time, now that they have your dead. Come. Show me the accommodations. I've apparently grown soft, because I'm actually tired of sleeping in a boat."

Fig. 82 · Glowing butterfly (insect)

CHAPTER FORTY

Starling did her best to avoid soldiers. She understood why they were needed, but . . . they made her uncomfortable. Her people had once raised armies against one another, making mortals fight on their behalf. Plus, one of the greatest duties of a soldier was to be obedient. That unnerved her.

Colonel Dajer left the strange tunnel and delivered the man who carried birds to some soldiers, who led him away. Then Dajer strolled up to her.

"Shall we chat, dragon?" he asked.

When they entered his office, the guards did not join them—though they did remain outside, ready to respond to a cry for help.

"You should know," Dajer said, sitting and tapping on his datapad, "that I respect your people greatly, Illistandrista. You in particular interest me, as the former companion of the most famous man in all the cosmere. The fool himself." He wrote a little more. "I do not fancy you lying about your age. Deception sets us off on the wrong foot."

So he did know her. Not surprising. How many leucistic dragons were there?

He looked up, face calm, and waited.

"Why," she said, "do you respect us?"

"There were no greater builders in history than the Yolish dragonkind," Dajer said, tapping his pad so an image appeared on his wall screen. The grand ivory city of Lar'Cal—built high along the glittering skyways of Yolen, far above the wild forests. Constructed by her people during their primordial service to Adonalsium, before the rivalry between the fain and the unfain. Long before she'd been born, back before even Master Hoid had been born. When Frost had been a youth.

Seeing it made her soul hurt. She stepped toward the screen, despite herself. The city had stood through disaster, war, upheaval, and the death of God itself. Its alabaster towers had seen millennia come and go, and she'd begun to despair ever seeing it in person again.

"The cities," he said, "the skyways. The palaces in Shadesmar, beyond the perpendicularity, at Silverlight. Even before we knew that Yolen was the source of all the Shards and of humankind, humans revered you. Your people were once the greatest builders and creators of all the cosmere. Once."

"It is for the best that we withdrew," she said softly, pulling her eyes away from the screen. "We caused others to stagnate—or worse, to bleed."

"And Xisis, your current master?" Dajer said. "Did he withdraw?"

Shards, he knew so much. Officially, all dragons had retreated from political life—they engaged in civil affairs, researched on their own, or kept to their religious duties. And yet, as Dajer seemed to know full well, few of her kin *kept* to that ideal, except in the loosest interpretation.

"What do you want?" she said. "What will it take to get you to let my crew go?"

"Now that," he said, clasping hands on his table, "is a problem. I will not play games with you, dragon. I've had dealings with your kind, and know how little you appreciate human attempts at familiarity. I also acknowledge and recognize your racial insistence on interactions you perceive as fair."

Every people wanted to be treated fairly, not just hers—but he was referencing the dragon penchant for bargains. Assuming, as many did, it was an innate part of them rather than learned behavior reinforced

ISLES OF THE EMBERDARK

over time. Many of her kind had stoked this particular stereotype, so she didn't blame Dajer for the perception. It was an odd thing to fight against what even some of your own kind had internalized as a truth.

"I am on the cusp of greatness," Dajer said. "According to the map that led you here, you are looking for the same thing I am. Your crew, therefore, knows something exceptionally dangerous: that a perpendicularity to the planet Drominad does indeed exist."

"That's the survey name," she replied. "What do the people there call it?"

"They call it First of the Sun," he said. "It's unwieldy to name things by local standards in our records, however. Every planet would be named 'planet'! But this is a tangent. Illistandrista—"

"Call me by my second name. Starling."

He sighed. "That is demonstrably less grand."

"As am I"—she raised her manacled hands—"these days."

"Very well, Starling," he said. "I have decided that I should like to have you on my staff."

She blinked. "Your . . . staff?"

"I have need of an aide-de-camp."

"I . . . doubt I'd be good in that role, Colonel."

"You're an immortal dragon trained by one of the most dangerous, and unfortunately knowledgeable, beings in all of existence. You know more than any mortal alive, I suspect." He stood up behind his desk and leaned forward. "And your kind demand respect."

"You want me to be a showpiece," she said. "To improve your stature among your peers."

"I want to hire the best I can find. Should a man not aspire to greatness?"

"Depends," she said, "on how far he can risk falling."

"What would it take?"

"More than you can offer."

"More than your crew delivered safely home once news of the discovery here becomes commonplace?"

"That could take decades," she said. "We both know that the Malwish will keep this secret as long as feasible."

"That is true," he said. "But Starling, you are immortal and virtually indestructible. Your crew is not, and many of them are criminals. You travel with an unbound shade, yah? I would not wish to be in your position, and I know how much dragons care for their followers."

She stared him down, using the tactics her master had taught her. However, inwardly she was sweating—as always. Did these kinds of negotiations ever get easier?

Dajer nodded to her wrists. "Sign a fixed contract of twenty years with me, entering service as a hired professional aide with strictly listed duties, not to be infringed or expanded by myself or any others. You would find it an invigorating position. I am soon to be one of the most important people in all of the cosmere."

If he found a new perpendicularity, then he was not exaggerating. The Malwish would own it, but the one who brought them that wealth would be powerful indeed.

But the idea of *service* and a *contract* made her stomach churn. Master Hoid would never have taken her on if she were the kind to agree to those kinds of constraints. She lived with manacles on her wrists only by force.

"I," Dajer said, "can remove those manacles."

This gave her pause. Why in all of creation would he make such a claim? "Don't be ridiculous," she said. "Nobody can, other than my elders."

"Do not be so quick to assume what can and cannot be done," he said. "The dragons have stagnated. Once, they flew, and mortals walked. Now any child with a coin can soar as they did—and even the gods tremble before what mortals create. I *can* take those manacles off. Scadrial is the most technologically advanced planet in all the cosmere."

Did you clear that claim with Taldain? she thought. *Or better, the planets Invention created? And for all your technological prowess, your ships run on aether.*

She didn't say any of this. She didn't need to antagonize him, and the Scadrians *did* tend to be proud of their mechanical wonders.

"You don't believe me," he said. "About the manacles."

"It's an extraordinary claim."

He tapped his datapad. The wall screen changed to a view of a crystalline cavern, with walls lined in silver. Dragonsteel, she realized, moving closer. One of the ancestral caverns? Which keeper would allow a camera to . . .

Wait. She knew this place. Her uncle had taken her to it as a dragonet, soon after she learned to fly. Those markings on the walls were the runes of the elders—a symbol that they had witnessed this location. Only, this view was wrong. The opening ahead, into that next room. It should have been shut tight, with an . . .

An impenetrable lock. For this was where her people had kept their Dawnshard, long ago. A human research team was studying the open metal doors, led by two people in black, old-style Scadrian masks. These were wooden, rather than the small metal bits people like Dajer wore grafted to their cheeks, under the ears and reaching toward the mouth. His was more jewelry than mask, though perhaps with a medical purpose, but these were ceremonial, and weighty with import. They indicated full Malwish arcanists.

Starling stared at that scene for far too long, her mind sluggishly accepting what it meant.

"I'm not supposed to have this footage," Dajer admitted. "But the head engineer of this project is a friend of mine. We've helped each other along the way over the years, as any good engineer knows that it takes more than one beam to span a river."

"How?" Starling asked, mouth dry, the word raspy as she forced it out. "How did you open one of our locks?"

"Concentrated beam of Investiture," he said. "Focused in the right way, with increasing vibrations that overload and reset the mechanism. We call this device, this weapon, the Intensifier. It takes an unholy amount of power—but also quite a bit of finesse, as the goal mustn't be to engage the lock's protections. You must instead flood it with so much power that it's oversaturated. Ancient draconic devices are fascinating, but cannot keep pace with modern technology."

She stepped closer to the screen. If what he said was true . . . She glanced down at her manacles.

"Do you know where they took the Dawnshard, by the way?" He asked it in such a casual way, as if he weren't inquiring about one of the most dangerous weapons in all of the cosmere.

"No," she said, truthfully. "It was decided that too many of us knew the location, so it was moved. By the time I made the pilgrimage, it was already gone. Only the lock remained. Closed, by tradition."

"Not just for tradition," he said. "A Dawnshard leaves a trace. If you know where it *was*, you might be able to ascertain where it *went*. Connection from something so powerful is almost impossible to purge. But that is a puzzle for a different department." He gestured, still sitting perfectly upright in his seat. She didn't know him well, but he didn't seem the type to lounge, even when alone. "I have sent a request to the man who oversees this machine. The Intensifier should arrive within a day or so."

She spun toward him. "What?"

He laughed. A forced sound. "No, I didn't know you were coming. I sent for it to try and deal with that entity outside. Some arcanists have had luck overfeeding the things. I might be able to put it to sleep and get a team past to the center. Therefore, you have an opportunity. While the machine is here, I might be willing to try other applications."

She considered it.

Shards, to be *free*.

Yes, she'd have to serve under this man, but only for twenty years—a short span for her kind. If the contract with him was airtight, then she wouldn't have to do anything morally compromising—other than the obvious fact of propping up an aggressive, expansionist regime. With the right negotiations, her service would even protect her crew.

Her exile would remain in effect even with the manacles gone. However, she'd be able to fly again, regain her powers, assume her other form. Recover the half of her that had been locked away by those who should have been her advocates.

It shocked her how desperately she wanted that. Freedom was a flavor she had not anticipated savoring anytime soon, lest she grow too anxious, then lose herself to depression.

Now it was like a meal sitting on the table, smoked, pungent, with juices dripping down the sides.

"Let me talk to my crew," she said, checking the clock. They ran on Scadrian time, of course, which was close enough to her ship schedule. The hour was technically late, and though she didn't feel sleepy like humans did, she would like some time to think. "We'll rest the night, and talk in the morning."

*Fig. 101 · Sak and Rokke
(Aviar)*

CHAPTER FORTY-ONE

The room they prepared for Dusk was virtually identical to the one he and Dajer had met in. Same short red carpet, same octagonal shape. It had a much smaller desk, a closet for clothing, and a simple bed that didn't match the rest of the decor—and which was attached to the floor by metal bolts.

He wondered if some bureaucrat had been kicked from their office to provide him with a room. Or maybe these were the quarters of one of the dead.

They brought his things, all except the boat itself, which he'd spotted nearby. Pulled up completely on the shore and overturned, likely so their scientists could inspect the glow on the bottom.

Using some adjustable bars for hanging clothing, he constructed a small play place for the birds. Two bars between the desk and the wall, with some rope netting up the back wall to climb on and hanging sticks to chew. Not the most active of entertainment, but the two were soon nuzzled together sleeping anyway. It had been a long day. Month. Decade, really.

Dusk longed to collapse into the bed himself, but instead he methodically went through his equipment and laid it out on the table. To their credit, the Ones Above had repacked his things quite well, despite their obvious time spent searching everything. The jar of worm paste showed the most apparent signs of tampering, but there were others as well. They'd replaced his boning knife upside down, and had left a few ties on his compass undone.

Everything was there, including his notebook and a map he'd made from strings and pegs on a board, helping him wayfind. Feeling a panic, he read his notes again, knowing they'd have copied them—but in this case, his terseness proved an asset. He hadn't mentioned the pulses, only drawn them in ways he assumed would be unintelligible. Other notes were framed as sightings, even the ones he'd felt with his new senses.

Hopefully, this meant they didn't know what he could do. He undid his string map, then used those strings to hang a few more toys for the birds when they awoke. Kokerlii had liked playing with his fork and spoons when he hung them together. Perhaps Rokke would be the same.

That done, he settled down—the implements of a former life arrayed on the desk before him—and forced himself to think. And to ask himself difficult questions.

What was he doing here?

He'd come out seeking proof for Vathi that his people could survive in the cosmere without making a deal with the Ones Above. Yet here he was, making deals with an enemy officer. Did this mean Vathi was right? That there was no way forward *except* to make allegiances with the powers that ruled the stars? How could they hope to outmaneuver, outdeal, or outthink people hundreds of years ahead of them technologically?

He put hands on his head, digging his fingers into his scalp, staring at his tools on the table. The tools of a trapper, used to travel to and live on Patji. Without them, he'd have been dead a hundred times over. Not one of them had been useful on this trip—no compass, sextant, or machete had relevance any longer.

Except . . . there was a tunnel on this island. One specifically overgrown with life from Patji. What did it mean? What was going on here?

Father . . . Why? What am I doing?

Though he'd hoped for a reply, like that singular time on the boat, he received nothing. The Father demanded they work out solutions on their own.

He felt he'd fallen so far from that wonderful moment when he'd reached the shore. Yes, he'd found the island. Great. He knew his kind could be bullied in this realm, just like the other one. Wonderful. Grand accomplishment. And . . .

And . . .

And he was too tired.

Nothing useful was ever accomplished by pushing on and on against fatigue like this. It would get you to make mistakes while trapping—so clearly it would also get you to make mistakes while *thinking*.

So Dusk did the smart thing. He quietly cleaned his tools and returned them to his pack. Then he went to bed.

Some hours later, Dusk awoke to insistent squawking. Not screeches, not yet. Not unless he kept on sleeping instead of doing his first duty—that of being a diligent bird-food-preparing machine.

He grumbled, but fetched some fruit from the guards at his door. He chopped that and added it to pellets and a handful of nuts. The birds hadn't been doing a lot of flying lately, and needed something less fatty and more nutritious.

He spread it out on the top shelf in the closet, then added a metal water dish from his tools. Then he pointed at each bird. "No eating just the nuts, then tossing away the less tasty things. And don't dump the bowl of water on the floor. I don't have anything to bolt it down."

They flew over and set out to breakfast while he showered in the small room for it, then dried off and fed himself, glad for anything that wasn't skullsnake meat. As he did so, he found that the sleep had worked. This time-tested method had revitalized his brain. Rested and fed, he didn't find his problem any less daunting—but he did have an inclination to do more than sit and mope.

So what kind of proof—or solution—could he find for Vathi? He wouldn't present it unless he believed in it, and traveling the darkness, or even the stars, by itself wouldn't protect his people. Surely there were many who traveled the stars who were still enslaved or subjugated. He had proof of that here, in the woman who had given him that translation device. She was currently locked up with her crew.

He needed to return with more than a discovery. He needed to return with a *solution*.

A clang sounded in the room. He sighed, turning toward the birds. Rokke was standing at the side of the shelf, looking with head cocked at the metal water dish on the ground. She chirped apologetically.

They never could resist.

Dusk threw a towel on the water, then told the birds to stay before stepping out of the room into the open air and black sky. His two guards fell into place behind him as he walked away. He was a prisoner, and they all knew it, but at least they had the good graces not to say so. And they seemed to have orders to let him wander.

He made his way to the Dakwara, which didn't do him the honor of facing him. She continued swimming in this inner sea of not-water, a glowing green force among the skullsnakes.

"You shouldn't get too close," one of the guards warned.

Dusk nodded, but he didn't intend to get close.

The Dakwara of myth had been defeated by Cakoban, the great Navigator. Once he'd untied her from her knots, she'd been forced to serve him. The stories said that Cakoban had set her to protect his daughter on her voyage.

So . . . if the Dakwara was here, did Dusk have to defeat her? But how? He doubted he could kill her, and that would make no sense anyway. How would you get a boon from something you'd slain? He didn't think he could trick her into tying herself in knots, as Cakoban had done. A demigod like her would not be tricked in the same way a second time.

He looked to his left, across the empty stone toward that strange tunnel. A challenge, perhaps? It didn't quite fit the myths, but perhaps he didn't know his lore correctly? He decided, right then, to do as Dajer demanded—travel through this tunnel and find what was on the other side. It was no coincidence that he was here. Patji had trained him, then sent him to this cavern.

Dajer would play him, though. How could Dusk avoid—or minimize—that? Only one possible solution came to him. So he decided to run with it.

Fig. 88 · Nose bug
(Sleepless)

CHAPTER FORTY-TWO

Starling did sleep.
Dragons could subsist directly on energy drawn from the Spiritual Realm. That included her, despite her other limitations. Eating wasn't required, and they had organs that would fabricate a nutrient or water by metabolizing Investiture through their Connection. Their immortality wasn't merely a matter of not aging; they were built to last.

Severing this Connection was an extremely difficult thing to accomplish, and was one of the only ways to kill them. The Connection powered her manacles by leeching away her own abilities and turning them against her. More importantly and soul-crushingly, the manacles blocked her from the Spirit Shores. The place where dragons went when they died, and sometimes when they slept.

For most, meditative slumber was a time to recharge their stores of Investiture. To gaze upon their fallen elders, and to meet with family members. For her, sleep meant darkness. She was conscious, unlike mortals, but in someplace black and empty. There, she sat cross-legged and attacked her problems.

It took her several hours, but she finally decided. She would not take Dajer's offer. She couldn't risk him keeping her people captive and using them as pawns against her for years. It perhaps shouldn't have taken her so long to make the decision. She only arrived at it after convincing herself that the weapon Dajer had sent for couldn't possibly free her anyway.

Now what?

Now, she thought, *I come up with a plan.*

Freeing the crew was her duty as captain. Coming up with the bones of a plan consumed the next five hours of meditation. Once the time was up, she forced herself to wake—but felt groggy afterward, something that had never happened before her exile. With a yawn, she climbed out of her bunk in the large octagonal pod her crew had been assigned. As Dajer wanted to stay on her good side, Starling had been allowed to bunk with them. They'd decided, after such an exhausting day, to turn in and tackle their problems in the morning.

Problem was, they were one hundred percent being spied on in here. So what could they possibly do to plan or strategize in the face of that?

She yawned again, sitting on the edge of her bunk, surveying their chambers. The Scadrians did camp in style. Having a freestanding building like this, with windows on all sides, was far preferable to going back aboard a gunship each night. Carrying detachable crew pods on the bottom also allowed the gunship to move into battle without threatening the scientists and engineers it deployed to study phenomena.

The result was almost luxurious. Each crewmember had a bunk on one wall they could climb into and a sliding panel they could close for privacy. Other than the head, the rest was one large room—well-lit, with sleek furnishings and red carpeting. Outside, several pods were connected together by a lattice of metal struts for power and water, which was purified back at the larger ship.

She was, surprisingly, the last one to get up. One problem with meditating as she did while sleeping—if she didn't pop out occasionally to see what was up, she'd miss things like everyone else rising early.

The crew sat together at a table near the kitchen side of the room. Their lodestars had been confiscated—as had Starling's, before she'd been let into the room last night. ZeetZi, though, worked on a datapad with his yellow and white crest ruffled. Aditil, still wearing her engineer's jumpsuit, read over his shoulder. It was good to see her interacting with the rest of them, even if the situation was less than ideal, and she seemed to be maintaining a perky attitude.

In direct contrast was Leonore, who sat with her cheek on the metal tabletop, hands flopped out in front of her, mask off and lying next to her arm. Nobody could sulk like Leonore. Ed was trying to entertain her by telling some long-winded story about a planet he'd read of with strange freezing winds that left icy sheets over everything.

Seeing them without Nazh gave Starling a sharp pain—which in turn caused her manacles to cool. No, she couldn't side with the Scadrians, no matter what fantastic promises they offered. They would *never* let Nazh go willingly. He was too dangerous, and his kind too hated. Plus, he was a possible bit of leverage over the Night Brigade, if nothing else.

Leonore perked up as Starling hopped out of her bunk, though Ed kept right on talking as Starling poured herself some kaftea and settled down with them. They really hadn't talked much the night before, but it was time. Ed trailed off. Everyone looked at her.

"Well?" Leonore asked. "Give it to us, Captain."

"The optimistic version?" Starling asked. "We're screwed."

"Eloquent as ever, Star," ZeetZi said, still tapping on the datapad. It wasn't his—probably part of the room's controls. Electricity zapped up from the surface to his fingers as he interfaced with it. "Warning, there are six cameras in this room, and a listening device secreted inside each bunk." He pressed a button. "I have availed myself of my ingenious nature, and deactivated them all just now."

"Wow," Aditil said.

"Scadrian arrogance is of a caliber easy to exploit," ZeetZi said. "They assume their technology is beyond anyone else, but I am of Invention's people—and we spent centuries struggling to escape the watch of the Sleepless and their experiments. This pod's surveillance system is porous—it's hooked into the same network as everything else, for one. And the datapad that controls the climate and lights in here—with a little creative bypassing—let me access the deeper functions."

"That's not arrogance," Leonore said. "Just military bureaucracy.

The people who work in this room would be told there are cameras, yah? The system is easy to exploit because this isn't supposed to be a prison—the cameras are there to have a backup recording of events. Nobody would bother hacking them because discipline would be swift."

"It doesn't matter either way," Starling said. "Turning it off will simply make them set up something more rigorous—or worse, it will make them split us up. Is there any way you can spoof the feed, show them something else?"

"I've been trying to think of how," ZeetZi said, "but I find myself at a complete loss. It would take relentless work and talented animators to fabricate a convincing feed—unless I were to merely repeat footage. But guards check on us periodically, and randomly. That would spoil the trick immediately . . ." He trailed off. "They're rebooting the system. Hmmm . . . They must think it glitched naturally."

Starling rubbed her forehead. She had formed a decent plan, but how would her people execute it if they were being watched constantly?

"I can fake your voices," a soft voice said. "Let the video feed come back on, but send me the network information and the method you used to hack it so I can proceed."

Starling froze. Then an insect—roughly half the size of her palm—climbed up on the table from underneath. Flat and winged, with brown colorings, it reminded her of a katydid from back home. A hordeling from Chrysalis.

ZeetZi shoved back from the table, showing uncharacteristic fright—then anger, his crest straight upright. The others gaped, and even Ed seemed disturbed.

"Chrysalis," Starling said. "I wasn't aware you were there."

"That is the point," the insect said, making the noise by vibrating its thorax and wings somehow, mostly replicating humanoid speech. "I hid this node in your things, a risky move. The Scadrians must not find me, or they are likely to destroy the ship just to burn me to death.

"They did not find me in their scans, but I cannot survive if we do not escape this place. Therefore, I take risks. Hurry, before the cameras reboot. Give me the information. I will interrupt the audio signal and send them a new one, with imitations of you all saying innocuous things. So long as you lean forward and keep your heads tilted down at the table here, they won't see your lips moving on the video cameras. I've been watching through them myself, but I had not yet figured out how to hack them further."

"ZeetZi?" Starling asked, glancing at him.

He remained standing as the insect crawled back under the table, where it would be hidden when the cameras came back on.

"Wait," Leonore said. "How can you imitate our voices?"

"They breed hordelings for the specific purpose," ZeetZi said softly. "A specialized insect, each one matched to a person, to speak with their voice—without a hint of a buzz. They did it regularly in the Grand Apparatus. You bred one for each of us on the crew, slaver? Already?"

The Sleepless was quiet for a short time. "Yes," she eventually said. "In the past I have found it useful on many occasions."

"What *kind* of occasions?" Aditil asked, her arms wrapped around her thin frame, as if trying to hold her warmth in. "Why would you need to imitate our voices?"

"Occasions," the insect said, "like this one. The information, ZeetZi. Quickly."

ZeetZi took a long breath, then gave a brief explanation of the exploit. A short time later, he settled down—hesitantly—at the table. "Their cameras are back on," he said.

"My imitation is working," the soft voice said from under the table. "Again, keep your chins tilted down. They will suffer a short delay between what happens and what they see and hear, but it shouldn't be too noticeable. I have my nodes imitating you, and speaking of trips to Scadrial in the past as a cover. I apologize. I have to make most of it up. I will try to represent you accurately."

"To do that, slaver," ZeetZi whispered, "you would first need to *understand* us."

"Hey," Starling said. "Let's look up, shall we? I mean, not physically. Keep your chins down, and all. But metaphorically. We can talk freely now. Which means you can listen to my plan for how we escape. We're going to fly out of here free as dragons before too long."

Leonore leaned forward. "Escape? From trained Malwish soldiers?

With a full flight of fighters and a gunship? Captain, I love you, but you're crazy. *We'd be blown to pieces.*"

"Maybe they'll just let us go," Aditil said. "Maybe we'll be too much of a bother."

"Um . . . no," Ed said. "Do you have any idea how rare it is to discover a new perpendicularity? This discovery will make careers, fortunes."

"More," Leonore said. "It's a discovery that will lead to military advantage. An advantage that decreases greatly when everyone else knows about it, yah? They won't let us go. Even if half of us *weren't* wanted criminals, we'd rot on Scadrial. Even Xisis won't know what happened to us."

"So we escape," Starling said. "We've been in tighter situations than this!"

"We have?" Ed said.

"Um . . . well, Master Hoid and I have been."

He always got out of them. Sometimes it was dicier for her. Traveling with him could be . . . an experience. She'd relished every moment, but then again, she was basically indestructible—and it hadn't been *his* fault he'd dropped her into a volcano.

"We can do this," she said. "I've got an idea. Look, we have to disable their ships. That's the secret. Leonore used to fly with this force, and if she says we can't outrun or dodge them, she's right. So we prevent them from chasing."

"You want to disable all the fighters and the gunship," Leonore said. "While imprisoned. Then find a way to unground our ship—they'll have locked it down—and escape, without being shot or recaptured by the ground forces?"

"And we need to save Nazh!" Ed said.

"Right, and we need to save Nazh," Leonore said.

"See, that's all," Starling said.

They returned flat stares.

"Hey," she said, "we could be trying to do something *actually* difficult. Like hauling Leonore out of bed the morning after she gets a bottle of ravamak from her mother." Starling looked to the others, forcing a smile. She waited, sweating, hoping.

Eventually, Leonore chuckled. "Good ravamak needs to be slept off. That's showing respect, yah?"

"I had a headache for *three days*," ZeetZi said. "One cup made Ed start speaking in gibberish."

"It was formal Yolish religious Draconic," Ed said, hand to his breast. "I learned it in school, and for some reason, it comes out when I have too much. I am, it seems, a very *refined* drunk."

Leonore leaned farther across the table toward Starling. "All right, Captain, I'll stop grousing. You're right, we need a way out. Sulking doesn't do anything. I'm just . . . not happy to be having a little reunion with my old employers."

Ed put a hand on her shoulder. "We won't let them have you, Leonore. No matter what. Not even if I have to break out the formal Yolish religious Draconic."

"It does have the best insults," Starling said.

"Nothing like a holy tongue full of religious iconography for some *real* vulgarisms," Ed agreed.

"Thanks," Leonore said. She pulled her mask down, which she probably should have done earlier, to obscure her lips. "Thank you. All of you. Captain, what's your plan?"

"Aditil gave me the idea," she said, nodding to the former aetherbound. "How do those ships fly? Like ours, I assume?"

"Sure," Aditil said. "They use aether spores as a power source."

"And you spend a lot of time on our ship," Starling said, "keeping those aethers vibrant, alert."

"Yes. Our cheap stuff tends to get groggy and lose power quickly. They'll have top-of-the-line aether."

"Can you talk it into going to sleep?" Starling said. "Like you talk ours into waking up?"

Aditil cocked her head. "I . . . well, I suppose I could. I mean, it's possible. I've had to do it before when encountering extremely dangerous wild aethers . . . But I never considered doing it to an engine."

"We have," Starling said, refusing the urge to gesture dramatically to Aditil, "the perfect weapon against the enemy ships. A way to sabotage them."

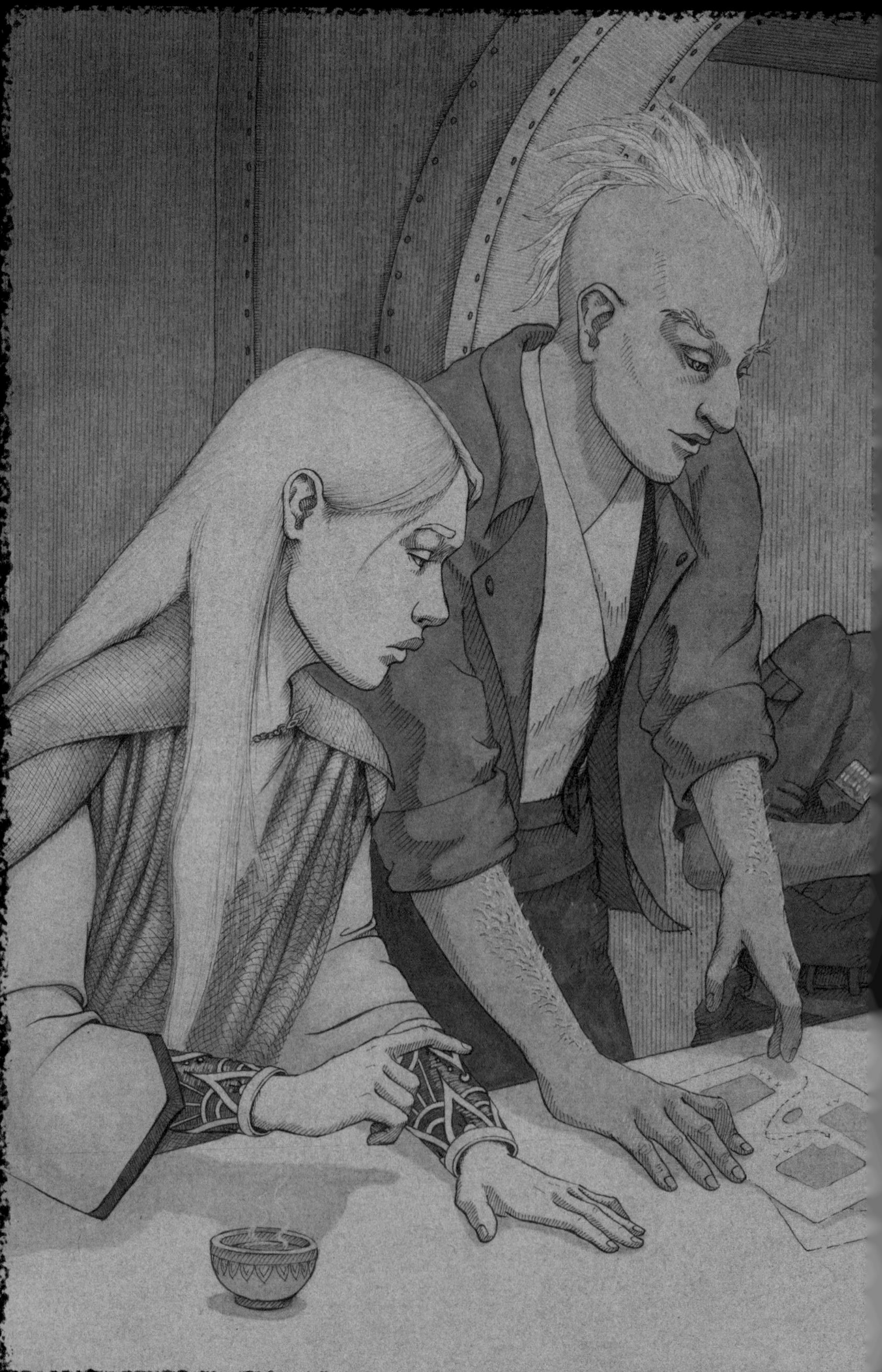

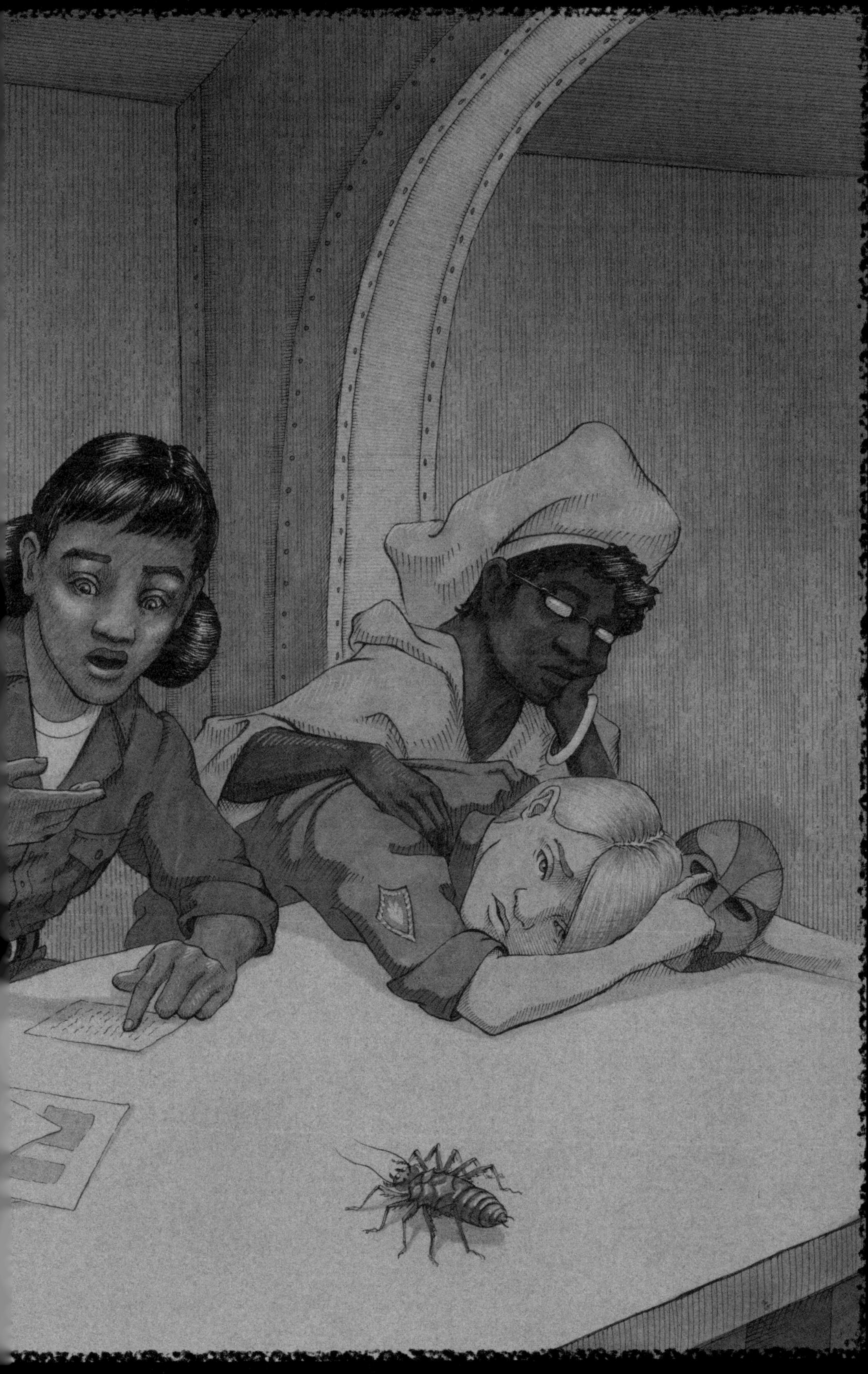

"Uh . . ." Leonore said. "Yah, but . . . we'd have to get her *to* the ships. Unseen. With time to talk to the aethers. I mean, it's something—but . . ."

"Aditil," ZeetZi said, "could you genuinely accomplish this feat?"

"Sure," she said, growing more confident as she nodded. "I wouldn't even need to open the tanks—I can do it through a little metal."

"But . . ." Ed said. "Um . . . I think Leonore has a point. We'd need to be free to do this."

"I'm working on that part," Starling said. "Their leader wants me to sign a contract with him—he is enamored with the idea of having a dragon attendant, though I don't think he's being completely honest about the reasons. Either way, I think I'll have more freedom than the rest of you. I'll need to come up with some kind of distraction. I'm working on that—maybe I can involve that stranger. The one who is probably from your bird planet, Ed."

"Drominad," he said, growing excited. "I've been reading about the place—the little we have, at least. Watch yourself with that one."

"Dangerous?" she asked.

"More stubborn than dangerous," he said. "Impressively so. It's been eight years, and his planet hasn't buckled before Malwish pressure *or* inevitable bribes from other planets trying to turn them. Drominad can't be conquered because of a technicality . . . Anyone care what kind, or shall I skip it?"

"I care," Leonore said, raising her hand. "I won't understand it, maybe, but I care."

"The planet has a higher-than-average presence of Investiture, indicating likely Shard involvement, even if none have claimed it," Ed said, his enthusiasm sparkling in his voice. "Might be some remnant of Ambition, and no one knows where Virtuosity is these days. Hell, it could have been Dominion or any number of other Shards that can no longer explain what they did. Either way, you can't conquer a planet like this—not without drawing the ire of *major* powers. Like, Invested powers."

"Gods," ZeetZi says.

"Depending on your definition, yes," Ed said. "And attacking, or even taking too much advantage of the locals, without knowing who is or was set up there would expose not just the Scadrians, but the Shards supporting them. So they really only have two choices. First would be to prove that the locals are a threat in some way, which—in the past—has really only worked for spacefaring cultures. What danger can a planet of people who can be bombarded to death present?

"Diplomacy is the only valid option. It can be a hollow shell of diplomacy, filled with bribes, threats, or manipulations—but you have to make the *smallest* effort to get local approval. And like I said, it isn't working. These folks have rebuffed the most important and powerful forces in the cosmere for *years*. Not biting on gifts, not bending to threats. Instead, they unified under a central government and began making demands."

"Dajer says he has a provisional agreement with the locals," Starling said.

"He might be stretching that," Ed said. "Before we arrived, I got the latest information the arcanists know—and we've got some insiders interested in the place. Offers have been made, and it looks good for an agreement, but nothing has been signed. For the moment, Drominad is still a free agent. That's got to be extremely aggravating to the Malwish."

Starling smiled. "A preindustrial society flipping off the Scadrians? I wonder if my master has been here. Sounds like he'd love the place."

"They're industrialized, but barely," Ed said. "Oh, and I could go on forever about those birds, but I thought you should know this part if you're going to meet a Drominadian. They don't give in easily. They've fared better than my people did."

Now it was Leonore's turn to offer support, fist up for him to bump. He did so, nodding to her.

"They're here for the perpendicularity," Leonore said. "They'll get their way eventually. Scadrians can be bastards when they're rejected. Trust me, I know."

"Everyone has their bastards, Leonore," Starling said. "My people included. But you're right. I doubt our friends on Drominad can isolate forever, not with this kind of pressure."

If we find the perpendicularity, she thought, *we might hasten their demise.* But Shards, that tide was coming for them; they were sitting on a proverbial dragonsteel well, full of riches beyond imagining. Eventually, even Shards would have difficulty staying away. Perhaps it would have been better if Ed hadn't told her about them, making her empathize.

But then . . . well, she'd empathize anyway, wouldn't she? That was what her uncle had taught her. At least now she couldn't pretend she wasn't part of the problem. A strange silver lining to find in the situation, but that was her way.

Guards peeked in a moment later, without bothering to knock. One waved her forward. "The colonel wishes to speak with you. The rest will stay."

She nodded and held up a finger to beg a moment or two. The guards reluctantly stepped back out, and she turned to the others.

"Keep positive," she told them. "We'll get out of this."

She pressed her hand, palm down, on the table and the rest reached in, hands on hers. Even Aditil, who in the past had complained that the gesture reminded her of some kind of sporting event ritual, though it was a draconic symbol of solidarity.

After that, Starling started toward the door. ZeetZi, however, hurried after her, stopping her before she could step out.

"Captain," he said. "Are we going to discuss the Sleepless upon your return?"

"Chrysalis," she said, pointedly using her name, "is helping us."

"Captain," he said again, then lowered his voice. "Star. It had our voices *ready to deploy*. It was preparing to duplicate us."

"They don't replace people. They're not kandra."

"It has our *voices*," he repeated.

"She's helping us speak in private."

"Because it's in even more danger than we are, here," he said. "Don't trust it. I know it's listening now. They're *always* listening, always playing with worlds, always observing them. Never helping. They don't *help* unless it benefits them."

"Zee," she said softly.

"What?" he asked, crest low on his scalp.

"Didn't you once tell me you hated how people looked at you when they found you were from the Grand Apparatus?"

He glanced down. But then nodded. "All people know is that we were . . . experiments to be observed. They kept expecting me to be some kind of simple, addlepated slave man, awed by the outside world—though my homeland is more advanced than any dared imagine."

She suspected the big words and elevated speech were things he occasionally exaggerated to fight this perception. She didn't blame him. However, now he looked to her again and seemed to understand.

It was a harsh thing to be judged before people even met you.

"You were first to call me captain," she said. "Back on the ship. Do you remember?"

"I did it deliberately," he said. "I knew Hoid would abscond some day; I saw him training you to take the ship."

"You said you trusted me," she said. "Do you?"

"I do," he said, hesitant.

"Then I want you to do something with that trust." She pointed back to the table—toward the node hidden beneath it. "I'm not asking you to forgive the people that did terrible things to yours. I'm not asking you to ignore the oppression, or the inarguable crimes the Sleepless perpetuated. But I am going to ask you for one thing: to try to work with this crew. All of it. And to give an *individual* a chance that needn't be offered to a *government*."

He sighed. "I don't know if I can do that."

"I just want you to try, and see what happens."

He took a deep breath. "All right. I'll try. As long as you promise not to let your optimism blind you, Captain."

She hesitated, but he *was* the expert. She nodded, and they parted.

Dajer wasn't in his office, but standing a short distance away outside. He was with the stranger who had the two birds, who gestured when he saw Starling.

"She is here," the Drominadian said.

"Yes," Dajer said as Starling walked up, "but why do you care?"

"I have decided," the Drominadian replied, "that I will perform the task you demand of me. I will go into the cavern, and seek its secrets on your behalf."

"Excellent!" Dajer said, rising. "What a *wonderful* decision, Sixth!

I cannot *wait* to see how you navigate the dangers inside. Once the pathway is open to your homeworld, we will *all benefit* so *very greatly*."

Shards. He emoted so hard, she thought he might strain something. With her, he had been cold, but now he turned it up—and way too far.

"How do we start?" Dajer asked. "What do you need?"

"I require only some tools," the stranger said. "A source of light, a pole for inspecting the way forward. Oh, and an accomplice to accompany me, as you suggested yesterday."

"I will send my best soldiers."

"No." The stranger turned and pointed to Starling. "I want her."

Dajer froze. Starling cocked her head. She was barely following this. Dajer wanted something from this man? But he wanted . . . her help?

"Why?" Dajer asked. "She knows nothing about this."

"Neither do your men, judging by how they died," the stranger said. "She doesn't like you. You don't like her. You're enemies. Therefore, she will tell me a different story than you will when I ask her about you." He shrugged. "She might lie, but they will be different lies than yours. I want her to come with me, so I can ask her questions."

Well he was a blunt one, wasn't he?

"We will . . . consider," Dajer said. "But come in, let's talk."

"I don't like talking," the stranger said. "You said she was hard to kill, and that will make her a good companion, won't it? You said I could demand payment, Dajer, and this is what I demand: the ability to take her, and speak with her."

"I . . . have no idea what is going on," Starling said. "Can someone fill me in?"

"Come," the stranger said. "I will show you the cave of death."

She cocked an eyebrow, following. At the location, she got a brief explanation. Full of deadly things. Possibly a way to the perpendicularity. Killed the soldiers who entered.

Dajer stepped closer to her and spoke softly. "Tell him you don't want to go. That you're afraid."

Instead she stepped away from him. "I think this is a lovely idea. Let's try it."

She still needed to confirm, for herself and Xisis, that the perpendicularity was real. And beyond that, it would buy her some time to sculpt her plan.

How bad could it really be in there, after all?

Dajer glared at her, but finally nodded to the Drominadian. "As you request, it will be done."

Fig. 59 · Masher wasp
(insect)

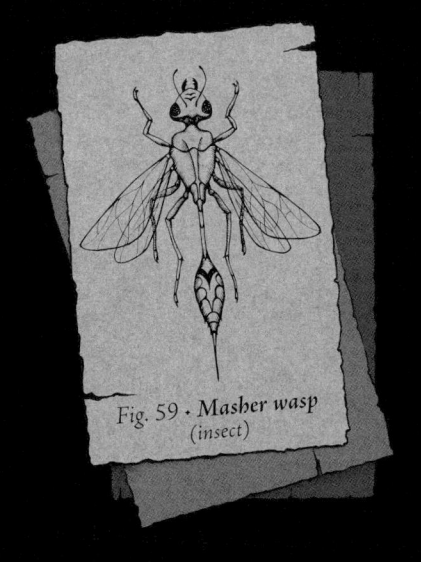

CHAPTER FORTY-THREE

Dusk again stepped up to the line of soil inside the mouth of the strange cavern. He knelt and dipped his fingers into the dirt, rubbing them together, feeling the wet loam.

Those *scents*. They oozed as if from another place, another time. Leaves, wet from the rain. But there was no rain here. Underbrush that grew more pungent with time as layers rotted into soil and new growth appeared. But how did it survive without sunlight? That one—that sharp scent—was distinctly the smell of a corpsebush, which coaxed insects into its gullet with false promises of aged carrion. How in the name of all the gods was a corpsebush living in this hole?

Sak squawked softly from one shoulder, and Rokke—riding in her increasingly familiar spot directly on his back—stuck her head into his hair. It was as if he were smelling ghosts. Figments of his past, come alive.

If it were so, they all shared the delusion, for Colonel Dajer joined him before the pit, arms folded, air hissing into his nostrils. Why did he keep his shoes that shiny all the time? That effort could have been put to something productive. Perhaps the Ones Above had shoes that remained shiny no matter what you did. Vathi would like to know about that. She'd order a dozen pairs for official functions.

He smiled at the thought. The world these people came from

seemed so terrible at times; other times, it seemed like a land where all things must be so easy, with miracle cures for birds and machines to do your work. Perhaps that was why they were grouchy—nothing to do but bother planets full of innocent people.

"Open the pathway," Dajer said softly. "Your reward will be immeasurable."

"I will not likely reach the end in one trip," Dusk warned. "I will want to explore a ways, then return, learning the route—and also taking time to investigate each danger. Assuming you want me to eventually lead you through to the other side in person."

"I will need that," Dajer said. "So yes. Go in a ways today, then return."

Dajer stepped back as the woman with the white skin joined them. She said she did not need to change for the task; she still wore the same flowing trousers and shirt from before, with a long filmy jacket. Simple flats for shoes. Clothing one might wear to an informal evening dinner, not for a descent into unknown terrors. Even Vathi had known to dress better.

Dajer had said she was difficult to kill. Dusk had assumed that meant she was capable. That as a treasure hunter, she'd be their equivalent of a trapper. But this was not a trapper's way of dressing for difficult work.

What was he getting himself into? Worse, what was he getting *her* into? He began to regret his request.

"Perhaps," he said, "I should go alone. This will be dangerous."

"I'll be fine," the woman said, moving away from the guards. "Lead the way."

"But—"

"I'll be *fine*," she insisted, making as if to stride into the cave.

Dusk warded her back by holding out his hand in front of her. He could keep her safe, couldn't he? He'd done so for Vathi. He needed to talk to someone from the stars who *didn't* work for Dajer.

"I do not know what dangers are in this pit," he said, "but it *seems* to carry all the burdens of the most dangerous jungle on my world. Those kill instantly, terribly, and without warning."

"I'm hardier than I look," she said, then met his stare with her own. "And besides, I'm *increasingly* interested to see what the fuss is about."

Well, he had given a warning, and she was confident. Perhaps he didn't know enough about the ways of alien trappers to say what was reasonable and what was not. He lowered his hand, then turned to enter.

"You will have one more companion," Dajer said.

Dusk frowned, but this was the type of statement that people often explained if you gave them time, so he did not demand anything. Indeed, Dajer gestured to a floating object, made of shiny steel, in the shape of a pill—only much larger. It was perhaps two feet across, oval, and marked by blinking lights like eyes. A long wire drooped behind it, like a hose, leading back to the buildings.

"An observation machine?" Dusk said, stomach sinking. "I thought you said those didn't work in here."

"It's a *marvel* how quickly you pick up on things so far beyond your comprehension, Sixth!" Dajer said. "Speaks well of how quickly we'll be able to civilize your people." He rested one hand on the device. "The previous machines were wireless, and we are confident this one—with the new and reinforced wire—will resist the entity's influence. I will be in the observation room, watching through the eyes of this machine, which we call a drone. You can ask me questions through it, and I will answer. Isn't that amazing?"

He waited for some kind of reply from Dusk.

"It is," Dusk said, "in line with other devices I've seen of your kind."

"Ha! How amusing you are." Dajer patted the drone. "We've lost *eight* of these so far. Even the ones we programmed to enter, continue after we lost contact, then return. None did. So be careful." Then he leaned in closer to the woman. "If you go on ahead without the drone, dragon, I will consider that an attempt to escape. I will be forced to retaliate against your crew. Stay in sight, please. And *do* enjoy the trip."

Yes, those two did not like one another. Not one bit. Dusk grew eager to interrogate her, but . . . that drone would be listening. He felt a fool. Of course Dajer wouldn't let him be with an enemy alone, without monitoring.

"If this device breaks," Dusk said, "you expect me to turn back?"

"Yes," Dajer said, unfortunately. "We have others we can send as replacements during your next try. I would rather have eyes there with you, Sixth; I don't want to miss any exciting discoveries!" With that, he waved them onward.

The woman started into the leaves, and Dusk caught her. Was she that eager to die? He shook his head at her, then stepped cautiously forward, leading them around the deathant nest, which he'd already stunned with a smoking brand.

"Walk," he said softly, "where I do."

He started into the cave, and the drone at least proved helpful for bathing the area in cool white light. As they passed through some thick fronds, Dusk cutting the way with his machete—avoiding some nightwind fungi—the woman kept stepping out of his footsteps and looking at things.

"This is dangerous," he said. "*Extremely* dangerous. Please. Do as I say."

She didn't seem annoyed at him. She just gave him a smile and nodded, then started stepping more closely into his footprints.

"You have a name?" he asked.

"Starling," she said, watching with curiosity as he used his exploration stick to lift leaves ahead of them, checking for more dangers. "You?"

"I am Sixth of the Dusk."

"Is that how you want to be called? The full thing?"

"Dusk is fine," he said. He could see the path Dajer's soldiers had taken, as they'd trampled vines here. He lifted those, crouching, then noted a hole in the bark of a small tree. It had a crust of wasp paper.

Masher wasps, he thought. Another insect that wasn't found anywhere but Patji. He took a small jar from his pack, then smeared some of the contents on a stick, which he propped up in front of the wasp nest's opening.

"What are they?" Starling said, crouching beside him, not even bothering to whisper as the things moved inside the hole, but stayed away from the pungent stick.

He never thought he'd find himself wishing for the day when he'd traveled with Vathi, but he calmed his annoyance.

This world, he thought to himself, *is as bizarre to Starling as her world is to me. And how well am I navigating that?*

He'd brought her into this. He could be patient with her.

"They're called masher wasps," he said. "The sting is extremely deadly. But they will not leave the hole with this stick blocking the way." He hesitated, then backed away, pointing toward the air. A worker was returning to the nest.

That was always a danger. He'd have to take care in here, as that worker wouldn't enter the nest with the stick in place. He watched it carefully as it buzzed down, inspecting the hole.

"This will do," Starling said, then let the wasp land on her arm.

Dusk gasped, freezing. She hadn't. She . . .

Starling poked the insect, and it started stinging her like crazy. Dusk scrambled back, kicking up dirt on the cavern floor. She . . . She . . .

Starling was dead. Even if she hadn't fallen yet, they'd stung her, and would lay eggs in her corpse. He put his hands to his head, disturbed by the woman's sudden foolish . . .

The wasp fell dead. Dropped to the soil, twitched a moment, then fell still.

What?

Starling eyed it, then cocked her head. "Huh. I actually *feel* something. Manacles cold . . . Slight lightheadedness . . ." She seemed genuinely disturbed. "That's no ordinary insect."

"I told you it wasn't. You . . . you should be dead," Dusk whispered. "Are you a god?"

"My uncle is," she said. "I never finished the training." She regarded the hole with the others distrustfully. "Your birds are Invested, so maybe the insects are too . . . I shouldn't even be able to *feel* the poison."

"It's the nephilim," Dajer said, "in the pool outside. We brought Feruchemical healing devices, and they didn't work in the slightest. Something's interfering with Investiture in this cave." His voice took on a gleeful tone. "You might actually be in *danger* here, dragon."

She considered, shaking her hand, though she recovered from the assault with remarkable speed.

"Why did you let it sting you?" Dusk asked.

"My kind are *very* hard to kill, and I figured I'd show you directly instead of having you doubt my word and—potentially—get yourself hurt trying to protect me." She wiggled her fingers. "But maybe I'll listen a little more carefully to what you have to say going forward . . ."

He breathed deep breaths, still trembling from thinking he'd gotten her killed. He looked at the dirt, where the drone's illumination showed the dead wasp. Struck down, as if by deity, for trying to claim her. Dusk reached up, and Sak presented her head in his hand, to comfort him.

"Always so dramatic," Dajer's voice said from the drone, replicated with shocking accuracy. "Sixth, she's no god—for all that some primitives worship her kind. I warned you dragons were charlatans and thieves. But she's robust, and you might want to let her go first."

"Why not just send her?" Dusk asked.

"I need someone who can lead me through the dangers," Dajer said. "Not someone who will stumble into them blindly. Besides, it seems she might not be as impervious here as she's used to being, eh, dragon?"

She didn't reply, still looking at her hand. The stings should have gone necrotic instantly, but on her, the red punctures healed and faded away. That was daunting, and he was amazed, but she still seemed to find any effect on her disturbing.

"Tell me again," she said, "what I'm to do?"

"Don't look at anything, or touch anything, without asking me. Stay close, and step where I step. It . . ." He hesitated, noting his own corpse ahead, lying face down. He breathed a whisper of thanks to Sak and checked the region.

Ah. There on the ceiling. Memist, emitted from the vines there, to knock one unconscious. Rarely would it be this close to a wasp hive, though, as the memist vines would starve if the wasps ate all of their kills. Strange. This place didn't make sense for a multitude of reasons. And . . .

Something else about the memist here felt odd to him. What was that thought, itching at the back of his mind?

He warned Starling, then held his breath past it, the birds both sensing from him to do the same. Though little Rokke breathed in too soon, and started to get drowsy. He cradled her as they reached a small clearing in the tunnel, and waited for her to recover. If she didn't do so quickly, he wanted to be ready to charge out of the tunnel to get her help.

Fortunately, she was soon perching easily on his wrist, and seemed embarrassed for having made a mistake. "You are not a trapper's bird yet," he whispered to her, "but you are brave. Do not feel ashamed."

"You . . . talk to the birds?" Starling asked.

"When there is something to say, I do," he replied, scratching at Rokke's neck. He scanned the tunnel, which was still tight, claustrophobic—overgrown with foliage. There was so much moss on the ground in this patch that he couldn't see soil—and the walls were obscured with hundreds of vines, growing in a hectic lattice.

"How is this possible?" he asked, studying it. "Do you have any idea? The plants should need light, fresh water, constant sources of meat for sustenance."

"Wait . . . meat?" she asked. "The plants?"

"Some of them," he said, then pointed. "Each of these are from the island where I have lived most of my life. Yet we are . . ." He trailed off. They thought the portal home was close, and he'd rather *both* of them continue to think it. "Yet we are in this land of darkness. Where nothing should grow."

"When a perpendicularity is near, strange things can happen. Plants can grow by the energy a pool emits—I've seen it on a dozen worlds, and numerous places in Shadesmar."

That made him even more curious what was at the center of this place. Could there be *another* portal? To another part of his world? He considered, but as Rokke chirped she was all right, he started them forward again—testing each step, checking leaves, listening for danger, and watching for his corpse. It was slow work, like exploring any new path. But they did soon find something exciting.

Dusk knelt on the moss and teased it out, careful in case something was hiding on it. A human rib. Followed by some pieces of metal.

"Rusts," Dajer said, the drone hovering close, its long wire rustling the leaves. "Well, that's Ensign Biord. Our other drones came this way, and while our visuals kept breaking up, I still find it remarkable that not a one spotted her."

"The moss grows quickly," Dusk said. "It has to if it wants anything to eat." He tapped with his rod, moving around. "Two skulls here. You sent them in together?"

"Yes," Dajer said. "Special ops."

"I suspect," Dusk said, "the wasps got these two. Probably angered the hive while passing, managed to run past the memist vines, but then fell here to stings. Impressive they survived so long."

He kept prodding at the moss with his rod.

"Poor people," Starling whispered.

"They're your enemies."

"They're just common soldiers," she said. "My problems are with those who lead them."

His rod hit something, and he smiled, tracing the outline.

"Is that a *third* corpse?" she asked.

He pulled out one of their large rifles, scraping off the moss. "No," he said simply, then flipped three buttons and powered it on. The sides lit up, and a display at the back indicated what he assumed was some kind of power reading.

". . . How?" Dajer asked.

"Your soldiers activated these yesterday, when facing Starling's crew," Dusk said.

"And you saw how?" Dajer demanded.

"I'm observant," Dusk said. "A requirement for a trapper. I'm not sure if I found the safety or not."

"On the side," Starling said. "Above your thumb."

He nodded. Wits were the best weapon when trapping, but he would not complain about having this as a backup. His wits didn't always come fully loaded.

They continued on. And he did not tell them that before finding this weapon, he'd located the outline of the other soldier's rifle as well. That would remain in the moss. Just in case.

"Come," he said. "I want to find out what happened to the drones."

*Fig. 53 · Tokka
(carnivorous plant)*

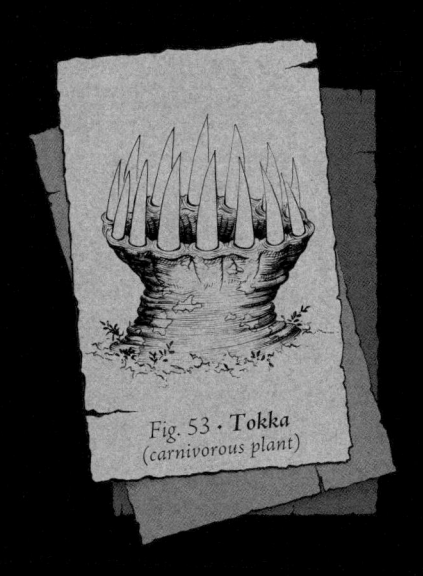

CHAPTER FORTY-FOUR

This man was fascinating.
Almost as if he were a bird. Always looking, head turning this way and that. Watching everything at once. Prone to bouts of quietude and terse replies.
You cannot adopt him, she told herself forcefully. *You have your crew to worry about already. You can't worry about him and his world. You can't fix every problem for every person you run across.*
She repeated these thoughts as they continued into the depths, Starling taking care to follow as he asked. She didn't think this place could *actually* kill her. The manacles had deeper protections that would engage if she fell unconscious, for example, letting her be recovered by her kin. That could take decades, maybe centuries, but they'd eventually notice she was gone and hunt for her.
Then again, that *was* an entity outside, and those *were* capable of killing dragons. No telling how far its influence extended. So she was diligent, following Dusk's commands—and though she *did* get bitten by something else on two other occasions, she didn't tell him. The effects wore off quickly, and she figured that so long as she didn't blunder into a full-on nest or the like, she should be fine.
Instead she focused on the trapper, and her innate desire to do something for him. He was so earnest, so determined. Her master had

warned her about this inclination to care for everyone she met. Apparently, it wasn't an uncommon problem among the people he chose to work with. If you were going to travel the cosmere, you were going to find people with problems. If you got embroiled in their conflicts, you'd never get anything done.

Thing was, her master always *said* he wouldn't get involved. He *claimed* that his eyes were turned toward bigger issues, that he couldn't get bogged down in details. The "details," however, were usually people. And he was very bad at ignoring people. She'd actually chosen Hoid over her uncle, no matter how much she loved Frost, *because* he chose to get involved.

So if Hoid couldn't do it, then how could she be expected to do so?

"Can you tell me," Dusk said, "why it is dark in here, but not outside? I see no sun out there."

"It's complicated," Starling said with a grimace. "Which is code for 'I'd rather have my arcanist explain it.' Basically, Shadesmar responds to our perceptions. There's a kind of automatic light in most places we perceive as 'outside,' but it doesn't extend to the 'inside' as we see it." She paused. "There are some interesting case studies about people with blindness—or races that don't use sight as a primary sense—visiting Shadesmar. But again, you really need to talk to an arcanist for that sort of thing."

"Arcanist?" he said.

"Specialist," she said. "In all sorts of cosmere lore. Half scientist. Half wizard."

"I do not know that last word."

"It's from my homeland," she said with a smile. "Most of the arcanists hate words like 'wizard,' as they reference people with magical knowledge. Most of them will insist nothing is 'magic' if you understand it."

He grunted, but nodded, accepting her explanations as they continued walking. So she decided to try a question of her own. "Your people," she said, ducking under a large frond as he gestured for her to do so. "You live in caverns like this?"

"Not caverns. But like this."

"How do you survive? Surely children can't be taught all of this."

He didn't reply at first. He didn't seem to trust her, which was valid. But he *had* brought her along, which said something, didn't it?

Or maybe it was the other participant who made him hesitant. That drone hovering along behind them, with Dajer on the other end.

"The birds," Dusk said from just ahead. "They find you strange."

"Honestly, I *kind of* am," she replied, smiling at the two birds. One was larger and black, of some breed that looked a lot like a crow. The other was smaller, though still somewhat large, with bright red along its face and a parrotlike beak and anatomy. That one spent a great deal of its time hiding in Dusk's hair, as if huddling behind vines in a jungle.

Both watched her with what she *might* have thought was hostility from a human or dragon. She didn't know birds, though. She stumbled and got close, and the red bird hid while the other one hissed.

It literally *hissed*. Mouth open, leaning toward her with a posture that instantly conveyed, "I *will* take your finger off if you get closer."

"Birds can hiss?" she asked, righting herself.

"Sak does it on occasion," Dusk said, calm. "They are wary of you; they can sense you aren't what you appear to be."

"They are smart!" Dajer said. "Dragons are duplicitous. Pretending to be like us when really, they are different creatures entirely."

Starling calmed her immediate burst of anger; she hated the implication that because a dragon had two forms, they were inherently untrustworthy.

Ahead, the tunnel narrowed. Dusk held up his hand to stall her, then knelt. He studied the ground, poking at it with his stick, for a good three or four minutes. Next, he tapped at the walls of the tunnel, which—here—were only about six feet apart. He moved methodically, tapping on section after section, stilling her with a finger when she tried to ask for an explanation. There didn't seem to be—

Teeth as long as her arm appeared from a section of the wall and *snapped* closed on Dusk's stick. It was frighteningly similar to a steel trap, like might be placed on the forest floor to hunt a beast—except it emerged *from* the wall somehow, and obviously belonged to some kind of animal.

Dusk calmly pulled his stick from between the teeth, bent off the broken portion, then continued on.

"Wait," Starling said, pointing at the jaws jutting from the wall. "Wait. What is *that*?"

"It will take an hour to reset," Dusk said from ahead.

"That's not what I asked! How did the *wall* try to *eat* you?"

"Tokka," he said. "They build a facade for themselves using mucus that they match to the colorings of their surroundings. They can strike up to four feet away, with jaws that extend, then they hold and wait for the prey to die." He turned toward her. "Watch for bare sections of ground or stone with mounds rising on them. The foliage and moss will try to claim every spot. Where nothing grows, danger often lurks."

He tapped to the side with his foot, dislodging something in the moss. Something metal . . . A drone, bitten nearly in half.

"Ah!" Dajer said, hovering the working drone closer to its fallen comrade. "You've done it, Sixth! Truly, the bond the primitive man has with the land is incredible. I'm in awe of your natural affinity for this jungle."

"I trained for years to learn these things," Dusk said. "A child from my people taken here would die, same as one of yours." He paused, then looked to Starling. "Most of the Eelakin do not live near these things. Our world is not all death. Death merely occupies it, as a challenge."

It took her a moment to realize he was referencing her previous question, about their children and how they remained safe. What a curious man. It was like . . . he knew the rules of ordinary conversation, but chose to live outside them, like a verbal conscientious objector.

"Here, here," Dajer said, hovering his drone down. "I'm going to download its recordings. Pause for a time." Little metal arms unfolded from the functioning drone and began working on the broken one.

Dusk pulled back, and—remarkably—took some nuts from his pocket and squatted, eating them and offering some to his birds. They didn't eat; they seemed too nervous, and she didn't blame them.

She approached, stepping in his footprints, then knelt before him, hoping to be far enough away from the drone to speak privately. "What

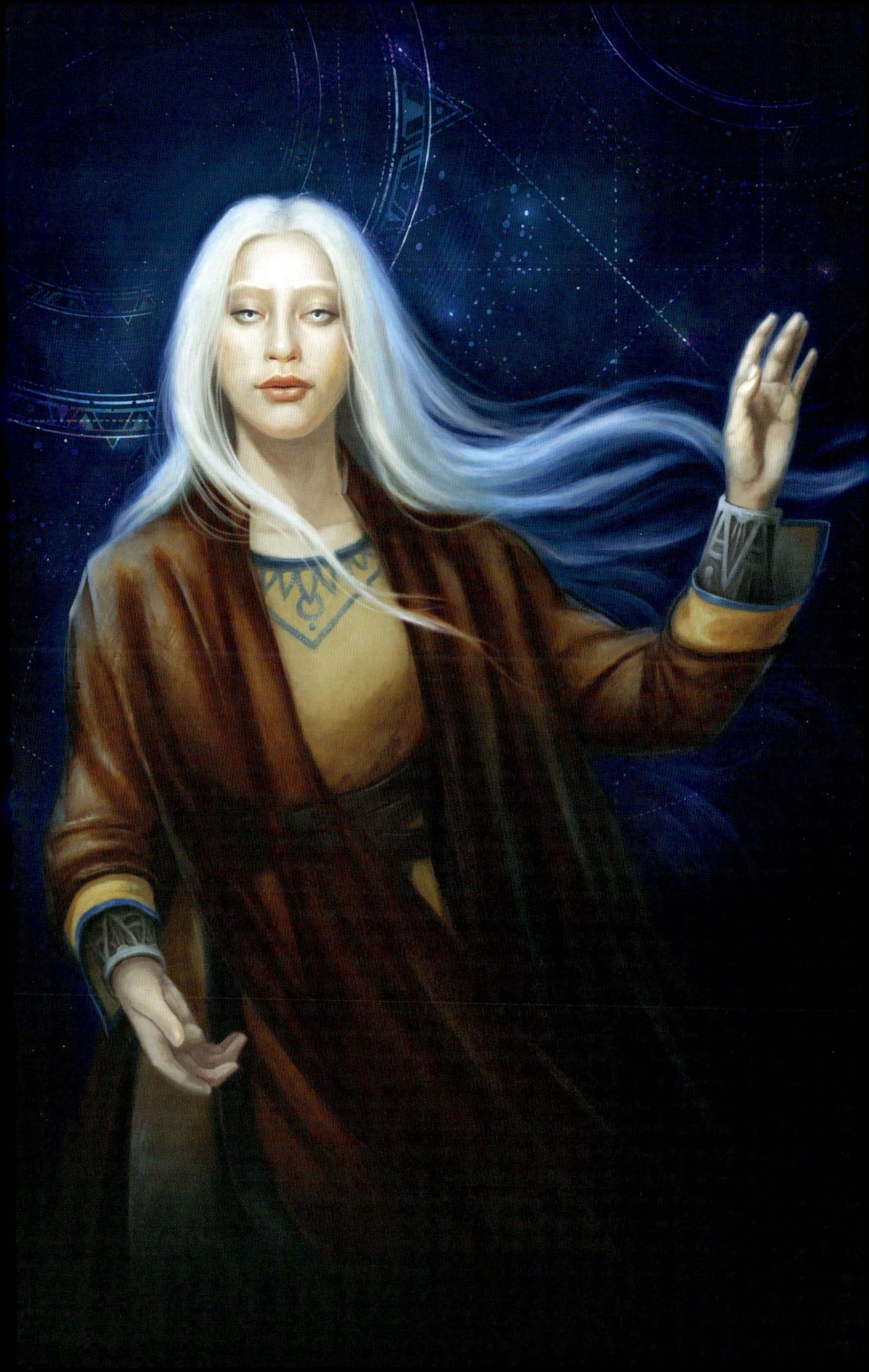

he said about me is wrong," she whispered. "I *am* what I appear to be. This *is* me. I'm also more, but it's not like this is a fake part of me. I'm not a liar by nature."

"Nobody is," Dusk replied. "Just as nobody knows *naturally* how to navigate the dangers of the jungle." He ate a nut. "He makes assumptions about you, as he does me."

"Yes."

"Is that common, outside?"

"Unfortunately, yes," she said. "Though some people are more prone to it."

He nodded. "It is common among my people too."

As they knelt, the black bird moved down his arm and opened its mouth at Starling again, warding her back.

"How," Starling asked, "do I make it like me?"

"How do you make anyone like anyone? Sak is wiser than I am. She recognizes danger when she sees it. And you are dangerous, are you not?"

"More than anyone probably realizes," she admitted.

He thought for a moment. "You cannot be hurt by normal physical means?"

"Nope."

"Let her bite you," he said, taking another nut. "But don't react to the bite."

Hesitant, trusting him, Starling reached out her hand. The black bird first warded her away again, then pecked at her, stabbing the skin. She bit harder, taking the side of Starling's hand in her mouth, pinching at the skin. Starling didn't feel anything other than a faint coldness as her protections activated. The bird clamped down and worked on her for a moment, then backed away and cawed, head cocked. The creature edged forward and pecked at Starling's hand a few more times.

Finally she retreated to Dusk's shoulder.

Dusk grunted. "She has decided," he said, "that you learned your lesson and properly respect her now."

"She got that from *biting* me?"

"More from the lack of a response," he said. "Birds like chaos and noise. If you make it when they bite, they are more likely to do so again. If you do nothing, then you're boring. They move on." He took another nut. "She still doesn't like you. Don't assume it's that easy."

"I won't," Starling said. "They're remarkable. Is it true that they're Invested? Um, that's our word for a thing that can grant interesting abilities, or has them naturally. It's . . . complicated to explain what constitutes an interesting ability, I suppose . . ."

He didn't reply, instead eating the nuts.

"I heard from a friend," she explained, "that your planet made first contact with outsiders from offworld a few years back. Everyone finds those birds very interesting . . ."

"I do not want to speak of it," he said, "because I might inadvertently give you information that hurts my people." He ate a nut. "I am not good with conversation."

She smiled. "I couldn't tell."

"I recognize sarcasm," he replied. "I'm not a fool."

"Sorry," she said. "It's just . . . I find it refreshing you're willing to say why you don't want to answer. Plus, you're not wrong. Most people will realize those birds can make a Nahel bond with people, then think only of the value to be exploited from them."

He grunted. "And you?"

"Dragons can't accept those kinds of bonds," she said. "We're already too highly Invested, and our souls reject interference. But I *can* see the value." She considered a moment. "It's been hard for your people, hasn't it? Scadrians come down from space itself, and suddenly you realize you're not alone. That's wonderful and terrifying all at once. They offer promises, technology, but always with a catch. And you know—you *know*—they're going to eat you alive. You're afraid there's nothing you can do about it. No more than the minnow can escape the shark."

"And is there a way out?" he asked.

"I . . ." Suddenly, she felt awful. The entire future of his people was being disrupted, and—if she knew Malwish practices—what was coming would be miserable. An entire planet scooped up and turned into yet another piece of their empire. Dusk's lands would be flooded with offworlders, who would soon own all the best real estate. The Scadrians would run the government in all but name, and would turn the planet into a cog in their machine.

ISLES OF THE EMBERDARK

Another planetary suburb working to fuel the war effort. Comparatively, the Scadrians weren't *cruel* masters, just *overpowering* ones. Dusk's people wouldn't be enslaved, but neither would they be their own anymore. And those birds would become a luxury item for the most wealthy.

It was inevitable as the rolling dawn, and she spoke of it callously. "I'm sorry," she whispered. "I . . . I don't know if there is a way out. They're relentless, and they're powerful enough that even *my* people are wary of them. You can try to hold out for better terms, but . . ."

"But the truth is," Dusk whispered, "progress will overtake us, whether we want it to or not. The opportunities coming are incredible, but they will crush us as we seize them."

"I'm sorry," she repeated, bowing her head and turning away. Shards . . . what a fool she was. She'd hoped to win this man over, so she told him his people were doomed?

"Thank you," he said from behind.

She turned back to him, frowning.

"For not lying and making it sound better than it is," he said. "We deserve to know. Indeed, we knew already. It is good you are not the type to dance around and make a tangled knot out of reality."

She nodded to him.

"Dajer," Dusk said, speaking in the same soft voice, "are you quite done listening in on us?"

From the drone, Dajer laughed. "You knew?"

"Metal eyes are better than flesh ones," Dusk said, standing. "It stands to reason metal ears are the same. Shall we proceed?"

"So clever!" Dajer said. "You must be remarkable among your kind. I am lucky to have encountered you."

Dusk heaved the slightest sigh, then continued on. She tried to poke him a few more times for further information, but the man refused her attempts—so if she *had* impressed him with her honesty, then he had an unusual way of showing it. Or . . .

Well, perhaps she could try not to underestimate him, like Dajer was obviously doing. This was another point her master had made, repeatedly, to her. Her people—as powerful, immortal beings that were regularly worshipped—had a habit of being . . .

Well, "distinctly insufferable" was how her master had put it. And for all that her uncle and Hoid had different worldviews, Frost had encouraged her apprenticeship. She still remembered what he'd said. *Learn from him. For he is one of the few grander than we are, and yet he treats all the same.*

While "same" to Master Hoid involved a great deal of mockery, she hoped she *had* learned what her uncle wanted. A little. So why would Dusk talk to her earlier, but now grow silent? Because he'd confirmed, through testing, that Dajer was listening. Yet he'd specifically brought Starling because she'd offer a contrasting opinion to the Scadrians.

Dusk wanted to talk to her but couldn't, because he'd be overheard. Therefore, he had questions he *did* want to ask her in private. Was there a way?

Wait . . .

Dusk deliberately stepped over a bare spot, then seemed to see something in front of him, coaxing the drone forward. She narrowed her eyes and stopped. Dusk glanced at her—seeming impressed when she stopped and fixated on the bare patch that might hold an unseen monster.

"Is something wrong?" Dajer asked as the drone hovered right above the patch of stone.

"The dragon," Dusk said, prompting the drone to stop and turn. "She—wait! Be careful. That's—!"

Dusk jammed his stick into the ground. Jaws flashed, quicker than Starling could track, and a moment later, the drone was a pile of scrap sparking on the ground—in the teeth of a presumably annoyed predator.

Aha! Starling thought. *If this drone falls, we're supposed to turn back—but walking to the entrance will take us time. Time during which we can speak freely.*

Such an elegant solution. Dajer was already accustomed to his drones falling, and they'd just proven how dangerous this place was to them.

"Pity," Dusk said, inspecting the drone. "I had hoped I wouldn't need to trigger the attack. It seems the beasts are learning these drones do not offer them food. Do you think Dajer will guess I triggered it intentionally?"

"I think," she said, "he'll underestimate you, and won't even pause to think you might have tricked him."

"Let us hope you are correct," Dusk replied, gesturing toward the entrance. "Give me a moment. I want to check something."

She frowned, turning as he walked back a little ways, then knelt beside a small fissure in the ground by the wall. She looked over his shoulder.

"Another deathant hive," he whispered. "So it's deathant, then nightwind fungi, wasps, memist . . . Here, tokka, deathant, tokka . . ."

"You seem concerned."

"It's a pattern," he said. "A highly improbable one . . ." He stood. "It took us roughly an hour to get this deep, and I would not want to continue on anyway. I have much to consider already about what we've found, and I would rather retreat and double-check the path we've taken so far. Indeed, that cord from the drone might have stirred up dangers that were otherwise slumbering. So we must be careful—and as we walk, we will talk. But take care, not just of the perils I mention. They may send another of these devices down to meet us." As he said it, he grimaced.

"What?" she asked.

"So many words. Vathi has practically made a politician of me. Come. I have many questions for you."

Excellent. Because, as her master had taught her, a series of questions could reveal a great deal about the questioner.

Fig. 36 · Memist
(vines)

CHAPTER FORTY-FIVE

The more Dusk walked in this tunnel, the more wrong it felt. On their way back, he tried to find another trap, another danger, that was new. He spotted nothing. He had indeed caught them all on the way down.

And they were all in the *exact same* order he'd encountered on that day when he'd first found Vathi. The day that dusk had arrived on Patji.

He went over them again in his mind. The exact list of dangers reaching his safecamp, followed by the specific dangers they'd encountered that night crossing the island. From the wasps to the tokka—every danger along this tunnel was exactly the same as they'd been that fateful night.

Patji had hundreds of deadly flora and fauna, but he encountered only the ones he had with Vathi? And in *precisely* the same order? No, his memory was not flawed. He remembered that night distinctly—and now that he'd made the connection, the sequence unnerved him.

"Invested," Starling was explaining, "means what it sounds like. It's a creature that has an extra amount of Investiture—and for most mortals, you usually need some kind of bond to make it happen. Like the bond to your birds, which are accessing Investiture somehow. I'd really like to know what powers they give you."

"One bird protects me from predators that hunt by sensing the minds of their prey," Dusk said, reluctantly giving away the information. But she had been so open. Distressingly so. He'd begun to trust her, but now she talked without holding anything back, and he found that suspicious. "On the islands I visit, creatures that hunt in such a way are plentiful."

"Ah . . ." she said. "That's actually a rather common ability, as these things go. Clouding, we call it. Though the Scadrians have their own similar term—because of course they do. If those birds can bond to any human, and offer the power organically . . . that's worth a great deal."

"They aren't for sale," he replied.

"Well, if the other powers are similar, then your birds represent one of the easier ways to gain a Nahel bond. Whoever accesses those birds is looking at a *fortune*."

"And the portal?" he asked. "Between worlds?"

She grew more subdued as she replied. "That's a prize," she said, "worth many times that of the birds. Many times what is already enough wealth to buy planets, Dusk."

Again, with the shocking honesty. "Let me go over it again," he said. "There are several major powers at war, out in space. One is Scadrial, which we call the Ones Above. Specifically an empire from that planet, known as the Malwish. But this conflict, it's not an ordinary kind of war, because none of those involved dares risk full-on invasion. They all jostle for position, trying to gain advantage, occasionally coming to a battle or skirmish—but mostly trying to threaten and dominate everyone who isn't involved."

"Exactly," she said. "And your planet is of extreme strategic importance if someone can get in and out of Shadesmar there."

"Because traveling through this endless darkness," he said, "is faster, easier, and cheaper than the other way."

"You were listening," she said with a smile.

"I always listen." He turned to her. "What is a dragon?"

For the first time, she seemed hesitant. "We . . . my people . . . we've kind of been around a while. Some of my kind are the oldest beings you'll meet. Older than the Shards, whom you might call gods. As old as some of the *aethers*."

"You hide among mortals," he said. "But are gods."

She winced. "To a lot of people, we are deities. We form our own bond—different, but similar—with followers. They pray to us, and we send them comfort through the bond, soothing their emotions, blessing them, helping them."

"And you seek to do this to me? Make of me a worshipper?"

"No!" she said. "I . . . don't really play that game. I just want to get my crew to safety."

"And the perpendicularity? Why are you here for it?"

She sighed. "I promised another dragon, an ancient one, that I'd confirm for him its existence."

Ah, so there it was. "You want the same thing from my people, then, as the Scadrians."

"Yes," she admitted.

"So the question, in your mind, is not whether or not my people can be free. Our decision is never for freedom. It is to whom we should become slaves."

"I'm sorry," she said. "But I don't see a way for you to avoid that. I . . . have trouble imagining any government being all right with this much power in the hands of, um, a . . ."

"Primitive people?"

". . . group inexperienced in the realities of galactic politics," she said. "You might be able to make a deal with a smaller power. Problem is, I don't think any of them are *completely* trustworthy. At least, not the ones who could even consider standing up to the bigger powers, like Scadrial or Roshar. Plus, there's always the chance the smaller power you choose will make a deal with the Scadrians, and then you're basically in the same spot as before, with a few extra steps."

"There are rules, though," he said. "They haven't simply conquered us—which they could undoubtedly do."

"Yeah, there *are*," she said. "They don't want to get the Shards involved."

"The gods, as you called them," he said. "We have our own gods. They are a jealous type."

"Chances are," she said, "your gods are one of the Shards, or used to be one of them. And in most cases, forces *can't* invade a planet of Invested people, lest they rile up the Shards. So they play nice by giving lip service to cosmere-wide treaties. They'll bully you, but won't force you, unless..."

"Unless we look like we're going to give our allegiance to their enemies," he guessed. "Then they'll invade, because it's not worth the risk."

"Or unless you somehow prove dangerous. They might try a ploy, at some point, to trick you into advancing too quickly on your own, or using powers that you don't understand, to make you seem like a threat worth suppressing."

"They started trying that years ago," he said, remembering the ploy with the strange device on Patji. "But my friend Vathi is too smart to be caught by it." He considered, standing still in the cavern. "We need to be able to protect ourselves. Be strong enough that they don't dare invade or bully us, but not so strong we're seen as a threat. If we can do that, *we* can give people leave to enter our planet, so long as they obey our laws. We can trade with whom we will, and modernize until we are like that place you mentioned earlier. Silverlight?"

"Yeah," she said, looking down as he started them walking again.

"Before," he said, "you were honest with me. Tell me what about my words makes you hesitant now."

"I don't know if your people can become like Silverlight," she said. "My people spent millennia building it up before modern militaries developed, and it's protected by the authority and power of the dragons themselves. Dusk... you don't realize how important your people have suddenly become."

"So we should side with you?" he asked.

"I don't have a side," she said. "If you mean the dragons in general... I'm afraid many would be just as quick to exploit you. The best of my kind don't take *any* interest in other worlds or politics, so the ones who *are* out in the cosmere interfering... Well, we're not generally the greedy monsters people like to pretend we are, but the ones who'd show interest in you are a self-selecting crowd."

Wonderful. All this work, and his big discovery? That the noose was even tighter than he'd assumed. Why had Patji sent him here, then? His loneliness returned, like an echo of a dying shout. He shouldn't feel *lonely*. Was there a word for a person without a home, because his home had evolved into something new? A person without a future, because the future had no use for him?

"I left my people," he whispered, "to find proof, Starling. But now I think that might be meaningless."

"Proof of what?" she asked, backing up as he pointed out the memist falling from the ceiling.

He watched the falling cloud of toxin. "It doesn't matter, for I am a fool. We speak of a woman, who long ago tried to paddle against the current of a tsunami. She turned around to do so, and couldn't see where the waters took her—and was crushed by slamming debris. That is me, Starling. Paddling. Furiously. Facing the wrong way."

"What proof did you need, though?"

"I thought," he said, "to show my people that we could explore the darkness of this place, like our ancestors must have done. I thought if I brought proof, the others would realize we could use this Shadesmar to find allies, or to trade on our own terms, or . . . anything to avoid making a deal with the Ones Above." He paused. "We are near caving to these Malwish from Scadrial. Their promises are too great, and their threats too dire. We know exactly what giving in will do to us, but we have no other options."

"Oh, Dusk," she said, deadly mist raining before them, "I'm sorry. But nobody can navigate this place like you say. Certainly not your ancestors. Modern technology can barely do it. Poorly."

He cocked his head. "You found your way here."

"With a map," she said. "Because someone found this island by accident, and recorded it." She pointed. "In vaguely that direction is the Knell—originally known as the Grand Disturbance of the Shard Ambition. The place where she died is kind of like a north star. Your planet has one of those?"

"I think I can understand the concept," he said. "A star that does not move, which you can use for navigation? We have one, but not in the north."

"It's the same idea here," she said. "We can point a direction and know which way the Knell is, using instruments. It releases waves we call the Current. With a map, and knowing where we're going, we can mostly get around. But even to most of us, these far reaches are a mystery. Navigating is difficult—most instruments don't work right—so exploring what we call the emberdark relies completely on luck."

He stared at her and, in the back of his mind, felt it. That pulsing from roughly where she'd pointed. The Knell. He now had a name for it, and for the Current it released. In addition, he could feel the ripples it made when things interrupted and added to it ever so slightly. At the moment, he could have pointed the way to a half dozen islands in the distance—much farther out than the one he'd found.

"You really don't know?" he asked. "You can't find your way in this place?"

"Off the well-used trails?" she asked. "No. Nobody can."

Nobody can.

But he could.

He knew *exactly* where he was.

Sak chirped softly. She felt his realization. There was one thing, in all this wide universe, *he* knew and the Ones Above *didn't*. How could he turn that into an advantage? He needed time to think. He tucked the gun he'd recovered into a spot where he'd be able to find it again, then led Starling the rest of the way out, which wasn't far now. They emerged to an agitated group of Scadrians, including Dajer himself, who smiled when he saw Starling had come with Dusk.

"Ah," the man said, clearly relieved. "You came back."

"You ordered us to," Dusk said, feigning innocence. "I told her we had to come back. So we did."

"You are delightful," Dajer said, and assigned a few guards to Starling. "Where is the gun?"

"I stowed it inside," Dusk said. "For the next descent. I should like to try again tomorrow. You have another drone?"

"Yes."

"I will take better care of that one," Dusk said, then started toward his own room. Once he arrived, a guard waited outside the door, as before.

He fed and watered the birds, then sat down at his desk, feeling overwhelmed. Not just by the realization that the Ones Above really couldn't navigate here, but the greater, more disturbing one. Why the cavern mimicked so exactly his experience on Patji long ago. That seemed a sign from the god who still refused to give him any direct answers. But what did it mean, and what did it have to do with what was at the center of this island, guarded by the Dakwara?

He sat back, closed his eyes, and tried *not* to feel overwhelmed. Then he felt a distinct spike of pain from his leg. An insect bite.

He bolted to his feet, realizing he hadn't done his customary patdown and change of clothing following a trip through the jungle. He had grown too soft from city living. Many a deadly insect could get trapped in the folds of clothing and work their way to the skin over time.

He was dead. He—

Please don't panic, a voice said in his mind. *It was me that bit you. Please don't alert the ones watching that anything is wrong, and I apologize for the pain. This was the only way I could initiate communication with you. My name is Chrysalis. I believe that we might be able to help one another.*

Fig. 86 · Chrysalis bug
(Sleepless)

CHAPTER FORTY-SIX

An insect was talking to him?
Dusk settled down at his desk again, feeling a chill run through him. An insect. With his fingers on his leg, poking the loose cloth, he could feel it clinging to his long stocking. It was maybe two inches across, and had a hard, smooth, round back—like a very large beetle.

It was talking to him. How?

I have grown, the thing said, *a specialized organ for the purpose of communicating mind to mind. This individual insect is not me, but is a piece of me directed by the whole.*

It could read his mind?

Yes, though it helps if you form the words specifically, slowly, one after another. The bite is necessary, as there is no actual bond between us, and I need access to your nervous system to speak to you.

What are you? Dusk tried, doing as it said.

Excellent, it replied. *That is perfect. What am I? Well, that is difficult to explain. You might think of me as a god, Dusk. An immortal being who has taken an interest in you.*

Another god? He had not expected the outside world to be so silly with them. What do you want, God of Insects?

I want what every being wants. To thrive. I believe we can help one another. You are being pulled between several very powerful forces. Well, those forces hate my kind with an irrational fury—and while I do not age, I can be killed. I am weakened for reasons I have not dared explain, even to my companions. If Dajer were to find me, I would be exterminated immediately. I have someplace safe to hide in Starling's ship, but I cannot remain there for extended periods, and I worry about a random scan finding pieces of me when I do not expect.

Does Starling know about you? Dusk asked.

Yes, and she says she accepts me as part of her crew, but she does not trust me. None of them do. I am forced to admit that I have no true friends or allies. Therefore, I come to you, hoping to engage your aid.

Why me? Dusk asked.

Because the birds said you might be willing to help. The creature paused. *It took work to persuade them I wasn't food. I thought the Aviar of First of the Sun were all herbivores?*

Every bird I know, Dusk said, *will have a worm or a beetle now and then. It's good for them.*

Occasional opportunistic carnivores, then, the thing said. *Curious. I've not been to your world, but several of my siblings reside there, watching your kind with great interest.*

"Wonderful," Dusk said, walking over to his birds on the modified perch he'd made. "Rokke," he said, "you have grown lax. Do better."

The small bird squawked suddenly, ashamed, and started using her powers again. The presence of the insect's mind vanished from his.

Starling returned to a room full of *very* excited people.

"We've got it!" Aditil said. "We've got a way to distract the guards and escape."

They ushered her to the kitchen table, where they pretended to be eager to feed her something ZeetZi had fixed. He was a good chef, but they actually wanted to obscure their mouths from anyone watching. Presumably, Chrysalis was still overwriting their voices.

"We considered the problem, yah?" Leonore said around some bites of ZeetZi's potato mash. Basically everything he fixed was a variety of mash. "How do we get Aditil time to touch the ships and put the aethers to sleep?"

"Yes," Starling said, "like I said."

"We," Ed said, "have an incredible idea."

Rokke chirped, bashful. But Dusk couldn't feel the bug's presence in his mind any longer.

Dusk rightly assumed that her protective shield could keep his mind from being influenced or spoken to, even from this being while it was biting him. He felt at it, and yes, it was still in contact with him. It buzzed with what he suspected was annoyance.

He should be able to think without it overhearing him. After all, it worked for the mindsingers, which would draw a trapper's attention in the forests and lure them with phantom music. And with the black leeches, which would affix and start driving a person mad.

He sighed, scratching Rokke's neck by pinching his thumb and forefinger together, and she clucked in satisfaction. So . . . talking bugs. He supposed he shouldn't be surprised. More importantly, this talking bug knew to call his birds Aviar, and was the first being he'd met outside which had done so. That alone proved it wasn't lying about its kind knowing his planet. He was dealing with something more informed than any of the others, which would require him to be extra careful. Not that he needed more reason to be wary of a *literal* talking *bug*.

"Patji," he whispered, walking back to his desk, "why couldn't you have sent Vathi to do this task?" The god had brought her to him, trained her, tested her, if in a different way than him. She was the future. He was the setting sun. All of it together made Dusk start to wonder. Was Patji himself a setting sun? What was one god to this greater universe full of them?

It was a disturbing thing to wonder. He'd spent his life trusting in the guidance of Patji. Without that, what did he have? *The wisdom of the past,* he thought, latching on to it. *The trappers, explorers, and ancients who came before me. Cakoban led them across long darkness, to the discovery and conquest of the homeisles, the taming of the Aviar.*

Dusk could do this.

He could talk to a bug god.

Dredging up memories of what he'd been taught, he settled himself away from the desk, on the ground.

"Rokke," he said. "Remove your protections, please."

"We discarded several plans," Leonore explained. "First, we talked about drugging the pilots somehow, which was foolish. They're not going to let ZeetZi cook for them."

"Alas, it is true," he said, combing back his feather crest. "Scadrians tend to watch what they eat extra closely, and will never accept a gift from me. This is obviously their great loss, for even were I to poison their mash, their final meal would rival any that they had ever had the delight of imbibing."

"Okay, now *that's* not a word," Leonore said.

"Imbibing?" he said. "Of course it is."

"You made it up," she accused.

"I did not!" he said. "It means to eat, but in a fancy way. So I suppose, Leonore, you can never accomplish the feat."

"Actually," Starling said, "I'm pretty sure it means to drink . . ."

"Well, mash is a liquid," ZeetZi said. "Of a relative sort." He glanced at her and shrugged, his feathers ruffling in a way that looked sheepish.

Leonore had frozen, a bite halfway to her lips. "Wait. He got one wrong? Did I *actually catch him* with one of his stupid words?"

"On the tiniest of technicalities," he said.

Leonore raised both hands in the air in fists, a spoon sticking from one. "I am a genius. It has finally happened. I have proven ZeetZi to be a blowhard who makes things up."

"I did *not* make it up! I stretched the definition a *tad*!"

"Genius," Leonore said, then pointed at him. "Blowhard."

Aditil watched all of this with bemusement. Ed leaned toward her. "Don't worry," he said. "They get this way when things are going well."

"It's a good sign," Starling agreed.

"Captain," Leonore said, "to you, everything is a good sign, yah?

You once found a corpse and said, 'Good sign, everyone! He died suddenly, so whatever's about to murder us is probably going to do it quickly!'"

"Are . . . we going to talk about the solution we found?" Aditil said. "Or what?"

"We're getting to it," Leonore said. "Any good plan involves some gentle mockery of ZeetZi."

"It's how you know we're on the right path," Ed said.

All right, God of Insects, Dusk said in his mind. He sat on the ground with hands out to the sides, palms toward the sky. *Let us speak.*

The rain acceptance pose? the insect said. *I'm honored.*

As we accept the sky's gifts, Dusk said, *so I am willing to accept your thoughts. Know that I am Patji's, however, and will not worship you.*

As you say, it replied. *Please, continue to speak in your mind, and not out loud. The enemy is watching, and if they get the idea that you're speaking to someone, they may begin hunting for me.*

First, Dusk said, *tell me specifically what you wish of me.*

I must reach the perpendicularity, the boundary between dimensions. You must find the pathway through that tunnel, then carry my core self through, so that I might escape these enemies and find my way to my siblings on your world.

He kept his mind calm, as his uncle trained him to protect himself on the island. He did not let thoughts intrude. *So,* he thought deliberately, *you know the perpendicularity is at the center of this island.*

Yes, the thing said, sounding impatient, *as everyone here knows. I must get there.*

Perhaps, Dusk thought, *you should rely on Starling and her friends, rather than me. Even if you do not fully trust them, you did so enough to travel with them.*

Unfortunately, the bug god thought, *they are trapped here, and do not have the freedom you do. I cannot rely on them. I will reward you handsomely, Dusk, if you carry me to freedom.*

I will consider it, Dusk replied, *but first, explain to me your nature.*

It is complicated.

I, Dusk replied, *am growing increasingly accustomed to complicated. Please proceed.*

"So," Leonore said, "we can't poison them. Unlikely to ever work."

"We hoped maybe Chrysalis could help," ZeetZi said. "We thought maybe the slaver could do something to distract the guards. However, Chrysalis refused to try."

Starling expected a reply. She didn't dare look under the table to see if her hordeling was still there, as that might expose her. Presumably, the Scadrians were watching, even if they weren't able to hear.

But Chrysalis didn't say anything.

"Chrysalis?" Starling said, face tipped down as she ate, trying to obscure her lips. "Is that true?"

"What?" the insect said. "Sorry. I was distracted."

Not good. "You *are* still replacing our words, right?"

"Yes," she said, voice muffled from under the table. "That is why I'm distracted, obviously."

"And why can't you help with our plan to divert the guards away from Aditil?"

"Starling, those are Scadrians," she said, voice buzzing with annoyance. "You know that they have weapons specifically designed for my kind—a single one of their greater interference clouds, and my entire consciousness will fall apart. What am I supposed to do? I'm just one individual."

"You could hack their ships for us," Leonore said.

"Hack advanced Scadrian military ships? I've tried in the past; I found protective shells around the most important equipment, preventing even my smallest nodes from entering. Worse, as I said, they'll have interference clouds ready to deploy. One *hint* of one of my nodes, and I'm as good as dead. The Scadrians are *unreasonably* paranoid about my kind."

"Unreasonably, it says," ZeetZi added. "Ignoring the small issue of one of their leading officials being assassinated by a horde two years ago. Those monsters."

Chrysalis did not reply. She seemed to understand. Even among all the wonders of the cosmere, her kind were unusual. Indeed, they might be the single strangest thing Starling had ever encountered.

Still, Starling reached across and put her hand on ZeetZi's hand. When he met her eyes, she mouthed two words. *Try. Please.*

He hesitated, crest down against his scalp. But then he did nod.

I am, **the insect god** said, *what you might call a group mind.*

Like a hive of ants, Dusk replied.

No, not exactly. A hive is a group of individuals who may have a certain swarm intelligence, but have no direct mind link.

So . . . Dusk thought, *more like . . . you are a hive, with one queen, and it directly controls the various drones?*

Again, not exactly, the thing said. *Though that is the most common mistake made about my kind. I am not a hive mind, I am not a swarm intelligence, I am not a group of individuals who contribute to one greater intelligence. I am me. An individual, made up of many pieces.*

I . . . don't understand how that could work, Dusk admitted.

Let me show you, it replied.

Suddenly, Dusk could see through the eyes of what must have been one of the insects that made up the god's substance. It was crawling someplace narrow, filled with wires in bunches, with metal paneling all around. Light filtered in through a set of holes and from cracks between panels.

The view was disorienting, as Dusk could see too many directions at once, and his brain had difficulty understanding. Though after a little bit, he got better by somehow focusing his attention only on one view, one eye.

This, it said, *is one of my observation nodes. A piece of me that I have bred to have better vision and auditory capabilities. Some call these nodes hordelings, and refer to my kind as Clemaxin's Hordes, after the being who supposedly first discovered us. We prefer to be called the Sleepless.*

You say "bred," Dusk thought, still himself though he could see through this . . . node's multifaceted eyes. *What do you mean?*

Do your people have an understanding of cells yet?

Yes, he said. *The little pieces that make up our bodies.*

Good. Just as you are made up of many, many little cells, I am made up of many nodes. From the outside, these look like any common insect hive—and the individual pieces of myself breed with other pieces, or with pieces of other Sleepless.

Over time, we can selectively breed specific strains of nodes, like humans have bred birds on your planet. We are more expert at it, and have bred certain nodes toward specialized functions. So while I'm made up of hundreds of different pieces, I have dozens of specialties among them.

For instance, the one biting your leg was bred specifically to give us a way to speak into the minds of humans and show them things we see. This node was first successfully developed by a relative of mine. Once she had it working, I interbred some of my nodes with hers until I developed a strain of my own that could replicate the function.

So you're . . . always a child of . . . yourself? Dusk said.

As are your cells. They reproduce asexually, but are constantly dividing, dying, being replaced. Yet you are always you, are you not?

Of course, he thought.

It is another mistake people make about us, the creature said, *that we are always dying and being reborn. While this is true, it is only accurate in the sense that all living things are always dying and being replaced. Like you, I have persistence of identity, memory, and personality. I am me, always changing, but always still the same.*

The node he was seeing through turned down a small tunnel between several sections of electronic paraphernalia. It crawled across the top of a large cord of woven wires and entered a hollow between sections of metal. And here, hundreds of individual nodes swarmed over one another.

This was Dusk's first good look at them, and he found them to be less beetle-like than he'd imagined. They weren't quite like ants either. Roach-like, though most were flatter, wider, with ten legs instead of six. It was like a city in here.

There, the god said, *those ones straight ahead. The large ones, to your right. You see them?*

This group of dozens of nodes had enormous growths on their backs, like tumors. They were so large, the nodes themselves seemed like they would have trouble moving. Indeed, one slipped, then climbed back toward the others—and its motions were slow, labored.

Memory nodes, the god thought to him. *Like the sections of your brain that learn and remember. That is the bulk of who I am—along with those processor nodes behind them that make up my personality. Those are the narrow ones, like fish, that come to a point at the front.*

Together, those are me—my core. All others I can lose, like you might lose a finger, and it will not change who I am. These memory and processor nodes, however, are essential. As one node ages, I grow a new one—blank—and then incubate and move the memories or personality paths.

How . . . long have you lived? Dusk asked, staring through its eyes at the many pieces. One brought water to others in a specialized chitin pan, developed from several of its legs. Yet another was like a mobile latrine, moving between individuals so they could deposit waste in its carrier for it to take away for disposal. And together . . . together it was one person.

I am six thousand, the creature said.

Young, for a god, Dusk thought.

Perhaps. Even the Shards are only ten. So I am of a proper age for a god. Though of course, many individuals in the cosmere would dispute my divinity.

That seemed odd to Dusk. A being thousands of years old, who could evolve itself to do specific tasks? Who could be many places at once, and speak into the mind of anyone it could touch? This thing was not as great as Patji, but it was certainly divine.

I think, it said, *I'm going to like your people, Dusk. Shall we discuss how you're going to get me through that perpendicularity, and earn your reward?*

Perhaps, Dusk thought. *But I still don't understand why you can't use Starling or her crew. She's a god, like you. Surely the two of you together are capable of defeating a group of soldiers.*

"So . . ." Starling said. "Back on topic. We can't poison the pilots, and Chrysalis won't help. Then what is your fabulous plan for getting Aditil to them?"

"Ah . . ." Leonore said, leaning forward and raising her finger. "Here is the important part. They're Scadrians. No aetherbound will serve them, so they don't have practical experience with Aditil and her powers, despite using aethers for their engines."

"They'll have a genuine understanding of how the engineering works," Ed said. "But even arcanists tend to have a bad grasp on the full range of aetherbounds' experiences or abilities—and they seem to encourage this mystery, not wanting to be subjects of our research."

"So while we can't poison the guards," Aditil said, practically bouncing in her seat, "we *can* poison me!"

"What do you mean?" Starling asked.

"I can make a tincture that will make her feel sick," ZeetZi said. "Nothing life-threatening, but it will give her a fever, to trick their doctors."

"I'll explain that I need to be close to aether to recover," Aditil said. "It's going to be believable, right? They won't know it's not really a thing for us." She paused, then grinned, leaning in. "I have horse-thief ancestors. I can tell a mean lie."

"So . . ." Starling said. "We tell them you're sick? Then somehow make them take you to each of the ships in turn to 'be near aethers'? So you can sabotage them?"

"Yes!" Aditil said.

"Aether spores will respond to the requests of an aetherbound," Ed said, "as you surmised earlier today. She can put their fuel into hibernation. No reacting to water—no explosion, no creation of propellant. No nothing."

They all looked to Starling, eager.

Problem was, this absolutely wouldn't work. That plan . . . it was awful. Starling surveyed the table full of eager eyes, and she determined something.

Their solution wasn't much of a solution—and optimistic or not, they seemed to realize it.

It is . . . not so easy as you imagine, the being said, switching Dusk's vision to a different view. One of the camp outside, as seen from an observation node that seemed to be hiding in a crevice on the surface of Starling's ship. *Do you see those fighters?*

It was indicating the sleek, smaller vessels that made up Dajer's fleet. *I see them,* Dusk said.

We have passed the era of gods, Dusk, the being said. *I am not ashamed to admit this, for I require no worship, and need feel no superiority to be satisfied with my life.*

Once, a being like myself was untouchable to anyone with a mortal heritage. No longer. Those ships have the firepower to vaporize someone like me—indeed, they have devices that interrupt my ability to communicate between my nodes, which turns me into a panicked swarm of barely intelligent insects. Powers like you used to cut me from your mind earlier, but far more potent.

Starling will fare no better against them. Yes, a dragon like her is basically indestructible—it would take a source of vast Investiture to do her permanent harm. Thing is, mortal societies are getting so that they can produce that kind of power, that kind of weapon.

Beyond that, dragons work best through followers, using them like I use my nodes. Starling is nothing without her crew, and Dajer can force her into impotence by threatening to execute them if she does not comply.

Technology has not killed the gods, Dusk, but it has made them smaller. I hoped, for a short time, to find acceptance with Starling and hers. There is one, a god like us—yet somehow something more—who invited me onto that crew. He is gone now, and without his stories clouding my judgment, I can see truth again. Starling and her crew will abandon me if they get the chance. I cannot rely on them, so I must find another option. I ask again. What will it take to convince you to take me through the perpendicularity, once you reach it?

Can you protect my people, the Eelakin? Dusk asked. *From the Ones Above, from the invaders. Can you help us become self-sufficient?*

There was a hint of hesitance when it replied. *Let us discuss what you mean by that.*

"I know it's not perfect, Captain," ZeetZi said. "Our plan . . . it has holes."

"Holes?" Starling said. "Zee, the 'our crewmember is sick' plan never works. Everyone has heard of it."

"Yah, but it's not impossible they'd listen, right?" Leonore said. "Aditil has no criminal record. The Scadrians might underestimate her."

"And how do we get Nazh free?" Starling said. "What do we do when, inevitably, they don't take Aditil to the ships, but instead get her a little aether from their stores? What if, worst case, they just don't care? What if they are fine letting her die?"

Starling looked around, meeting their eyes in turn. And now that she looked, she saw their desperation. Dajer had every reason to make them vanish, even *if* she gave him what he wanted. Her crew was outgunned, outmatched, outmaneuvered. They'd been barely holding together before this expedition; now they'd been captured by a hostile empire, locked away, unable to do anything but sit and wait.

It would have been easy to give in to the hopelessness. Instead they had found something, the only thing they could consider. An edge they hoped to exploit.

Yes, they knew their chances were slim, but they were putting a bold face forward. They were a smart group, and better than she deserved.

But this plan was untenable.

"Look," Starling said, "I'm glad you're trying, but I can't let us go through with this."

"What, then?" ZeetZi asked. "What do we do?"

"Leave it to me," Starling said. "I promise you: I'll think of something."

My kind, the god of insects said, *prefer to work in the background. We've learned that mortals—be they human, Sho Del, or true Vaxilian—fear us. They do not like beings that creep, and hate that which does not fit their definition of grand or impressive.*

But if you help me, we will help you. We can advise your people on how to ride what is coming. For access to the perpendicularity, we can aid you in your negotiations, and advise on the evolution of your society. I am not authorized to negotiate for all of us, but take me to the perpendicularity, and my kind will look favorably upon you for it. You will be rewarded, I guarantee.

That is what I needed to hear, Dusk thought. *I will consider. For now, I will ask you to leave my mind to itself.*

As you wish, it said, sounding displeased. *But do not make me wait long for an answer. My need is urgent, and so my desire to reward you is at its peak.*

Dusk gave no reply to this, keeping his mind calm and clear—deliberately avoiding considering too much about what he'd been told—until he felt a small spike of pain, followed by blood running down the side of his leg. He used a blanket to obscure the node climbing out, then placed the blanket in the corner.

Then, finally, Dusk let his thoughts flood in, none of which were particularly calming. They set him tossing, turning, bothered and annoyed. Until, closing his eyes, he focused on the thrumming pulses.

Those, blessedly, reminded him of waves rocking a boat. Of nights sleeping with stars overhead and the quiet sounds of the ocean enveloping him. They helped him, at last, drift off into a somewhat fitful sleep.

Fig. 44 · Cakoban's Finger (flower)

CHAPTER FORTY-SEVEN

The next day, Dusk was tasked with leading Starling and a new drone back into the depths of the cavern.

A restless night and fretful morning had left him feeling tired. Patji, as usual, remained silent—and all of this made it dangerously difficult to focus. He could almost hear his uncle chastising him as he worked by rote, barely pausing to note the rot on a nearby tree. Stepping over a deathant crack without caution.

Focus. He'd never had this problem before.

He'd never had so many thoughts before. The coward in him wished he could ignore them forever. The man he'd become, with Vathi's influence, refused.

Strange, how he should look back upon his past self and find a coward. A man who wanted to hide from the future like a rat hid from the rising sun. He was no longer that man. And shockingly, it was being around other people that had urged him to change. Not just Vathi, but Mother Frond and a dozen others he'd come to interact with. Around other people, you couldn't keep doing the same thing. They forced you to adapt. Grow.

Fortunately his thoughts were his own today, as he had refused the touch of the insect god, who had wanted to join him on this descent. Either way, he was a poor companion for Starling. His attention—already divided—could not make room for conversation. That meant she had only Dajer to talk to—and in the amusing way of most people, she went ahead and did so. They might hate each other, but found silence a common enemy.

"So how do you think all of this grows?" she was saying to him. "I asked Dusk, and he says that plants work the common way on his planet—sunlight, water, nutrients from the soil. Or meat, I guess."

"The perpendicularity should be enough to replace a sun," Dajer said through the drone. "Aren't you from Silverlight? How do you think the plants there grow? It's by the power of the perpendicularity."

"Yes," she snapped, "thank you for the lesson about something I am well aware of. That was my initial explanation too, but you're missing something, as I was. In Silverlight we need to *expose* the plants to the light, as well as the proper tones. Here? No tones. No light—at least not in this cave."

"Perhaps," Dajer said, "the tones here are simply inaudible to our ears. I know of multiple places in the cosmere where unique kinds of Investiture emit a variant of radiation. That could be what the plants live by."

"I suppose," she said. "Though *all* Investiture emits a kind of radiation—at least when it's being used. Otherwise, sand wouldn't recharge, and Seeking wouldn't work."

"Which means," he said proudly, "I'm *obviously* right. It required only idle thought and basic competence. You are not impressing me with your abilities, dragon. And I'm *very much* relying on you to be *impressive*."

Blessedly, she did not reply, and Dusk got some time without them blabbing.

Everyone wanted something from him. How had it come to this? He was nobody—a trapper who knew birds, not politics, yet now he had to choose between forces that were each trying to crush and manipulate his people.

He didn't trust the god of insects, of course. It had danced around the issue, but the "fabulous reward" it promised him was just another collar. His people could accept its guidance, but he'd heard stories of gods offering deals.

Patji offered no such deal. You survived or you died.

Dusk's grandfather had—before joining up with the military for one of the companies—purchased land on a far island with his brothers. When he'd returned from deployment, he found that his brothers had already divided up the land—and given him the worst plot. Though he had been quiet about it, Dusk's mother had engaged the services of solicitors to fight for her father's rights. The brothers had, in turn, engaged the services of other solicitors. All of the family had been too poor to afford high expenses, so they'd paid with part of the land.

The result? In Dusk's day, the lawyers had the nicest part of the island. And the descendants of the original three brothers still squabbled over what remained. If his people were to accept the help of the god of insects, that would be their fate, he had no doubt. Help in negotiating would have a price equivalent.

So, no accepting Dajer, and no accepting the god of insects. That left Starling, but she made him uncomfortable, because nobody was *that* open and *that* helpful. She wanted something from him, though he hadn't yet figured her out.

He stopped them for a time, drinking from his canteen, feeling the humid air—too still. There was always wind somewhere on Patji. If you couldn't feel it, because of trees in the way, then you could hear it. Along with the surf—sometimes a roar, sometimes a rumble.

Here it was too quiet, too still. It made him think that a predator was near, and then there was the other problem . . .

Next will be Cakoban's fingers, he thought. If this tunnel really did follow the exact sequence of dangers as his trip with Vathi so many years ago, then the deadly tree—with the flowers that imitated thought—would be next. That had been when it all had changed, hadn't it? The moment Vathi discovered that plants could think on Patji, which led to her connecting why birds that weren't ordinarily Aviar could gain powers. The path from those trees had ended at a pool with glowing worms.

Down a little farther . . . and there the trees were. Crowded impossibly into the tunnel, bark trunks pushed against the stone walls, flowers drooping from the ceiling. It was all here. Which meant there would be nightmaws to deal with at the end. He would use Vathi's same solution for those—this time, via an advanced rifle from the Ones Above.

"Water," Starling suddenly said. She turned to the drone beside her, its lights shining on the plants ahead and reflecting off their leaves. "How is there water in here? The perpendicularity explains the plants growing, but this soil is wet. There is no rain in Shadesmar."

"There are some aquifers," Dajer replied through the drone, "here and there. Maybe some water spilled in through the perpendicularity."

"I don't think inanimate objects can just . . . flow through a perpendicularity," she said. "It requires Intent."

"And I say we don't know all we assume we do. I suspect we'll find a reservoir of water down here, and with the cave being mostly enclosed, the system refreshes itself—like a terrarium. Sixth, you said that the perpendicularity is in a pool, right?"

"A shallow pool of water," he agreed. "I believe the portal is somehow at the bottom. There is real water in it, and fake water too."

"Like used to exist on Roshar," Dajer said, triumphant. "Same thing."

Dusk led them past the trees. Even the god of insects thought there was a portal at the end of this tunnel. What if they were all right, and Dusk was the one who was wrong? Could this place have appeared in his absence, somehow? Had he made a grand circle back to where he'd started, but didn't recognize it because of a great number of sudden changes?

Starling stepped up. "Hey, you all right?"

Years living among people again had taught him not to snap his response. Not just to be polite either. He was proud of how he forced down annoyance. She was asking after him, showing concern. To snap was not only rude, it was unthinking.

"I am overwhelmed," he admitted. "I do not know the right decisions to make, and I am left questioning everything I once believed. My god, my heritage, my purpose . . . even how I got here."

"I'm sorry," she said. "That sucks."

That use of the word didn't make sense to him, but he'd noticed that the translation mechanics weren't a hundred percent accurate. He fingered the coin she'd given him, which he now wore like a wristwatch.

"My people," he said, carefully leading them around the expected patch of stinging terror vines—then using his stick to hold the plants up so the drone could hover beneath. "We did travel this unsea and this emberdark, as you call it."

"You have primary accounts confirming it?" she asked. "Written records from those days?"

"Well no," he said. "Why would we? That was long, long ago, when we had only the simplest of runes. We don't even have knot-tales of it, not ones that date back that far. But we do have the stories, passed down from loremother to loremother—under the direction of the kingmakers themselves."

"Oral tradition," Starling said.

"Exactly," he said. "So extra trustworthy."

"Extra trustworthy?" Starling said, sounding amused. "When there are no written records?"

"The oral tellings are far more accurate," he said, confused. "Anyone can write whatever they want—and they often do. But the loremother covens are not faulty. Those tell that we crossed the darkness, coming from distant seas. That Cakoban challenged the Dakwara and won our land. So it must be true."

"Oh, Dusk," Starling said.

"Don't try to dissuade him," Dajer said. "I find his innocence endearing."

He frowned and turned to Starling, expecting her to contradict the drone. She didn't.

"Look," she said, "I'm sure you have *wonderful* stories. But Dusk, my people have tens of *thousands* of years of written records. We chronicled the Shattering itself—my uncle was *present* at the event. Written words are forever. The memories and minds of people, passing stories . . . well, don't you worry. We'll see they get recorded so they are never forgotten."

She seemed, again, genuine. Dusk finally felt like he got Starling.

She wasn't here to exploit him—she really wasn't. She wanted to *save* him instead.

Which was almost as insulting.

Her intentions were good, it seemed, but she also didn't see his people as capable of ruling themselves. As she'd said, she saw no way for a "primitive" people to stand up against the might of "modern" ones. Still, she didn't use the words, and wasn't intentionally insulting—she tried to be respectful—and he found that he was growing to appreciate her attempts.

She saw him and his kind as children nonetheless. It was, in this case, like the god of insects had said. When you were an indestructible immortal, you had trouble finding equals. You ended up regarding everyone as inferior, even if you tried to be benevolent.

Understanding her was . . . refreshing. Perhaps he should have disliked her for her attitude, but now he could at least frame their conversations. Besides, perhaps she was right to look at them this way—with these people, he certainly did feel, at times, like a child among adults. That said, she was a prisoner and he—ostensibly—was not. So perhaps he was doing better for himself than one might assume, and perhaps his people could do better for themselves than any of these assumed.

"Ah," Dajer said. "Yes . . . Look!"

Dusk froze, surveying the tunnel. He saw nothing of note, save for some red grannymoss hanging down nearby. That wouldn't kill you, but it *would* leave you itching for hours.

"What?" Starling asked.

"We've leveled out," Dajer said, shining the drone's light on the ground. "See? It's working! If we continue this way, I'm *certain* we'll start *ascending*, then come up inside that cavern on the inner island. We're nearly halfway to our goal."

Dajer hovered the drone forward, towing its cable behind it. It was a miracle that it hadn't been snapped in half by something along the way, though Dusk had been careful to trigger any tokka he saw.

They continued onward, Dusk inspecting each few feet of the route before letting Starling follow, and found that he didn't want to reach the end. Not yet. He hadn't made up his mind on what to do with any of these people—and if there was a portal here, he didn't want to start giving them what they wanted. Or, potentially as bad, prove to them that there was no perpendicularity. They'd then start hunting elsewhere in the region—which might lead them to the actual location.

"Dusk," Starling said, "your people have steam engines, I assume? Powered by coal?"

"We have started using gasoline," he said. "Because of some things we learned from those who visit from the stars."

"What do you think?" she said. "Of our flying ships?"

"They're nice," he said.

"Just . . . nice? That's all?"

"Birds can fly," he said, scratching the neck of Sak, on his shoulder. The bird had stopped being so fidgety when Starling drew near, as he'd hoped. She respected anyone who could take a good bite.

"Yes, but flying machines are pretty incredible, aren't they?" she asked.

"I suppose," he said. "I like the feel of the ocean as you sail it; that reminds you of the pulse of the planet, beating at the shores with waves. I think I'd miss that. But a flying machine can take you places the ocean doesn't reach." He shrugged. "Seems useful."

"Are you curious how they work?" she asked.

This was . . . a strange line of questions from her. Though she might be unimpressed by his people's ways, he was increasingly certain she *was* trying to help. Perhaps this was just another way.

"I do not know," he said, "if I'm the person you should tell about things like flying machines. I don't even have the technological understanding to fix the motor on my boat. That said, yes, I do find your machinery curious."

"They work on something called aethers," she said. "A compact power source even more useful than gasoline or coal."

"How do we mine for this resource?" Dusk asked.

"You can't," she said, amused. "We get the spores from a certain couple of planets—but they're plentiful, and not too expensive. Or you could have an aetherbound who makes them for you. Like I have on my crew."

"A rejected aetherbound," Dajer said, hovering past, "with a cracked aether bud. Do you think I didn't do my research on your crew? She's incapable of creating aether herself."

"Aditil is still a genius with aethers," she said. "You should see what she can do. I think you'll find that I'm not the only member of the crew who can be of use to you, Dajer."

"Trying to manipulate me?" he said. "To what end?"

"We could serve you better as a whole team," Starling said.

"Not interested," he said. "Can we continue on, please? We have our own aetherbound serving back on Scadrial, and I'm certain they can do anything your friend can do—better, even, as *their* buds still work."

"Wait," Starling said. "There are aetherbound serving the Malwish? How? Who?"

Dajer moved on, leaving her stewing. Dusk wasn't completely certain what she'd wanted out of that conversation, but she hadn't gotten it. Either way, Dusk pointedly let Dajer take the risk of floating ahead on his own. Maybe he'd get that drone destroyed so they could turn back, giving Dusk another day to . . .

What was *that*? The drone had pulled to a stop in front of a wall of vines, interlaced and woven together like thick netting. A swipe of the machete would have gotten through that easily, except there was a sign hanging from it, tied in place by vines. It was wooden, with symbols carved at the center. The sort that trappers would hang to give warning.

The fact that some trapper had been here before would, alone, have been enough to floor him. But there was more. Enough to make him gawk, his jaw dropping, his mind reeling.

"What?" Starling said, looking to him, then to the hanging slab. "What's wrong?"

"This," Dusk said, "is one of my signposts. Using my mark of ownership, carved in my handwriting, with letters I devised myself." He paused. "It implies that I've been here before . . . But I do not remember ever having done so."

How? What?

This was *impossible*.

Dusk reverently took the sign off the vines, then held it close. Could it have been . . . copied? But then . . . how would anyone know he'd

ISLES OF THE EMBERDARK

reach this place? Why would they position it down here at the bottom? How had they done so, past all those dangers?

"We need to leave this place," he said.

Before they could complain or contradict, he started back, feeling cold sweats all the way.

What in Patji's holy name was going on?

Fig. 38 · *Nightmaw*
(predator)

CHAPTER FORTY-EIGHT

"**One of your people must** have brought it," Dajer said via the drone as they left the cavern. "To give you encouragement on your spirit quest. Oh! I'll bet this is something they do for everyone; you just don't know it. One last boost, so you can push the final distance and finish your ritual. Let's return and press on!"

"I need time to think," Dusk said, noting that a new ship had apparently arrived during their descent.

"Think instead about how it will feel!" Dajer said, turning the drone toward him. "Savor the victory of your quest fulfilled, Sixth! I've read of rituals such as this one, practiced by many preindustrial people, marking the passage to manhood. Won't it feel wonderful to be a man?"

". . . I'm forty-three."

"Late, I should think, for you to be undergoing this ritual. Why did you say you waited so long again?"

He didn't reply, as he honestly didn't remember the exact lie he'd given to Dajer. He was reasonably certain, however, he hadn't said anything about coming of age.

Dajer hovered the drone along, like a fledgling hoping its mother had a few more worms to regurgitate. When Dusk didn't show any signs of turning back, he finally let the drone drift backward, and the customary pair of not-guards hastened to join Dusk. Rokke, showing increasing levels of bravery, wasn't hiding in his hair at the moment. Instead, she'd hopped onto his wrist, and was pecking at the wooden slab he held—the sign with his handwriting on it—as if trying to discover why it troubled him so.

Someone had put it there *specifically* to unnerve him, but why? It didn't make any kind of sense.

Perhaps Dajer or Starling was lying to him. Perhaps they'd been among his people, and knew who he was. His mind reeled at the implications of that. They'd have needed to know *he* was going to sail the unsea, then beat him here so they could prepare the surprise. They'd have needed to somehow sneak into the tunnel—not impossible, as one was immortal and the other had drones—but still. It seemed wildly implausible they'd know about these signs.

Maybe . . . maybe someone could read his mind? His memories? The insect god had done that; perhaps it had prepared this sign using his memories? Or maybe someone else could do the same thing? That seemed . . . *slightly* less insane, though it disturbed him incredibly that someone reading his mind was the *more* plausible scenario.

He felt at the slab. This was too much for him. He was so far outside of his depth that he wasn't just drowning; he'd already sunk down to where light itself was dying. Down into the lair of the shadows beneath. Down to—

A voice spoke behind him. Words that shocked him to the core. "I know there's no perpendicularity on the other side of that tunnel," the voice said. "And I know that you are lying."

Starling left the cavern to a stunning sight.

A large Malwish cargo ship had set down on the side of the island, and was unloading some device. While Dajer's drone followed Dusk, jabbering at him and trying to get him to go back down, she froze in place.

That was it. The gun Dajer had mentioned—the Intensifier. The machine his people had used to destroy an ancient draconic lock. A chance for freedom. She'd pretended it couldn't work, but now that it was here . . .

She knew the stories about her kind, the deals mortals were said to make with dragons. Contracts with devilish beings who would, in some cases, demand a human's very soul. She wished the stories were complete exaggerations, but she'd unfortunately heard of some of her kind making Cognitive Shadows or other Invested entities out of the dead.

Today, she felt like she understood those mortals: put in a position where their deepest wishes faced off against their morality. What did you choose when everything you'd ever wanted was presented before you?

I could be free already, Starling reminded herself. *All I need to do is accept the judgment of the dragons.* Accept that she'd done wrong by saving the people she had, years ago. Give them up to draconic retribution.

She wouldn't do that. Therefore, imprisonment was *her* choice. The dragons had no real power over her; neither did the manacles. Dajer having a way to free her didn't change her convictions—and besides, she wasn't convinced he could manage it, Intensifier or not. So she steeled herself, and started back toward her quarters.

Dajer soon gave up on Dusk. The drone floated off for maintenance and to upload its data, and Dajer himself emerged from the nearby gunship—the domineering vessel that dwarfed the others on the island, even the cargo ship. He made his quarters on board, in the safest possible location.

The red-haired man trotted down the gangplank while several of his guards kept her in one spot. She was certain Dajer was playing Dusk somehow with that slab, though she didn't know how Dajer had planted it.

Games beyond games. Ever it was with these Scadrians. They loved their secrets.

Dajer jogged toward her, then gestured toward the cargo ship, which was hovering into the air to leave, its delivery made. It had left a small crew of engineers, who guided the large device—which did look something like an old-fashioned cannon, though several times larger, and with a narrower front—on a hover platform to join the main complex. She noted with amusement that the platform was Rosharan tech. The Scadrians couldn't help using the tools of their enemies in situations like this, without a steelfield.

"Wait here," Dajer said to her, then ran ahead to speak with the other engineers. Finally he pointed, likely indicating the right spot to position the device. In clear firing sight of the great green entity that guarded the center of the island.

That done, he strolled back to her, smug. "Your time, and that of the primitive, runs short, dragon. Soon I'll be able to blast my way to the center—and I'll owe him nothing. He really should have accepted my counsel that he return to duty today. I don't look kindly on people who shirk."

She said nothing, glaring at him.

"So spicy," he said to her. "You know, I've always been disappointed that your kind don't breathe fire, like in the stories."

"It was metaphorical," she said, "you pin-faced mosquito."

"Ha, lovely," he said, then motioned for the guards to step back. He walked right up to her, and spoke softly. "It is time. You will decide upon my demands. Will you serve me?"

"Why do you even care so much?" she said, gesturing with frustration. "You're that insecure, that you think having a dragon as a servant will make something of you?"

"Ah, Illistandrista," he said quietly. "I thought you'd have figured it out. But I haven't explained, and you are young. Have you heard of Yadramak?"

"The name sounds familiar."

"Prime minister," he said, "of the Malwish Empire."

Her stomach sank. "The one who was killed two years ago."

"Assassinated. By one of the Sleepless. You know them, don't you? You've heard of the terrible creatures made all of crawling, creeping, murderous bits? Terror incarnate?"

"I've heard of them."

"Well," he said, "I know for a fact the detestable creatures respect your kind. And while the others of my crew are afraid of ghosts, and shades, and incarnations that walk Shadesmar . . . none of those frighten me. They have, in general, posed only a minor threat to those in power."

So much suddenly made sense. About what he'd done, and what he was doing. She followed his gaze as he looked toward the glowing serpent—and beyond. Discovering a new perpendicularity would make him extremely powerful, but he was a service man. Most of the wealth of that discovery wouldn't come to him—more, he would gain the notoriety. The fame. And the influence among others in his industry.

"So," she said, "your sights are set even higher than I assumed."

"New minister appointments are soon," he said. "*Perfectly* timed. Everyone fears the Sleepless will strike again, but one of us will *not* fear. One of us will be under the protection of the only race of beings longer lived, and more intimidating, than the insects."

"You don't want a servant. You want a bodyguard."

He clapped his hands, then waved to the side. An attendant there, who had been waiting out of earshot to give them privacy, trotted up. They were carrying a datapad, which displayed a woman of Aditil's same ethnicity, with light brown skin, though she was wearing a Malwish uniform.

"Esandi," he said to the screen. "Thank you for taking my call."

"Anything to repay the favor, Dajer," she said in accented Malwish.

"Will you show my friend your palm?" he asked, and the woman raised her hand—exposing a fully alive aether bud.

Though Ed and Aditil had been certain no aetherbound served the Malwish, here was proof otherwise.

"You realize," the woman said, "that this reveals closely guarded state secrets to that woman."

"Don't worry," Dajer said. "She'll soon be in my personal service." He looked to Starling. "Isn't that so?"

"An aetherbound, *actually* serving you?" she asked. "How? The aethers allow it?"

"There are ways around that," Esandi said. "Anyway, I have answers to your questions, Dajer. Do you want them now?"

"Absolutely," he said.

"You are correct," she said. "A former aetherbound, so long as she still has her bud, will be able to speak to the aether spores you use as fuel. Even if her bud is cracked and disconnected, I wouldn't let her anywhere *near* your ships."

"Wonderful information," he said. "Thank you." He nodded to the attendant, who withdrew with the screen, again leaving him and Starling alone. Still standing on the black, coral-like ground of the island, near where the engineers were setting up the Intensifier.

Starling felt a fool before his grin. She had thought herself so clever, but she'd again been solidly outmaneuvered. By talking to him about Aditil earlier, Starling had revealed what she was trying to accomplish. He'd seen straight through her, and he seemed to know *exactly* how humiliating that was.

"You cannot beat me," he whispered. "You cannot outthink me. Oh, I have no illusions that I could match skills with an ancient dragon, but you are not ancient, now are you, Illistandrista?" He waved to the side, and another attendant stepped up. This one had a screen with a view of her crew, locked in their room.

With mounting panic, she at first worried he knew about their subterfuge with the replaced voices. Blessedly he didn't seem to know that, as he was pointing at the climate controls at the bottom of the screen—with which he could change things like the temperature and oxygen content of the room.

"These bunks," he said, "are built to accommodate several of the more exotic species who work with our empire, including some that need it quite hot to survive comfortably. Hot enough that it would cook a human being alive." He inched his finger toward the controls. "Such a curious power to have, wouldn't you agree? Push one button, and the heat in this room would slowly increase. Step by step. Until they start to feel it, terrified—the very surfaces they touch start to burn them. The air in their lungs scalding their throats . . ."

"You'd so flagrantly violate the Silverlight Accords?" she said. "You might be able to execute some of my crew—probably just Leonore—but with such torture? Your own crew would turn you in for discipline."

"You are smart," he said. "But you also underestimate me. Accidents happen. Heating elements get stuck. And besides, tell me: Do the Silverlight Accords protect shades?"

She followed his gesture toward the bunker in which his people had set Nazh's prison, visible through a window, with an Aonic forcefield around it.

ISLES OF THE EMBERDARK

The Silverlight Accords, like most laws, did not protect the dead. Dajer could do to Nazh whatever he wished, no matter how excruciating.

"My intel," Dajer says, "indicates you and the shade have traveled together for quite a while. He was involved in the events that got you imprisoned, was he not? A good friend, always by your side." Dajer looked to her. "He will die to negative Investiture, just like any shade. Or maybe a little silver, to burn his essence? Make him scream, his eyes reddening, losing all semblance of personality before the terrible agony of—"

"Enough," she said. "That weapon can release me from these manacles?"

"Yes," he said.

"Prove it."

Fig. 24 · Meeker
(rodent)

CHAPTER FORTY-NINE

"I know there's no perpendicularity on the other side of that tunnel," a voice said. "And I know that you are lying."

Dusk stopped in place, and became aware of his surroundings. He'd walked almost all the way to his room, and the person who had spoken to him was one of his guards. It took Dusk an embarrassingly long time to process all this, during which he just kind of stared at the guard. A woman with long black hair, auburn skin, and a round face. Her metal mask wasn't full sized, but did cover her entire chin, unlike Dajer's. It seemed of a different style, and her uniform also bore a few unusual insignias.

She *knew*?

She gestured, and the other guard stepped away, looking around, as if to . . . maintain a perimeter. Give them privacy? From whom? Other soldiers?

"Let's step inside," the woman said, pulling the door open, then glanced back at him. "Come on. The lie is over. It's time to tell the truth."

The truth?

He would love the truth, for once. Still in a mild daze, he walked into his room, thinking on what she'd said. *I know there's no perpendicularity on the other side of that tunnel.*

Maybe she was the one who had placed the slab. Maybe he was *finally* going to get answers. He walked past her—Sak snapping to warn her to keep her distance. Inside he turned, hopeful, as she entered and closed the door.

"If you tell me the complete truth," she said to him, "I can make sure that you get no sentence. Just testify against Dajer, and that will be enough."

Testify?

Sentence?

Father . . . he thought. *I'm never going to make sense of this, am I?*

Starling's optimism was collapsing.

For the first time she could remember, she was losing her belief that everything would work out. She'd maintained her optimism when being banished. She'd held to it in those first, difficult years alone. She'd kept it when her uncle vanished, then when Hoid abandoned them. All along, she had been the one others could trust to see the light in every situation.

That light was stuttering. And the replacement light she could see came from a terrible device in Dajer's control. How did she save her friends? She gave in to him.

No, she thought as Dajer's soldiers settled her in a seat before the Intensifier. *No, he won't let them go, even if I agree to serve him. He might let them live, to maintain control over me. They, however, will never be free again. They know about the perpendicularity, and what Dajer was willing to do to obtain it. They are extreme liabilities.*

She could find no optimism in this. Leonore would essentially be back in jail. ZeetZi again a slave, after escaping his homeland and the tyrants there. Ed locked in a room, never able to see the sights of the cosmere. Aditil . . . Starling had promised her a chance to go home. But she'd never see Dhatri again. Not if Dajer won.

How could one be optimistic in the face of that? Starling slumped in her seat, even after the engineers counseled her to sit upright. She slouched there, staring at the glowing light from the front of the machine.

My friends have more optimism than me right now, she thought, *because I told them I'd solve the problems. I made them put their trust in me . . . I promised them. And I'm failing.*

Shards.

For the first time in her life, she saw only darkness. She was their captain. She was supposed to find a way out. She was supposed to *protect* them.

The device fired.

Contrary to her expectations, it released only a tiny beam of light—intense, so bright that everyone else put on shaded goggles. She couldn't be harmed by sights like this, but the tiny beam filled her vision with light.

They'd locked her arm in place so the beam hit the manacle. She heard Dajer instruct them to put the power output to a certain number, and the light intensified.

At first, she felt nothing except the normal chill that came whenever something attacked her or the bracelets.

Then . . .

Then Shards, she felt a tremble. The air around her quivering. The sense of cold from the bracelet faltering.

She strained against it, and felt something she hadn't in a long while. A well of strength inside of her, the innate Investiture of her species, constantly replenished directly by the Spiritual Realm. She couldn't access it, but she could *feel* it waiting for her.

Her senses expanded. Her kind didn't just claim to be gods. Dragons were Connected to their followers—and to each other. With the manacles weakened, she reached out, searching for her uncle. As she'd been trained as a child, she slipped her mind out of her body and entered the Spiritual Realm, going where dragons went when they slept, meditated, or died.

The ancestral ocean.

It took the shape of a vast shoreline—a beach like back on Yolen, with glistening white sand and rolling waves. All along the shoreline, dragons stood like incredible statues, towering over a hundred feet tall. The line of them ran as if into infinity, some more weathered than others.

They weren't actually statues, but neither were they alive. Something between the two. They were the dead who still meditated, and this was a place living dragons could visit—assuming they were old enough to have the training.

And that they weren't locked down by manacles. The only times Starling had been here following her exile were when she'd been brought by powerful dragons to stand before judges and answer whether she was willing to give in to their demands or not.

Today she came here on her own, appearing directly on the beach. Feet in the sand. Rolling waves like familiar friends, calling their greetings. She spun around, searching for her uncle, hoping he'd hear her unique call—for the first time in years—and join her here.

He did not.

But someone else did. A white-haired being in human form, with a prominent nose and a smirk to match.

Her uncle might not have heard her, but her master had.

Fig. 88 · Nose bug
(Sleepless)

CHAPTER FIFTY

"**Don't look at me with** that stupid expression," the guard woman said, walking into Dusk's room. "I know everything. It will be so, *so* much easier for you if you tell me, rather than making me force it out of you. When did Dajer hire you? How did he get you here?"

"He hired me," Dusk said carefully, "in his rooms after I first arrived. I came via boat, as you probably saw."

The woman rolled her eyes. She wore stark white gloves, something few of the others did. He again noted the way her mask outlined her chin and sides of her face, though the front was open. It was the only one like it he'd seen here.

"Please," she said, "the 'stupid savage' act isn't fooling me. Your arrival is far, far too convenient. A simple tribesman *sailing* to these shores out of the darkness, with a story of a perpendicularity matching Dajer's fancies? Right after he loses so many soldiers that he's in danger of having his operation shut down? It was *obviously* scripted."

Scripted?

She thought he was an actor paid by Dajer to pretend to be . . . well, a man from First of the Sun. He found a logic to what she had guessed, as it must have looked convenient indeed that Dusk should arrive. Particularly if you assumed, like all of these outlanders did, that a man such as himself could *never* have sailed the unsea without help.

"Not going to talk?" she asked. "I'm Saja, of the military police. It's my *job* to watch Dajer. I don't know if he's told you, but what he has made you do is *highly* illegal. Lying to us, leading him to be able to requisition sensitive and important equipment?

"If there is a perpendicularity in this region, it's not here—but Dajer can't afford to admit that. He's caused the deaths of six soldiers pursuing a barely authorized personal crusade. He knows that when the truth comes out, and everyone knows how much money, time, and blood he's wasted . . . his career will be over. He'll be thrown in prison." She pointed at Dusk. "You'll go with him—unless . . ."

"Unless . . . what?" he asked. Because she expected it, and Vathi had told him he should at least try to facilitate conversations.

"I have a deal for you."

Dusk quite nearly laughed. *Of course* she did. Why wouldn't she? Why wouldn't *everyone* in this insane place have some kind of role they wanted him to play in their machinations? Who was next? The chef who brought his food?

"Agree to testify against Dajer," she said. "I'll call it in now, and we can stop this farce, then keep looking for the perpendicularity elsewhere under my leadership. You'll get to be a hero instead of a villain. Just tell me you're willing. I've been gathering *quite* the case against Dajer, and while I don't need you to bring him down, this is your chance to set things right."

Dusk settled the birds on their makeshift perch, then refilled their water and food. Sak gave a chirp that sounded . . . ashamed.

Now this was something important. He ignored the woman for a moment, leaning down. "What?" he asked the bird. "Why are you sad?"

She chirped again, and he thought he got it. All her life, she'd helped him by giving him the unusual ability to see his corpse. A unique gift among Aviar. But here . . . she'd barely been able to do that because the dangers he currently faced were the kind you had to navigate with a sharp word, not a sharp knife.

"Please don't be like that," he whispered, scratching her. "You're wonderful. And you've been helpful during our descent into the cavern. Don't forget."

She cooed, more hopeful.

The cavern. The sign. He took that from around his wrist and hung it for the birds to play with. He still needed to deal with it, but first, the woman. Who was displaying signs of impatience as she stood there, arms folded.

"I'll admit," she said, "the birds are a nice prop. Almost believable."

"I will consider what you said," he told her. "And I will not tell Dajer you approached me. Will that settle us for now?"

"It would be better if you just agreed to help me."

He did not reply. Because that had not been a question, and he did not need to facilitate conversations *that* much. Particularly with those he would rather throw from his rooms so he could get some rest.

"I suppose I can give you a little time," she said. "To consider."

"Thank you," he said. And though he was annoyed, he acknowledged that under other circumstances, this might have been the right person to side with. She seemed the most reasonable of them all, wrong though she was. Perhaps if he turned in Dajer, everyone would leave.

They would find out I'm no actor, he thought. *The reports of this place, and what Dajer saw, would bring others. Even she thinks there is a perpendicularity somewhere, just not here.*

So he walked to the door and opened it. Thankfully, she left. This allowed him to, at long last, lie down to consider what he'd seen. The wooden slab. His own handwriting.

Unfortunately, the toll of so much happening—so much to think about—had to be paid. He needed rest more than he needed answers. He started to drift off. Then felt a sharp pain in his leg.

He groaned but, with annoyance, had Rokke turn off her warding field.

What happened today? the insect god immediately asked. *I don't understand why you're so distraught.*

Am I distraught? Dusk asked.

I can feel that you are, Dusk. The tension hovering in the back of your mind. The desire to escape it, for a time, with sleep. The guilt for that desire. What happened?

We found a sign, he thought, *with my own markings on it. I used to leave those when trapping, as reminders and warnings. I made up each symbol so* no other trappers could read them—and as far as I know, none of them ever cracked my code.

And what, the creature asked, *did this sign say?*

It said . . . "If you pass this point, you will never have a home again."

Curious words indeed. I see . . . None of your people know the symbols? You are sure?

Reasonably sure, he thought, careful to keep the rest of his mind blank. To not think things that might give away information. *Either way, the sign let me turn back. I'm not ready to find what's at the end of the tunnel.*

Not ready to finish your quest? Or is there more? What aren't you thinking, Dusk? What are you hiding from me? The skill to do so is not one I'd have expected from a person unfamiliar with my kind. Ah, but beasts on your homeworld hunt by tracking minds? Fascinating.

The thing was close to teasing the truth from Dusk, despite his efforts to hide it. He needed a distraction.

How would someone have placed that sign? Dusk thought. *How did they know to put it here, and how did they traverse the tunnel?*

No one placed it, Dusk, the thing replied.

What? But they must have. I didn't—

Take my node with you when you return, the god of insects thought. *I have the answers you want. I will show them to you. But only if we go together.*

With that, the thing released him, pulling its fangs out of his leg and crawling away under the sheets, hidden from observers. Dusk groaned and felt at his leg, but like the day before, the bleeding wasn't bad—the thing probably had a coagulant in its mind-reading venom.

What a strange life he led, these days.

Still, he was free for the moment, so he allowed himself to lie down to get some sleep. He focused on the thrumming pulses of the Knell, and the phantom Current, but they were growing softer. That made him panic a moment before he remembered how the worm paste ran out when applied to a boat.

He might just need more. He probably should have waited, as he didn't need those pulses at the moment—but he realized he'd begun to find comfort in the constant, if quiet, rhythm. So to cover what he was doing from both the insect god and the soldiers, he did an account of all his tools—including the jar. During this, he oiled equipment, sharpened knives, checked that the birds' pellets weren't rotting. He unscrewed the lid of the jar, sniffed the paste, and covertly got some on his finger.

With the lights on, he hoped that wouldn't be noticeable. He didn't eat the stuff until he'd gone into the bathroom, covering the act by brushing his teeth.

The thrumming, blessedly, returned. Indeed, it felt louder than before, almost insistent. Feeling relieved, he switched off the light and turned in. There, he drifted off, and . . . as he was going . . . he was sure he heard the gentle lapping of waves on the beach, and the soft voice of a loremother speaking to children.

He reached to touch the medallion around his neck, taken from Sky, a fallen brother of Patji. Something seemed to lift from Dusk as he fell asleep.

And he thought, for a moment, he saw his ancestors.

Fig. 100 · Dragon (head)

CHAPTER FIFTY-ONE

It *was* him. Master Hoid, strolling along before the shimmering spirits of the ancient draconic dead, studying their statuesque forms. Only dragons were supposed to be able to project themselves into this place, but Hoid did a great number of things he wasn't supposed to be able to do.

He turned to her and grinned, then extended his hands as she rushed up and gave him a hug. Some of her facade of confidence fell away, and she felt—for the first time in a long while—like a youth again. She pretended she was an adult, and mostly felt like one, after eighty-seven years of life. It was hard to feel otherwise around mortals who were so young.

But here was one who was legitimately wise. Someone whose life rivaled that of any living dragon.

Hoid was here.

Hoid would fix everything.

"Master!" she said, holding to him. "I need you. Please. The crew is in trouble, and I think I've ruined everything. You have to help us."

"That's going to be *rather* difficult, Star," he said gently.

"Why?" she said, pulling back.

"Well, it's frankly embarrassing," he said. "There's this vault, and it only opens once in a very long time, and . . ."

"You're trapped inside, aren't you?"

"I was *sure* I could find another way out . . ." He looked around. "I was hunting for your uncle when I sensed you. He hates it when I bother him with my quandaries."

"Master," she said, finally stepping back. "Uncle Frost . . . I haven't seen him in years. Nobody has. I thought you knew."

"Oh, I'm sure he's hiding somewhere," Hoid said. "He's one of the few I assumed I could reach from inside this vault. I'm surprised to find you, considering. Have you escaped the manacles?"

She shook her head. "But there are Scadrians, Master, and . . . well, it's a complicated mess. Please. Surely there's something you can do."

He contemplated her, then looked to the line of ancestral dragons. Each with eyes toward the distant, rolling horizon. "Walk with me, Star," he said. "Tell me about it."

She did, hurrying alongside him. She explained what had happened with Crow, how they'd found the map, and how she'd led the others into danger. Embarrassed, she explained her simplistic plan to rescue them, and how Dajer had outmaneuvered her.

"I can't do it," she finished. "I'm no captain, Master. Not like *you* were. We have to find a way to get you out, so you can come save us. Maybe your wife can get you free? Have you tried contacting her?"

"She and I aren't on speaking terms," he said softly. "Partially because she doesn't remember ever having been my wife." He stopped, then found himself a nice walking stick among the flotsam on the beach, though she'd never known him to need any such support. "If you see either of the twins after you've gotten out of your mess, I'd appreciate you warning them I could use some help."

"Yes, Master," she said.

Hoid then fell silent. They walked the endless beach, leaving footprints for the surf to play in. They passed dragon after dragon, each one enormous. All settled with necks out, looking across the ocean. Each distinctive, but in a similar posture. The farther back you went, the more faded and transparent they became. Dragons were so Invested that they needed a place to fade away after they died—a process that could take millennia.

It had been a while since she'd been here, but she'd always wondered what the ancient dragons thought about as they waited for eternity. They wouldn't speak to you, no matter how you tried to get their attention. The concerns of the living no longer interested them. They only cared about those rolling waves, and the deep thoughts of ones who have seen worlds rise and fall.

She gave Hoid time to think, not interrupting him. She did wave to Design, however, who dimpled his long jacket. This was technically the Spiritual Realm, so Design could have appeared as she wished, but today the spren just spun her pattern a little more vibrantly by way of acknowledgment.

"Star," Hoid said. The surf tickled their toes—neither of them wore shoes. It would have felt wrong. "Do you know why I left you and the crew?"

"I assumed something important came up," she said. "Someone who needed your help. I . . . admit I felt abandoned at times, but I knew you must have had a good reason."

"Yes. I got bored."

"Oh," she said, thinking through those words. Why would he say that? For her benefit, obviously. "You mean . . . you needed to do something dangerous, and you didn't want to bring us, lest we risk getting hurt."

"Amazing," he whispered. "All this time, and you still think the best of me. Makes me wonder where I went wrong with the others . . ." He smiled at her. "I lied. I didn't get bored, Star. I saw something in you . . . saw that you were ready. I knew you needed to do the next part without me. That, I'm confident, is still the case."

"But I'm ruining it."

"You protected the ship and the crew from Xisis."

"I just moved the debt collection down the road, then led everyone into a disaster trying to find a way to pay it! I . . ." She took a deep breath. Optimism. She needed to be *positive*. "I . . . I'm protecting them now. I'm coming to *you* and letting you help."

"And if I can't help?"

Then . . .

Then . . . Shards. Then she was *terrified*.

They walked a time longer, but she couldn't enjoy the curling waves

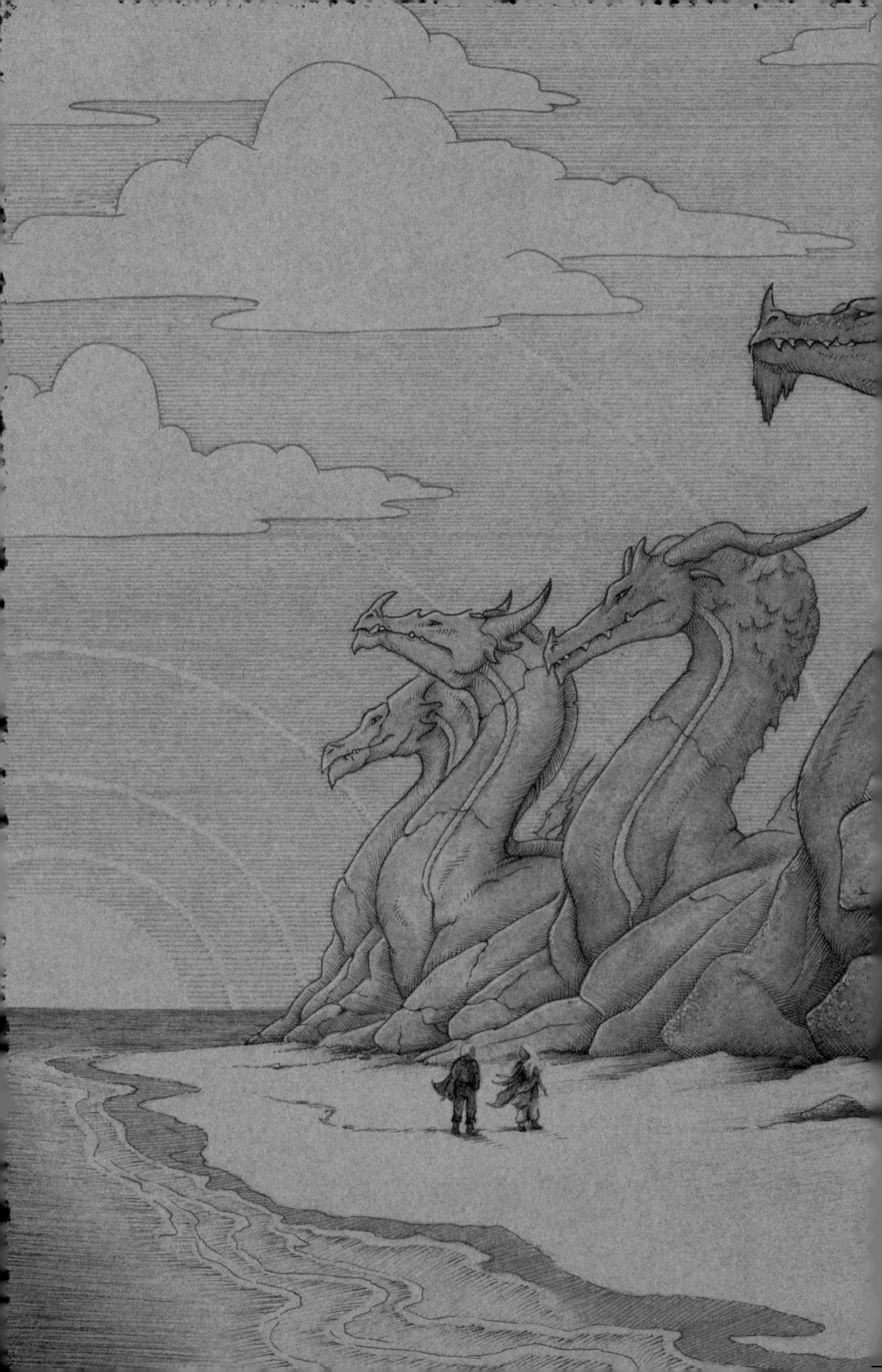

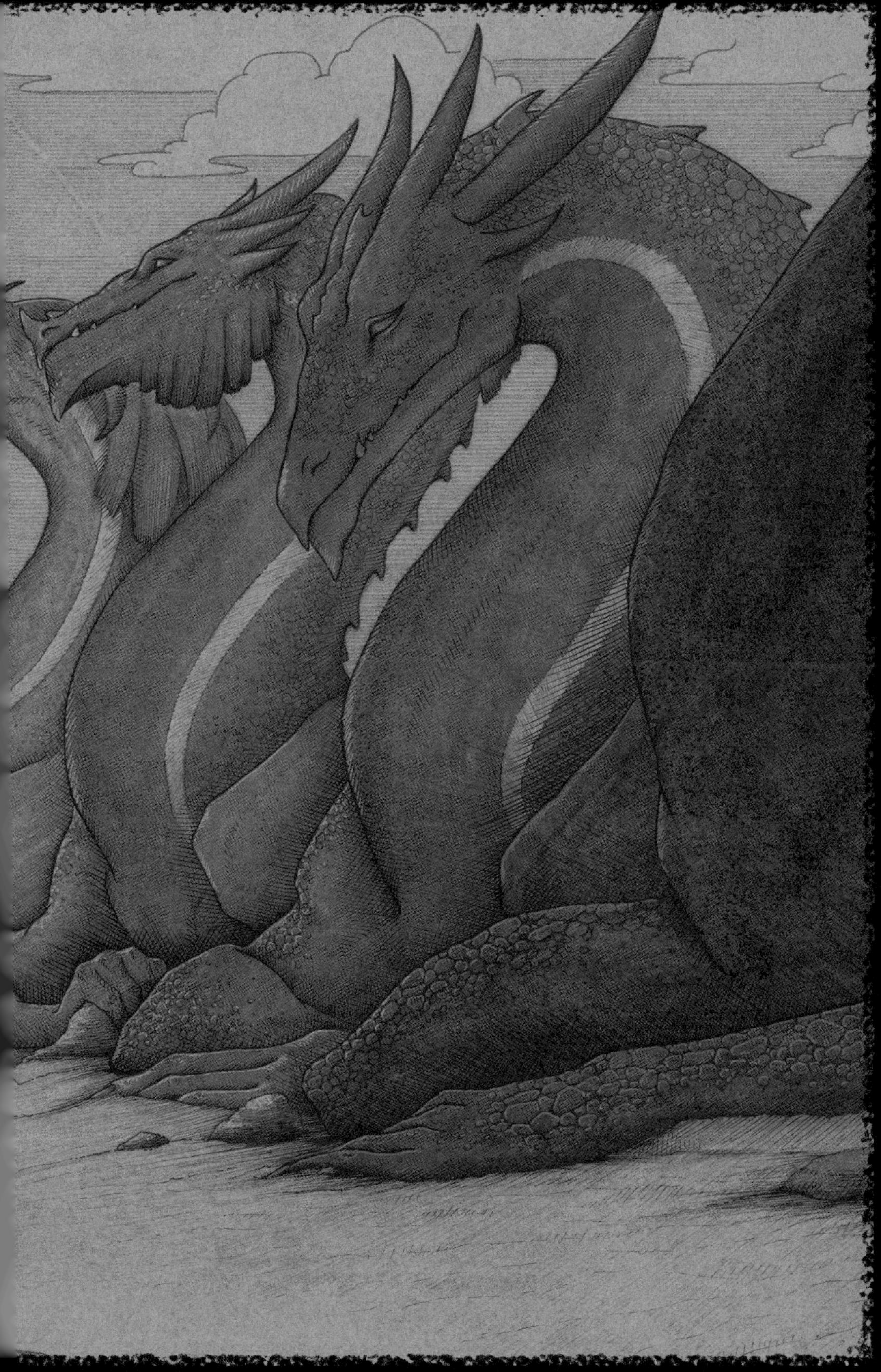

with silvered heads, the deep blue expanse whispering mysteries, the stoic ancestors with shimmering scales. Partly due to her worry, but there was more. Each time she'd come to this place in recent years, it had been because the judges had called to demand she accept their will and end her exile.

In that, this place of peace and beauty had become—to her—just another prison.

"Star," Hoid said, planting his staff in the sand with each step, "would you like a story?"

"Please," she whispered.

Ocean wind blew his hair like a capped wave. "This," he said, "is the story of wise King Nohadon, and how he saved Roshar."

Starling put her hand to her lips. Stories of Roshar were among the best; Hoid had a special affection for the planet.

"On the planet of storms," Hoid said, "the gods imbued ten warriors with power beyond what almost any soldier has known. They could fight with the help of the wind itself, and were virtually unstoppable in battle. They could kill hundreds, sometimes thousands. They protected the people each time their enemies came upon them—a nightmarish force of immortal spirits."

"Those ten were the Heralds," she said. "I know of them. They're said to be the greatest warriors the cosmere has ever known."

"If not the greatest, then in contention for the title. But here's the thing, Star. Each time, soon after they fought and defended the land, society collapsed."

"It did? But . . . why, Master? If the warriors were so incredible?"

"You anticipate the moral of the story. Good, you're learning. I shall, then, turn the question back on you. Why? Why would having *incredible* warriors not be enough?"

She looked at all aspects of the story, and imagined it as described. Ten incredible soldiers, Invested to incredible levels. Who would fight, then leave, to seal away a demonic enemy. It involved a planet with powerful soul magnetism of some sort.

"They died," she said, "and left behind . . . ordinary people. Shards, people had never learned to fight for themselves because the Heralds always did it for them."

"Yes," Hoid said. "Starling, I left you an incredible crew. ZeetZi is a genius with machines. I've rarely met a pilot like Leonore, and she has untapped understanding of Scadrian tactics. Have you asked her for help with them?"

"She's reserved," Starling said. "She doesn't like going back to those days."

"She will, for the good of the crew," he said. "And don't discount Ed. He's a shade overeager, but brilliant. Aditil has unharnessed power she doesn't recognize, and neither does anyone else. Then, of course, there's Chrysalis."

"She . . . doesn't like us, Master. And frankly, I don't trust her."

"That's because you're smart," Hoid said. "Chrysalis is undoubtedly working on multiple ways to escape this predicament and abandon you. The Sleepless have learned self-preservation at all costs."

"That doesn't sound very useful to us, Master."

"That depends," he said. "Star, do you know why I took you on as an apprentice?"

"Because of your friendship with my uncle?"

Hoid chuckled. "No, Star, he tried to talk me out of it. He didn't want you getting into more trouble, and for some baffling reason, he assumed that I would attract it!"

She didn't say anything, though Hoid eyed her, expecting a wisecrack. She'd found that if she just smiled, he'd imagine one better than she could make.

"I took you on," he continued, "because you got exiled."

"So it was pity?" Her stomach turning at the thought.

"Pity? Illistandrista, child, you took on the entire draconic society! You spit in the face of some of the most distinguished, self-important, powerful beings in the cosmere. And you did it because you cared."

He turned to look her in the eyes, standing beneath the powerful figure of Karokandriamast the Mighty, a dragon some three centuries dead. Her soul was the color of new steel before it was polished, marked with the char of the coals that had given it birth.

"You *cared*, Star," Hoid said. "You took a stand, despite what it cost you, and didn't back down. I don't consider someone for an apprentice because they can turn a phrase or memorize stories—I learned that lesson. I can teach those skills anyway. But someone who *cares*, even when the cosmere does everything it can to beat that sensibility out of them . . . well, that's impressive."

She stood a little taller.

"Now," Hoid said gently, "you need to stop protecting your crew, and start *leading* them."

"Like . . . Nohadon the wise?"

"He realized that people couldn't continue to lean on the Heralds. His was the era where powers came to the ordinary people, not just their demigods. He was the one who realized that without change, they'd always fall once the Heralds left. Because the Heralds couldn't always protect the people. Just as I can't always protect you."

"And . . . I can't always protect the crew."

Hoid nodded. "Your powers are locked away, you're watched, and this Scadrian is considering everything you say with an eye to outmaneuvering you."

"But the crew . . ." she said. "He threw them in a room, and is basically ignoring them."

"They can do more than you're letting them, Star. Every mortal can. It's our failing, with the gifts we've been given, to assume that everyone around us is incapable."

She wanted to object to that, to contradict him, to explain she *didn't* think the others were incapable. But . . .

But she'd learned to listen, really listen, when he spoke. Especially when he said things she didn't want to hear.

"I . . . tried to make up the plan myself," she admitted.

"And dismissed their attempts to help."

"But Master," she said, "their plan was *terrible*. It was little more than the 'fake sick' routine. It's the first thing everyone tries! Followed closely by 'two friends start a fight.'"

"So their first plan was bad. You made many bad plans when we traveled together. What did I do?"

"Made fun of me."

"After that."

She thought back. "You pushed me."

"As you need to push them. *That's* your job. We're not captains at war, Star. We don't lead by running ahead with weapon raised. We lead from *behind*."

"How does one lead," she said, "from behind?"

"By standing at the back of the wagon," Hoid said, "and *pushing*."

"I . . . All right, I'll do better."

"Do more than what is better," he said, leaning toward her. "Do what is *amazing*. I'll come check on you once I get out of this vault. If you run across Sigzil, smack him for me."

"Master, I could never."

"What? It's a sign of affection among his kind."

"The Azish?"

"No, incredible bastards."

He smiled, then started to fade. Or . . . no, it was *Starling* who was fading. Out of the ancestral ocean, back into Shadesmar, where she was still in front of Dajer and his enormous cannon.

She drew breath and shook herself. She hadn't ever left this place physically—they'd have seen her just sitting there in a daze, probably for only a few moments.

"It worked," Dajer said, taking off his goggles and stepping closer. "Don't lie and pretend it didn't. That *weakened* your manacles."

"It did," she admitted.

"We used barely a fraction of the Intensifier's strength." He smiled. A wicked, self-satisfied smile. "You know for certain now. I *can* save you."

She nodded.

"So do we have a deal?"

"I will . . . consider," she said, then met his eyes. "For real this time."

"You have one day." He gestured for the guards to haul her back to where her people were being kept—a way to remind her, she was certain, of the costs of not agreeing.

She didn't care at the moment, because it put her with her crew. They were sitting around the table as she entered, playing cards.

Hoid was right. Dajer had been mostly ignoring them. And so, despite her best intentions, had she. Her master challenged her to lead them, but what were the specifics? He so often skipped that part—the practical *how* of what he suggested someone do. If she had a criticism of him, that would be it.

Be better, he said. *Soar,* he challenged. *Be amazing.*

Suddenly, despite how uplifted she'd felt moments before, this seemed like just another problem she had to juggle. She walked through the room as the others smiled and greeted her, then sat at the table with them, trying to project optimism. Trying to be what they needed.

But today it was too much. She found herself shaking, holding herself. Not crying, but trembling. They looked at her, horrified, as she spoke.

"I don't know what to do," she said, her facade of control crumbling. "And I think we're all in serious, *serious* trouble."

They stared at her. As far as she knew, none of them had seen her this way. Nazh had, but he was still locked in that shade prison.

She was worried seeing her flaws would break their wills.

Instead, it did something else.

"Rusts," Leonore said, pulling her mask down over her face. "If Captain is worried, it must *really* be bad."

ZeetZi dropped the tray of puffs he'd been cooking and slid into a seat. Ed put his cards back in their box. Aditil pulled her hands to her chest, a sign of concern.

"All right, then," ZeetZi said. "No more playing. We need to *fix* this."

Fig. 95 · Dakwara
(Entity)

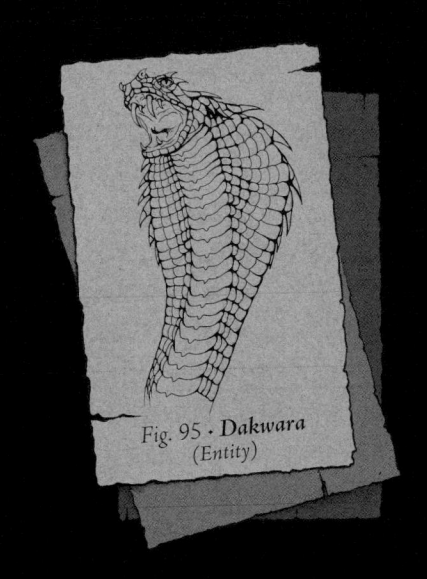

CHAPTER FIFTY-TWO

Dusk dreamed he was Cakoban, the great explorer.

Perhaps it was real. Perhaps it was imagination. But the ropes felt real as he gripped them, tying rigging, sweating, working as they sailed . . .

The unsea.

A black sky. A deep nothing beneath. A horizon that was too far away. Cakoban yelled—no, Dusk yelled—to those working with him. A three-person catamaran, bigger than Dusk's canoe, but not by much. Yet this boat had a *sail*. Shimmering and golden, iridescent with its own light. Somehow, though there was no wind, it billowed and moved the ship.

The Current. It was a sail that could sense the Current.

Cakoban was a large man, by the lore—but in the dream he was lean and wiry, not fully five and a half feet tall, but with muscles that bulged as he moved along the boat and took over the rudder. He glanced down, and saw that it glowed with a shining light that matched the sail—and matched a glow on the bottom of the boat. More golden than the worm paste, but obviously something similar.

"Still back there?" he asked, holding firm to the rudder as one of the other men—wearing no shirt, dressed in the wrap and loincloth of the ancient days—peered backward.

"Still there," the man said.

"It thinks we will lead it to more prey," Cakoban said. "Smart. Dangerously smart."

"Either that," the other man said, "or we are the prey now. Where is your friend? Is he close?"

"I do not know," Cakoban whispered. "I wish I did."

In the dream, Dusk knew his ancestor's mind. They'd dropped most of their people at the new land—the one with the deadly islands. Cakoban had left again on a long expedition, with three other ships, to search the darkness. They'd been separated during a strange storm, and when he'd used his senses to find one of the other ships, he found it wrecked on an island with no survivors. But something else had been watching it.

Death. A monster that immediately gave chase and prevented his team from fishing—for it ate each of the skullsnakes they tried to catch. They'd barely stayed ahead of it, and had been fleeing for weeks now without food.

But who was the friend Cakoban spoke of?

"How far?" the third man said, from the prow. "How far to the island? Surely we're close. Surely we can make it."

Cakoban gestured for the closer man to take the rudder. He did so, and Cakoban climbed along the ship to the center, where he took out a small glowing jar. Filled with worms? No . . . a thick golden liquid. He drank, then hit his chest—which released a sound, almost like that of a tuning fork.

In a moment, Dusk could hear the pulse coming from that distant place—the one that washed over this darkness, unheard by most. Cakoban's eyes began to glow, and he hit his chest again, releasing a distinctive golden sound.

"There are days yet until we reach the place with the portal," he said. "I'm sorry."

The other two wilted. Days. They would not survive. Cakoban pointed, however. "There *is* a small island ahead."

"The monster will kill us," one of the men said. "Land didn't save the others."

"It will not kill you," Cakoban said. "I will not let it, my friend." He pointed. "Veer that direction, just slightly. That's it. Good."

Then he turned to face the monster.

It was not what Dusk had been expecting. He'd heard many stories of Cakoban and the Dakwara—but this thing was no serpent. It was a many-armed horror, rising from the unsea on two spindly legs, bearing a hollow face full of pits. It moved without moving. Frozen in a position one moment, then in another position the next. Dusk felt something pulsing from it, a longing for life and a *fury* at all who lived. Confusion, and terrible regret. It had been destroyed, yet pieces of it lived on.

It had to consume. For it knew no other purpose.

Cakoban returned to the rudder and took his knife, then notched the wood ahead of it to indicate a heading. If one kept the rudder even with that line, it would lead somewhere. "Keep it on this heading, Jope," he said, pointing ahead. "Right there. You have enough light to make it, so long as you maintain your mindshield."

"But Cakoban . . ." the man said.

"The thing wants our light," he said, picking up the jar. "And it wants me, for having had too much of it. I can feel its mind each time I Navigate. But I can best it. You know the stories. Best the monster, and it must serve you."

"I . . . don't think that is one of the daccwaga, Cakoban," the man said. "It is something born of terrible darkness. It will not follow our rules."

"You deny me the honor of trying?" Cakoban demanded.

"You're just trying to put me off from arguing," the other man said, tears in his eyes. "You know it will kill you."

"You must return to my sister, Jope," Cakoban said softly. "You are her entire world."

"I see your fear," Jope said.

"Well, when you tell the story, tell it more bravely than that, eh?" Cakoban laughed. "Tell them I knew I could defeat it." He tossed the jar of light up a foot and caught it as it fell. "Tell them I did defeat it. And then I sailed on, for new adventures, eh? My children will like that."

They could see the small island ahead now, the one that Dusk had located, with the tunnel. Cakoban smiled to his friends, then threw the lid off the jar of glowing light and tipped it back, drinking it all.

Then he started to glow golden.

They zipped past the island, and he dove into the unsea. Glowing as he was, he could swim in the not-water. The ship, with his friends, continued on.

He didn't reach the island. The boat could barely outrun the monster, and he was a lone swimmer. Before he'd gone a short distance, the thing snatched him in one of its many arms. Him, the size of a worm to it.

He should have died, but with the glowing power within him, Cakoban resisted—struggling weakly in the monster's fingers—and his defiance seemed to *hurt* it somehow. The beast tossed him to the island.

There he broke, bones snapping.

The thing loomed overhead, but . . . as Cakoban's life slipped away . . . he thought he heard . . .

Wings beating.

He whispered, eyes fluttering closed. "You are too late, my friend. But thank you."

"Cakoban." A deep voice. "I could not find you. I am sorry. I had no Navigator."

Light shone across Cakoban, and something reached to lift him. The deep voice continued, "I will take your body to the others."

"No," Cakoban whispered. "It will follow if you do so. But . . . I defeated it . . . It came to kill my friends, and by my sacrifice, they escape. I faced it with courage, so it must follow . . . my rules. It must follow . . . me . . ."

He slammed his fist to his chest, and when his eyes opened, they shone golden.

"It must *follow me.*"

Dusk shocked awake.

To the sounds of people screaming.

Fig. 82 · *Glowing butterfly*
(insect)

CHAPTER FIFTY-THREE

"**They know about Aditil's abilities,**" Starling explained to the crew. "Dajer guessed what I was trying to do. They won't let her anywhere *near* their ships."

"Then we have to do this another way, yah?" Leonore said, all business.

"And soon," Starling said. "He's given me one day to agree to his terms. He really, really wants a dragon bodyguard. He thinks it will protect him from the hordes."

Leonore tapped the tabletop with one finger. "That weapon he brought in—maybe we can use that."

"Oh!" Ed said. "The Scadrian Intensifier!"

"What an ineptitudinous name," ZeetZi said. "Sounds like the sort of device you'd use to occupy a toddler."

"I like it," Leonore said. "But sometimes I have the temperament of a toddler. What do you know about it, Ed?"

"They've been developing it in 'secret' for years," he said. "But the Malwish can never resist an opportunity to show how powerful they are, so they let a few external arcanists witness it. It makes a highly focused beam of disruptive Investiture, intended to unravel permanent Spiritual bindings. Like anti-Investiture, but less destructive."

"It flickered the lights," ZeetZi noted, his eyes narrowed.

"Sure," Ed said. "It takes an *incredible* amount of BEUs to power something like this." He paused. "Is it warm in here to anyone else? We should tell the guards."

Starling felt a spike of alarm, but the heat didn't increase further. This was just Dajer making another warning. She forced her thoughts back on track. "The device," she said. "Dajer said he used only a little of its possible power on me." She held up her manacles. "He thinks, with a stronger blast, he can get me free of these."

ZeetZi nodded, obviously considering something.

Leonore perked up. "Oh!" she said. "We can get him to let you go, then you go all giant reptilian predator on the lot of them! Gobble them up."

"We don't eat people, Lee," Starling said.

"But you'd do it this once, yah?" Leonore said. "For me?"

"Wouldn't work," Ed said. "He'll only let her go if she agrees to a contract, the sort that are extra binding on dragons. Like the one Star refused to agree to during her exile, which got her the manacles in the first place."

"He's right," Starling said. "Dajer will insist on something my powers would bind me to. He isn't going to make the mistake of doing otherwise. And if he does get me under contract, the first thing he'll do is vanish you all. He considers you too much of a liability to keep around."

"Intimidated," Ed noted, "by my good looks. Sorry, all. I keep earning us enemies that way."

"The gun . . . the Intensifier," ZeetZi said softly.

"What?" Aditil said. "We steal it?"

"Doesn't matter," ZeetZi said, practically bursting. "The lights flickered! It takes a lot of power, Ed?"

"An insane amount."

"Power that comes from . . ."

"The gunship," Leonore said. "This is a standard Jada-class, long-range support cruiser. It has an amazingly powerful engine."

"It's powering all of this," ZeetZi said. "Right?"

"Sure," Leonore said. "Cords to each of the habitats, which is why when it fired the Intensifier, our lights . . ." She sat up. "Our lights flickered."

"Magnetic locks," ZeetZi said. "If he fires the machine too much, or too long . . ."

"We get free," Ed whispered, then grinned.

"That doesn't solve the main problem," Starling said. "If we get out, great—but our ship will be on lockdown."

"Zee has overrides," Leonore said.

"Indeed," he said. "There isn't a Scadrian alive who can lock me out of one of my own systems."

"They'll *still* hunt us down with those starfighters, though," Ed said. "So Star is right—we're back to our original problem."

The group grew quiet, stumped. Until Aditil, looking embarrassed, raised her hand. "I have an idea."

"Oh!" Ed said. "Is this about the aethers? Is there something you can do with them?"

"Ah," she said, glancing down. "No, it's not about that. It's . . . I'm sorry."

"Aditil," Starling said, putting her hand on the woman's, trying to do as her master would. Only without the insults, since those never worked well for Starling. "You're a member of this crew. What you have to say is important, whether or not it has to do with aethers."

"Yah," Leonore agreed. "You're not here just because you got a hole in your hand. Just like Zee isn't here simply because he has a hole in his head."

"Well," Aditil said, fidgeting—but smiling—at the attention. "I was thinking . . ."

As she pointed out something the rest of them had completely missed, Starling started to get excited. This could work; it could *really* work. A much better plan than she'd come up with, and one she could *never* have come up with on her own.

She'd worried that being weak before them would erode their confidence in her. And yet somehow, being weak was exactly the sort of leadership they'd needed. Together at the table, it all started to click into place.

Nurtured by their determination, optimism rekindled inside of Starling. They *were* going to get free.

All she needed to do was get Dajer to overextend that Intensifier until the gunship engine stuttered—and the lights went out.

She nodded to herself, confident. Until she heard the people screaming outside, and knew that something had gone terribly wrong.

THE END OF
BOOK THREE

BOOK FOUR:
THE DAKWARA

Fig. 45 • Cakoban's Finger
(fruit)

CHAPTER FIFTY-FOUR

Starling ducked out of their habitat and entered chaos. Soldiers ran and shouted as they crossed the obsidian beach, while weapons fired with sharp cracks in the near distance. She ducked out of the way of a passing squad and positioned herself to see what was happening.

The entity at the center of the island had decided to attack.

Squads of soldiers unleashed varieties of gunfire on the thing—but the weapons, both conventional and Invested, had no discernable effect, save perhaps to annoy the entity. It reared high, like a cobra well over a hundred feet tall, eerily reminiscent of her draconic ancestors posed on the Spirit Shores.

Shards. Had she set the thing off somehow?

Accompanying the entity were hundreds of smaller snakelike creatures with prominent bone protrusions on their faces. Physical beings, not creatures made entirely of glowing Investiture like their god. Normally, these swam around it in circles, like currents of writhing flesh, some going one way, some the other. Today they boiled up onto the land, slithering across the ground to strike at the soldiers. At least here the gunfire did something, blasting the creatures to pieces and spraying blood across the black stone.

Then the god struck.

As Starling watched, the monster snatched up a soldier. Though the entity was not made of traditional matter, it could touch a person easily enough, and the unfortunate soldier vanished. His soul devoured by the ancient, broken god; his body instantly dissolved into dark mist.

One part of her acknowledged the tragedy in this. The rest of her realized the opportunity. She turned to gather her crew, hoping to flee—but though the guards at her door had orders to let her pass, the same was not true for her people. One guard warded Leonore back with a gun while the other slammed the emergency lock, sealing the door shut.

"What's wrong with you!" Starling shouted, waving toward the chaos. "Your friends are in danger."

"My orders," a guard snapped, "are to keep these prisoners *prisoners*."

Starling gritted her teeth, locking gazes with the woman—but while the Malwish Scadrians had many flaws, their military force was incredible. Discipline reigned even during an attack.

Nearby, fighters lifted off into the sky to provide air support against the entity, and her team's newly minted plan depended on those fighters being grounded. If Starling and her crew *had* managed to escape their pod right now, they'd still have the same old problem: fighters would make quick work of them. She had little doubt that the pilots would spare a moment, even during all the killing, to shoot at the *Dynamic*. Starling—indestructible but unable to transform into her winged form—could safely be allowed to fall through the darkness of the unsea until the crisis was over. Then she could be recovered from the still-plummeting wreckage, snatched from among the corpses of her friends.

Her team couldn't escape now. They needed those fighters on the ground first—which meant the fact that Dajer was out among the soldiers, visibly calling for the Intensifier to be set up, was another problem. She couldn't risk that weapon draining power now, opening the locks. It was too soon.

She started toward the Intensifier, fully aware that the entity—like the one they'd faced before—was one of the few things in the cosmere that could kill a dragon. She crossed the ground at a low run—one of her guards following to keep an eye on her—and spotted someone else on the beach.

Dusk, carrying a rifle but seemingly unconcerned, walked straight toward the entity, as if facing a giant glowing snake monster were the most common thing in the world.

Dusk strode amid shouting soldiers, and was impressed. The Ones Above formed groups and took turns firing, a tactic that kept the Dakwara actively disoriented, looking one way, then the other. A separate group of soldiers put down their rifles—which seemed little more than irritants—and picked up harpoons.

Dusk had noted those earlier: dozens of rope-bearing harpoons lined up near the edge of the island's inner moat. He'd wondered at the purpose, but now it seemed evident. The soldiers quickly dipped the ends of the harpoons into a glowing liquid. A rank launched them at the Dakwara while she was distracted by gunfire, then held to the ropes.

They weren't trying to kill her, if such a thing were possible, only hold her down. Clever indeed. At least if his people were going to be conquered, it would be by competent soldiers.

"Dusk!" Starling said, emerging from the chaos and running for him. "What are you doing?"

"In the histories," he said over the noise, "it is said you must never run from the Dakwara. Her body extends through the entire ocean, and she can be anywhere she wishes. Only confidence and bravery will allow you to survive—and only if she is impressed enough to spare you." He looked at Starling, noting how frantic she seemed. "But those are just our stories. You think they are silliness."

"I didn't say that," she replied.

"No, you didn't. Thanks to some learning I've done these last years, however, I can understand what people *don't* say." He turned back as the Dakwara reared, easily lifting the dozen soldiers trying to restrain her. They shouted and fell. It had been a valiant effort.

"Shards," Starling said. "Some of those were wearing medallions to increase their weight tenfold—and it lifted them like dolls . . ." She waved for Dusk to join her beside a large chunk of obsidian coral jutting from the ground nearby.

He walked over but stood tall, in case the Dakwara looked his direction. "What does your knowledge say of a creature like this?"

"I don't think you'll like it," she replied.

"If you think that," he said, "you have not been paying attention. I am of the dusk—the boundary between the dying day and the one to come. Your learning is useful to me, even if it contradicts what I know from my experience."

"All right," she said. "Will you at least take cover?"

"She doesn't appreciate those who take cover." He pointed as it slammed down and ingested a man who had been running. "Both soldiers she has eaten so far tried to flee."

The skullsnakes were different, of course, but most of them now retreated into the moat. They left dozens of their dead behind, but hundreds still churned in there. What did they eat when there weren't convenient soldiers nearby?

"That is not some creature from your mythology," Starling said. "It's what we call a negative-Investiture entity, a . . . type 3? Type 2? Shards, Ed knows. Anyway, a long time ago—when the Shards were newly born—one named Odium attacked and killed his *sibling*. A god was destroyed, torn apart, its Intent removed and its pieces made into some kind of terrible negative energy. They roam the emberdark, seeking souls to consume."

"That," he said, "sounds reasonable."

"Not outlandish?"

"You're speaking of gods," he said. "I don't believe anything is outlandish for a god. It sounds like the myths we tell. The ones you say cannot possibly be true because they weren't written down." He tipped his head back, studying the thing, remembering his strange dream. "That *is* the Dakwara from our lore. But it wasn't always that way, was it . . ." Could this thing be both? The creature of her legends and the one of his?

Why not? He found that did not bother him.

"Entities like this," she said, "change based on the thoughts and perceptions of the people nearby."

He looked at her sharply. All shouts faded, gunfire dissolving to nothing. He felt as if his vision had snapped into place—what had been blurry suddenly sharpened.

"They *change*," he repeated, "*based on what people think of them?*"

"Well, yeah," she said. "That's how all Investiture works. Especially Investiture like this, which is free from direct influence of a Shard. The thoughts, perceptions, and dreams of a society over time are particularly powerful."

"And stories?" he said. "What of stories?"

"Of course stories will have an effect," she said. "They shape people's perceptions. As I understand it, the more structured and unified the way people think of something, the more likely free Investiture is to latch on to that idea and embody it."

"So that *is* the Dakwara."

"It's untethered Investiture—a fragment of a dead god—that has, over many centuries of living here, been molded by the perceptions of your people to imitate the Dakwara."

"And how," he asked, "is that *functionally* different?"

She considered, still crouching beside the rock. Then she stood up beside him, adopting his same posture. "I suppose it really isn't. It will see itself the way you see it. And . . ."

"And she will follow the rules of the stories," he said. "Because she *is* the Dakwara—and perhaps Cakoban himself made it so . . ." He narrowed his eyes. "You think this is foolishness. In the stories, the Dakwara was born of a god . . . from far away. It fits. And if she is riled, then someone must have tried to cross her threshold without first proving himself worthy."

Dusk spun on his heel and walked to Dajer, who was shouting at some men near the big cannon-like machine. During all their interactions, he had never seen Dajer so irate. Usually the man was the very *model* of control. Now he waved toward the Dakwara. "I brought you here specifically for this, Tague!" he screamed. "I don't have time for excuses!"

"Look," Tague responded—while several engineers in simpler uniforms worked frantically with the equipment. "I can listen to you shout at me, or I can try to make the Intensifier work. It is new technology. Hiccups are common."

"Hiccups!" Dajer screamed. "I've just lost another soldier! Two! That means . . ." He hesitated, voice lowering. "I've lost too many. Mandatory review . . ."

"I am ready," Dusk said, "to return to the cavern."

Dajer focused on him, seeming to see him there for the first time. "We're under attack!"

"She is retreating," Dusk said, turning and pointing. "Her warning has been made. Did one of your people try to cross to the center? This is retribution for such an event."

"How could you possibly know that?"

"From the stories," Dusk said.

"Quaint," Dajer snapped, but the serpent *was* calming down—retreating back into the moat, lurking there instead of attacking. The soldiers stopped firing and formed back into squads, helping the ones who had been injured. They left behind a few still-writhing, dying skullsnakes.

Dajer pointed to one of his attendants. "Find out if anyone tried to cross without my permission."

"Yes, sir," the guard said, running off.

"How long?" Dajer demanded of the lead engineer. "Until you can fire this?"

"A half hour, perhaps," Tague said. "It's new te—"

"New technology, splendid, so you keep saying." Dajer spun on Dusk. "And you? Diving back in now, after you ignored me earlier? Why? Have you realized that if this machine *functions*, you are out of a job?"

"Your machine cannot kill the Dakwara," Dusk said, certain it was so. "I must return to the cavern because I know now what it is and why it is here. It exists to let me prove myself worthy to challenge the Dakwara."

"Nonsense, nonsense, and *more* nonsense," Dajer said. "Well, I suppose I have nothing to do for a half hour, other than contemplate upcoming discipline because of the casualties I've incurred." He took a deep breath. "This is coming to a head, savage. Home command can often take days to come to decisions—but many there wait for my failure. I would guess we have but a few hours before I am ordered to return in shame. I will have to abandon this project, or risk . . ."

He'd been about to say more, but his better sense obviously got ahold of him. Dusk had been certain he'd been about to say something like, "Risk seeing if my soldiers will follow me in violation of superior orders."

Dajer called for his drone to be prepared, though as they were waiting, the attendant he'd sent away earlier—to see if anyone had tried crossing the moat—scrambled back. "Sir!"

"Who was it?" Dajer said, eagerly turning toward her. "Oh, please tell me it was Saja."

Instead she held up a small object, the size of a pebble. It had been crushed, but Dusk could still make out the remnants of ten legs, an abdomen, and a thorax.

"Hordelings," the attendant said, breathless from running. "There are a dozen such corpses by the shoreline. One of *them* is *here*."

Fig. 88 · Nose bug
(Sleepless)

CHAPTER FIFTY-FIVE

Dusk was unceremoniously confined to quarters.

Not, he suspected, because they knew he'd had contact with the insect god. More because too much was happening, and a "dumb savage" standing around was more than any of them wanted to deal with. Just when he'd finally been excited to delve into the tunnel.

He settled down on his bed and was not surprised when he saw something creeping under the covers toward him. He slipped a leg underneath and soon felt another characteristic bite.

I'm sorry, it said. *I could not wait on you. I thought to fly to the center with some of my scout nodes. The thing was too observant.*

An understandable decision, Dusk said, *considering your desperation. What happens now? War between you and the Ones Above?*

The thing responded with a chuckle. *Do you remember earlier, when I told you that the days of gods had ended? It is time for you to witness why.*

Dusk frowned at the fatalism in its tone. The creature showed him what was happening outside, from the eyes of one of its nodes. Soldiers quickly setting up some device—not the cannon from earlier, but instead one that had disks on its front. They plugged it into some cords coming from the largest ship, all while Dajer—looking legitimately panicked—supervised.

You know the funniest thing, Dusk? the god asked. *We didn't kill the person they all are worried we assassinated. Their leader? He engaged my services as a spy. I was there when partisans killed him. But some of my nodes were killed as well, and where people find us, they assume malice.*

Even now I can feel you doubting. Because who would trust a mass of talking insects over the official reports? You have no stake, and yet you are suspicious. As we deserve. For always watching. For never acting.

Dajer gave the order. The machine turned on.

Their search before didn't miss my hiding place, the voice said. *They used deep scanners, which noticed part of the ship mimicking a false reading. Now this new machine will prevent us from speaking further. Before they kill me, I wish to tell you something. I know why the cavern confuses you. Those plants, those creatures, they exist because—*

I know, Dusk replied. *They are manifestations of what you call Investiture, created by the perceptions of my people. That cave is a creation of the thoughts and worries of trappers who worked Patji for generations. That's how plants survive here. They are creations of Investiture, like the Dakwara.*

Yes, it thought. *More, you are strangely Invested. You've done something to Connect yourself to this place—and to the emberdark itself. The cavern is adapting to your own perceptions and memories. That's where your sign came from.*

It appeared there, Dusk thought, *because of my own insecurities and worries . . .*

Yes, the insect god replied. *You are so much more than they think you are. I am glad we met, even if briefly.*

The machine engaged, and Dusk's vision vanished. The node attached to his leg started to spasm, pulling out its fangs, working its legs erratically and scraping his skin. He was left with a distinct impression of panic and terror.

This device didn't kill the god of insects. It did something worse.

It made the one become many.

"The Scadrians have Chrysalis," ZeetZi announced.

"How can you be sure?" Starling asked, stepping over to him after being forced back to their quarters.

He tapped his watch. "I have the *Dynamic*'s access hatches rigged with sensors to tell me if someone tampers with the wrong systems during dock. They found the bay where Chrysalis was hiding, and I'll bet they overrode the locks on the secret smuggler's chamber."

Starling checked under the table. Maybe it was unwise and would reveal too much—but she hoped their enemies were too distracted to spy right now.

The node that Chrysalis had been using to talk to them lay trembling on the floor.

"They'll have an interference cloud set up," Ed said. "Those are usually a bad idea—they interfere with *all kinds* of essential systems. While that's up, Dajer will have no sensors, no FTL communication, no nothing for any of the ships. But it will *also* prevent the various pieces of Chrysalis's body from linking—like a coordinated group of drones that lose all wireless capabilities."

"Glad someone finally found a way to disrupt them," ZeetZi said. But then paused. "I hope it's not too painful."

"I'd be curious what it *does* feel like," Ed said. "Do we even have words to describe the experience of each part of your body suddenly . . . going off on its own?"

"They'll ground the fighters," Leonore said. "Protocol. To make sure that no hordelings are in the systems, secretly piloting the ships. I don't even know if it's possible, but the manual dictates positioning every nearby ship within the interference cloud."

Dajer would only grow more unhinged—his time running out, his paranoia activated. He would be dangerous to her crew. *He's already dangerous to one of them,* she thought.

"They could still be listening to us," she said to the others. "Remember that." Chrysalis's protections would no longer be in place. Starling made eye contact with each of them, and they nodded. Even Aditil, who sat by the wall, looking sick.

The fighters were grounded. The Intensifier was here, ready. This was as good a time as any. Her team's signal would come when the lights went out; all she had to do was get that weapon to fire and drain the power. Then she would need to trust them to execute the rest of the plan themselves.

With that in mind, she went to the door and pushed the call button to address the guards outside.

"One of you run to Dajer," she said. "Tell him I'm ready to sign his deal."

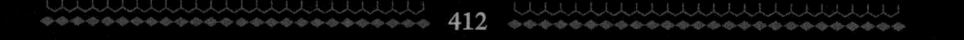

Fig. 99 • Dragon (claw)

CHAPTER FIFTY-SIX

They were moving Chrysalis with a shovel.

A flat, wide shovel, meant for moving snow or ash. Several soldiers carried her nodes, which they'd knocked out with some kind of foul-smelling gas, and deposited them none too gently into a new housing pod that had been released from the gunship.

At least they're not burning her, Starling thought forcibly. *She's alive—for now.*

Paranoid or not, Dajer didn't throw away tools. Starling's gut said he'd at least interrogate Chrysalis to determine if she was the one who had assassinated the prime minister—because if he captured *that* horde, it would be a political victory of sizable weight.

Starling found him sitting in a chair right beside the bulb that emitted the interference cloud. Not taking any chances, was he? Her manacles grew colder as she drew close, a warning she didn't need. Within this cloud, her ability to contact her kind—or draconic followers with a tamukek—would be blocked. But the equipment of her exile did that already, the manacles having recovered from the short jolt they'd been given earlier.

"So," Dajer said. "You were hiding one of *them.* I should have shot your ship down the moment we spotted it."

"If you'd done that," she said, "you wouldn't have any way to confirm the identity of the horde you killed."

He leaned forward. "You say you'll take my deal. You assume I'm still willing to offer it."

"You are," she said. "Because I had a horde on my ship, and she *obeyed me*." It was a stretch, but he wouldn't know that. "There's only one thing they fear: dragons."

He smiled, then nodded to an aide, who brought the contract. She'd already thoroughly read the one he'd drawn up, and this was the same. Unfortunately, it was reasonable. He knew as well as she did that her age would be an excuse if the contract were otherwise. It required thirty years of service—up from twenty—in a standard employment position. She had to protect him, and do reasonable tasks—as outlined in the contract—as requested.

This would make her his pet dragon, his bodyguard, his showpiece. A prison within a prison . . . but for only thirty years. A blink of an eye for her kind. It would be a small price to pay, and under other circumstances one she'd genuinely have considered. Except for her crew.

"You must let them go," she said, pointing to a clause. "Not simply promise 'best efforts' to see them 'appropriately treated.'"

"Without that clause, we have no deal," he said smoothly. "I have the law on my side, and even your draconic elders would not claim I'm pressuring you by threatening them. The truth is, I *should* see all but the aetherbound executed. You are trading for their lives, Starling."

"Lives spent in a cell."

"Lives," he said, "*lived*. Sign or do not sign. Your time is up."

She signed. "You realize," she said, "Chrysalis is on my crew. This protects her."

"Unless she killed the prime minister," Dajer replied. "See the footnote."

She'd read it.

Shards, but she hoped she was wrong and Chrysalis hadn't been the one to do that. Still, this would ensure that Chrysalis was given a fair trial. As fair as one could get in a Malwish court, at least.

It was the best Starling could do, especially since she didn't intend to go through with this contract. The agreement was void unless he actually freed her from her manacles. The plan was to stall, get him to engage the Intensifier, and cause a blackout.

He took the clipboard with the contract, reading it over eagerly—as if to admire his handiwork. An attendant approached and whispered to him, just loud enough that Starling—who had better hearing than most mortals—could overhear.

"We located eighteen memory nodes," the attendant said, "and twelve personality. That's an appropriate number for a horde this size. We believe we got them all; they do need to stay near one another, unlike other nodes."

"Excellent," he said. "Seal the door and bring me the temperature controls so I have some insurance."

Dajer crossed the black coral ground toward the Intensifier. Starling followed, breathing deeply, preparing herself. It would all come down to whether her people's ancient binding could withstand his device. She found herself disturbed—she had never had reason to hope for the strength of the prison that held her. But if it failed before the power source did . . .

Once they arrived at the Intensifier, Dajer didn't lock her into place. He pointed toward the moat and the entity. "Are we ready to kill it?"

The engineers nodded.

"Then fire," Dajer said.

"Wait," Starling said. "What about me?"

"You are of secondary importance. We need to find and reveal the perpendicularity before orders return regarding my . . . activities here. Fire at will, Tague."

"But . . ."

They ignored her, starting a short countdown. Starling stilled herself. The entity was easily as powerful as her manacles, likely far more so. Firing at it might be enough to drain the power. Moments later, the device emitted a tight beam of concentrated light, which struck the entity square in its serpentine head.

It blinked. Then closed its eyes. And seemed . . . happy. At a nod from Dajer, the lead engineer, Tague, turned up the power—making the light grow brighter. This didn't have any discernable effect on the creature.

"It's feeding on the Investiture," Tague said. "As I warned you might happen, sir."

"What key is the Investiture?" he asked. "Unkeyed?"

"Yes, sir. Positive aligned."

"Try negative."

They did. She couldn't see a change in the light, but it . . . felt wrong. Or, well, sounded wrong. But not to her ears. She thought she could see a slight warping to the air.

The entity didn't respond. Unnerving, considering the tantrum it threw earlier.

"Maybe," Starling said, "you're not using enough power."

"The ship can't give much more," Tague said. "Not without crashing the system. If this isn't working . . . sir, you have to accept it. This is a good data point, and a test we've been meaning to make, but I'm sorry—I can't imagine this accomplishing what you want. The entity is indifferent to our interference." He paused. "This is one of the better outcomes. It *could* have tried to eat the machine."

Dajer did not seem pleased. Starling almost encouraged them to try upping the power again, but she held her tongue. Last time she'd pushed too hard, she'd tipped Dajer off to her plans.

"Well," Dajer said. "I guess I'm going to have to put my life in the hands of the primitive after all. Someone fetch him. Our time is extremely limited."

Fig. 38 · *Nightmaw*
(predator)

CHAPTER FIFTY-SEVEN

Where Dusk had once been distracted, now he was focused.

He made his way through the tunnel one last time, carrying with him the rifle he'd discovered on his first trip, Starling close behind.

He devoted his entire attention to the descent. He found each tokka mound, avoided each danger, leaning fully into his training, his skill, and his memories. He knew why he was here. For the first time in *years*, he knew what he was doing. Why he was doing it. What it meant. It felt incredible to have purpose again.

Once through this tunnel, the questions would rise again. What was a trapper's place in the modern world? The question he'd been unable to answer with Vathi all those years before still loomed, like a sunrise. That was distant. He was the dusk, and this was his sunset—his last time among the deadly plants and animals of Patji. His final opportunity to prove himself their equal.

He had trained all of his life for *this*. Even if this had appeared because he expected it—even if it was made of the phantom energy that created so many things in this place. This cavern was real enough for him, and he knew it would kill him if it could. The challenge would be meaningless unless that were the case, so he welcomed the danger.

He always had.

Rokke offered a chirp of encouragement from behind Dusk's

ponytail. Sak picked up on his determination and stared forward, showing him each and every careless death that awaited him. Together they descended, as they once had, back when their lives meant something.

The only thing that could have distracted him was thinking of the insect god, who had fallen. Such a great loss. The deity had helped him in the end, offering to explain the nature of the cave when it didn't have to. In his pocket he carried the node that had bitten him. It was still alive, but it twitched, disconnected from the core.

He thought idly that if he saved it—and took it to safety—something of the insect god would remain. Foolish, because this was not its personality or memories. Saving this was like keeping a finger as a memento of a dead loved one. Perhaps he should bury it.

He could think about that another time. For now, he maintained his focus. He smiled grimly to himself as he led them deeper and deeper.

"You're different today," Starling said, kneeling beside him as he checked a patch of soil.

"We are all different every day," he whispered. "Each day, the world changes. And we must change with it."

"Profound words," she said.

"Words from my friend, Vathi. On the day I first met her."

"Is she your . . ."

"No," he said, smiling.

"Can we hurry this up?" Dajer said from the drone, hovering along behind.

Speed? No. Dusk intended to do everything with precision.

"I've been thinking about what you said," Starling said as they moved on, "about stories. And I wanted to apologize."

That was the first unexpected thing in this descent. He turned back to her, walking in his footsteps, as she'd always done since that first day after being bitten.

"I was dismissive of your ways," she said, "and what you were trying to share. I . . . When you live as long as I have, you get used to being right and doing things for yourself. I shouldn't have dismissed your stories. I'm sorry."

"Accepted," he said.

ISLES OF THE EMBERDARK

"Will you tell me more of your storytellers?"

"The loremothers," he said, "have kept our histories for millennia, since we crossed the sea at night to escape killers who would have destroyed us all. We struck out, navigated the darkness, and found our way to the homeisles. I mean to prove it—to you, to my government, to all the cosmere. Prove that we don't need any of you."

"Can we stop chatting about pastoral idealism?" Dajer said. "We are on a *deadline*."

Dusk continued on, remaining methodical. As he knelt by the next patch of ground, Starling whispered, "I don't know if I believe what you just said, Dusk."

"You've already said you don't believe the stories of—"

"Not the part about crossing the darkness," she said. "Maybe you did—the Iriali crossed it. Ancient dragons crossed it. I don't know why I responded to you the way I did. I guess it's because I know the emberdark can't be *navigated* even with modern equipment. Either way, that's not the wrong part. It's the part where you said your people don't need anyone. You might be strong, but you're never so strong that you can go without help. Not even a dragon or a god can do that. Everyone needs allies, and friends."

He frowned, then considered. Because she had actually said something worth considering.

Was she right?

"The Eelakin loremothers," he said as they stopped at the place they'd reached before—the one with the veil of woven vines, where his warning had been. "They are more trustworthy than writing, Starling. We have records too, not as old, but written ones. Sometimes a man or woman would write something foolish, to confuse everyone. A political attack, or a false account.

"The loremothers are forced to be impartial. The words they memorize? They are overseen and tested by the covens, as it has always been. They meet every year to repeat the stories and check for inaccuracies. Just because something is oral, and done an older way, does not make it untrustworthy." He looked to her, and felt it was the right thing to say, even if it seemed silly to reveal. "Starling, I *know* our people used to navigate the emberdark. I can do it myself."

She pursed her lips, as if to object. Instead, she nodded slowly. "I believe you."

"How?" Dajer said from the drone. "How could you possibly navigate the emberdark?"

"I just do," Dusk said, not wanting to give away anything more. "I can sense the way."

"Sure," Dajer said. "I'm sure you imagine all kinds of interesting things on your little spirit quests. I'll let you try to prove it to me another time—but can we *please* dispense with this chatter and keep moving?"

"Fine," Dusk said, then turned, put the rifle to his shoulder, and fired on full automatic.

The shots—like little bits of fire—burned through the veil of vines, ripping flaming holes through them. A fresh corpse collapsed toward the burning foliage: a giant nightmaw, with a vicious beak and terrible claws.

It thumped to the ground, smoldering, holes as wide as Dusk's fist blown clean through it.

"Good weapon," Dusk said. "Can I keep this one? I believe it's mine by right of salvage."

"How . . ." Starling stared at the nightmaw, then Dusk. "How did you know it would be there?"

"Because it was here when I did this in a similar cavern years ago," he said, stepping around it, past the veil of vines.

To reach a dead end.

A simple cavern wall, marked by his energy blasts. In the real jungle, no nightmaw would have sat here in this alcove, waiting. But this wasn't quite the real world; it was a test. Dusk approached the wall, frowning.

Shouldn't . . . there be more here?

"What?" Dajer said, hovering his drone forward. "*WHAT?*"

"I'll admit," Dusk said, "that I am stumped. I thought there would be a pool, or perhaps a stream . . ."

"Gaaaaah!" Dajer shouted. "No, no! We missed . . . missed a secret passage. Or . . . or this wall is fake. This wall must be fake! Shoot it. Destroy it."

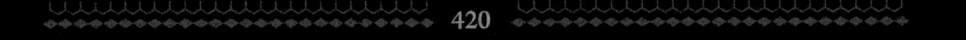

Dusk sighed, as he'd obviously already blasted it. He did so again, then shot at the other walls. "If there is a hidden passage, I do not see it."

"The sensors . . . the sensors should have . . ." Dajer said. "It can't be. It can't be! But if we try to fly to the center, the thing attacks us. It destroyed a fighter . . . There has to be a way. This was supposed to be it!"

Dusk heard a bang from the drone and suspected that, on the other side, Dajer had thrown his chair. Muffled curses and shouting followed. The man that Dusk had assumed was calm and collected was proving himself . . . less so, under stress.

The drone finally hovered away. Recalled, he suspected, by one of Dajer's attendants. As it left, he could still hear the man swearing.

I should not like, he thought, *to take that man trapping.*

"I need to go, Dusk," Starling said. "I've got a plan to get free, and I need to execute it before Dajer gets recalled." She hesitated, stepping closer to him. "Is it *really* true? Can you somehow *navigate* the emberdark?"

"I feel vibrations," he said, pointing. "From there."

"The Knell," she said. "You *feel* the Current? Like a Seeker can? I suppose that explains some things. We can sense the Knell with instruments. It would certainly help your people . . ."

"There's more," he said. Again, it was *right* to admit this, he was sure. Just as it had been right for Vathi to trust him about the truth of Patji's Eye and the worms.

Sometimes, words were right.

"Starling," he said, "I can feel interruptions in the Current. My ancestors traveled the islands without modern equipment—and one way they did was by noting patterns in the waves. Certain patterns of interference indicated an island was near." He tapped his chest. "I can feel the same thing here, though the interference tends to add instead of subtract. I can *hear* objects, like islands, in the Current. I could point you toward a dozen of them right now."

Her eyes grew even wider. Then she grinned a wicked kind of grin. "All this time, Dajer had *you* in his hands . . . And he didn't realize . . ."

"What?" he asked.

"Dusk, if you can *actually* navigate the emberdark, do you know what that means? Exploration, trade, *spying* opportunities . . . Can others of your people do this?"

"I suspect so," he said. So long as Patji believed they'd been tested enough, if they had access to the light, he was certain they would be able to do as he did. For he was not special. He would not want to be.

"The perpendicularity is worth so much because of the tactical advantage it offers," she said. "You offer so much more . . . Dusk, you are worth *more* than the perpendicularity. Be very, *very* careful about the people you share this information with."

Then she gritted her teeth and turned back up the tunnel, following his footsteps, as they'd done previous times. She would be safe enough, if she did that right.

She had an escape plan, did she? Well, he wished her the best. He did not trust her completely, but . . . it had been right to speak to her. For now he knew the true value of what he could do.

And that . . . that was the answer, wasn't it? "Is this why you brought me here, Father? Tested me again? You wanted me to know the importance of this gift I bear?"

Dusk had passed, and the sun would now rise. On a different man, with a different purpose.

He turned to follow Starling, but then stopped. There, in the mud of the cavern, something glistened. He bent down, pulling it free. A medallion . . . Cakoban's medallion. Like the one he'd given Vathi. Like the ones all good trappers carried.

Pure gold. He held it up and compared it to the one he wore. This new one—found in the mud—depicted Cakoban just as Dusk had seen in his dream.

His task on this island was not finished yet. The Dakwara had not been defeated.

It was time for Dusk to face the monster and find out what was at the center of the island.

Fig. 100 · Dragon (head)

CHAPTER FIFTY-EIGHT

Starling managed to reach the lights near the cavern entrance without major incident, though she *did* get bitten twice and had to wait to get over the dizziness. She shook out her clothing best she could, then left the cavern and marched over to the nearest guard.

"Get Dajer," she said, then stalked toward the Intensifier.

When Dajer arrived, she was trying—unsuccessfully—to talk the engineers into showing her how to work the thing. Dajer's skin was flushed, the tubes to his nose hissing oxygen. He had changed to a larger mask—metal that extended from nodes at the sides of his face, plating his forehead, his cheeks, and the ridge of his nose in a way that outlined his eyes with sharp angles. A war mask. Great.

"I might be able to protect you from not just the Sleepless, but other factions in your government," she said. "The contract is signed. Do your part. Free me."

He considered only briefly, then nodded to Tague and the engineers—because it was true. With a dragon serving him, the balance of power could shift in his favor. She might be his only way to avoid court-martial and imprisonment—if not execution—for what he'd done. Soldiers killed, resources lost, and deals made without authorization. They both knew how it went when a politically minded Malwish aspirant fell from grace.

They moved to strap her in, but she shook her head and placed her wrist into the spot. "I can hold it."

The engineers took her word for it, then looked to Dajer.

He put on tinted goggles and whispered, "Engage the machine."

A brilliant beam of light shot from the tip of the device to Starling's manacle. Her eyes adjusted as no human's could, letting her see the manacle begin to glow. The one on her other arm mirrored it; they were paired. Break one, and the other would fall—but they also shared power, resisting the beam as one.

Like before, she felt her powers stir. Through the frozen chill of the manacles, something *moved*. Strength welled inside her.

"More power!" she shouted. "It's working!"

They complied, and the manacles' coldness intensified. All of their energy turned to resist the attack, which left her unobstructed. And in that moment, she remembered what it was to be a dragon.

Awareness. She could sense all living things around her, and many distant—those who had devotion and were seeking her kind. The prayers of the faithful Connected to all of her kind, who answered questions and gave support.

Power. She felt *power*. The ability to take away pain from followers, or influence emotions. Investiture she could release as attacks of her own, for while dragons could not breathe fire, they had defenses equally glorious.

Above it all, she felt her other form. The part of her that could fly.

For a moment, she was again soaring with her uncle on that day of her first transformation. Higher, higher. Toward heaven itself, and the home of gods. Toward her dreams, her family. Sunlight glittering around her in an open blue expanse.

Home.

Freedom.

"More!" she shouted. "The manacles are weakening! I can see them melting!"

It was working. *Legitimately* working. She could be free, be herself again. Complete.

And if she did . . .

If she did, her crew would be imprisoned instead. She would be free, but they never would be again.

The beam intensified, and the light grew until even she had trouble looking directly at it. This was it. The moment. It was going to happen. It . . .

It couldn't.

With a scream, Starling gathered her power and fed it *into* the manacles. She bolstered them, holding shut the door to her own prison with everything she had. She kept them from breaking, sealing her fate, and whispered: "More."

"It's too much!" Tague warned.

"Do it!" Dajer said. "This is my only chance!"

The beam came to a crescendo. Light surrounded her. In that glory, she was a dragonet again, standing before the first sunrise of her new life, embracing the warmth. She took that hope, and she fed it into the manacles.

Be strong, she thought to them.

They melted against her arm and . . . were confused.

She held them tight, supported them, and fought against her own freedom *just* long enough for . . .

The beam went out.

The machine died.

And all through the camp, lights extinguished.

Starling's powers vanished, her awareness retreated, and she blinked. She found herself not in the sunlight with her uncle, but here, on this lonely island.

Her manacles, distorted, had held. She wasn't certain if they would have broken before the machine or if they would have managed on their own. She probably wouldn't ever know, because they *had* held. With her help.

"Damn it!" Dajer said, seizing Tague by the front of his jacket. "It can't even do this? What good are you?"

Starling wiped tears from her cheeks. Oh . . . Oh Shards . . .

She'd done it. She . . . She'd done it again.

She'd locked herself away.

Right now, Aditil would be sneaking out of the crew's quarters. Starling needed to mount a distraction to hold everyone's attention and buy time. Pieces were in motion. The escape was already happening. She . . .

"Hey," a nearby soldier said, pointing. "Hey, what's *he* doing?"

Tague and the device engineers, even Dajer, turned and looked. It seemed she wouldn't need a distraction after all—for Dusk had left the cavern and decided, for some crazy reason, to step right up to the edge of the moat.

Harpoon in hand, he was going to fight the entity.

Alone.

Fig. 95 · Dakwara
(Entity)

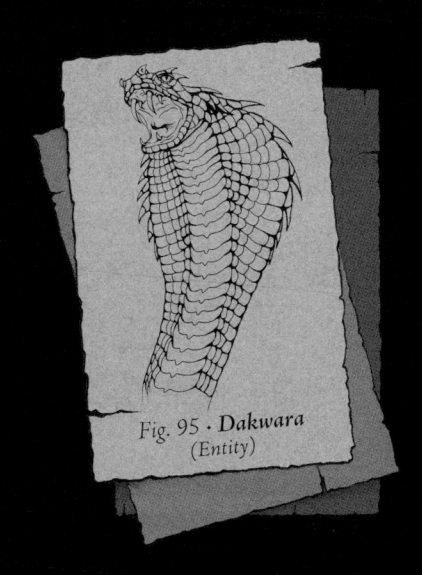

CHAPTER FIFTY-NINE

Dusk saw his corpse out there among the skullsnakes, which flowed in rings, some clockwise, some counterclockwise.

Well, good. He'd not expected this to be easy. Sak squawked softly as he pulled his small boat—ignored by the Ones Above all this time—up to the moat. With the light the soldiers used earlier to coat their harpoons, he coated the hull, then turned it back over. So much easier than the last time he'd done that . . .

Sak squawked again. Rokke nestled in his hair.

"I know," Dusk whispered. "I see my body."

Sak squawked louder.

"I'm not turning back," he explained, "because we can't always turn back. Sometimes the only path is forward, Sak. Terrifying though that may be." He carefully piled harpoons inside the boat—more than any trapper should need, each with rope still attached—and made sure they didn't tangle.

"I'm not ignoring your warning," he promised her. "I appreciate you. But today I have to continue anyway and hope I am better than the future thinks I am." He hesitated, watching the Dakwara slowly rise from the unsea, a huge shape with thousands of smaller skullsnakes streaming around her, making an eternal round in the moat. Concentric spirals of worship.

People were starting to notice. They'd been distracted by the beam of light from the strange machine, which had let him get into position, but now that had gone out. So he shoved his boat into the moat on top of the writhing skullsnakes. It rocked and shook.

The Dakwara, he hoped, would not attack as she had when the god of insects tried this. Because Dusk had gone about it the proper way. He'd defeated the challenge of the cavern and proven himself worthy.

"You two should remain behind," he said to the birds.

Sak gripped his shoulder tightly and hissed. Rokke dug deeper into his hair.

"Suit yourselves," Dusk said. Then, with the Dakwara rising and unfurling her hood, he raised a harpoon high and stepped into the boat. "I challenge you in the name of my ancestor, Cakoban the Navigator!"

With his other hand, he raised the medallion he'd found, now tied around his neck next to his original one. "I have passed your test and proven myself in the cavern. I have the right to challenge you! Whatever you might once have been, today you are the Dakwara and must abide by these terms."

The beast opened her mouth and dove for him.

Dusk threw his harpoon.

Not at the monster.

He threw it down into the unsea, spearing the back of one of the moving skullsnakes. Dusk seized the rope, and the boat launched into motion.

Pulled straight out of the way of the diving monster.

Starling gasped as the thing almost ate Dusk.

But though there was not a lot of space between Dusk and the monster as it crashed into the unsea, there *was* a great deal of space between *almost eaten* and *eaten*. Dusk crouched low, pulled on his little boat by a rope in front of him, a little like . . . well, someone on water skis. Except with a boat, a rope, and a speared monster.

It was remarkable, particularly with that black bird on his shoulder, wings spread wide.

All around, soldiers stopped what they were doing and either cheered or jeered at Dusk. Perhaps without this glorious distraction, someone would have realized the danger in the lights going out. But they soon turned back on, and the power reset.

Nobody put together that, during those few brief moments, the locks had gone down.

All of them.

The beast crashed into the unsea behind as Dusk crouched, rope pulled tight with one hand, front foot braced against the prow of the boat. The skullsnake he'd speared pulled him with a speed that rivaled his engine.

He grinned at the wind in his face, feeling a wild exuberance. "Rokke," he exclaimed. "Look!"

The smaller bird peeked out.

"We're beating her," Dusk said, leaning to the side where—with his free hand—he seized a second harpoon.

Rokke screamed. Dusk's body appeared in front of the boat, and he glanced over his shoulder, seeing the Dakwara looming again. She was faster than the skullsnakes, of course. She was a demigod.

Dusk saw anger in her eyes. Indignance that this little beast would challenge the queen of the snakes, the monster whose length was the entire ocean.

"Let's see," Dusk said, "how well you turn."

It dove.

He let go of his current rope and hurled the second harpoon at a skullsnake farther inward.

Traveling the other direction.

The harpoon hit, and Dusk made a wicked smile, feeling *alive*. His boat lurched as he held the rope, bracing against the side of the small boat. In this, the not-water having no weight was a huge advantage, as he spun—even gained some air—and was yanked the other direction by this new skullsnake.

The Dakwara again crashed down without getting him. Dusk held the rope tight, speeding after the new skullsnake. The medallions felt warm against his chest, and he suspected he knew why.

He wasn't on this quest alone. He never had been.

An entire people rode with him.

Starling gaped as Dusk worked his way inward, going one way, then the other, moving with . . . not *grace*, really. More stubbornness and brutality, but it worked.

"Have you ever seen anything like that?" asked the soldier next to her. Starling didn't know him, but in the face of something so bizarre, they became spectators together.

"Never," she said.

A sudden alarm blared through the camp. Soldiers shook out of their stupor, glancing around. Someone grabbed Starling from behind, spinning her. Dajer?

"The guards at your quarters are missing," he snarled. "What have you done?"

"I was right here with you," Starling said. "What *could* I have done?"

He frowned. Then his eyes went wide. "The blackout." He whirled toward the *Dynamic*—still sitting where they'd first landed it two days back.

The lights turned on as Leonore powered it up.

"Idiot," Dajer said, then tapped part of his mask. "Scramble fighters. Shoot down the *Dynamic*. I want to watch it explode. Our dragon no longer gets the privilege of knowing we're treating her friends with respect."

Silence. Starling waited, praying, hoping.

A voice spoke from Dajer's mask. "Sir . . . the fighters, sir. They've been sabotaged! Control panels destroyed!"

"All of them?" he asked, then shook Starling. "What have you done? How? *How?*"

"The locks went down," she said.

"The fighters were guarded! I had soldiers watching them! You couldn't have gotten to them without alerting us, unless you could . . . could . . ."

"Travel through the ground, unseen, and pop up underneath them?"

Starling said as something rose from the ground behind Dajer. "Remember how you said you were more afraid of the Sleepless than you were of ghosts? You might want to revise that."

Brilliant, bloody red eyes shone from behind Dajer. He spun, then went absolutely *white* with terror.

"Do you have any idea," Nazh growled, "how uncomfortable those shade prisons are? How hungry for *human flesh* an *experience like that* makes an individual?"

Dajer screamed and started running.

Dusk careened to one side, and the Dakwara roared, affronted again by another near miss.

The birds screeched, not in terror, but in exultation. Even little Rokke, having learned bravery these last few weeks, clung to him and yelled with enthusiasm.

The Dakwara turned with difficulty, needing a great deal of space to maneuver. But as soon as she started toward him, Dusk grinned and threw another spear at the skullsnakes, to lurch in the other direction.

The creature's roar was like applause. Dusk knew he was grinning stupidly, but he couldn't help himself. He'd never understood Cakoban's joy in the old stories, his humor and trickster wit, but now it made perfect sense.

"I should be dead, it's true," Dusk said as the Dakwara screamed. He threw another harpoon, and pulled the boat inward. "Somehow, I'm not. Somehow, this is working." He looked over his shoulder as the beast loomed again. "And by the Father himself, it feels *good*."

The thing dove, and Dusk let go of his rope, this time leaping forward. He threw himself off the boat, which was destroyed behind him with the force of the Dakwara's hit.

But Dusk's feet landed on solid ground. The inner island. He spun, and met the monster face-to-face—hers wider than his by many yards, slit eyes level with his head.

You didn't beat the Dakwara by killing her.

You survived. Just as Patji taught him to do.

"I," Dusk said softly, "have defeated you."

Fig. 84 · Skullsnake
(creature)

CHAPTER SIXTY

"Hungry for human flesh?" Starling asked, running toward the *Dynamic* with Nazh gliding beside her. "Really?"

"Humans expect certain things," he said. "Many wait their entire lives, afraid of ghosts—and I'm the only one they'll ever meet. Star, imagine their disappointment if I didn't say something appropriately grisly. Honestly."

She grinned, reaching the ship. "Leonore is flying without her lodestar?"

"The pile of them was near my prison, with a few other things confiscated from the ship," he said. "One problem, though. I couldn't sabotage the gunship. It has a silver layer in the hull, a standard precaution—and it has multiple bridges anyway."

"We can outfly it," she said. "It will take time to get going."

The *Dynamic*, which was already hovering, opened the cargo bay for her. She leapt up, and ZeetZi grabbed her hand, hauling her on board. Nearby, Aditil hugged Ed with one arm and—grinning a stupid grin—held something high with the other: the smashed-up shade prison.

ZeetZi and Leonore had dealt with the guards outside their room. Aditil's job had been to sneak out and find this, after Leonore explained that a shade prison would almost certainly have a local power backup.

There was no reason for a power outage to lock your own soldiers in their bunkers—quite the opposite. But a shade prison would have a separate system.

The power outage *had*, however, opened the pod where Nazh's prison was being kept—and brought down the forcefield protecting it. From there, a little creative smashing had been all that it required.

"You did it, Aditil!" Starling said.

"Horse-thief parentage is good for something, I suppose. Other than getting me into trouble." Aditil grinned, then threw the prison away and grabbed Starling by the shoulders. "It worked! I can't believe it worked!"

Starling grinned back as the ship turned to make an exit. A large gunship was meant for firing at other capital ships, but if Leonore flew them well—with no fighters harrying them—they could use the island itself as cover and fly far enough away to dodge any gunship shots. They really could escape.

Except.

"Wait," Starling said. "We've forgotten something."

Within the cavern in the island, Dusk found bones.

Cakoban himself, judging by the clothing and, well, where Dusk was. He knelt, reverent, and touched the skull's forehead. "Greatest Grandfather," he whispered. "It took us a while, but the ones you saved have finally returned for you."

Of course, the bones did not reply. He liked that about bones. This cavern was quite small, and the corpse was the only thing in it. No plants, no deathants. Just the remains.

"Your final orders to the Dakwara were to serve you," Dusk said. "You kept her here, protecting your corpse, for eternity—where she could do no harm to those who sailed to our new home. Until someone could best her."

His vision had been true. He would have to tell it to the loremothers for recording. He looked out of the cavern, though, as he heard shouting.

"If what Starling says is true," Dusk whispered, "then the Eelakin will never be left alone. First the birds, then the portal, now me. My ability to sense the Current. It's like . . . the gods themselves won't let us remain alone."

Silence from the bones.

"Is that the point?" Dusk asked. "Is it like she said? We need each other, don't we? Not just individuals. But peoples. We can't be alone any longer. Just like . . . like I couldn't be alone on Patji anymore."

He stood, then noticed something. The wall of the cavern was covered in strange symbols—some kind of writing. He'd need a light to see it better.

Something squirmed in his pocket.

Dusk started—he'd nearly forgotten the little node he'd placed there. He got it out, placing it on his arm, and it bit him. Strange, to be happy for that.

God of Insects? he sent.

. . . Yes . . .

You are alive! That is good.

There was an . . . interruption with the power . . . and their cloud went down . . .

Dusk frowned at the weakness in the creature's voice. *What is wrong?*

It seems . . . it replied. *It seems . . . I am to be . . . eliminated.*

Starling stood in the cargo bay with the others, save Leonore, who was flying. The base below was—for the second time in one day—a mass of chaos and confusion.

The Scadrians would soon regroup. They were capable.

But somewhere out there, Dajer was alive. Angry. Reckless. And he had the means to get revenge on Starling in only one way.

By killing Chrysalis.

"It takes time," Ed said, "for one of Clemaxin's Hordes to establish Connections and regain sapience. The power failing probably let her begin the process, but she wouldn't have been able to do much. She's almost certainly still locked away."

They all fell silent. Their plan had counted on Chrysalis still being hidden on the ship. Since her discovery, everything had happened so rapidly, and there hadn't been any chance to plan further—especially not with the Scadrians listening.

"We have to go back for her."

Starling shook herself. She hadn't spoken, nor had Aditil, or Ed. It had been . . .

"ZeetZi?" she said, turning to him.

He stood with one hand on the wall by the cargo bay opening, his crest feathers blowing as the ship moved. He met her gaze. "We have to go back," he repeated. "Chrysalis is a Sleepless, but she's on the crew. We can't leave her."

"Quickly," Starling said. "I know which pod is her prison."

The god of insects was too weak to speak. Instead it showed Dusk what its nodes saw.

The horde had been repositioned into one of the habitat pods, but the light inside had gone red, and the heat . . . the heat was *incredible*. Hundreds of hordelings had died already, and the rest furiously beat their wings to try to cool the most important ones—the memory and personality nodes, which huddled against the wall opposite the heating vents.

As the god died, it had pulled roughly into the shape of a person made from clinging insects. Despite himself, that sight made Dusk nauseous.

No, it thought with despair. *No, not you. I thought . . . with the insects you respected . . . with the island . . . I thought you . . .*

In that moment, Dusk felt its feelings, not just its thoughts. He knew the creature, what it wanted, and was not surprised.

It wanted to live. That was all it had ever wanted. Yes, it was dangerous. Yes, it was strange.

Dusk thought of insects in a jar. Of a man in a jar. Of an entire people in a jar.

Suddenly he was angry.

Very, *very* angry.

"Hold on," he said. "I'm coming to get you."

How? it asked, sounding exhausted. *What can you . . . do . . . One man? They are . . . many . . .*

"You make a mistake," Dusk said, running from the inner island's cavern. "I have defeated the Dakwara." He reached the moat, where the thing reared up.

Then she bowed her head before him.

"By the stories," Dusk announced, "she must now serve me."

Except Dusk's boat was broken.

He knew, without needing her to tell him, that touching the Dakwara would be deadly—even for the one who controlled her. Their natures were not compatible. So she couldn't lift him.

Instead he started stepping across on the heads of the skullsnakes, which lined up for him at the Dakwara's command. This, however, was slow.

Frighteningly slow.

He tried to run, but nearly slipped, and had to catch himself, then pick carefully as he moved. With each step, he knew he was failing to make good on his promise to help. For he could sense the god of insects grow weaker as more and more of its nodes died. He could see its sights overlapping his own, its many eyes failing one after another.

Dusk was crying with its pain as he reached the halfway point. That was when he knew he'd be too late.

But then, the doors to the prison opened.

Starling, haloed by light, stood in the doorway. She smashed the controls on the wall with a weapon, and the terrible heat began to dissipate. She crossed the floor, her shoes melting but her feet untouched as she reached the insect god. The surviving nodes stood on burned lumps—remnants of the ones who had died. The god was still roughly in the shape of a person, just a very lean one, made entirely of insects.

"S . . . Starling?" the god of insects whispered.

"Can you walk?" Starling said. "We have to go."

"Why?"

"Why what?" Starling helped the figure manage its feet, walking on the dead that the bottom nodes of its legs clung to as a buffer against the scorching floor.

It was a terrible, yet glorious, sight.

"Why . . . care?" the insect god asked softly.

"You have to ask?" Starling said. "Shards. Your life has been a hard one, hasn't it?"

"You," the god said, "have no idea."

Starling reached the door and helped Chrysalis out. She didn't know a lot about the Sleepless, but . . . well, there were a *lot* of dead hordelings back there. The central ones, though, seemed to still be alive. At least, Chrysalis seemed to still have her senses and mind intact. She stumbled as she walked. All the skin-imitating hordelings had died, leaving her innards exposed.

This completely destroyed the illusion that she was human—she was a collection of insects clinging desperately together, their legs locking to one another, forming limbs, joints . . . like a child's block toy that snapped together roughly in the shape of a person.

Starling continued leading her as Ed ran beside them, rifle in hand. But Shards, she hoped Nazh was keeping the Malwish ground troops busy, because most of her crew was not going to last long against a trained military.

They rounded a habitat and, unfortunately, encountered two Malwish running toward the gunship. They immediately pivoted to fire, and Ed yelped.

Starling stepped between the enemy and the crewmembers right as the enemy opened fire. One had conventional rounds, the other Invested—and both aimed with deadly accuracy, striking half a dozen killing shots within seconds. Her bracers, once again eager to do their job, cooled as the energy blasts hit Starling mostly in the head and the bullets ripped through the clothing at her core and chest.

Ed leaned out behind her and returned fire, but missed—though he got closer than he had any right to, considering. Perhaps Leonore's training actually was paying dividends. Of course, the real value of the gunfire was that it kept the soldiers' attention while an apparition with glowing red eyes surged up behind them.

Starling turned aside as Nazh ripped the souls from the bodies of the two soldiers. Their corpses dropped, eyes sunken into withered faces, flesh sucked dry. Starling returned to help Chrysalis, who had formed into a worried huddle behind her.

Nazh fell in with them as they hurried forward.

"How are you doing?" Starling whispered.

"Worse," was all he said, glowing red eyes forward. "Killing is . . . dangerous . . ."

Fortunately, they reached open ground and the *Dynamic* hovered down beside them. ZeetZi—kneeling at the back of the open cargo bay—fired at another few soldiers, making them scatter.

"Most of the enemy," Nazh said, "were recalled to the gunship. Hurry."

ZeetZi lowered his rifle and reached out a hand to help them up. Chrysalis hesitated when she saw that hand. She raised a head with no discernable human eyes—those hordelings had probably died—and looked at him. Saw him.

"I don't trust you," ZeetZi said, "but we *don't* leave crewmembers behind." He seized her hand, apparently unbothered by the insects that made it up, and heaved her on board.

Starling and Ed jumped up after. Chrysalis crawled to the corner of the chamber, then fell apart into her components. When Starling stepped up, a dozen insects spoke in rasping, weak voices. "Thank you. I will live. *Thank you.*"

Nazh hovered up, then turned glowing eyes to the side as gunfire from enemy soldiers ripped through the cargo bay door. Ed cursed and ducked, while ZeetZi flattened against one wall. The *Dynamic* didn't have a military-grade hull. Even small arms, if Invested, could rip it apart.

Starling hit the comm as more shots tore through the wall. "Leonore. Get us—"

The gunfire stopped suddenly. Silence claimed the cargo bay, save for a groan from ZeetZi, who had been shot in one arm. Ed quickly grabbed the first aid kit from the wall.

"Captain," Leonore said over the comm. "We're in trouble."

Starling reached the bridge in a mad dash, then scrambled to Leonore in the pilot's seat, looking out the front windshield.

She didn't need to be told the problem. The soldiers had stopped firing because the gunship had launched, and was pointed right at them.

"Can you dodge it?" Starling asked.

"At this range?" Leonore said. "With nothing to hide behind?" She had her mask down. "We took too long. A little more distance, and yah. Here? Dodging would be one in a hundred, Captain. Then it will fire again. And again."

Starling's stomach fell. She hit the comm, assuming Dajer would be waiting for her to do so.

"All right," she said as the communication was picked up. "We'll land."

"No need," he said. His image appeared on the small viewscreen at ZeetZi's station. Behind her, the others—save Chrysalis—arrived, ZeetZi holding a bloody bandage on his left arm. They didn't rush in. They stood at the back of the bridge, quiet.

"Dajer," Starling said. "Please."

"Begging now?" he said. "Orders have come. I'm ruined. And you? I don't need you. I don't need any of you."

The massive cannon on the front of the gunship began to glow—a redder, harsher light than the Intensifier.

Leonore grew tense, ready to dodge.

Except . . . what was that below? That green light?

Starling edged to the side, peering through the windshield at the island below—where Dusk, looking tiny, stepped out of the moat. As if he'd walked on the unsea itself.

The entity—the vast snake of lore and mythology—erupted from beneath the island and *crashed* into the gunship, throwing it off as it fired. With enormous jaws, the entity crushed the front of the ship—holding Dajer and the bridge—releasing an explosion of gas and fire.

In a blink, Dajer disappeared from the viewscreen as it snapped off, black. The rest of the burning wreckage dropped into the abyss.

Then, remarkably, the creature snatched the back half—burning and broken where its mouth had touched it—and raised it from the depths before it could fall too far. There would be survivors in that, and the beast . . . the entity that reviled life . . .

It wanted to help them?

What?

"I don't understand," Leonore said, hesitantly raising her mask. "Are we saved?"

Starling looked closer, squinting, making out Dusk with arms upraised. His eyes glowed a bright green, the same color as the entity. He pointed, and the entity put the wreckage of the gunship down carefully, so the living soldiers inside could escape rather than plummet through the unsea until they died. That did demolish the Intensifier, however, as the ship rolled to the side, on top of it.

"Well I'll be damned," Starling whispered. "I guess his legends *are* true."

Fig. 74 · Mirris
(Aviar)

CHAPTER SIXTY-ONE

President of First Company Vathi—leading elected official of the planet First of the Sun—sat with head in hands, waiting for the news. A vote of no confidence in the parliament, instigated by both the traditional house—containing chiefs and kingmakers—and the elected house of senators, was occurring.

While she wasn't there.

Her political opponents had waited until she was visiting Patji's Eye—a several-day trip by ship—to call the vote. It wasn't unlawful, just unprecedented. She'd left after months of political wrangling as one final delaying tactic.

It hadn't worked. The others would abandon precedent to get to her. So she waited for the telegram that would proclaim her fate, the results of the vote.

She could win it. Maybe? She'd won two so far since Dusk's departure. Sweat dripped down the sides of her face. This one would be closer.

It was hot on Patji. She always forgot how hot until she returned. She claimed to prefer the heat—a way of reinforcing her "tough as tree bark" reputation. Today she wouldn't have minded a fan, though. The Ones Above claimed to have technology that could cool a room to any temperature you wanted. What would happen to her people when they got such conveniences? Would they lock out the world itself, make their own new world inside? Would they forget their heritage?

We didn't forget our heritage, she thought. *We gave it grand parades, locked it in cages, put it on display. No, we didn't forget the trappers. We made another monument out of them.*

Dusk was no such monument. A part of her was glad he had talked her into letting him leave, so he could die an explorer rather than wasting away as a man on display. Pinned to a board, like an insect.

The rest of her was horrified to think of her friend that way.

You think about when *your people get the conveniences the Ones Above offer,* she thought. *Not if. You know the tide is coming. You told him it would wash him away. Now it's going to take you.*

The future claimed everyone eventually. Because the past was all anyone could ever become.

A knock at the door. She turned, hoping she didn't look too eager. Tough as bark. Even on a day like this.

It was Second of the Soil, her vice president of the interior, holding the telegram.

"Go ahead," she said. "Open it."

He slit it open, read the lines in his head.

And relaxed.

"Seventy-three against," he said. "Three abstaining. We're still a government. No dissolution."

"By a margin of *two* votes," she said.

"It doesn't matter how close the margin is," he said, waving the slip of paper in the air, his Aviar snapping at it gleefully from the top of his head. He really needed to carry her on his shoulder, like most people. The pictures in the broadsheets were getting ridiculous.

"It matters," Vathi said, "when the last vote was won by a margin of fifteen. And the one before that by a margin of thirty-six. We won't survive the next."

"The people want progress," he said as she stood, Mirris fluttering onto her shoulder. Vathi slipped past him into the hallway, and he fell into step behind her. "They want the wonders being promised. They don't understand what it will cost, Vathi. Winning this vote is a sign— the senate *wants* you to lead us. But they *will* act if you keep stalling."

She entered her offices here on Patji, then took the telegram from Soil. She pinned it—with her trapper's side knife—to the corkboard. Tough as bark. Wouldn't it be wonderful if that were true? She moved through the office as aides and lesser ministers took up the news, cheering. As if this were a *victory*.

Two votes. She was as good as done for.

"Vathi," Soil said, stopping her as she reached the porch of their offices near the shore of the island. "Please tell me you'll say something. Let's have Kuko write you a speech about how you've decided at last to accept the provisional terms the Ones Above sent."

"I promised Dusk two months."

Soil groaned. "It's been almost that long. He's *dead*, Vathi."

"Then we respect him in death," she said. "Two months. I promised . . ." She trailed off.

"What?" he said.

"Silence. It means death in the jungle."

He cocked his head, ever the city-born, utterly confused. She pushed past him—Mirris batting her wings on Vathi's shoulder—back into the office, where everyone had suddenly grown quiet. Standing not around her corkboard with the "good" news, but around young Flumi—who held the service phone, her eyes wide, the receiver dangling in her fingers.

Vathi's stomach dropped. That seemed like bad news. What had happened? What hadn't she accounted for? What had she missed? She slept so little these days, it would be no wonder if she made a mistake.

"What?" Vathi demanded.

Starling opened her eyes on the other side of the perpendicularity, and saw a blue sky.

It wasn't *her* blue sky. It wasn't Yolen, the home she'd been forbidden, but seeing it made her tremble anyway. She floated in the pool, enjoying the azure gradient, like watercolor paint.

Her personal experience would do as proof for Xisis. She'd confirmed the perpendicularity existed, though Dusk's cautions rumbled in her mind. This island was safe now, but he'd given her a list of seventeen things she wasn't supposed to do, lest she get bitten, poisoned, eaten, or—remarkably—hanged. By vines.

She smiled and stood up. The water was a blue mirror of the sky—but dark. Saturated like acrylics, painted on so thick that they had a visible grain. Within it, Dusk appeared—his birds remaining behind, as they hated going under water—then floated to the surface.

She'd been worried about leaving the entity, but he insisted it would stay as ordered. And after flying with it trailing behind—like a giant, murderous, soul-eating puppy—she was inclined to believe it actually *would*. Gods, Ed said, could not be contained by steel, ceramic, or even an Invested shield.

But a story . . . well, that was another thing entirely.

Dusk stood up, then sighed, holding his hands to the sides. "Sunlight," he whispered. "I'd begun to forget the feeling of sunlight on skin." He eyed her. "You *sure* you won't burn to a crisp?"

"I'm literally indestructible."

"I've known albinos," he said. "They sunburn easily."

"Not exactly an albino. And still indestructible."

He smiled, which . . . well, she couldn't remember seeing him do that in all their time together. Granted, "all their time" hadn't been long, but she still thought it remarkable. He was always so stoic, except now, as he grinned and strolled out through a narrow gulch to an area with a waystation and a rugged track, where they waited until . . .

Cars, of an old-fashioned style, drove up a road alongside the stream. The lead one arrived, pulled to a stop, and a distinguished woman of his same ethnicity leapt out, wearing a fine suit.

"Dusk?" she cried. "Did you *really* bring an outlander here? Through the pool?"

They pointed weapons at Starling, of course. She'd have been offended if they hadn't.

"I did," Dusk said, seeming dutiful—like he wanted to answer her question honestly. Clearly.

"Why, Dusk?" the woman said, hand to her face. "What could *possibly* have possessed you to give away its location?"

"I believe," he said, "the ancient spirit of a fragmented god, deified by our own stories and perceptions of it, is the thing that possessed me.

But that doesn't have any *direct* connection to why I decided to trust Captain Starling." He walked back toward the pool. "Come. I have important revelations to show you. I think you'll like them, Vathi." He paused. "You *did* wait, didn't you? To make the decision?"

This Vathi woman heaved a sigh. Then she chuckled. "Everyone told me you were *obviously* dead, you know."

"Now you'll get to tell them how wrong they were. I know you like that." He nodded to Starling. "Come. Vathi waited, as I said she would."

At Vathi's order, the soldiers lowered their weapons. Starling followed Dusk back to the pool, which he stepped into and vanished. Starling hesitated on the bank—her clothing soaked by the water that skimmed the top of the Invested liquid below—and waited for the others.

"President Vathi?" Starling said. "I'm sorry. He wouldn't let me call ahead, and forbade me to make introductions or formal requests for admittance to your planet. He . . . um . . . was rather dismissive of my suggestions that it was proper for an alien to do that sort of thing."

Starling held out her hand. Vathi regarded it, but Dusk had said that shaking hands was a thing they did. So Starling kept it extended, hopeful.

"Dusk hates bureaucracy," Vathi said, finally taking the hand. "He has this infuriating sense of entitlement to the island here—as if it belongs completely to him. He gets offended whenever I mention the need for a permit to visit."

Starling smiled. "I hear you're having troubles with Rosharans and Scadrians."

"'Trouble' seems a mild term for the potential enslavement of our entire planet to offworld interests. Can you help?"

"I'm not very important," Starling admitted. "And I don't have a lot to do with their conflict. I mostly just try to stay out of their way. But that also means I don't have a claw in this fight, so to speak. If you have questions for a neutral third party . . . well, I can give you some honest answers."

Vathi withdrew her hand, but seemed interested. She was more politic than Dusk—who, Starling was coming to learn, wasn't reserved or diplomatic, despite seeming that way at first. He was really an enormous grouch, which made a fair approximation of both at first glance

"That would be appreciated," Vathi said. "Captain Starling, is it? You . . . have a ship? Like the Ones Above?"

"Not as grand," Starling said. "But it's mine."

Shards. It would be. All hers, the moment she delivered her pronouncement to Xisis: the perpendicularity on First of the Sun was real. She wouldn't be *completely* free with these manacles on, but there were gradients to freedom, like the sky itself.

Something emerged below, and Dusk popped up through the pool again. "Are you coming?" he said. "Sak wants to see you." He dipped down again, as if to vanish.

"Dusk!" Vathi said. "I need an explanation. You brought an offworlder here without even asking. Do you have a way to protect us? Is she it?"

"What, her?" he said. "No, she's just my ride. Only way I could get back here in time, as traveling via my boat would have taken too long. Also . . . the Dakwara smashed it."

"The *Dakwara*," Vathi said. "Dusk, that's a myth."

Starling felt vindicated that one of his own had that initial reaction too.

"A myth," he said, "will be what saves us. Are you coming? I bonded an ancient god of destruction to my will, and she wants to meet you." He vanished below again.

Vathi seemed stunned by this, as well one should be.

"It . . . does get easier," Starling promised. "You folks are jumping off the high cliff the first go, I'm afraid." She paused. "As ancient gods of destruction go, this *is* the nicest one I've met." She gave a little shrug, then stepped into the pool and sank down—with a mental command to transfer to the other side.

A short time later, Vathi's bodyguards appeared in Shadesmar, followed by the president herself.

Dusk waited patiently as they gaped at the Dakwara, which swam through the unsea around their island, trailed by her skullsnake entourage.

"Yes," he answered for what felt like the seven-hundredth time. "She does what I say. I bested her. The Dakwara has to serve me for a hundred years—longer, if nobody else arrives to best her after the century passes."

That should be long enough, he figured, for his people to get their feet under them and build a stake in the cosmere at large. A hundred years, during which no unauthorized ship could approach this island to use its perpendicularity. Starling had explained how they could expand the pool to accommodate even the largest vessels.

Patji, which had once been a proving ground for trappers, then a center for research, was to become a spaceport. He no longer felt bad about that, for this was his Father's will. Proven in the tests that Dusk had survived. Those, at long last, were through.

Now on to others.

"Are you done?" he asked Vathi, leaning closer to her. She stood on the shore of the small butterfly island in this strange dimension, still staring at the enormous snake beast.

She, in turn, was prancing a tad. As she slithered. He figured a god could prance while she slithered—at least, he wouldn't want to be the one to try explaining that she couldn't.

He nudged his friend. "Well? President Vathi? Done staring? Can we get on with it? I have more to show you."

She blinked, and a tear rolled down her cheek. "I thought you were going to die, Dusk. I thought you sailed off *to* die so you wouldn't have to witness what was going to happen to us." She looked at him, finally. "I wanted to go with you so I wouldn't have to either."

She embraced him, and he held her, realizing this was what he'd needed as well. "I know," he said. "I nearly did die. I should have. Patji led me, Vathi. He *spoke* to me. There's more, so much more. Come with me."

"What more could there be than this?" she said, gesturing.

He smiled, and led her to the *Dynamic*, which hovered with its cargo bay door down. Vathi's bodyguards followed, of course, though she didn't need them with Dusk there. They probably didn't know a tokka from a dunghill.

Together they walked up to the bridge, where Starling had made room for Vathi to sit at the ship's small screen.

Dusk knelt beside her chair. "I told you," he said, "about the island where I found the Dakwara. Inside there was a cave."

"The place you claim was Cakoban's tomb."

"I saw a vision confirming it," he said, then pointed. "There was writing on the wall. We took pictures."

The screen showed images of the cavern, taken after he'd brought Starling and her crew there with lights. Strange runes covered the wall.

"It's my people's language," Starling said from behind.

"Your . . . people?" Vathi said, turning around and frowning. "You mean . . ."

"Yes, dragons," Starling said, then pointed at the screen. "One was there when this man died. It reads, 'I was too late to help, but I laid him here. The hero Cakoban died with honor.'" She hesitated, then said the most important part, "It's signed by my uncle's individual mark, President Vathi. Our people have long lifespans, and my uncle is still alive, though lost. If I can find him, he can authenticate this—though the writing should do that. No dragon would use another's sign."

"It means . . ." Vathi said.

"Our people *did* travel this darkness long ago," Dusk said. "Proof, Vathi. When few others even tried, *we* traveled the darkness—and we met others. Gods, monsters—lands aplenty. We met dragons, and befriended them." He took her hand. "We can do it still. Don't give in. Don't accept either deal. Find other partners, build up our nation, and stay *independent*."

"Freedom," Starling whispered from behind him, "is difficult to win back, once lost. I know I don't have much say in this, but . . . listen to him. You can get a *much* better deal than you're being offered. I once thought otherwise." She watched out the front window as the Dakwara passed, continuing a circular route. "It feels good to be wrong."

"I think," Vathi said, "this evidence—and the presence of the Dakwara itself—will change a few votes. We'll need starships of our own, though. We can't rely on the god forever. We have to find a way to earn money, and I can't stomach selling the Aviar."

"What if we sell something else?" Dusk asked.

She looked to him, frowning. And he felt a thrill.

"They need guides," he explained, "in this darkness."

"And you think we can do this for them?" Vathi asked.

He let himself smile, a bird on each shoulder, squeezing her hand in his. "We are Navigators, Vathi. Of *course* we can guide them."

THE END OF
BOOK FOUR

Fig. 101 • Sak and Rokke
(Aviar)

EPILOGUE

Six Months Later

An entire entourage of government officials gathered to watch the First Company Expeditionary Navigators return from their inaugural solo excursion. Dusk didn't see the need for such a formal name for them, but the bureaucrats with their ledgers and their hats needed to fill their time with *something*.

He'd suggested they keep calling them trappers.

"What are they trapping?" they'd asked.

"Our future," he'd explained.

They hadn't understood, because it didn't make sense in their little books. As if words, like ideas or people, couldn't evolve over time. Still, he *did* like the term Navigator, so he supposed he could live with the decision.

They were all in Shadesmar on the perpendicularity island, waiting. Dusk refused the polite company and dainty seats set up for the senators and important chiefs, who presided over larger islands. He instead stood on the beachhead, hands at his hips. Searching. Until . . .

There. Three small ships, with lights flashing.

They'd done it. His first team of trainees had made it to the waypoint and back, Navigating solely by the pulse of the cosmere. It turned out that not everyone—not even every trapper—who ate the worm paste could hear the sounds. Many could. And only trappers.

As per Patji's words, this was a gift only to them. Ed had an explanation—close proximity to a perpendicularity could change people's souls. He was confident nobody but those from First of the Sun would have this talent unless they spent time living on Patji or the other Pantheon Islands, close to the power of the pool.

Dusk didn't need such explanations, as he had the word of the god himself. But it was good to hear, so they knew who to test for the talent. They hoped that some of the guards posted at the pool might develop it—though they needed to devise proper tests. Perhaps a training protocol in wayfinding and survival . . .

Also, he wondered at the few trappers who hadn't manifested the ability. They were strong and capable. Why not them? Were there . . . other powers they could give their birds instead?

Regardless, it was done. The skill he had discovered would live on in his people, no matter what happened to him. There was just one more thing to take care of. He reluctantly approached the others, with their dinner party on the beach. Captain Starling—whose ship hovered nearby—had given her crew these six months of shore leave. A welcome rest on a new planet, following their years of difficult service.

Now she stood with Vathi and the planetary leaders, holding up a small viewing device—which showed what appeared to be a human with a bald head and dark skin. The dragon had been able to watch through this device, which had been delivered along with the rescue ship he sent from Silverlight to collect the Scadrian troops.

"Will that do?" Vathi asked him through the device, which—apparently—was very expensive, as it could communicate through the less explored places in Shadesmar when many could not, at least not at long distances.

"For now," Xisis said. "Yes. I will publicize this news of your Navigators. I suspect that you will have little trouble with outsiders threatening you in the near future."

"It can't be that easy," a senator said, looking over Vathi's shoulder.

"Easy?" Xisis said through the device. "I was led to believe that these Navigators were developed at great tribulation. Regardless, it won't be easy, but you now have excellent leverage. Before, everyone merely wanted to conquer you. Now they need something far more difficult: your *cooperation*."

Vathi glanced at Dusk. She, like him, thought it would take more. And it would. There was always a hidden deathant waiting to strike. However, he *did* believe this would stop the threats for now, as the dragon indicated. Everyone would need these Navigators and couldn't afford to let them fall only into enemy hands. Yes, one power could decide to attack and conquer, but that risked unifying all others against them. Plus, did anyone really want to rely on Navigators with grudges, working under duress?

Or did it make sense to just pay the required price, same as everyone else? It wasn't an arms race, so long as the Navigators could be hired by all. In an instant, First of the Sun became a place that everyone needed to keep happy—which would involve its own delicate balancing act for Vathi and her government. He was certain she could manage. Her tests had proven her, just as his had proven him.

They turned off the device and, at Starling's suggestion, put it in an aluminum box to prevent it from "accidentally" overhearing too much. They'd keep it, to talk to Xisis—but as soon as possible would purchase others, opening lines to impartial Silverlight communication hubs.

"Well," Starling said to the group on the shore. "If the Navigators have returned safely, I guess the *Dynamic* won't be needed for a rescue effort. Time to make my farewells."

"Thank you," Vathi said. "For all your help."

"It is my pleasure. Your deal with Xisis is a good one, and I'm not just saying that because I was the negotiator. Don't trust him, mind you, but understand he *will* keep to the terms."

"I still don't understand what he gains," Soil said. "He offers to spread the word as we asked, and has given us free translation devices, lodestars, information—even the chance to travel to and from Silverlight—all without an actual promise of payment."

"Xisis plays very long games," she said. "Right of first negotiation for reduced tariffs—once you open the perpendicularity for trade—will be worth a very great deal in the future."

To Dusk, this Xisis seemed like a dragon who understood. Progress was a wave, and it wore away even the strongest stones, with time. First of the Sun would open to foreign ships. Probably someday soon, once infrastructure was built and the skeptics swayed. Already, the shore leave of Starling's crew had introduced some on the homeisles to the idea of foreigners visiting. The future would come whether you wanted it or not. Best be ready, then, to shape it.

That was what he'd earned for his people—the right to be the ones doing the shaping.

Starling made her farewells while some on shore waved and shouted to the approaching Navigators, but Dusk was impatient. He grabbed Vathi by the arm and pulled her aside, leaving her to hastily make an excuse. He glared at her bodyguards, who glared back. As they should. Good men.

"Vathi," Dusk said. "We need to speak."

"I can see that, from how you pulled me away," she said. "Can it be quick? I want to welcome the Expeditionary Navigators personally."

Quick. Yes, he could be quick. He towed her to the other side of the small island, a five-minute walk, to where the Dakwara waited. It could go mostly invisible, they'd found, and seemed perfectly content spending its days a few hundred feet beneath the island, swimming in circles. Most of the skullsnakes had left it. Only one or two dozen remained.

Dusk felt that the Dakwara enjoyed the light of the perpendicularity, which fed and refreshed it, so it found this duty preferable to its old one of guarding a grave. It reared up as he arrived, and it became a vibrant glowing green again, hood extending, mouth opening. Rokke chirped hello, and it chirped back. He wasn't certain when it had learned that.

"You," he said, pointing to the thing. "Serve her now instead of me." He pointed to Vathi. "If another is elected in her stead, serve them."

Then Dusk nodded and started to leave.

"Dusk!" Vathi said, spinning on him. "What? Don't just walk off! What did you do, you insufferable man?"

"You wanted quick."

"You are such a pain," she said, then waved toward the beast. "Why did you do that? You are the hero, the one who defeated it."

"I don't want to be a hero. I want something to do."

ISLES OF THE EMBERDARK

"Commanding such a powerful being isn't enough?"

"No," he said, then sighed and stepped back to her. "The Dakwara needs to stay here to defend the perpendicularity. So the one who commands it . . ."

"Needs to stay here," she said. "On our planet."

He nodded.

"Dusk . . ." she said.

"If I remain," he said, "I become a man in a glass jar once again. To be admired. Gawked at. I don't want that. I want to be *useful*, not *important*." He pointed at the Dakwara. "That's too much power for me. The president should command it. You can figure out laws about its use. You're smart like that."

"But . . ."

"Tell me I'm wrong," he said. "Tell me that a single random man should command our greatest weapon, rather than an elected servant of the people. Tell me."

"You're not some random man."

But she did not contradict, or answer him otherwise. She stared at him, and remained silent, for he had not asked a question. She had indeed learned a few things from him.

"Where will you go?" she said.

"I have a boat. I have birds. I can feel the Current. I will go where these things take me." He hesitated, then took her hand. "I will return periodically, if I am not dead. I am . . . honored to have guided you on your first trip to Patji. I never saw his hand in delaying you until I arrived so that we could meet, but I should have. Thank you."

She nodded. "I'm glad for your freedom, Dusk, but I don't think you should go on your own."

"With some of these others, then?" he asked, waving. "Your Expeditionary Navigators?"

"No." She glanced over her shoulder. Toward Starling, as her crew bade farewell and began walking the short distance to their ship. "What was it she said to you? That we can't be alone?"

"It is good to need others," he whispered. "I used to disbelieve that. I liked being on my own."

"And now?" she asked, turning back to him.

And now...

Now the sun had risen on a new day. He embraced Vathi, then—birds flapping excitedly on his shoulders—started toward the ship.

How strange, he thought, *to seek out other people.*

And how strange to look forward to doing so.

Starling entered the *Dynamic* and called for the crew to go to their posts. They ignored her, however, waiting in the cargo bay.

Six months on Dusk's planet had been good for them all. They'd spent the days enjoying the local food, petting magical parrots, and reveling in the panicked sounds Scadrians made over the comm channels when one of their ships traveled too close to the perpendicularity island in Shadesmar. The Dakwara, it turned out, was *very* good at chasing away starships.

Now that Dusk's people had proven they could Navigate, though, it was time to go. She'd done what she could for them, negotiating the deal with Xisis, honestly answering their questions. She'd also spent a great deal of time listening to their stories.

Because her people, somehow, factored into all of that. She now had even more questions for her uncle, once she found him. So she wanted to get going. She hesitated in the doorway into the corridor, worried by the way the crew all looked at her. Even Chrysalis was there, skin partially regrown as she created new hordelings for the purpose. It was patchwork, but the rest of them pretended not to notice—and she conscientiously made herself scarce when anyone else was eating.

"All right," Starling said, leaning against the doorframe with arms folded. "What's going on? Is there a birthday I missed? Does someone expect more shore leave? What's up?"

"We have been discussing," Ed said, "how close you got."

"To..."

"Freedom," ZeetZi said, wounded arm looking pretty good now that the bandages were off. The word had weight, coming from him.

"We noticed the manacles," Ed said. "That machine almost worked, didn't it?"

"Almost," she said. "It's possible if it had more power, it would have."

ISLES OF THE EMBERDARK

She left out that she'd strengthened the manacles. They must never bear the burden of knowing what she'd done for them.

"The Intensifier was destroyed," Nazh said, arms folded as he floated halfway through one wall, "but they will build more. We could steal one, try it out."

"Even if we can't find another of those," Aditil said, stepping up beside the others, "there has to be a way to get those off without sacrificing your integrity."

"We have decided, Captain," ZeetZi said. "Our first mission as a vessel is to help you obtain your freedom."

The others nodded, even Chrysalis. Shards. She felt an overwhelming flood of emotions—gratitude, embarrassment, love—seeing them there in a line in the cargo bay.

"We can't do that, though," she began. "I mean . . . how would we even start? Plus, we need to earn money for our upkeep."

"We can take a job that brings us near the Grand Apparatus," Chrysalis said, naming ZeetZi's home planet. "Few take that work, and it pays well. My kind might have suggestions on how to free you."

"I can put the arcanists of my order on the problem," Ed said. "They will be fascinated to know how close we got to defeating dragon technology. Plus, the pictures I took might help our engineers recreate the Intensifier."

"Really," Aditil said, "it's the least we can do after you got us out of this."

"You guys did all the work of the escape plan," Starling said. "I just got out of the way!"

"Difficult trait to find in an officer," ZeetZi noted.

"Downright impossible," Leonore agreed. "A captain who *doesn't* muss everything up? Rusting incredible, that is." She smirked. "Just accept it, Captain. From this day forward, our main goal is to get those manacles off you, yah?"

They filed out, clapping her on the shoulder, giving her grins. Nazh hesitated a little longer, then winked at her. "You were right," he whispered. "We did find a way through it."

"No ghosts for dates, though," Starling said.

"Alas," he said. He saluted with one finger and floated off. Starling forced herself to appreciate their praise and help. Because, as she was beginning to understand, leadership was sometimes about accepting you didn't get to make all the choices. Shards . . . she loved this ship. And this crew. There were still going to be problems—she didn't miss how ZeetZi kept an eye on Chrysalis as they left. The crew had its divisions, and she was sure they'd manifest more as immediate danger grew distant.

But it was *her* ship. *Her* crew.

They'd find a way.

Aditil was the last one left. As she passed Starling, the aetherbound held out something in an envelope: a ticket to her homeworld. The one Starling had given her.

"Aditil?" Starling said as the woman put Starling's hand around the ticket, then let go. "It's all right if you use that. I'll buy you a return one, even. You can go home, then come back."

"Knowing that," she said, "is enough. And honestly, Captain, I'd rather you hold on to this for now. I'll use it someday. For now, I want to be part of this. Fully." She leaned closer. "I'll go home once *you* can go home. Captain."

Hesitant, Starling tucked away the ticket. Aditil gave her a smile, then hurried after the others, a bounce in her step.

Starling moved to close the cargo doors, then hesitated. Someone was standing on the gangplank—she'd missed him arriving. Dusk loomed there, shadowy, with a bird on each shoulder. Shards, but he could be an intimidating sight.

". . . Dusk?" she asked.

He stepped more fully into the light, and she saw he was carrying a pack over his shoulder. And he was crying. A pair of quiet, solemn tears ran down his cheeks.

"Dusk!" She hurried to him. "Are you all right?"

"I," he said, "am finally coming to terms with the fact that I no longer have a home."

She gave him room to speak. He seemed the type to appreciate that. He wiped the tears, and took a deep breath, steeling himself.

"I once lived on Patji," he explained. "I suppose every child must leave his father's home eventually. I should like . . . I think . . . to not travel alone any longer. I did that. I conquered it. It is too easy to accept, and too hard to survive." He looked to her, fumbling his words. "I believe you could use a Navigator."

"Dusk . . ." she said. "We absolutely could, but we can't afford you. Your people need to be charging extreme amounts, like I told you, to leverage your unique abilities! That's the only way you'll build a starship fleet of your own."

"I have done my duty to my planet all my life," he said. "Now I have brought them into the sunlight of the new day. The rest of the crew, do they work for you?"

"No," she said. "We're partners on the ship."

"Then I will forgo my fee," he said, "for a piece of whatever you discover. Somewhere out there are people like the Eelakin, who do not know what the stars contain—and the dangers that will soon approach, now that nations can sail the emberdark. I would like the chance to see them first, if I can. To explain, and pass along our wisdom. If, that is, you will have me."

"Are you kidding?" she said. "With you, we can go places nobody has ever gone! We can see things even *Master Hoid* never saw! We can"—she glanced at her manacles—"maybe find solutions to problems everyone thinks unsolvable. Yes, we'll have you, Dusk." She smiled. "Do . . . we pay the birds separately?"

"Yes," he said firmly. "Fortunately they work for head scratches and the occasional nut." He walked around the cargo bay, scanning it, then turned to her—and she realized he hadn't been inspecting the room, but searching for echoes in the pulse. Islands in the emberdark.

"Where do we go first?" he asked.

"I have no idea," she said. "Do you have any suggestions?"

"That depends on what we're looking for."

"I suppose . . . we're searching for tomorrow."

"Well that is easy, then. In my experience, it will find you on its own." He hefted his pack. "Shall we?"

THE END

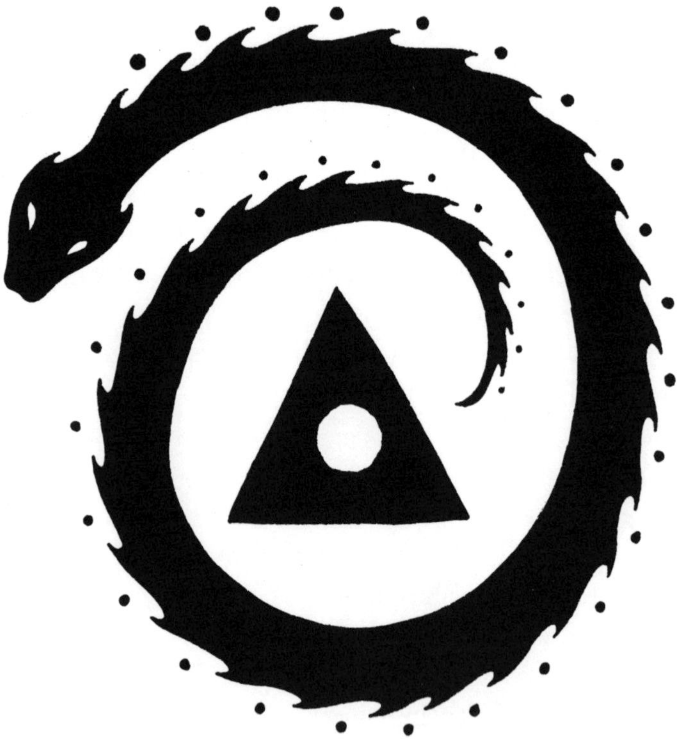

ACKNOWLEDGMENTS

Every book that reaches readers has a team of people launching the author's story into the world. This book is no exception. Dusk and Starling had a talented group of behind-the-scenes heroes helping their story sail from first draft to finished tome.

Below is a list of all those Navigators. The number of names in this list continues to grow, but every one of them contributed to making the story better, making the book more beautiful, or getting it to more readers. I couldn't do this without them.

Let the credits roll!

—Brandon

Artists: Esther Hiʻilani Candari (for the interior art) and Rebecca Sorge Jensen (for the cover). Also Elena Hyde, Esther's assistant, and Howard Lyon.

Audiobook narrators: Jennifer Jill Araya and Kaleo Griffith.

At JABberwocky Literary Agency: Joshua Bilmes, Susan Velasquez, Christina Zobel, Valentina Sainato, and Brady McReynolds. At Zeno Literary Agency: John Berlyne.

Printing partners: Bill Wearne, Kim Wearne, Landry Evans, Dan

Deardorff, Jim McCafferty, Tedd Litty, Joe DiMauro, Robert Carrier, Charlie Smith, Tracy Shelby, Melvin Faust, Dan Clippinger, and Chad Dillon.

At Dragonsteel: COO Emily Sanderson.

Creative Development: VP Isaa< Stewart, Art Director Shawn Boyles, Art Director Ben McSweeney, Rachael Buchanan, Jennifer Neal, Hayley Lazo, Priscilla Spencer, and Anna Earley.

Editorial: The Inductive Peter Ahlstrom as VP, Editorial Director Kristy S. Gilbert, Continuity Director Karen Ahlstrom, Jennie Stevens, Betsey Ahlstrom, and Emily Shaw-Higham.

Publicity & Marketing: VP Adam Horne (a.k.a. the Godzilla Expert), Marketing Director Jeremy Palmer, Octavia Escamilla-Spiker, Tayan Hatch, Taylor Hatch, and Donald Mustard III.

Operations & HR: VP Matt "the HRinator" Hatch, Operations Director Jane Horne, Lex Willhite, Jerrod Walker, Kathleen Dorsey Sanderson, Ethan Skarstedt, Becky Wilson, Christian Fairbanks, and Makena Saluone.

Merchandise & Events: Kara Stewart (VP of Merchandising, Events, and Writing Big Checks), Merchandise Director Christi Jacobsen, Events & Support Director Kellyn Neumann, Richard Rubert, Dallin Holden, Ally Reep, Brett Moore, Joy Allen, Katy Ives, Daniel Phipps, Braydonn Moore, Mem Grange, Michael Bateman, Alex Lyon, Jacob Chrisman, Camilla Waite, Quinton Martin, Hollie Rubert, Gwen Hickman, Isabel Chrisman, Amanda Butterfield, Logan Reep, Pablo Mooney, Rachel Jacobsen, Hayden Stillman, Zoe Hatch, Owen Knowlton, Laura Loveridge, and Kathleen Barlow.

Narrative: VP Dan Wells, still the only member of the Narrative Department, because with his One Direction fan fictions being so good, why would we need another?

My writing group: Kaylynn ZoBell, Kathleen Dorsey Sanderson, Eric James Stone, Darci Stone, Alan Layton, Ben Olsen, Ethan Skarstedt, Karen Ahlstrom, Peter Ahlstrom, and Emily Sanderson.

Arcanists: Eric Lake, Evgeni "Argent" Kirilov, Joshua "Jofwu" Harkey, David Behrens, Ian McNatt, and Ben Marrow.

Authenticity reader: Lehua Parker.

Beta readers: Kendra Alexander, Ellie Frato-Sweeney, Kathleen

ACKNOWLEDGMENTS

Holland, Frankie Jerome, William Juan, Valencia Kumley, Erika Kuta Marler, Eric Lake, Jeremy Levao, Kierynn Levao, Ben Marrow, Rahul Pantula, Kalyani Poluri, Jennifer Pugh, Kendra Wilson, Kyle Wilson, and Deana Covel Whitney.

Gamma readers included many of the beta readers as well as Krystl Allred, Amir Kasra Arman, Jessica Ashcraft, Sam Baskin, David Behrens, Siena "Lotus" Buchanan, Tim Challener, Brandon Cole, Darci Cole, Trae Cooper, Poonam Desai, David Fallon, Aaron Ford, Joshua Harkey, Ted Herman, Brian T. Hill, Alyx Hoge, William "Aber" Juan, Evgeni "Argent" Kirilov, Bob Kluttz, Jayden King, Ari Kufer, Jessie Lake, Eliyahu Berelowitz Levin, Zenef Mark Lindberg, Chris McGrath, Ian McNatt, Lauren McCaffrey, Shannon Nelson, Ross Newberry, Ene Nytch, Donita Orders, Tyler Patrick, Aubree Pham, Becca Reppert, Gary Singer, Billy Todd, Sean VanBlack, Paige Vest, Glen Vogelaar, Philip Vorwaller, Rob West, Dale Wiens, Rosemary Williams, and Lingting "Botanica" Xu.

Brandon Sanderson grew up in Lincoln, Nebraska. He lives in Utah with his wife and children and teaches creative writing at Brigham Young University. His bestsellers have sold 34 million copies worldwide and include the Mistborn saga; the Stormlight Archive novels; and other novels, including *Tress of the Emerald Sea*, *The Rithmatist*, *Steelheart*, and *Skyward*. He won a Hugo Award for *The Emperor's Soul*, a novella set in the world of his acclaimed first novel, *Elantris*. Additionally, he completed Robert Jordan's The Wheel of Time®. For behind-the-scenes information on all his books, visit brandonsanderson.com.

Esther Hiʻilani Candari is an Asian-American artist from Hawaiʻi. That upbringing taught her to see the beauty, power, and sacredness in the diversity of the people, the majesty of the land, and the delicate balance of nature around her. She now lives in Utah with her husband Dr. Steven Christiansen. You can find her work at hiilanifinearts.com.

Rebecca Sorge Jensen has always loved stories and the art they inspire, so becoming an illustrator made perfect sense. She currently lives and works in Utah, creating art for books,cards, posters and anything else people will let her draw on. See more of her work at rebeccasorge.com.

Author portrait by Howard Lyon